Blood at the Root

Blood at the Root

a novel

Lee Meitzen Grue

ALAMO BAY PRESS
SEADRIFT•AUSTIN

Cover Art: Moonyeen McNeilage
Graphic Design: Valentine Price
Author Photographs: Kichea Burt
Book Design: ABP
Epigraph: "Strange Fruit," by Abel Meeropol

For orders and information:

Alamo Bay Press
Pamela Booton, Director
Lowell Mick White, Editor / Diane Wilson, Activist

825 W 11th Ste 114
Austin, Texas 78701
pam@alamobaypress.com
www.alamobaypress.com
www.alamobaywritersworkshop.com

Grue, Lee Meitzen.
    Blood at the root / Lee Meitzen Grue.
    pages cm
    LCCN 2015933128
    ISBN 978-0-9908632-3-6

    1. New Orleans (La.)--Fiction.   I. Title.

PS3557.R79B56 2015   813'.54
                            QBI15-600070

To my mother, Bernice McCullar Meitzen,
and to the three Meitzen women,
who were my other mothers.

"Here is a strange and bitter crop...."

Contents

Blood at the Root

Elliot

ELLIOT HEARD THEM SAY IT. HE HEARD THEM SAY it lots of times.

He said, "Moo, who is High John the Conqueror?" She closed her face down like a rat trap with the rat in it.

She said, "Where you hear that, Elliot?"

He said, "I hear it lots of times."

"Little pitchers got big ears," she said as she swished soap around in a mason jar, rinsed and laid it upside down on the dish drain before answering. "You better let that subject lay."

"Took told Hall the iceman that Camilla Jane's got High John the Conqueror all locked up and that she can have any man she wants because she's got him, and I don't know him. He's not from High Castle. Is he from New Orleans?"

"Yes, sir. You got it right. That's where he's from."

She was laughing a mean little laugh she laughed sometimes when she knew something—like what he was going to get for his birthday and it was something he didn't want.

"Moo," he said, "I'm worried about your soul. You're old and you're mean. It won't be long before you're dead and some people won't be sorry to see you go. I hope you have somebody other than this family to say masses for the repose of your soul."

She turned her back on him, and her back could close down even better than her face.

"I'm going next door," he said to her back. She didn't answer but he had to tell her anyway or he'd get in trouble.

Elliot climbed over the back fence because it was the shortcut and the handiest way to go. Aunt Mag's kitchen was out back. He climbed through her butterbean vine strung up by a string lattice on the back gallery, his thin body passing through without knocking off a bean.

He ate a couple of raw butterbeans, not only because they were half decent to eat but because he liked to watch Took at the end of the season store the dried beans in a mason jar with tobacco to keep the weevils out of next year's seed. He felt obliged. In order to keep seed somebody had to eat butterbeans.

From the gallery he could see Took in the kitchen walking slow to the coal oil stove, to the sink, to the ice box — going back and forth because she never remembers what she wants to get the first time. She was making coffee and something else. He stayed low so he could see what she was doing, walking to the ice box, taking out a couple of eggs, walking over to the kitchen cabinet, taking down a batter bowl. Then she walked back to the ice box and got the milk. She must have made ten trips around the kitchen before she got everything she needed. The last thing she got is the vanilla bean so Elliot knew she was going to make French toast.

"You going to make French toast?" he asked through the screen.

"Where you come from Creeping Jesus? Come on in here. Can't you make some noise when you walk?"

He came in to watch. She stuck the vanilla bean in a bowl

of milk which swallows it up, but he could see tan stain the milk where it was beginning to work. She turned around slow and started back toward her old rocker with its rusty looking blue seat cover. There was something about her seat that looks like the seat of the rocker, soft and sort of worn. She grabbed the arms of the rocker, let go with her feet and fell down into it. She sighed in time to the creak of the rocker. "Now, what you want?"

"Who's High John the Conqueror?"

"You don't talk about High John unless you got a use for him and then, you don't talk about him loud." She leans forward and looks into his face. Took smells like coal oil and bacon grease. The smell of it comes out of the pores of her skin and grabs him before she puts out both arms and says, "Come on, Sugar, sit on my lap and I'll tell you." Elliot gets on her lap, but his feet are hanging over onto the floor. He knows he's too big, but he likes the bacon grease and coal oil smell. He leans back and she tells him in his ear.

"High John the Conqueror is a man root. He a man when he wants to be and he a root when he wants to be."

"Where's Camilla Jane got him locked up?"

"Who said she got him locked up?" She looks down her nose at him, pulling together the dark skin around her eyes which are little and dull as four o'clock seeds.

"You said that to Hall."

She grabbed both his arms and held onto him. "You don't go saying that. Miss Mag says they's no Hoodoo here and they's no Hoodoo here. So you watch what you say, Sir, or something bad is liable to happen to you."

"I won't say anything. My lips are sealed with an X." And he showed her with his finger making a big X over his mouth.

"Get up, Mister. You too heavy for old Took. Too heavy." She let him go and moved to finish the French toast. She beat two eggs into the vanilla milk then soaked pieces of French bread in the milk and egg mixture. She fished the bread out with a slotted spoon, put it into a hot iron skillet, fried one side in butter, flipped it once with a spatula, fried the other side and moved it onto a piece of brown paper bag on the enamel shelf of the stove. In a few minutes, she had five pieces of French toast laid out on the paper. She let him shake granulated sugar over it with a teaspoon. He held the handle of the spoon in the upturned palm of his left hand. To suit her, he had to slap his left wrist with little taps of his right hand to get just the right amount of sugar on the French toast. After it looked right, she moved the toast onto a small white plate with yellow and orange narcissus flowers painted on it. She poured a big cup of coffee and put in four tablespoons of condensed milk then gave him the tray to take upstairs to Camilla Jane.

"She sick," Took said.

He got out of the kitchen screen by pushing it with his bare foot. Took helped him but he had to walk down the back gallery and all the way up the side gallery by himself, open the screen door to the hall, close it, and then open the wooden door to the attic stairs. The stairs were steep, narrow, and hot. He had to do all this without spilling a drop because sure as he did Camilla Jane would jump out of bed and let the toads out of her mouth.

Whenever Elliot did anything for Camilla Jane he could hear Moo's voice in his head, "Old Miss Elise had four daughters: Your mother's the best, but she's wore out from miscarriages. Two of them live up North and Mag a throwback. Now we got this disgusting generation—you and your cousin Camilla Jane. She some sort of remnant, messed up piece at the end of a bolt of good material. Her and her Hoodoo sister. I don't know why you want to hang over there all the time."

But he knew why he hung around. Why he wanted to go up the dark stairs that smelled of old secret things to Camilla Jane's room on the right at the head of the stairs.

The other side, at the top of the landing, was a junk room. He always stopped by this wall, where there was a hole like a rat had been chewing into the brown, papery composition board. Every time he came up he peeled off another piece. He could see in deep, count the ends of the layers, see how the walls were made, how each piece of paper held up the other pieces into something that appeared solid. Except for the hole he'd made, you'd never know it was all paper. The door to the junk room had a brown china door knob. He wanted to go in there, look at the yellowed sheet music, read *Sea Serpents* in the box of old books, but he had to bring the coffee to Camilla Jane because he was going to ask her.

She was sleeping on her stomach, wearing white batiste pajamas with ruffles on the legs, one knee bent up to her chin. When he came in, he shoved the door with his foot and struck the end of her metal bed with his heel. It rang like a gong. She turned over and kicked off the sheet. He could see a big reddish-brown stain at the top of her wrinkled pajama leg. At the other end of the bed he could see her black hair, sweaty curls stuck to her face. Her skin looked thick. It had a special kind of pink to it that could look good when her hair was all fluffed out and she had on lipstick. Right now she looked hot and cross as two sticks.

"Well, if it isn't Skinny-Marinky-Dink making enough noise to wake the dead. Aren't you sweet, bringing me break-fast in bed—French toast and cold coffee. Same thing every day. Took only knows how to make two things—both cold. She the only cook in the world knows how to cook without heat."

She sat up and motioned him over. "Jesus, Elliot, every time I look at you you're skinnier. I hope you fill out by the ninth grade or some dog's liable to carry you off for a bone." She grabbed the French toast and started tearing it into little pieces and stuffing it into her mouth with her fingers. He didn't say anything. Just looked around. Camilla Jane always ate like she was starving. There was a big picture of her twin, Pamel-la Jeanne, on the dresser, a piece of palm from Palm Sunday stuck in the metal frame; a plate of dried red beans sat in front of the picture. Keeled over on its back, a big outside roach lay on top of the beans. Elliot didn't know if the beans had killed the roach, but they looked poisonous enough to kill a cow.

There was a circle of flour around the plate and the picture, two burned down candles in front of it. In the frame Pamella Jeanne looked timid, milky-faced, not much like Camilla Jane. She was only four years old when she died from stringing oleander blossoms and biting off the stems. Moo said, "Colored kids always die from swallowing lye and white kids die from stringing flowers."

"Why don't you go now, Sugar. I have things to do." Camilla Jane gave him her sweet smile.

"Where's High John?" he asked.

She put down the bread and stared at him. She didn't growl but she might have. She looked like a dog does when it's eating and thinks you want to take its food.

"What did you say?"

"High John the Conqueror Root—where do you keep him?"

"Get yourself out of here. You ask stupid questions about something you don't know anything about. I'm going to tell your mother how smart and sassy you act, and Moo's going to whip your butt."

"You tell my mother I'm sassy and I'm going to tell Aunt Mag you mess around with Hoodoo and you've got a Hoodoo altar to Pamella Jeanne in your room."

"Now wait a minute, Elliot. Let's leave our mothers out of this." She sat up higher in bed, plumped the bolster, fluffed her hair out and put on the "sweet mouth," which was what Moo called the face Camilla Jane made when she wanted something.

"It's hard to leave your mother out of things. She don't miss much," he said.

Camilla Jane looked like she was dividing pecan pie and figuring out how to get the biggest piece without showing it. She said, "I guess you'll just have to cross your heart and hope to die so I can tell you." He crossed his heart.

"Elliot, come here and give me a kiss before I tell you." She pointed to the side of the bed next to her, then she patted the sheet.

He could feel himself getting red. The bottom of his belly felt like it did when he went to Baton Rouge and rode up in the elevator. Camilla Jane had been kissing on him since he was a little kid. She'd catch him in the pantry or the closet. Hot, sloppy kisses right on the mouth, and he always got some of whatever she was eating but he didn't care. It just made those kisses different and special. He would have sold his mother if he could have stayed with Camilla Jane in her hot room and gotten sloppy kisses all day long. He got up on the bed right next to her. She took his hand and put it on her neck above the ruffles and she kissed him.

He squeezed his eyes shut and dreamed about what he always dreamed about when Camilla Jane kissed him. In the dream he was little, but he couldn't even let himself think about what else he was. She hugged him real hard for a long time, and she seemed to enjoy it, too. He knew there wasn't too much she didn't enjoy.

She said, "Elliot, you are the best kisser I've ever known." Then she finished the French toast, dropping crumbs all over the bed, turned up her coffee cup and drained the coffee in one swallow, some of it running down the dimple in her chin and ending up as a light-brown stain at the top of the white ruffles across her chest. She gave a belch that sounded like it came from her toes, laughed and said, "Better an empty house than a poor tenant," as she stretched her arms up over her head, bowed her back and stretched her feet toward the bottom of the iron bed until her back cracked like a .22.

Elliot moved over to the cane-backed chair next to the bed. "Are you going to tell me or not?"

"Or not."

"Okay," he said, and started out of the room.

"Wait a minute, Elliot," she said very fast, "High John is in the kitchen in the false-bottom drawer of the *garde-manger* — but don't tell Mama because I need him."

"Why?"

"Mama's sending me to some sort of school in North Carolina to finish me. I can't go there. Took says if I go too far I'll get sick. If I went to New York I'd die."

He laughed at her. "You didn't even have chicken pox when the rest of us did. You're never sick."

"If he wants you sick you're sick; if he wants you dead you're dead. Took said so. I'm scared." And it was on the edge of her eyes.

"Don't believe if you don't want, Elliot, but don't tell where he is. Promise?"

Took yelled up the stairs, "Moo wants you."

Elliot ran out, down the stairs past Took and out the front door. He jumped over the porch railing and headed back down between the two houses. He hid under the hedge to make sure Took was still in the house then went into the kitchen and pulled open the bottom drawer of the kitchen safe. It was a click drawer with a false bottom. He'd watched Took open it a dozen times, whenever there was going to be a party. She kept the good silver oyster forks with the grape leaves on them in the drawer. He always watched her before he went in. He fancied himself a slick cat burglar, and spying on Took was practice. The latch was on the bottom of the napkin drawer. He pushed the button and the bottom moved back a crack.

It was lying on the second bottom of the drawer looking like this old wrinkled something, like an old dark finger dead a long time. He picked it up and it was just an old root like Moo made medicine tea with sometime — every day and ordinary like Hoodoo, but he felt a warmth in his fingers and an electric feeling up his back like he felt when a magnet moved pins.

He clutched the root and said aloud, "High John the Conqueror, I want to marry Camilla Jane."

He heard Took opening the screen door so he threw High John back in and closed the drawer.

She said, "What you doing here, Creeping Jesus. I thought I told you to go home. What you running your fingers over this time?"

He said, "Moo wants to borrow some damask napkins for Camilla Jane's party."

"Moo got more damask napkins than this house ever seen. You're lying, boy."

All the creases were shook out of Took. She leaned over very slowly and opened the drawer, pressing the bottom latch as she did so. When she saw the High John she shut the drawer and turned to Elliot, looking old in the eyes.

"You poor, dumb little boy," she said. "You already stuck on Camilla Jane; now you stuck for life. Go on home, Elliot. I can't do nothing for you, and Moo can't either—much as she wants."

River Road

NOW THE KITCHEN DOOR WAS CLOSED. THE ONLY time Took closed the kitchen was when she took a bath in a galvanized tub. Camilla Jane was inside there with Took. What were they doing in there? Camilla had dropped a hint that she was going to be in something special on All Saints' Day. While she tantalized him with little bits of information, she kept shaking her shoulders in time to a fast piece playing on the radio, and she made the sweet mouth, as if she were the most wonderful thing on two legs; acting the same way she had when she was to be Sugar Plum Fairy in the dance review at The Gayle Parnelle School of Dance before Mag suggested to Gayle Parnelle that the Maynards should get a discount.

"After all, the Maynards are the oldest family in High Castle. If Camilla Jane Maynard takes lessons from you everybody will," she said. But Gayle Parnelle said she was more interested in getting money to pay her bills than in old families.

"Most old families don't have a pot, just a couple of dirty old windows with broken shutters." Camilla Jane cried, but Mag didn't have the money so Camilla Jane had to drop out of the review.

Took pulled down the shade. Elliot could see in through the crack at the bottom. Took and Camilla Jane were thick as thieves for the last week — Took sewing on something she kept away from Aunt Mag. Now he knew it was a dress. Camilla Jane was trying on a dress — a long dress, almost ankle length. It was different watching her through the window, even though he couldn't see the top of her, only the ends of her arms. Her hands looked heavy as they hung against the white satin, more awkward than he remembered.

Looking through the window at this part of her, he found her to be very young — even younger than he was. Took's back blocked most of his view but he could see enough to know Camilla Jane was going to wear a long dress in something. But listening to Took talk with pins in her mouth he figured it was on All Saints' Day — early. It had something to do with Pamella Jeanne. He heard her name mentioned twice. They were going to get "Camilla's *Gros bon-ange*" — whatever that was. And, as usual, Camilla and Took didn't want Aunt Mag to know anything about it.

He waited on the screened side porch at Aunt Mag's, sunk down in the green and white glider to keep warm. No one could see him there. It was early morning; he loved the thought of Moo's face when she came to wake him up for mass and the trip to the cemetery to whitewash tombs but found, instead of Elliot, an empty bed. He was past needing Moo for every little thing. He was almost a man. He'd probably get punished. Today was a Holy Day of Obligation, but he didn't want to pull grass or trim the grave of his grandfather or that endless procession of dead babies with his name. He might not get punished if Took and Camilla Jane had to cover their tracks. If they had to cover theirs, they'd have to cover his too.

He heard Hall's truck and wondered why he was delivering ice on All Saints' Day, but when Elliot heard the front door shut softly, he realized that Camilla Jane and Took were riding off with Hall in his ice truck. Elliot rushed around to the front of the house just in time to see the truck pull out. It shuddered and shook as Hall gassed it. By the time it picked up speed, Elliot was in the back with the ice. Through the warped and yellowed isinglass, which replaced the missing rear window, he could see the outlines of three figures in the front seat. Elliot had jumped in, afraid they would take off without him. Now he found himself with very little room.

Huge blocks of ice with canvas covers filled the truck bed. Metal grommets laced with cord held the canvas down. Elliot hung on at the tailgate but if he stayed there the others would surely see him when they stopped. By pulling his belly in, he squeezed under the tent next to the ice.

It was cold under the canvas. Slabs glinted and sweated like ice cliffs in the dim light. He thought of Eskimos in their warm ice houses lit by radiant oil lamps which kept them warm. Soon his clothes were soaked. Small rivulets of water searched for exits in the bed as the truck, which had no springs, bounced along some unknown road. A bleak Stonehenge surrounded him as he shivered under the flapping tent.

Ice. Water but not water. The weight, shifting as the truck bounced, threatened to crush him against the side. The truck careened to the right and then to the left in a snaky, breathless motion, which knocked and bruised him. The road followed the river. Hours passed. The temperature of his body dropped. His mind slowed and he felt as if he were floating above himself watching the tight canvas from above. He would freeze here but not drown. He thought how his frozen body would be found by the side of the river road—his death a mystery. A stiff body wheeled into the Baton Rouge morgue—stone cold as a slab of meat at Kimburger's Market. The puzzled doctor chipping into his frozen arteries—crystalline blood cells packed like a nectar snowball. These thoughts flew above the truck, aerial and light.

At last they came to a stop, and he flew back into his body which crouched shivering in the back of the truck. He waited to make his exit without being seen, but it was only Hall going off into the bushes by the side of the road. Where were they going? It was a long trip for Camilla Jane and Took to make without permission from Aunt Mag. They didn't have permission. He knew that. It was a big risk. It must have to do with High John.

As it started up again, the truck groaned like Took getting out of a chair. The skin of Elliot's shoulder burned with a red ant bite. It had been numb from leaning against the ice while he waited to leap out of the truck. Now it burned. If the truck didn't get where it was going soon, he would have frostbite—what craziness, frostbite. The pain in his shoulder was constant, now his hips, where they joined his legs, ached with the bony equivalent of a four a.m. earache he'd had last winter. Now his mind became crystal. He could die. He'd never thought of death before. Old people died. He'd learned something in the back of the truck. Young people too could die. He could die—too proud to give up. "False pride," Moo called it. "Your family's all swollen up with false pride. Can't learn nothing new. Don't even see what's here. Don't know how anything really works. False pride's an ice crust over deep water."

He wanted the pain to stop, but his body knew better than he that pain is a symptom of life. He wanted to be numb. He welcomed it. When there was no longer any pain he would go with the ice to the morgue where they'd slide him from the truck into a long, cold drawer.

The truck stopped. He heard doors open. A long time passed as Took struggled to get out, and then a loud bang as Camilla got out and slammed the door. He could hear a number of people talking. A man with a bass voice, who was addressed as the Reverend Simmons, said, "So this the *serviteur? Bonjour. Passe blanc, eh?*"

Camilla Jane was unusually quiet.

"*Bonjour*," Took said. "This the *serviteur*. She needs the support of her sister to succeed in life. She is a *Marasa*."

"*Marasas* are much trouble, Mother Took. Always hungry. Stubborn. I don't like to summon *Marasa*."

"Don't worry. The *Marasa* you'll summon is timid and the one you'll strengthen is willing. You'll have no trouble," Took said.

The voices moved away. Elliot shook his stiff arms as he listened for anyone who might come back and discover him. Now he felt it safe enough to come out. Hall had parked the truck in shade under pecan trees but to Elliot, who had spent hours in dim light, it was as if he'd come from the underworld into the full glare of a lifeboat at sea, an open sea of heavy clover broken by white waves—headstones that stretched down the curving road. Elliot jumped out stiffly and crouched by the truck. He soon realized he didn't need to hide. There was no one around. Everyone had gone into the church. A constant drumming vibrated the earth and entered him from the soles of his feet up the conduit of his legs into his genitals, his belly—up in his throat, as if the drum were his own voice seeking exit. The sound came from the wooden church. He could hear voices raised in litany. It was a French church. He'd heard the sacred litany before. There were high windows, clerestories that rose above the side aisles to light the interior. A scaffolding of rusting iron painted white pushed against the sides of the church to hold it up. There were three of these buttresses on the side where Elliot stood. He climbed one like giant stair steps and peered into the church.

The inside was unlike any church Elliot had been to. The entire congregation wore white. Two drummers sat near the nave of the church beating tall drums. The reverend was a tall, thin man who stood before an altar piled with burnt candles in green wine bottles, clay jugs in canvas bags, assorted feathers, beads and odd drawings. It was the man of the deep voice who now spoke of the *Marasa* again. He spoke above the drumming and his voice carried to Elliot perched on the flying buttress.

"Today we call the *Marasa*."

Elliot didn't know the word but the congregation did. There was a disgruntled hum, as if someone had announced to the kids at his school that lunch was going to be liver and boiled spinach. "I know. I know. The twins are unpredictable. Capricious. They're always hungry. They eat and leave nothing for the congregation. But remember, they are only children; they cannot provide for themselves. When one serves food they eat it all at once without caring to leave some for another day. We must be generous. One of our *serviteurs* is here to join with her sister. Now I am calling:

> *Marasa si map rélé loa io mian mian.*
> *Marasa nago map rélé sin an mian mian.*
> *Marasa a si nago min rélé loa io.*
> I am calling the twin spirits to eat.
> These twin spirits. I am calling you to eat.
> Mago twin spirits, I am calling you.
> We have prepared food.

Elliot kept switching his gaze from the Reverend Simmons, who was working himself up into something big, to Camilla Jane, who didn't look at all afraid. She was lying down with four other girls to the right of the altar, but Elliot got a little worried when he saw that their legs were tied with white pieces of cloth. Camilla could have been reclining on the porch-glider for all she appeared to worry. She watched the reverend with that bright-eyed bird-look she laid on anything of real interest. Suddenly, her head slumped and she appeared to be sleeping. The girl next to her slumped at the same moment. The other two just kept quiet. The Reverend went over to them to untie their legs. Elliot let out his breath and realized he'd been holding on to it until he could see what the Reverend was going to do.

Elliot's heart thudded like a jackhammer against his breastbone. In all the comic books he'd read; in all the Tarzan stories engraved in his brain—virgins were sacrificed! He didn't know about the other girl, but he thought maybe

Camilla was one, although he didn't know for sure. She was liable not to be just because she didn't like to wear any kind of label. Two women with white cloths on their heads walked Camilla and the girl next to her to the middle of the circle. They were big women and they supported the girls under the arms to keep them from falling. The limbs of both girls were flaccid, as if they'd been asleep a long time. Two straight-backed chairs were set up in the middle of the floor to receive them. Elliot wanted to yell out, but his changing voice sat still in his squeaky throat. The girls now sat on the two chairs in the center of the circle. Two large platters of food connected by a bar were placed before them. *"Le plat-Marasa,"* said the Reverend Simmons.

The Reverend called out:

> *Marasa simap rélé loa io mian min.*
> I am calling the twin spirits to eat.
> I am calling you.

Camilla awakened with a toss of her head and a petulant mouth. Everything about her was different—the way she cocked her head, her hands. A sour little expression sat on her face like a small toad. The other girl woke up doubling Camilla's every display of emotion. Both looked as if they'd cry if they didn't get their way immediately. They found the food in front of them and fell on it like a pair of starving Pekingese. Elliot, long accustomed to Camilla's big appetite, was appalled. This was ridiculous. She'd lost all control; stuffing bread, squash, okra—things he knew she didn't like— into her mouth with both hands. Her twin did the same thing. The congregation hummed along while the twins stuffed their fat little faces. They began to sing in earnest when Camilla and her twin found whole chickens and started tearing meat off the bones, flinging the remains up onto the altar where, as natural artifacts, they didn't look terribly out of place.

> *O Marasa min dlo min mange, Fammi Marasa pran io.*

Twins here are water and food for you.
Parents come and get them.
Help me, *Marasa.*
I provide you with food so you will help me.

While the congregation sang this plaintive refrain, Camilla and Pamella Jeanne (that's who he'd decided the other girl was) didn't miss a beat on the vittles. Camilla had some kind of red sauce from the squash all over her face, and when the twin looked up, she had it on her mouth and cheeks. He didn't know how they managed to get it into their eyebrows but Camilla was using the back of her hand to smear it up toward her hair.

Two women from the congregation rushed up with hot towels scented with Florida water — Elliot could smell it all the way outside. The women washed the girls' faces tenderly but Camilla pushed the women washing her away, and the twin was just as impolite. Elliot thought about how spoiled Camilla could act at eighteen. He was glad he hadn't known her at four — Pamella either. They picked up the *plat-Marasa* and licked it clean. Elliot was shocked to see Took sit through this whole display of bad manners without correcting Camilla Jane. He didn't figure she had too much control over Pamella Jeanne since she was dead anyway.

There didn't seem to be any more food arriving. The twins stood up and linked arms together, and then, like some sort of sister act, they began to sing in the sweetest soprano voices he'd ever heard. Elliot didn't know Camilla Jane could sing. At home she always tried to sound like a blues singer. They sang:

Loa Marasa nou rivé
Sa ki mande pou loa Marasa nou rivé
Ba nou sa o nou rivé.
We are the twin spirits, your protectors.
We are saying that we are here.
Who has asked for the twin spirits?

Here we are, give us what you have prepared for us.

But no one moved to get more food, and Elliot heard a fat woman in the congregation say, "I wish they'd go back where they come from. They always hungry." He thought about the pecan pie on the table outside in its nest of dishcloth, and wished he had a piece. The congregation began to sing again:

> *Marasa nou nan noi e*
> *Olicha Nago.*
> Twin spirits we are in misery.
> Good spirits from Nago, we are in misery.
> We say keep your ties with us.
> When next you come there will be food.
> We won't let you beg.
> We are strong and we'll feed you well
> next time you come.

The girls answered:

> *Marasa io dosa min ianvalou moin.*
> We are female twins and our eyes are
> wide open to see what's going on.
> Our mother sent us from Guinea
> to see what's going on.
> *Marasa prété nou ché-z pou nou chita pou moin gadé io*
> *Bouch io pou io is di sa io vle.*
> Bring us twin chairs so that we can keep
> our eyes on them.
> Their mouths are theirs;
> they can say what they want to.

The twins sat down again on the chairs brought for them. They sat staring at the congregation with their arms folded and disgusted expressions on their faces.

The congregation began again:

> *Marasa,* we went to the wood.

We went to the sea.
We went to the river.
We are asking your blessing and your forgiveness.

To Elliot the singing had begun to sound a little frantic, like his mother's polite conversation when she was trying to be nice to guests who'd stayed longer than three days and had begun to stink like fish.

But now the Reverend Simmons moved back before the congregation, and he sang in a very deep voice:

You are very tired, *Marasa.*
Go to sleep now, little girls.
Your bellies are full. Go to sleep.

They didn't answer back and Elliot saw their heads drop. In a few moments they opened their eyes, and it was Camilla Jane back inside her eyes, all grown up and making the sweet mouth to the whole congregation, who grumbled, "Who does she think she is?" and didn't smile back. The other girl had ceased to look anything like Camilla, and acted like she had some kind of attitude all the time. They were called back to their earlier positions, and once more Elliot's stomach jumped as the Reverend bound their legs. "No," Elliot said aloud, but no one heard him. How could anyone as free as Camilla Jane Maynard allow some man to bind her legs? It made him sick.

He was afraid his heart would burst out of his chest and run up the aisle screaming. But his heart did not burst out and he was too sick to do anything but watch.

"Damn," he said aloud, and in his own litany: "Boy, boy, boy, little boy."

The Reverend carried a jar like a flower pot with a cover and placed it by the head of the first girl. The women in the congregation began to dip and sway to the music which was insistent — constant. Elliot's brain was aswirl with ideas to save Camilla Jane from some indignity worse than making a pig of herself. He was puzzled that Took, her friend, would put her in this unsafe situation. But Took was an adult even though she usually sided with children. The deacon, or whatever he was, continued to bring out clay jars — one at a time from the sacristy — to place by the head of each girl lying there like a tied calf waiting for the branding iron. The knot in Elliot's stomach tightened when the deacon placed one by Camilla's head.

But now something had happened to the floor among the dancers. One woman had gone blank in the eyes and begun to quiver. Her shaking added to Elliot's excited feelings.

A man from the congregation brought an enamel basin and a towel. The woman washed her face carefully and motioned for the other man to bring something else. A mirror. The dancing woman began to fix her face with powder and put on perfume. The fragrance drifted out to Elliot. Each thing to make her pretty was brought by a member of the congregation, mostly by men. There was something very exciting to Elliot about the woman's concern with her appearance. She put on a *peignoir* of thin cloth and a delicate rose silk scarf she wound around her hair, her arms high above her head, and Elliot saw the rounded tilt of her breast which inspired in him a terrible longing. As the last act of toilette, she put on a necklace, two bracelets and three gold rings.

"*Erzuli, Erzuli,*" whispered the voices in the room.

He noticed one of her legs is rooted to the floor, and she begins to spin on it like a top, loosening it only to get stuck again. Many men were there watching the dance, but not taking part. In the eyes of Elliot they now took on a sinister expression. The rooted woman was helped by other dancers; each time she gets stuck it was harder for her to pull her foot out. Elliot tried to see better. He thought there might be a hole in the floor because it had gotten so hard for her to pull her foot out. Suddenly, she becomes unstuck and her whole demeanor changed. She flirted with him because she knows he's there. She seemed nothing special to Elliot before the powder, perfume and flirtation, but now she moved her body in such a sinuous way that Elliot couldn't take his eyes off her. Her face lit up the way Camilla's did when she was pleased with herself or him and when she knew how pretty she is. Beautiful—as if she wanted to belong to every person in the room. The woman moved her hips in a rocking motion—back and forth, back and forth; Elliot could feel his own body thrusting back and forth. He knew she was directing her dance toward him—the same way he knew the band at the circus played for him. It was like they were dancing slow drag together. In fact, he moved back and forth so much and got so warm, and then warmer, until suddenly he felt terribly relieved, as if a terrible burden had been lifted off his mind. He was embarrassed to notice there seemed to be some physical evidence of this relief but no one could see him—except maybe the dancer, and he wasn't sure of that anymore.

But now the woman's demeanor had changed again. She danced slowly over to a skinny old man who sat on the front row; he looked sick or starved or both. The woman who dominated all other figures in the room embraced him. She petted his head tenderly and placed her mouth on his lips. After she kissed him her face clouded up and she began to cry. The congregation called out, "*O metres, o Zili, Freda Daomé, help us.*"

The old man began to sing:

> *Erzuli, oteeeourieyou pa oue moin n dlo.*
> Don't you see I am drowning? You pass by.
> I say, *Erzuli,* where are you?
> Don't you see I am drowning?

Terrible sobs poured out of Erzuli; she wrung her hands in a washing motion, and spilled out sweet words into the old man's ear, who sat like an ancient battle-scarred tomcat too sick and old to react to her kisses. Again Elliot felt an ache at his own root. But then the old man took life, responding "*Mon cher, Mon coeur.*" Erzuli and the old man clung together in an agony of sorrow until some of the women ushers appeared with cups of water to restore them. The woman was led away, still crying miserably, to a straight-backed chair on which she flung herself. As the ushers tried to comfort her she stiffened and changed; the light went out within, and an ordinary woman sat limply in the chair.

Elliot, fascinated by the woman with the rooting leg, had not been watching Camilla Jane. As he looked at her now, he saw the deacon was holding open a clay pot tipped on its side. It had not been placed by Camilla but by the head of the girl lying next to her. The jars by the other girls stood upright with the tops on them. Elliot felt he had missed something. The Reverend Simmons stood over the girl. He passed his hand from her feet to her head. Her body lifted as if a charge of energy like electricity flowed invisibly along her spine. Again Elliot felt he had missed something. The Deacon quickly capped the pot and stood it upright. Now the Reverend Simmons stood over Camilla Jane. Elliot's heart palpitated wildly.

As the Reverend lifted his hand, Camilla's body shivered from toe to head as something flowed into the capped pot. Elliot saw it move in like a snake into a basket. At least he felt he had seen it. There was no visible thing that had passed in but he had seen it go and something of Camilla or from Camilla was in the clay jar. He was too late. He felt a cold fury, and now he could not help himself. He flung open the window and cried: "Stop." And his voice came out in its deepest tone. The whole congregation looked up to see him standing above them poised on the window ledge. The Reverend did not bend to cap the jar.

Camilla Jane sat up abruptly and said, "Elliot, you get down from there right now. You have no right to mess this up. You'd better let Pamella Jeanne go on and get in that jar so I can get some use out of her." And then, turning to the reverend, she said, "You get right on with our business. That's just my little cousin."

She lay back down and closed her eyes. Elliot, who should have felt dismissed but didn't, said, "Okay, have it your way but I'm here if you need me," in the same deep voice. The Reverend Simmons stooped and capped the jar. When he stood he said, "The ritual is finished. The *govi* is full—nothing is lost. The community is served." And he turned to Elliot, who was still standing on the window ledge, and smiled. "Come in young *serviteur*. I see you have given yourself to *Maitresse*. Come in. Come in, young devotee. *Maitresse* is a generous mistress. You won't be sorry. Now your cousin is well and it is time to feast."

At these words the congregation rushed outside, and Elliot got down to get some pecan pie.

Buying Back

THEY DIDN'T GET HOME UNTIL WAY PAST DARK—late. A light was on, which meant someone was waiting up for him. Camilla Jane went on home to bed. He was glad because the sight of her set Moo off. Took had come into the house with him armed with an alibi. As soon as he saw Moo sitting up by herself in the rocking chair in the double parlor, he knew the alibi wouldn't do any good. Moo didn't say anything when they came slinking in. She never did, just waited for them to hang themselves.

Took started out pretty good: "Moo, I want to tell you how sorry I am you was worried about Elliot. He went with us to Bayou Goulah to the cemetery by my *parain*'s house. We had a picnic, and then he helped us clear up the graves. I didn't know you hadn't given him permission to go, or I would have come right over here to see if he could—" Her voice trailed off.

Moo's eyes were hard as flint and her words shed sparks.

"You ruined him. Elliot got ruined with you and your alley cat. I can tell by the way he walks. He walked in here like he thinks he's got something big in his pants, like some old tom cat. You didn't go by your *parain*. You didn't go by your *tante*. You went to some spiritual church and got Elliot chained up like you been chained all your life. Don't come around here with your lies and your poor mouth how Miss Mag treat you bad and you got to get some *gris-gris* or Boss Fix Powder to help out. You trying to act so gracious to me about Elliot. I know what I know. Now you always afraid of the *bokor*. You better be afraid of me. I'm stronger than the reverend. If Elliot's ruined it's going to fall on your head. I'm telling you something you know about. There's going to be a *coup l'aire* or *poudre* in the shape of a cross on your doorstep tuned to your footstep and blood in your bed. Now you tell me the truth and I'll see what I can do to help you."

Elliot was trying to lay low. He was glad Took had come because she was getting it all. Took was shaking and begging now. She said, "Moo, I promised to tell you and I will; don't set nothing on me, Moo. I didn't take Elliot there on purpose. I took Camilla because she's got nothing to start with. She needs her *gros bon-ange* because her sister's dead, and she don't have nothing to work with. Her mama's about to go to the poor house. Half the time Miss Mag don't have milk in the house. She's going to sell Camilla off any way she can. Camilla Jane's got to have some strength to deal with it all. Creeping Jesus so sneaky he just laid in the back of the truck and came along for the ride. We didn't know he was there until he jumped out to eat pecan pie."

"Don't you call him Creeping Jesus. His name is Elliot—Mister Elliot to you. You sure nothing happened to Elliot?" Moo pulled out her most suspicious look. "He looks different to me. He looks ruined to me."

"Oh, no, Moo. All he did was eat a whole pecan pie by himself. He sat outside and watched through the window. He didn't get serviced or nothing. He just sat outside and then, when the Reverend Simmons saw him after the ceremony he invited him to eat."

"That's it?"

"That's all."

"Well, you got off this time, but if Elliot shows up any worse for the wear I'm going to get me a piece of your hide and the Reverend Simmons too. Miss Mag know anything about this?"

"Lord, no. She's off in Baton Rouge at some bridge tournament trying to make some money to run the house on."

Elliot couldn't believe his good luck. It was Took Moo was mad at. He didn't even get punished. If anything, she was much nicer to him than usual, cooking him special things he liked and ironing his pajamas. He loved to have his pajamas ironed. The soft cotton felt slick as talcum powder against his skin, and everything that smelled good or felt good, felt better these days. He was stronger, too, and he worked his muscles out every day on an exerciser called a SuperToner he'd ordered from a Superman comic book. It was a coiled spring with two handles and it came with a set of exercises written on tissue paper in very small print.

He was breezing through school. Moo had kept him at the books through eighth grade, now high school was a snap. He'd skipped one grade, and developed an erudite style of speaking when he was not excited or upset. It was similar to Took's church style. The brothers kept talking about a scholarship to Tulane he'd be eligible for when he got ready to graduate in a couple of years. Later he would be going to Tulane Law School because his dad had gone there. He wasn't interested in law, but nobody had ever asked him what he was interested in. He saw less of Camilla Jane these days. It was getting close to time for her to graduate, and Aunt Mag had been turning over every rock looking for a way to get the money for Camilla to go to Newcomb in New Orleans. Camilla was willing to go to Newcomb. She'd flat out refused to go to finishing school, which was where Mag had made a deal to send her. Mag hadn't yet found a way to get her to college so there was an impasse, which was the usual state of affairs next door. Camilla's grades were terrible. The nuns had suspended her for disobedience and insubordination at least once every year since the fourth grade. Sister Mark didn't like Camilla Jane. Obedience was the rule of the order, and Camilla Jane had never obeyed anything but her own nature.

Elliot felt less needy. Took saying High John had bound him was a myth. If anything, he was less dependent on Camilla's lead than he could ever remember. He had found another mistress, someone stronger than Camilla, and she was willing beyond his wildest dreams.

Elliot was now a regular attendant at the Reverend Simmons's church. Took and Camilla had not been back since the *marasa* ceremony. The acquisition of Camilla's *gros bon-ange* had not seemed to make a big difference in her life, but in truth, Elliot had not been keeping count of Camilla's successes. Instead, he had managed, by increasing the number of imaginary tennis games he played on Sunday, and the imaginary bus trips he took with the good brothers, to fool Moo into thinking he had become a good Catholic boy who athletically rid himself of all impure thought through the diligent use of exercise and cold showers. He had become addicted to Erzuli.

He spent much of his time as a sort of fly on the wall of the Reverend Simmons's church, watching the *hounsis* dance. He hitchhiked, often arriving after the service had started. He stationed himself at different windows hoping for the appearance of Erzuli. Sometimes he was rewarded, often not. Her embodiment was different each time. He learned the habits of all the *loa:* the hunger of Legba who can't be fed enough even by all the deaths of the world; Damballah the great serpent, Ogun the warrior; Marasa the hungry children; and Erzuli the goddess of love. It was Erzuli who made the back of his tongue ache like aspirin; it was Erzuli who released him from desire without touching his body. It was she who kept him coming back for more.

And the congregation was not unaware of his visits. Sometimes the Reverend Simmons would call out when a beautiful young woman was ridden by the *loa*. "Ah, *Maitresse*, you have a secret admirer. He's spilling seeds from his pocket onto our graves. Now no one can steal our dead. There are too many seeds. A thief would count seeds until daybreak."

But no one came to accost him. No one said, "Get off our church, you Peeping Tom." They accepted him with light-hearted grace as a real devotee of Maitresse, one who was slightly removed — outside of things, as Moo, who sat outside the family pew on the side of the Catholic church in High Castle.

But nothing ever stays the same. It was Moo. It was Moo, as it had always been Moo, who changed this, put things in perspective.

She was dressed in her best, and it was only Saturday morning. His mother came through the dining room carrying a portable easel and wearing a sun visor. "Where are you going all dressed up?" she asked Moo.

"I've decided to buy some land, and I'm taking Elliot with me to help me."

"That's very nice, Moo," his mother said. "A little house for your old age?" And she passed on about her business without waiting for a reply. Elliot stood there sweaty from shooting baskets in the backyard. He hadn't known he was going anywhere. Moo sent him to bathe, commanding him to "Dress in your blue blazer." When he tried to ask where they were going, she wouldn't answer any questions and was stern as she'd ever been with him. He came out with wet hair. She sent him back to shave off the few blond hairs clinging to his upper lip. He had been in hopes of growing a moustache. At last he was dressed to her satisfaction, which left him seething with poorly concealed resentment. They went out the front door and got into a new Packard chauffeured by Took's brother, Little Robert.

As they left High Castle by the river road, Elliot began to

have real fears about their destination. Moo was carrying her cane which was the dried and stretched penis of a dead bull. She'd had it forever, but she seldom carried it because Ann Elise considered it disgusting. Moo saved it for great or cere-monial occasions. There was an unwritten law that his mother would never comment on the cane if the occasion was great.

The back seat of the car was a vacuum, impossible to breathe in. His nose was so stopped up his upper palate clung to the roof of his nose—a physical impossibility. In a panic Elliot rolled down a window, but suffered burning eyes from noxious fumes escaping from the exhaust. He remembered reading that Pliny the elder died of noxious fumes when his curiosity led him to investigate an eruption of Vesuvius by climbing to peer over the rim. He couldn't believe a new car would have such a bad exhaust.

"Whose car is this?" he asked.

"Never mind. It runs, don't it?" They lapsed into an op-pressive silence. He would have welcomed carbon monoxide; it was invisible, painless, but no less deadly than Moo's wrath. He knew now they were going to the church, and he rode along with an anticipatory dread that was the exact opposite of his usual dreams of future delights.

As the church came into view, Elliot kept his eyes on the brown and white cows placidly eating grass on the levee. When the Packard drove right past, he was overwhelmed with joy and thanked High John, Erzuli, and St. Jude the Saint of impossible causes. His joy was premature, however, as Lit-tle Robert soon stopped and went into a tin-roofed lean-to with one room attached and a hand-lettered sign above the door that announced it was The Sweet Shop. Robert came out shortly and said to Moo, "It's over there," pointing to a neat green house with a white picket fence. They pulled up out front. Little Robert got out and rang the bell on the gate. El-liot recognized the good looking woman who came out. She was one of the dancing *hounsis* from the church. Elliot blushed when he thought of the last time he'd seen her.

She went into the house, and after about ten minutes came

back out to the car. She said, "The Reverend Simmons will see you now." Elliot felt like his hands hung out from his coat sleeves about two feet. The blazer sleeves were only about an inch too short, but he felt like Sammy, the boy in town who stuck his head out of a moving train when it was passing a concrete bridge pier and lived. Sammy just kept getting bigger, but he didn't get smarter or any less soft. Just bigger.

Moo said to the woman, "We've come to buy property. Does he understand that?"

"Yes," said the woman, "he does."

Elliot was glad the Reverend Simmons understood because he sure as hell didn't. They followed the woman inside. Robert didn't come with them. Elliot held the front door for Moo, and she gave him one fierce look before they went in.

"Remember, Elliot, you don't open your mouth. No matter what happens." They were led into the living room, which was small and close. There was a long, hard bench set out in front of a high-back black wicker chair where the Reverend Simmons sat looking for all the world like a Roman Catholic bishop. He even had a big ring. Elliot let out a strangled little laugh. Moo gave him the look. Behind the Reverend was a plain shelf with a big statue of St. Expedité sitting on it. There was nothing else around that reminded Elliot of the altar in the church. The Reverend Simmons was downright *fraicheur*. Elliot had learned that word by watching Erzuli. She was big into being *fraicheur* because she started out hot, always fanning herself to get cool. The reverend indicated the bench with an imperial wave of his hand. Moo did not sit down. Elliot stood beside her, still feeling like Sammy, sort of simple and useless. The Reverend Simmons gave no indication that he recognized Elliot.

"Won't you sit down," the reverend tried again.

"No," said Moo. Her head well above his. Elliot noticed the Reverend Simmons picked up his own cane which had been leaning against the wall. He closed his hand over the ebony carving on the top before he said, "As you wish. I like my guests to be comfortable. I realize old bones are often more comfortable standing."

"We've come to buy property," she said, and banged the bull cock on the floor so hard it made a thunderous hollow sound like there was a deep cavern under the floor.

"I have no property to sell you," the Reverend said and banged his cane even harder.

"You can find some. I have the price," said Moo using the cane like a hammer with a flexible handle pounding invisible nails.

The Reverend, becoming agitated said, "Go see a real estate man," and he banged his cane twice. The sound was less persuasive.

Moo pulled herself up taller and shot her bull cane out like a custom cue to hit the wall right below the statue of St. Expedité, which fell into the wastebasket like a ball dropping into a pocket.

"I need some property right now. I've got your price right here." Without aiming this time she banged the metal wastebasket, St. Expedité rattling down from his nest of paper in the top of the basket like plaster dropping from a ceiling. When the metal can stopped dancing, it tipped over, spilling out the saint in three distinct pieces. One of which was the Saint's head.

The Reverend, obviously undone, picked up the pieces.

Moo smiled, "Oh, Reverend Simmons," she said. "I owe you for your property. Sometimes this cane has too much kick, and I can't control it. I'll have to pay you for your property. I hope fifty dollars will take care of it."

She reached into her purse and peeled off five ten-dollar bills as if she did it every day and laid the cash on the shelf where the statue of St. Expedité had stood. The Reverend's eyebrows were strung together like storm clouds, but he didn't say anything about not accepting the money.

Moo said, "I'm leaving now," and gave one more mighty clap on the floor with the bull's pizzle. The Reverend Simmons jumped like he'd been shot. When she turned to the door, Elliot was already there to open it. They went out to the Packard, where Little Robert stood with the door open. She got in and Elliot followed, feeling more and more like Sammy. As they passed the church, Elliot took a good long look at it because he figured he wouldn't be visiting there much anymore.

The Shed

ELLIOT LAY ON TOP OF THE SHED STARING OUT through green while rubbing his stomach with a slow steady rhythm. Through the overlapping branches of the fig tree, he heard Moo call him from far away in another world. He would not come down. The earth had been shifting under him. He had to stay above it. The roof of the shed was solid. The world of the fig tree small. It was not an earthquake that moved the world. It was a slow shifting of dirt too full of water—grass that looked solid until you put your foot through to sour water and muck sucking at your legs—a shifting world that made you feel dirty and smell bad—unsure of how to go on.

His body was changing. Hair was growing on his stomach. It was a straight line moving downward. Now today there was more hair; among the soft down were three black hairs on his balls. The only thing worse was hair on the ears; hair on the ears was death. His grandfather grew hair on the ears and it killed him. He'd once heard his cool, seersuckered father chewing his thin cigar telling off a truck driver who'd dropped a Mallard chair. "You've got a pair of hairy ones," his father said in some heat. Elliot didn't know what he'd meant at the time, but today, with a sudden flash, he knew because now Elliot had a pair—although the hair was sparse.

"Elliot, are you up there?" she called.

He didn't answer. Camilla Jane came up by the jagged cypress fence, clambering up to the solid cross-bar that held the fence together, walking along behind pickets, balancing on bare feet as she hoisted herself up to the tin roof where Elliot lay flat under the branches. Slightly out of breath and smelling of soap, she dropped down beside him where she sat on her inner thighs with her legs bent behind her, knees forward. She took over the roof the way she took over a room. He sighed with great weariness.

"I don't know why you like to lie down under fig branches. The leaves are sticky and they don't smell nice like sweet olive."

"I like to be by myself," he said pointedly.

"No, you don't. You like to be with me," she said, unfolding her legs and scooting down beside him so that they both lay on the cool, corrugated tin up under the overlapping branches of two fig trees and the taller half-shade of an ancient bay leaf tree. The wavy no-man's-land of roof between the trees was hot enough to fry corrugated eggs, and a hot smell came up from the tin behind him when he turned to look at Camilla Jane. She pressed the bay leaf she was carrying up to his nose, cupping his face the way he cupped his cat's nose into the palm of his hand to feel the wet softness. The scent rushed him into the pleasant daydream of dry bay leaf floating in a delicious brown gumbo.

"Took said you were fooling with my High John."

"I touched it."

"Then you can have anything you want."

"It wasn't anything, just an old medicine root."

"I said, you can have anything you want."

"I bet."

"Elliot, the trouble with you is you're too smart; you out-smart yourself because you're smart about the wrong things. Things people know in their heads. You can do anything you want if you feel toward it. High John draws—he draws what you need, so you can use it for what you want.

"Yeah, well it's not going to help me. What I want is too hard."

"What do you want?"

"Can't tell," he said, still feeling the line of hair beginning at the top of his shorts.

"Can't even tell me? I thought we could tell each other anything—"

"You didn't tell me about High John or your *gros bon-ange*."

"I did when you asked me. I didn't want to think I needed him or her."

"Why not?"

"Because I should be able to do what I want—anything." Her voice was unexpectedly fierce. "My mother can."

"No she can't. She never has enough money, but she can make other people do things they don't want. It's always just next things next. If somebody else wants something then she knows what she wants—just the opposite."

"Don't talk about my mother."

"Sorry."

"She's always trying to make me do something."

"You've gotten good at fighting her, Camilla."

"Doesn't work—we get what neither one of us wants, and we tire each other out. Women shouldn't work against each other. Nobody wins. We wouldn't have the strength for a real enemy. We'd be too tired from fighting each other."

"Hmmm," he said. He'd lost interest in the warfare between Aunt Mag and Camilla. It tired him out too. He could see stilt-legged spiders stalking around. Their tiny bodies were like spots of red cayenne in the green tent of the tree as her urgent voice moistened his ear with words he'd stopped hearing; he'd stopped hearing her but he could still smell her.

The smell of Camilla's body was stronger than bay leaf, tin shed, or fig leaves. The dreamy rubbing of his stomach had gained some insistence now.

Her voice dropped again, and he heard it. "Tell me what you asked High John for."

"I don't think I should."

She put her hand on his arm and the tiny hairs under her fingers felt like electric wires connected to his body. He sucked in his breath so that she tightened her fingers."

"Does something hurt?"

"Sort of," he said.

"What?"

"I can't tell you," he said.

She leaned closer. Her hair against his cheek, those hairs plugged in too, so that the part of his body that hurt began to nose up to make itself visible and known.

He hadn't stopped rubbing his stomach. Now her hand dropped to the waist of his drawstring shorts, and she too began sliding her fingers over the short hairs on his belly. His eyes closed and he held his breath until it came out in short gasps—rapid as the shallow breath of a bird. He had gone inside himself now and couldn't hide anything from her as it passed before his eyes.

"What is it you want, Elliot?"

"You," he said, and the word croaked out of his throat in the deeper voice that came and went now.

"Well, why didn't you say so?" she said with one of those deep chuckles that made him so happy.

Her hand now moved under the drawstring and down, holding him. Just as slowly as he had been rubbing his stomach, she began rubbing his hard flesh, which strained and bent again his shorts and her firm grip. Her hand was the most he'd ever felt. All other sensation—smell, taste, feel—was concentrated on this point of contact between her hand and his flesh. As she pushed down his shorts and held him openly, a new insistence rushed him to some conclusion, and as it did she turned and bent over him and kissed him on the mouth. Her mouth was all the wide, deep kisses she had ever kissed him. He felt himself rushing into her hand as his tongue rushed into her mouth, and an electrical current shot up his spine. He felt closer to her and more distant from the world than he'd ever felt in his life.

"You see, Elliot. High John will get you anything you want." Her voice sounded calm and slightly amused. "Did you like it?"

Like it? He was nailed to the shed. He couldn't answer. She began rubbing again, and he felt a cold wet stickiness on his shorts. He groaned, but he felt his body respond again, and once more he moved into her hand as if it were home. She took his hand and moved it inside the wide leg of her shorts. Like the disembodied hand in a movie he'd seen once, his hand found its own way under the tight elastic leg of her underpants to something warm and slick with an unbearable softness. His finger barely moved, but he felt her body quiver and stiffen as her hand relaxed against him. He had to move himself against her to join whatever was happening. They lay up under the fig trees holding hands, and a cool breeze began to play over their bodies in such a delicious way that he felt as if no time or place could be any better.

"Things look better, don't they?" she asked.

But he had begun to feel a little sad.

"Did High John give you what you want?"

"Yes," he said.

"Is that all?"

He didn't answer, because already in the back of his mind was the thought that there might be—there just might be something else.

The Party

SISTER EUPHEMIA SAID, "CAMILLA JANE'S OUR FREE bird. She'll fly high, if nobody shoots her down." Camilla Jane was to graduate from St. Basil's Academy in May but it looked like a near miss. She lacked half a credit. After many dramatic visits by Mag, they finally agreed to let her go out of sheer weariness.

There was to be a tea at Elliot's house — at least his grandmother called it a tea. Mag called it open season, and Mag organized it. Everyone in the family was pressed into service. For three days Moo and Elliot's mother, Ann Elise, cleaned silver and argued. "Moo if you were any kind of a housekeeper the coffee service wouldn't be blue-black."

"You're right. And if you was any kind of a manager, you'd have told me in plenty time to clean it. All you do is paint Morning Glories. If you seen one Morning Glory, you seen them all. And why we got to hang ugly Morning Glories on the wall when we got pretty Morning Glories in the yard I don't know." She held up the coffee pot. "What you think about morning glories, Mr. Pot? I think they ugly. I think they crawl all over everything and choke it to death."

Ann Elise, who hated parties and wanted nothing more than to go back to her easel, scrubbed at the silver grape leaves, her mouth pressed thin as a dime, while Moo, laughing because she'd got her goat, rubbed the moon side of the coffee pot to a shine.

In April a dress had appeared on the cover of *Vogue* magazine; white, imported Swiss organdy, it had a pale blue satin cummerbund and giant bow in the back. Mag couldn't afford the original but she made a deal with Miss Tweet Lemoine. If Miss Tweet would copy the dress cheap enough, Mag promised to get her a new and fashionable following. Miss Tweet, consumed by ambition, kept Camilla Jane standing on chairs and tables for three weeks to make sure the hem hung right. She was so pleased with her own artistry, and with the promise of a new following that she had business cards engraved: ***Clothilde Lemoine, Modiste***. When Mag and Camilla came for a fitting she whispered, "Miss Magdalene, only give the cards to the best families."

On the Wednesday before the party, Mag passed the cards out at bridge but couldn't resist saying with a curled lip, "I wish High Castle had a real *modiste* instead of Hot Seam Lemoine."

Three days later, when she went to pick up the dress from Miss Tweet's house, Miss Tweet acted funny. Elliot was sitting in the kitchen with Took and Camilla Jane, when Mag came in and told them about it.

"Hot Seam finally lost her mind," she said. "She wouldn't talk to me except to say, 'It's in that gunny sack over there. Take it or leave it. I was sewing a pretty *hot* seam last night after I heard about the bridge party.' She closed her Singer up with a snap, turned out the light, and pulled the flowered curtain that shuts off her bedroom from the shop right in my face.

When I tried to get her out, she said, 'This shop is closed, Sister.' She let me stumble around in the dark and put the dress in the car by myself; it's probably a mess of wrinkles. I don't know what got into her. But she was never too bright. Anybody who sews that much for that little has got to be crazy."

Camilla Jane went into the house to try the dress on, and Mag collapsed in the blue rocker by the kitchen table. Took gave Mag a demitasse and a glass of ice-water on a little side table. Mag took her shoes off and put her feet up on the cane-bottomed chair.

"This hasn't been my day," she said.

"Thank God, I've got my old servant to take care of me." And she patted Took's hand. "You are my old servant aren't you, Took?"

Elliot couldn't breathe. He knew Mag was working up to calling Took some bad name. Mag was pouting now, drinking her coffee with a sour look on her face.

Took went to the sink and started washing dishes. Her back expressed such weariness that Elliot picked up the dish-towel to dry. In a few minutes Camilla Jane came stomping back wearing the starched petticoat, "It's limp as a damp dish rag. And the dress is falling apart. All I did was pull a piece of thread and the whole hem unraveled. You're cheap, Mag. You had to bad mouth Miss Tweet after she did you a favor. I'm going to be standing bare-ass naked in the receiving line because you couldn't keep a bargain. My dress is going to fall off because you had to save ten cents."

"Well, I'm glad my daughter can afford complete honesty. I can't. Don't ever marry a poor man, Miss Priss."

"What's going on here?" Camilla looked at Took's back and Mag sitting in the rocker. "I said, what's going on here? What's wrong with Took?"

"Aunt Mag patronized Took. She was getting ready to call her a bad name."

"I don't know what you're talking about. She and Moo call each other names all the time."

"You don't know—what do you mean you don't know?

You know, Mag. You know. You're petty and you're mean, Mag. It's a wonder Took doesn't fix you some elephant ear tea. You'd better apologize or there won't be any Camilla Jane at your fine party. I don't want to get married anyway."

"Don't be silly. Took knows I didn't mean anything. Forget it, Took. I'm sorry. I was just all disgusted with Miss Tweet for being so unreasonable."

"It's not much, Took," Camilla said. "Consider the source. It's probably the best you're going to get from Mag."

"Good thing you didn't say that to Moo," Elliot said as he skipped out the screen door.

Mag sat up half the night whipping in a new hem. Took re-starched the petticoat and hung it over the stove to dry. The next morning the whole kitchen smelled sweet; the starch had dripped onto the stove, sizzling and giving off a perfume that kept Elliot pointing his nose to the petticoat like a spotted bird dog. Took, wearing a seven-pointed black doo-rag tied on her head, stumbled over Elliot sitting by the stove. "You'd better get out of here, Creeping Jesus. That nose of yours always gone to get you in trouble," she said.

It was early evening. The tea at Elliot's house was in the double parlor. Aunt Mag had invited eligible men as well as ladies. She said, "I can't afford to outfit Camilla Jane for every jackass party that comes along. We've got to get as much mileage out of this shindig as possible. God help the genteel poor."

She dominated the receiving line, not looking at all like a poor relation. Elliot's grandmother, who was paying for the party did, however. Her thin, nervous hands and rusty black dress belonged to someone who was never quite sure. Aunt Mag wore violet crepe and a string or pearls that dangled from the mountain of her bosom like a lifeline. A climber could have swung himself over the crevasse between her breasts. Elliot had been afraid of her all of his life—ran when she called, hid when she passed. This evening was no different but he hung nearer than usual because Camilla Jane, wearing the white dress off the cover of *Vogue* magazine, stood next to Mag in the receiving line; his grandmother in black and his mother in pale grey also stood with Camilla Jane, offering their hands to people they saw only at weddings and funerals.

There was no Uncle Mag. Elliot wouldn't have known why except for a minor accident one day at Kimburger's store. He was carrying the basket for Took when she sent him to get Pine Oil. He picked up Lysol by mistake; it slipped from his hand to the white tile floor, where it broke, flooding the store with a strong medicinal odor. Took jumped like she'd been shot and screamed, "Mr. Horatio's walking," then folded herself over the broom and mops, holding onto the handles. Elliot stood by while the butcher fanned her face, but it was the Lysol odor that revived her. When she came-to she made the sign of the cross and kissed her thumb. Mr. Kimburger took them home in his new two-toned blue and white Studebaker.

They helped Took to her quarters, a small neat room in the back of the house with a lavatory and a big toilet hidden behind a brown curtain. After Mr. Kimburger left, Elliot immediately used the toilet. There was something daring about using a toilet where people in the room could hear him pee. Then Elliot sat with Took to keep her company while she told him about Uncle Horatio. "He was a gentleman didn't care about or know how to make money. He swallowed Lysol on purpose — put it in a whiskey sour with ice and a cherry in it, then said to Miss Mag, 'Here's to you my iron darling.' It blistered his esophagus and weakened his lungs. He was sick for a week and died of pneumonia. Miss Mag worried they was going to bury him in unconsecrated ground, but Dr. Parker signed the death certificate 'Pneumonia,' and didn't say nothing about the Lysol."

"How come you think he's 'walking,' Took?"

"Because of Camilla Jane. He's looking out for her. Mr. Horatio's nurse was a Mambo. That's why it was Lysol that broke not Pine Oil. A Mambo's breast gives milk one day and vinegar the next. Children who teethe on Mambo milk crave acid, that's why he took Lysol — and they spiritual too — don't care too much for the world. Miss Mag don't care for nothing else, so he drank acid and left her to it. That was a mismatch anyway. That's why Miss Camilla Jane's spiritual and worldly. She's got them fighting in her. She put a splint on a roach's leg one day and step on him the next . He wants her spiritual, so he's walking. And he was walking at Kimburger's because that's where the Lysol is."

Elliot didn't like what she said about Camilla Jane so he said, "You're talking hocus-pocus, mumbo jumbo."

"Why you think Miss Mag outlaw Lysol and Hoodoo in this house if that ain't so?"

"My Daddy says your head's full of superstition."

"That's alright for you, Mister. Wait until Moo fixes your little red wagon. I'm going to tell her what you said." That night at supper Moo wouldn't give him bread pudding for dessert. She told his grandmother he'd sassed her. "I can't have that, Miss Elise. He'll spoil and salt won't save him."

"You're right, Moo. You should be ashamed of yourself, Elliot."

He said, "I'm ashamed." And excused himself from the table.

Moo, Took, and Robert David, Took's little brother who was fifty, passed up and down among the guests with artichoke leaves stuffed with shrimp dressing, fried oyster in garlic-butter sauce, shrimp rémoulade and little finger sandwiches. They had some kind of pink punch Elliot liked so much he almost finished the bowl.

The party had a hot band. The musicians were two second cousins from Corinth, Mississippi: Alissa Donleith, whose hair hung so long her hands got tangled in it when it swept the piano keys, and General Wathon McLean, who played drums. They were going through their repertoire of standards "Smoke Gets in Your Eyes" and "Dancing in the Dark," because the party was just getting started, but they could play fast dance music too. On the day before the party Elliot and Camilla Jane had danced and jumped around the room while the cousins played "Give Me a Pig Foot and a Bottle of Beer." Alissa sang it and Camilla strutted it in her blue short-shorts and Citadel sweat shirt. They danced until they fell in a sweaty heap on the floor and Moo brought in cherry pie. Camilla Jane wolfed down her piece then pulled up her shirttail to wipe the red juice off her chin. General got mad at her because it was his sweat shirt.

But now—tonight—Camilla Jane was not herself. She didn't move to the music when General went as crazy as Gene Krupa on the drums. She didn't tap her foot or move her fanny. She stood between her mother and Elliot's grandmother with her stomach sucked in and her chest stuck out, shaking hands with everybody who told her how beautiful she looked. And she leaned stiffly from the waist, presenting her cheek to be kissed. Her eyes looked sad to him, but she had a superior expression on her face, as if she were speaking to red orangutans, when she spoke to Mag's bridge ladies and thanked them for coming.

Elliot didn't see her eat anything, not even oysters with garlic butter. Usually, she was the first one in on the food, and she always spilled something on her dress—she was partial to red or brown stains. Took chasing Camilla Jane around with a wash rag was his favorite part of birthday parties. "You just stop, Miss. You stop dead or I'm going to trip you," Took would yell, and Camilla Jane would be turning around like a top. Once at her own birthday party she sat up in the Japanese plum tree because Took wanted to clean her dress, and Took sat under it with a peach switch for two hours waiting for her to come down.

Dr. Parker came in the front door with a man Elliot had never seen before. He tried to steer him in the direction of the receiving line, but Elliot watched the man do a neat sidestep to avoid it. His hair was prematurely grey and his face shone with a silvery sheen as if the barber had dusted him with talcum powder. Next to him Dr. Parker looked like the guy who didn't get the girl at the movies. Elliot's mother stepped out of the receiving line and came over to Dr. Parker and his friend since they hadn't come to her. Dr. Parker introduced him as Public Service Commissioner Soltice Busteaux of Crowley, Louisiana. In about fifteen minutes So Busteaux had six ladies around him asking questions about rice farming and the Public Service Commission. They were screaming at the top of their lungs so he'd hear them over the music because General Wathon McLean was flat out on the drums.

He answered even the silliest question as if it was the most important in the world. He made jokes in English, but Elliot heard him whisper in French into his mother's ear—lots of *jolies* and *belles*. She was blushing and looking very young, but Moo came by passing oyster patties. Moo said, loud enough for Elliot and So Busteaux to hear, "Swamp rat Cajun." His mother was eating it up; she ignored Moo, and acted as if So Busteaux was *gentil*. The only person who snubbed him was Moo, who passed him the artichoke leaves and said, *Cochon de lait?*" as if she were passing roast pig or calling him a pig, when it was really shrimp artichoke. He caught on right away and said, "Give me a piece of dark meat."

Elliot's mother turned red up to the dark roots of her hair, and left—just sailed right across the room with her hand outstretched to cousin Angeline Delahoussaye, who had already been received. Cousin Angeline looked confused, but she'd had a brain surgery and was out of it anyway. His mother said, "Cousin Angeline, how good to see you."

Moo cackled at what So Busteaux said. She topped him with, "You can't have a piece of dark meat; too tough for you. Try a mantel piece." She nodded over to Camilla Jane who was standing by the mantel greeting people. So Busteaux looked in her direction and it was a *coup de foudre*—one look and he was goners. He got into the receiving line by cutting in. Camilla Jane was the focus of everything. For Elliot she was a magnet. Hanging from a silk cord at her waist, she had a little satin pocketbook shaped like a flower, and suddenly—Elliot noticed—a long, dirty black fingernail stuck out of it. He felt his backbone drawn—he knew what she'd done with High John. He could see So Busteaux drawn to her, too, just like a dressmaker's pin.

When So Busteaux got in the receiving line—to Elliot it seemed a year before he took her hand—Camilla said, "I thought you'd never get here. I'm so tired of shaking hands," and she walked out of the line and left Mag standing there. But Mag, grateful she'd stayed as long as she did, passed off her leaving by telling everyone that Camilla Jane had a slight indisposition to seafood. Elliot knew she hadn't had anything to eat. Camilla Jane and So Busteaux went out on the gallery to talk. About half an hour later she took off with him in his yellow Cadillac and left Aunt Mag and Elliot's grandmother to explain the honoree's absence. Miss Elise said, "She's gone upstairs to recuperate."

But everyone knew what had happened: Camilla Jane Maynard took off from her own coming out party with a rice farmer from Crowley, Louisiana. A lady in a magenta taffeta dress sidled up to Aunt Mag and asked, "Tell me where *is* your lovely daughter?"

"Enjoying her life," said Mag through her teeth. Later Mag said, "If I'd been standing there with my hair on fire, I wouldn't have squirmed for that woman's satisfaction."

When Camilla Jane left, Elliot had a lost feeling in his chest; his clammy skin felt like something was crawling on his neck. He ran outside and jumped on his bike to follow them. It wasn't hard at first; they stopped at the drugstore in the next block for an ammonia Coke. But Elliot was pumping so fast he didn't brake in time, and his bike banged into the back fender of So Busteaux's car. Camilla Jane turned around and gave him a withering look, the kind that could kill flies. But when she saw who it was she said, "Oh, Elliot, I wish you were grown up. It'd be nice to marry family." Then So Busteaux came out of the drugstore with her Coke and they left.

Elliot pumped and pumped; his legs were moving automatically, moving closer to her. Camilla Jane kept looking back but then she laughed and said something to So Busteaux. He laughed too, and hit the gas, leaving Elliot weaving in the empty road. When they were just a dot in the distance, when he knew he could never catch her, he turned in front of a Breaux Bros. truck that had come from nowhere. It swerved to miss him, and the bike hit a concrete culvert. Elliot went down under his bike in a dry gravel ditch. The driver, who was one of his father's third cousins, brought him home. His mother and grandmother thought he'd gotten drunk from spiked punch, but he didn't get well that day or the next. In fact, he didn't get well.

Sick, Getting Sicker

TOOK CAME TO SEE HIM. SHE SAID, "POOR, LITTLE baby. I told you not to touch High John. Running your fingers over Camilla Jane's mojo got you stuck. She's going to marry So Busteaux and move up. You better get undone or you'll be sick for love all the time like Rose of Sharon love the invisible worm."

Elliot stayed in bed all that summer. His mother thought he had TB, but Doctor Parker called it rheumatic fever. Moo and Took knew better. They brought him nasty things to eat and drink—and some things not so nasty. Moo killed six roosters, soaked their gizzards in Jack Daniels, and put it in a green cork-bottle. Elliot, going on sixteen, found out how whiskey and chicken gizzards kill pain. He stashed his bottle behind the bed. All summer he drank whiskey and read Baum's *Oz* books—all 14 of them—and *Les Fleurs du Mal* in French. He thought of Camilla Jane as Glinda in the slick purplish Oz illustrations, sometimes as a dark red passion flower with a face. Her lips the color of the flower. She was a fairy nimbus around the light bulb, the dark brown stain of coffee-medicine spilled on his sheet. Sometimes the calf of his leg was the calf of her leg, and the hot rumpled sheets of summer sickness were the hot rumpled sheets of her attic room. He didn't get better. Dr. Parker said, "Rheumatic heart."

Elliot awoke with a lurch. A voice was speaking to him with clipped British calm, speaking to him from the radio in his room: *The princess is marrying her prince*. The princess was closer to him than Camilla Jane in Baton Rouge, who now seemed more distant than England, more distant that the moon. In his mind he saw his heart as a pale heliotropic sunflower with a heavy head, the flower fallen forward, the plant trembling at every breeze. Arrhythmically, the sunflower thumped its brown head in his chest, wanting and wasting with a constant ache of unrealized desire. Life was less than life when she was gone. He couldn't think of good things to do on his own. Not exciting things like the trip they'd taken to the towhead.

Camilla Jane had been reading *Life on the Mississippi*, and she decided they should canoe out to the towhead in the middle of the river. Once she got an idea it was on its way to reality. Elliot wanted to go with her but they had to convince Moo it was alright. Not alright to boat to the towhead but for him to go for the afternoon with Camilla Jane. Camilla told Moo they were going to the dime store to get some green thread and a thimble for Took. Moo was always suspicious of Camilla Jane. She didn't like for Elliot to go anywhere with her because Camilla loved to run the streets and Moo wanted him to read until he knew everything. Moo looked her straight in the eyes (she believed she could tell if a child was lying by looking in their eyes), and asked, "What's Took want green thread and a thimble for?"

Camilla looked straight back and said, "To sew up the cavity and bind the legs of a rooster she killed so he won't be mad at her because she killed him." And Moo believed her; it had the ring of truth. They took off walking toward the dime store, but once they were out of sight of the house they started running toward the levee. Gregory Landry had gotten a boat for his birthday, and Camilla Jane had talked him out of it by telling him her cousin from New Orleans would take him hunting in the Rigolets if he'd just let him borrow his boat today.

When they got to the levee, Camilla was the one who carried most of the canoe on her shoulders. Elliot couldn't keep his end of the boat steady. As Camilla pulled up the levee with the boat on her back, Elliot was able to help on the incline, but the boat began to slide off and Camilla started to sink to her knees. Hoisting it up again, he was able to hold up the back end. Getting it down the other side was a breeze. They bumped and slid it all the way.

But then they were at the river and although it was low river, the towhead seemed far away. "Come on," she said and got in and pushed off. There was a sluggish current still working; it almost capsized them. His tongue and mouth went dry as he tried to hold the canoe steady. Camilla Jane had been to camp one summer where she'd paddled around a brackish lake for two weeks, when Mag had gotten a windfall from Uncle Horatio's brother who died. He'd left something to "my brother's poor widow and destitute child." Elliot had never been in a canoe before. Half-way across he begged to go back but Camilla said, "Shut up, Yellow Belly. We've reached the point of no return. I'm Calamity's Child. No river can conquer me." Her strokes were surer as she kept up a constant monologue about how brave she was. She told him when to dip his paddle and pull. They had to ride the current down to the towhead.

The towhead had a small sandy beach. She dragged the canoe up while he pushed. After they beached they found themselves alone on the edge of a fringe of trees on an island in the middle of the Mississippi.

"Let's build a fire," she said. And they began to gather

pine knots and small white sticks of driftwood. At a clear spot on the beach, away from the trees, Camilla Jane crossed the sticks, added pine knots, and let Elliot tuck in a few handfuls of dried grass. She squatted down by the sticks like a print in a mahogany frame his grandmother had. It was called "Indian Campfire."

"How're you going to light it up? Rub two sticks together?" He was serious and sure she could do it.

"Nope, I brought matches." Rummaging in her pants pocket she pulled out a shiny, metallic case about five inches long. It had a neat little clasp that lifted and rolled back to open it. She took out a kitchen match and struck it on the rough side of the case. There was a wonderful smell of sulphur as the match kindled and lit in her hands and eyes.

The first curl of smoke raised a certain wildness in him, and he wanted to let out a war whoop as a little flame began to lick the sticks. A real fire began. He danced around laughing and moving his feet in a regular shuffle like he'd seen Indians do in a movie. She was still squatting down, both knees near her face, her head thrust forward as she stared into the fire, but then he called out, "Camilla Jane, Camilla Jane, there's a ship coming down—a big ship," and they both ran down to the water to look.

At first, it seemed to be bearing down on them, as if it would beach on the sand as neat as the canoe, or as the size of it impressed itself on them, slice right up the middle of the towhead—slice down to brown water. But then it began to slide off, and Elliot could see it had looked that way rounding the point and now it was passing. They were standing on the sand when a man—a pilot—came out on the wing of the bridge and began to shout at them and wave his arms frantically. They waved back but then a great suction of water pulled at their feet; he could feel the sand sliding out from under him. Camilla grabbed his arm and they scrambled to safety and ran back toward the fire which was still burning. The suction from the ship continued to peel back the water from the edge, sucking it out until he could see the bright green of an old glass bottle rolling up from the bottom right where they'd stood. As the ship passed on, the man waved in a friendly manner, and the waves came back with a rush, lapping half-way up the beach.

Now it was Camilla Jane who was jumping up and down singing, "I'm Calamity's Child, Queen of Nottoway, a gap-toothed, gold toothed Mambo. I'm gutsy, brass-bosomed and steel-hipped." She jumped up and clapped her heels together and said, "I can swim like a snake and fin like a catfish. I'm going to be whatever I want to be, like a pilot on the old Miss-a-sip-pee. I got my mojo to ride."

Elliot, too, clapped his heels together. He said, "I can drink whiskey and I can eat pie. I can walk barefoot on asphalt in the summertime."

Camilla Jane started to laugh at him. She said, "What kind of a flat-boat, bull-alligator cry is, 'I can drink whiskey; I can eat pie?'"

"It's good as what you yelled."

"No, it isn't. I'm going to be a pilot on the Mississippi, and I was giving flat-boat, bull-alligator yells."

"There aren't any hen-alligators." "And there aren't any women pilots. I'm the one who's going to be a pilot."

"Well, it's about time there was, but as long as one of us does it's okay. I might just as well be governor. There aren't any hen governors, either. Look, what I've got—Took's whis-key." She pulled a half-pint out of her pocket, brandished it like a trophy. "You got any pie?" And she turned the bottle bottom up to the sky.

But that seemed eons ago, now it was June. His grandmother and Moo had arranged a bed-birthday party. His father, of course, didn't come. He had tried when Elliot was twelve to convince him that he was the tennis hope of the world. It happened, however, that Elliot had inherited his father's weak backhand, and now his weak heart. His father couldn't stand to see all these weaknesses in one room at one time, so he didn't come. There was cake. A massive dobérge with butter icing. People Elliot's own age had been invited. They clustered around his bed in blooming health. A faint smell of chlorine surrounded them as if they'd recently been disinfected. They'd come from a morning swimming class at the High Castle pool — antiseptic children gathered by a parent to visit the sick. His classmates were all taller, stronger than he. They clutched the cardboard favors — carefully preserved from his fourth birthday party: Dopey, Grumpy, Sleepy — each and every dwarf smiling foolishly over a cup of cinnamon red hots. Only the candy was new, the rustling red tissue slightly faded, had been revived from a more innocent time by his grandmother's frugality. "Where's Grumpy?" Elliot whined. "He should be mine. My favor." Louis Landry immediately surrendered the Grumpy, candy and all. The kids were polite. They had come to visit their unfortunate classmate, Elliot, confined to bed on what might be his final birthday.

The cake was cut. Each child had a piece, heavy with butter icing, with a lump of rapidly dissolving vanilla ice cream sitting on top. In the room one small oscillating fan described a brief half-circle, like a fan at a tennis match turning its head from left to right, as it sat on the oak dresser. Each swipe of the fan reduced the mass of ice cream on the plates, as a hot breeze took turns around the room.

The kids sang "Happy Birthday," but no one could carry a tune, and the song melted with the ice cream before they came to the end of it. Moo continued to dole out ice cream long after anyone wanted it. She fixed Brett Harding with her good eye and made him finish the last warm, sweet swallow.

In bed, Elliot tried melting back into the vanilla sheets, so that none of that healthy crew would be offended by his lack of energy. His mind, the only thing about him capable of flight, made sickening swoops; chewing on stoicism it longed to be Superman.

His grandmother came to the door of the room with the air of someone bringing the big surprise. "Ta-ta-ta-tuh," she mimicked the sound of a trumpet, holding her hands up to her mouth as if she held one. They all looked up. Embarrassed at what appeared to be his grandmother's ultimate foolish act in her efforts to please him and help him get well—he stared at her with hatred. She had become the warden of the prison, and this some new kind of punishment.

A figure swept into the room wearing an expression of infectious glee, extreme self-satisfaction that seemed, in light of the person, justified—the sweet mouth. Where the classmates and their lifeguard friends had been pictures of robust health, they now seemed sallow as old photographs. Camilla Jane carried her own light. It jumped out of her black hair, clipped by fingernail scissors, and moved around her head like an electric current sparking a short in a wire. The kids at the party receded into the dark corners of the room. Elliot felt his own strength, vibrating like the needle of a compass, shaking and plunging toward magnetic north.

She came toward him in a pale blue dress and bent over him on the bed. Hanging out from the dark valley of her breasts a pendant of lapis lazuli on a silk cord dangled over his chest. On the pendant, a phoenix and dragon entwined around a small glass oval; as her face came down on his in one of those kisses he lived on, he saw High John in miniature, nesting like a buzzard between the phoenix and the dragon as it swung against his neck. High John's black fingernail scratched at his throat as he thrust his mouth back at hers, and he held onto her with his boney arms as if he could suck life out of her. His arms had the strength of the dying, and finally she put her hands out and pushed him back on the bed.

"My goodness, Elliot. You're better off than I thought. I was led to believe you were almost dead; I made a special trip to see you before you passed away. I think you're fooling your Mama. You just want attention, Elliot."

"You're right," he said, and started to get up.

His grandmother and Moo rushed over to contain him. He didn't know where it came from, but a gurgly sound was building in his throat. Moo supported his back to help him if he was going to vomit but when it came rushing up out of him it was only sound and he cawed, trying to clear his throat. His grandmother put her hand over his mouth to help him or shut him up, but the sound flapped its wings and stood up on the post of his throat and he threw back his head and crowed like a rooster.

Elliott in New Orleans

ELLIOT SKIPPED DOWN THE STEPS OF THE TILTON Memorial Library. When the sun hit his cheeks, he felt the sunburn he'd picked up playing tennis in Pass Christian over the weekend. Red, white and blue like a flag. No. Khaki, pink and blue—his pants were not white—pink face, oxford blue shirt. Still pretty conservative. He stopped a minute in front of the library to light a cigarette and look around. Students were milling and dividing off down Tulane's concrete paths, a few set off across the grass to their next class, but one figure caught his eye—a jogger. Joggers were ubiquitous, but this one wore high-topped leather shoes, and khaki pants pulled up under his armpits and held in place by black suspenders. His long hair circled a smooth round bald spot and a long pig tail hit his back with the impact of every step. The jogger held his arms up in an exaggerated posture as they flapped from the elbow. He looked like an early experiment in aviation—flapping wings that never got off the ground.

Elliot laughed before he realized the figure could only be one person—a person he'd never expected to see running, but then he should never be surprised at anything Gorky did.

"Gorky—Gorky," Elliot called out, then set out to catch Nathan Gorky who was high-tailing it in the direction of Broadway Avenue. Elliot ran in easy strides. He ran every morning, three miles rain or shine, and played tennis twice a week but the odd figure flapped on with incredible speed. As Elliot began to hear his breath, he thought how typical this was of Gorky who never seemed to work at any real job, but worked constantly on his own projects—projects that related to nothing and to everything. The most recent was a giant, abstract sculpture in front of his family home on Gentilly Boulevard where the houses all boasted guardian animals, concrete lions and dogs in pairs. Gorky had painted his sculpture bright pink and christened it with a party at which Lilah and Elliot had drunk potent punch until five a.m. The guests, mostly from uptown or the Quarter, felt they'd been part of some witty happening. The neighbors were less amused.

There had been many letters to the editor of the *Times-Picayune*, and petitions signed by homeowners for someone to do something, as the sculpture, which was made of some sort of expensive weather-tight plaster, crumbled in grotesque decay. There had finally been a lawsuit. Elliot had put a lot of free time in court representing his friend, but while Elliot was busy with a conventional defense, Gorky had done something original: He bought seven concrete dwarfs, two with small pick axes, and he set them on the lawn where they appeared to work vigorously on the sculpture—there were a number of dwarfs on other lawns; the monolith continued to crumble like Miss Haversham's wedding cake, worked on by industrious little men who never seemed to get ahead of the problem. The trial and its solution was to Elliot a typical Louisiana legal transaction. The judge lived uptown so he didn't care what they put on the lawn in Gentilly. The defendant had a certain personal style that appealed to the judge, and would have appealed to the jury if there'd been one. There was a tongue-in-cheek recognition by government of the problem without effecting change. The only real difference Elliot could see between this and other look-the-other-way cases was that no money changed hands.

Gorky disappeared on Willow Street, and Elliot figured it was just as well. Gorky's conversation could be brilliant, but exhausting. He assumed Elliot knew as much as he did, but Elliot lacked the competitive drive to keep up. His own mind took tangents while Gorky talked. The programs on the radio were easier to deal with than Nathan Gorky in the flesh: WWL let him record his dialogues and inspired insanity for a weekly jazz show, and Elliot listened and laughed with pleasure. No interaction expected. Elliot walked back to the library to wait for Lilah to pick him up, but some part of him still raced after Gorky, that invincible figure in high-topped shoes.

Elliot saw a Mercedes double-parked on Freret Street, an impossibility that Lilah had managed to achieve by gracefully motioning the cars around her with a long, tanned arm. The fact that the cars moving around her were in jeopardy as other cars moved toward them at an unhealthy speed didn't perturb her. She held her spot, and he remembered the first time he'd seen her in Haiti. There was a certain authority to everything she did. Elliot found himself running again to avoid someone else's automobile accident. He grabbed the handle of the mustard colored door and swung into the leather seat. Lilah immediately stepped on the accelerator and gave a wave and a bright smile to the truck driver behind her, which resulted in the truck driver opening his whole hand to wave back instead of giving her the finger. "Hi," she said to Elliot. "I've been missing you."

Her face had a placid glow that always amazed him. He leaned over and kissed her. "Did you get what you need from the library?" she asked.

"Yep, I guess I could have gotten that information elsewhere, but there's something about the carrels at Tulane. Makes me think I'm twenty.

"You are twenty—eight."

"Yeah, well twenty-eight—."

"It feels good." She dropped her hand to the inside of his leg, where a muscle bulged against the khaki. He felt his face get pinker, and a slight stirring in his groin. He liked for Lilah to make sexual gestures, but knowing Lilah he realized the gesture was more affectionate than sexual. She would express surprise if he followed up on it. Since they'd been married, she'd never allowed sex to get in the way of other things she wanted to do. The stirring ceased. He began to think of the tax case. It was convoluted and he'd been working on it a long time. Tax law could be rewarding, but it was criminal law that interested him; he liked the vicarious thrill of being on the wrong side of the law, and that was a career jump he'd silently considered. A safe life has its rewards, he thought, but there are long stretches of boredom.

They were turning into the driveway on Octavia Street; he looked up at the house. It was similar to Aunt Mag's house in High Castle; the high gable could be Camilla's room, and he knew why he liked this house. Why he insisted on buying it. There was a promise of danger there in the attic. It had nothing to do with Lilah and nothing to do with the kids. No matter how much Lilah wanted to redecorate and open up the attic. He would always say, "Let's add on," and the attic would stay as it was. It was someone's past, and when he looked up at it, it was his.

He closed the iron gate behind them. It needed an automatic switch, but that would come later, and he walked into the wide hall which was still musty and damp in its old wallpaper. Lilah was deep into renovation. There were constant consultations with the painter over decorator colors for the inside walls.

"How about a cup of tea?

"Not now," he answered. "I've got to talk to the window man."

Lilah's efficiency confounded him. His own mind, which was sharp and quick on a case, reaching into voluminous files for a point of law, had difficulty with the coordination of workmen; the swirl and flow of children and their friends; the phone which rang incessantly. He moved away from Lilah's telephone conversation with a man who had installed casement windows in the sun room, the only completely finished room in the house, where light came in glorious bursts as clouds passed over the sun. The clouds opened and closed the shadows of the room which was cool but sunny. There were dappling patterns of outside bamboo on the white sofa, and he coveted the peace of the room. He carried in a book of Roethke's poems with a cup of black tea and sank into a down-cushioned chair. He read the poems slowly as some men read the Bible, taking time to lift his eyes to the outside green, letting the words sink in and his mind fly. They were a comfort to him in the deep and sorrowful part of his soul which was never truly comfortable in his life.

He felt himself drawn home to cool, dark, mysterious moments lit by translucent green butterbeans on the back gallery. The toad in him hopped under the gallery to cool, packed dirt for conversations in the kitchen above, secrets and smells that were always there under today.

"Daddy, Daddy—DADDY?"

The voice was loud as the boy peered into his face.

"Daddy, were you asleep? Your eyes were open."

"No, just thinking, Davis."

"Daddy, can people sleep with their eyes open."

"I think so—yes, I definitely think so. Have you ever tried?"

"No."

"Well, I want you to try when you take your nap. Is it time for your nap?"

"No, I've had my nap. It's time for dinner. Mama said for me to call you. We've got fried shrimp."

Elliot heard Lilah's brisk footsteps and he straightened up.

"Here's a gin and tonic. Have you ever considered narcolepsy? It could be an inherited condition. Your mother was on the sleepy side." She smiled at him, but there was an edge to her voice as she stirred her gin and tonic with her index finger, pushing a half-moon of lime around the rim of the glass. "Run along, Davis, and let your daddy have a drink with me. He's awake now."

Elliot's office had just been painted dark blue—a shiny midnight blue. The smell of paint followed him. At home, he had awakened with clogged sinuses and a dull headache. At home the woodwork now had a matte finish. A decision which had taken two of Lilah's days in deep conversation with the painter—whether to leave the cypress bare or to varnish it. He felt as if he'd been poisoned with *coup l'aire*, but if he'd said that to Lilah she wouldn't have gotten the joke. He went to the office early only to find the fumes following him. He sat at his desk in a state of terminal disgust with his body and its allergies, but when he picked up the newspaper in his desk he saw her picture was on the front page. GOVERNOR'S WIFE FINDS DEPLORABLE CONDITIONS. She had on a dress with a very wide skirt and a tilt brim hat. He couldn't see her face; it was a mass of tiny, inky spots, but he immediately recognized the figure. It was the way she stood. And his body reacted the way it always did. There was a point, a meaning to existence. He hadn't seen Camilla Jane since Christmas when he'd gone to the nursing home to see Moo. He carried a number of small gifts: RJ's snuff, which Moo dipped incessantly; a bottle of Florida water to purify the room, a ten-pound box of hand-dipped chocolates from D.H. Holmes, and four cotton nightgowns made by a Creole seamstress on Desire Street.

He'd been waiting in the lobby of Ransome's Nursing Home for about fifteen minutes, but the receptionist told him she was on her way down.

"Psst." The sound was like steam leaving a tea kettle—insistent and watery. He knew who it was. Moo standing behind a Daetera plant. She liked to watch him when he didn't know it, had been doing it since he was a kid. She could tell his true state of mind if he didn't know she was watching, and she always managed to find some way to fool him into thinking she was where she wasn't. "Mister Elliot," her voice came down hard on the first word. It was her way of saying, "You won't ever be a Mister to me." Never tall, she had shrunk another three inches. Her eyes, however, were as imperious as ever.

"You got any money?"

"Some."

"Well, that's good. Get it ready." In a medicinal cloud she walked ahead of him down the linoleum hall. He wanted to put his hand on her arm, pull her back from the odor of sickness which slowly claimed everyone in the nursing home. But Moo wouldn't take his arm, she never touched him. She had stopped touching him when he was ten years old, as far as he could remember she had never touched him since. He'd fallen off the roof in Aunt Mag's back yard, and Moo, as tiny as she was, carried him into the house alone; she nursed him and babied him with special things to eat, but when he awakened from a terrible nightmare and cried for Moo to rock him, she hissed at him, "What's the matter with you, Boy? You want to be a freak? You too big." His mother had come in and put her cool hand on his hot forehead, but she'd gone away again. It was Moo who was there through the night.

They had reached the sun porch now. Women in wheelchairs kept rolling in. Everybody wanted to take a look at him. At a wicker table an old man with large, hairy ears was hanging over a Bible with tiny print. He didn't seem to see the words but mumbled the prayers aloud.

"Give him something," Moo said.

"What for?"

"He prays for you. Probably the only person who does."

"What should I give him?" Elliot asked.

"Give him five dollars. He likes ice cream."

A round-faced aide in a blue smock walked around fluffing pillows behind backs and straightening atrophied limbs that hung in cracks of wheelchairs.

"Give her ten dollars. She don't make nothing to speak of."

A tall, bright Creole woman, with a white uniform and flying nurse's cap came in. Each movement she made was crisp, and her full thighs rubbed together in a silky sound as she moved around the room in her starched uniform dispensing white pills in pleated paper cups.

"How do you do, Mr. Gilbert? I'm Mama Moo's nurse, Alita LeCroy."

"I'm not your mama, girl," Moo said.

Alita LeCroy pulled herself up, smiled at Elliot, ignored the remark as if she hadn't heard it, and moved on passing out pills.

"What should I give her?" Elliot asked.

"Don't give her nothing. She's too proud. Send her flowers. She likes carnations. Send her two dozen red carnations and sign them Mrs. Moosha Glondile."

"But you were never married, Moo."

"She don't know that."

Suddenly, there was a heavy smell of jasmine synergizing with the Lysol and a commotion at the door. Everyone looked up. Camilla Jane posed a moment in the doorway, an electrical aura framed her like blue neon lights around a figure of the virgin. Camilla, too, in Mary's blue. A small, cocked hat on her head dispelled the vision. She could have been a movie star in the way she moved into a room, working it. Everyone there was an old friend, and she passed through pressing hands and kissing cheeks, and within a few moments everyone was sn old friend — except for Moo, whose back came up like a cat's.

"What you doing here?"

"Moo, I'm so glad to see you," Camilla said as she put both hands on Moo's face and kissed the older woman's cheek.

"Jesus, I'm bound to be crucified. I've been kissed by Judas."

Elliot wasn't listening. He stood transfixed as his cousin came to greet him. He tried to deflect her kiss by kissing her Creole style on the cheek, but she turned her face and he found himself, as he did in every dream, kissing her on the mouth, and there was a faint taste of something sweet, not the aftertaste of sugar, which is sour, but something like Juicy Fruit gum. He pushed his body against hers — they were alone in the room — it was only when he heard the clicking sound of wheelchairs that he realized they were the hub of the room; wheelchairs in an agitated state of excitement were wheeling around them. With a burst of static a loud voice came on the loudspeaker saying, "The wife of Governor Soltice Busteaux is here today with special gifts for all of you. She'll be passing them out in the recreation room before the movie. You'll meet her before the movie, which is *Laura*, starring Gene Tierney, Dana Andrews, Clifton Webb and our own first lady, Camilla Jane Busteaux. Let's have everyone move to the recreation room. Everyone, please move to the recreation room."

"Why, that's me" she said tucking her arm into his. "You can take me there, Elliot. It's so good to see family."

Saturday morning the doorbell rang. Alita LeCroy said, "I'll get it," to her mother, a little ball of a woman with pale, lemony skin, and a brown knot skinned to the top of her head. Gold hoops hung down from her stretched earlobes. Her curiosity could hardly be contained as Alita went to the cut glass door.

A tall man stood on the porch holding a bouquet of red carnations. "Be careful," her mother said. Alita opened the door on a chain. As she peered at him, he grinned at her appreciatively and bowed as he presented the flowers. She closed the door in his face just as quickly but before she threw the latch he said, "Wait a minute, Miss. I'm just delivering them."

"Well, next time don't be so cheeky. I don't know you."

He grinned again, in a very appealing way and said, "Maybe you should."

She ignored the remark and took the flowers. He tipped an imaginary hat, skipped down the steps like a football player skipping rope, landed on the sidewalk, did a military right turn, saluted and jumped in a florist truck. By this time Alita's mother had come to the door and was standing behind her, stretching to see through the cut glass panel. "I thought he had brought those to you himself. Thought he might be full of himself to be black and ugly as the wrong side of a shovel bringing flowers to a woman in the Seventh Ward in the day time. Hmm — uhh."

"These are not even from a man, Mama. The card says, 'Mrs. Moosha Glondile.' That's the old lady I was telling you about. She's the one who think's she's white."

"The one at the home?"

"She's got this grandbaby who's white. He comes once a week, and she leads him around by the nose — must have some money because she tells him to give it around and he does."

"He ever give any to you?" Her mother's face was stern and disapproving.

"Of course not. But I think she fixed him a long time ago. When he comes in he talks to me like he's white and lives on State Street, and when he talks to her it's some gumbo from the country sounds worse than the projects."

"Why is she sending you flowers?"

"She's putting on. She's always putting on around me."

"What color is she?"

"She's as bright as me. And she gets him to bring her books, but she asks the priest to help her when she doesn't know the words. She acts like she knows everything when she's around me. She doesn't have any education but she knows how to read, and she's always studying like she's going to be twenty tomorrow and go to college. Wouldn't ask me for any help if her tongue was about to fall out — too proud."

"How do you treat her? If she's old you've got to treat her with respect no matter how she treats you."

"I'm respectful. The one thing she wants me to do is take red beans to St. Jude all the time. Once a week she gives me money. I buy the beans across the street at Pickett's, but I send them to St. Jude's shrine by Wilson, the orderly. He lives downtown."

"Is Wilson getting those beans where they're supposed to

go?"

"Oh, he teases. He says they smell so good he eats the sausage right out of the carton before he gets to Canal Street on the streetcar, but he takes the beans and puts them by the statue. He's honest. He wouldn't pick up a dime didn't belong to him."

"How come she's making flying novenas to St. Jude?"

"She says her grandbaby Elliot had a spell put on him by a woman with a High John the Conqueror root when he was thirteen, and it's up to her to save him because his mother's dead. She says if it hadn't been for her prayers he would have been under this woman's thumb a long time ago."

Mrs. LeCroy sat down heavily on her TV chair which was covered with a neat, white linen cover. "That's something. What else?"

"Remember when I told you the governor's wife was coming?"

"Well, she came yesterday."

"How does she look?"

"Oh, she looks good. I would too if I had as much money as she does. It turns out he's her cousin."

"The grandbaby?"

"That's right. And he was there."

"What about the old lady? She must really have had her nose in the air, since her people are so important."

"No indeed. That old lady hates with precision. Right before the governor's wife sits down she spits in her chair—the governor's wife, cool as a cucumber, takes out a lace handkerchief and wipes this big old gob of spit off her chair—before any of us could even think to do anything—then she sits down real fast before the old lady could spit again. The old lady had her mouth all puckered up, but we rushed over and took her to the back of the room. She was fighting and shoving Wilson and me. She said the governor's wife is a Hoodoo Queen, and she'd just come there to put a binder on her grandbaby."

"Where was he all this time those women were fighting over him?"

"Oh, he was gone by that time. They'd got all the old people upset with their French kissing, so he'd walked out of there before all of this like he was stoned."

"You mean to tell me he was kissing his cousin on the mouth—the governor's wife?"

"He had his tongue halfway down her throat, and those old people were clicking their wheelchairs like castanets." She laughed remembering. "Then he walked out."

"When did the old lady spit in her chair?" asked her mother. Her eyes avid for more detail.

"That was at the movie. After all the kissing I had to take them over to the auditorium. The governor's wife got some spirit. After all that, she acted as if nothing unusual had happened—acted just natural—cool. Asked me about my mother and where I'd gone to nursing school. I think she would have kissed him on the mouth if the governor had been standing right there."

"She looks like an 'I-don't-care,' from her picture in the papers."

"Oh, she's better looking than her pictures—like a movie star. She has a round face, pinky with pretty, pretty skin, but there's something a little too free about her for her position, even when she isn't kissing her cousin."

"What's he look like?"

"He's got eyes like icy green grapes and blond hair. You'd remember him if you saw him."

"I thought you said he was bright? Sounds like an albino to me."

"I'm telling you, he's white. The old lady just thinks he's her grandbaby. She reared him. It's one of those funny arrangements from the country."

"Your job is better than TV. What else did the old lady do?"

"Well, we had to take her back to her room. She kept hissing, "Bitch," at the governor's wife from the back of the auditorium. The governor's wife acted like it was a natural state of affairs, but the old people were all excited and couldn't settle down until we got her out of there. It all caused so much of an uproar we didn't get the movie started until four o'clock, which messed up the cafeteria staff's feeding them on time. The governor likes to help the elderly—you know—it's election time. But they didn't pay much attention; they were all talking about the kissing and the spitting. After Mrs. Busteaux left I went upstairs and took three aspirins. That old lady is something else; she gave me a headache."

"She sounds like she's something else."

"The next morning Wilson told me Miss Moosha was down in the assembly room at 7 a.m. with a broom, a bottle of Florida water and a mop bucket full of water and some chlorine bleach. As old as she is, she brushed down all the walks, purified the corners of the room with Florida water, and washed all the statues of the Virgin Mary with Clorox bleach."

"I can't believe it!"

"You better believe it. She says the governor's wife is Queen of the High John, that she's a bad woman who's got the power, and that if it hadn't been for Miss Moosha fighting her all these years, Louisiana would have gone to the dogs by now. We'd be having the next thousand years of yellow fever, malaria, leprosy, cholera, and boils—."

"That old lady's got some vivid imagination, but you look at the paper, she's not too far wrong. She'd better pray some more; there's lots of stuff she's not taking care of."

"She was so worn out after she purified the room she couldn't bathe herself, so I went in to help her and she let me. I guess that's why she sent me carnations. But she still calls me 'girl.'"

"Maybe it's because she's so old. Maybe you just look like a girl to her."

"Oh no. She's smart that way. She just wants to see me get the *go-go rouge*."

Lilah

"WHAT'LL IT BE?" A LARGE LUMINOUS WOMAN IN a white shirt moved behind the bar wiping it with a cloth glowing like neon.

On St. Louis Street the door stood open. A dark current of air flavored with hops flowed out. Lilah had drifted in, but couldn't see a thing; the pupils of her eyes, still dilated from the glare of the street, didn't adjust quickly. This woman was the purple-white something glowing in the dark, toward which she stumbled, blind and groping.

The idea of drinking in a bar was foreign to Lilah. In Texas she'd drunk whiskey on the run, speeding from one drive-in to the other with Clay Semens, drinking out of a bottle in a paper bag. Alcohol went with white-hot kisses in the back of a Thunderbird.

"Sitting on a barstool sipping some kind of pink drink would be death to me. I'm from Texas. Can you make a lemonade?"

"Sure. That's a Tom Collins without gin. This your first time in New Orleans? It's a wiggy town."

Lilah thought about the bar, how she was then, but that was all a long time ago.

This morning Lilah had dropped Davis and Elise at the Montessori School on Zimple. A blue skirt floated out from her bare legs as she pressed the gas pedal. A draft from the floorboard of the jeep accelerated her sense of freedom. Depositing the kids made her breasts feel lighter, buoyant. She felt slim, pubescent, returned to a single state for at least four hour of free conversation with Lane Clayley. Lane was always saying, "You're somebody's mother, kid. Suits you damn well."

Today she wanted something riskier—the other life. Like these memories.

The big woman talked as she worked pouring simple syrup over ice, cutting and squeezing fresh lemon, adding water from a black hose, and a cherry on top. She presented the drink to Lilah and said, "Look at me. I came here green as grass from North Louisiana—the Bible belt. I moved into the Two Lion Hotel on St. Louis Street. It wasn't anything like it is now—they've been restoring it to something or other. It was a flea-bag then. But what did I know? I was being real careful with money. I wanted a clean, second-rate hotel. It was second-rate alright. I didn't have much — no job and no prospects."

"Like me," Lilah said.

"Maybe. I was green—I can't tell you how green. I didn't even know what dope was much less smoke it. All these cats in the hotel got little flower boxes out the windows, and they're always making with the water cans. So I said to this blonde who lived down the hall. 'Honey,' I said, 'that's nice the way you kids love flowers.' She said, 'What? That shit? That's marijuana.'

"The people who lived under me made sandals. Their pad smells to high heaven. They've been saving their pee in galvanized garbage cans on the balcony to tan leather for sandals. The blonde's old man's got to take a leak and he whips it out and leaks in the garbage can. In the summertime everybody in the hotel shifts over to one side, doubling up just to get away from the garbage cans. The desk clerk doesn't care what they do as long as they buy their pills from him.

"The same blonde I was telling you about brought the heat down. She'd just come back from Mexico. The police raided, checking ID room by room. The blonde's old man stashed her quick in an old restaurant icebox out on the gallery by the garbage cans. The police are looking for her, not anybody else. They don't bother with the window boxes or the shipment of grass she's just brought in. Now everybody's waiting on grass. There's been a dry spell—nothing to smoke, nowhere. So now the police split, and the dudes want to turn on out of relief. No one remembers the blonde stashed in the icebox. A couple of days go by. Her old man's stoned. There's pads full of guys digging their navels and saying, 'That's some fine weed, man.'

This guy's not selling it. He's giving it away. The blonde's the business end of the twosome. One day somebody goes to dig some leather out of the piss cans on the porch, and hears this funny little Donald Duck voice coming out of the icebox. He thinks maybe a cat's crawled in somehow. So he gets some people and they open it up. There's the blonde doubled up—her mouth wrapped around the drain pipe sucking air like a soft drink. They drag her into the pad with her old man and all the heads. Her old man says, 'Groovy, dig the shape of the chick's mouth—crazy. Just what I always wanted in a woman.' That was some hotel. Where're you staying?"

"Mrs. LeBlanc's—down the street."

"Oh, yeah. She's the lady from Ville Platte. Used to be in show business. Must be older than God."

Lilah liked thinking about Nan's stories, but she couldn't stop thinking about Elliot. He'd awakened in a groggy, semi-drugged state, complaining of paint fumes in the bedroom.

He dressed in a distant manner and left without kissing her goodbye. Love?—she loved him, but his blond good looks were glaciers sliding over her life. She never knew why he turned off—got cold. He was annoyed with the renovation, could see no reason for it. He was perfectly happy living in the usual scene. Always talked of family as some sort of inherited blood poisoning you lived with or died from. God knows, considering his own crazy family she could understand it.

Her own sense of family made up for it. The steady, deliberate family life she'd seen in her grandmother's house or even one of those good families from TV—a proper father as concerned with the children as he was with making money, and a mother who turned the everyday trials of life into eventual triumphs like the give and take with the window man, who was going to do it her way after all. What she didn't want was her mother's way. Not the concrete traditionalism of her mother's house, which sent her tearing off in a fury to the bus stop in Geograph, Texas. Geograph was the nearest escape route from Rule, Texas, where her mother sat so smugly in her big house on her big, traditional pile of horse manure or bullshit, whatever it was Lilah had been smelling all her life.

She'd run off mad to New Orleans' French Quarter, which was just a name in a book until she arrived on the Trailways bus. She left those non-complaining Rule women talking pregnancies, the new preacher, Jimmy Evelyn's skirt-chasing husband, and the little girl they were collecting toys for because she wasn't going to make it to Christmas.

Lilah was still mad walking down Toulouse street carrying a suitcase she changed from hand to hand as it got heavier and she got sweatier. The heat from the street made her stomach quiver. The air above the sidewalk shimmered like a fever dream. Lilah wanted something extraordinary to happen—didn't want to be the ordinary tourist. The man walking ahead of her wearing hot-pink Bermuda shorts and carrying a camera probably didn't want to be an ordinary tourist either.

The odor of stale beer floated up from bar boards hosed off by a young man in front of the Golden Slipper Club. He held the hose down and shut it off as she passed.

She was looking for The Christian Women's Exchange. She needed a cheap room and it was the only place she'd heard of. Crazy how her mind, even its violent rejection of the big, flat church in Rule, had returned to Christianity as a symbol of something good now that she was trying to find a place to stay. When she saw the brass plaque attached like a medal to the chest of the old building, Christian Women's Exchange, she felt the same disgust with her life she'd felt when she ran away. This was the place where Rule could grow long arms and grab her. She might as well run back to her mother crying: Here I am, Mother. I can't make it on my own. I'll be one of you. A good, strong woman who never complains. I'll have a few new appliances—won't have to slop hogs, shoot geese, or hoe the garden while producing and reproducing for the old man who sits tall in the saddle even when he hasn't got a horse. I may add a new last name, but who am I? Who am I? She passed the Christian Women's Exchange as if she'd had words with the manager. She sighted down Toulouse Street—narrow, dirty. Linked houses of crumbling plaster and exposed brick leaned together like drunks struggling to keep each other up. This kind of thing—honky tonks and garbage—had always been back of town in the South she knew. This was the heart of the city. She took in the rusting iron grillwork, the sidewalks greasy as dirty dishes with a sense of familiarity. Trash overflowed the battered tin cans sitting in muddy gutters, but the sun struck the bright colored buildings with impressionistic light. She was glad to be here.

About a block down she came to a house the color of green enamelware, a sign permanently affixed to the door, ROOMS FOR RENT, as if the tenants came and went. This was it. Nobody stayed too long. A tall building with a balcony overhanging the sidewalk, fresh paint sloppily applied over pitted erosions on the front of the building, faced the street like a woman trying to stop time with lipstick and makeup base.

Lilah rang the bell within the doorway where an iron grill protected a screened door. After the bell sounded there was a long pause, and then footsteps in the corridor. It was dark inside. A piece of flowered cloth tacked behind the screen kept Lilah from seeing the person who answered the bell.

A woman's accented voice asked, "Who's that? What you want?"

"I'm looking for a room to rent. I saw your sign." The only parts of the woman she could see were tan house shoes with Indian Chiefs printed on the toes. From the slippers rose two toothpick legs wrapped in flesh-colored stockings both rolled, one slightly higher than the other.

"Oh, *chère*, is that so? Sure I got a room. Why don't you say you want a room? Come on in." She opened the screen and Lilah saw a square, petite woman in a cotton dress with a blue print apron tied over it. Black hair, carefully finger-waved into a thirties hairstyle, had rusted at the ends and at the scalp around the piquant, wrinkled face.

"It's clean, *chère*. Very clean. I cleaned it just one hour ago. The young man left to be a monk at Grand Coteau. I give it to you cheap. Twenty dollars a week, paid in advance, and you use the bathroom across the patio. I'm Mrs. LeBlanc."

She led the way down a corridor. The hall opened onto a small crowded patio where hundreds of plants lined up in French Market Coffee cans along the bricks under the balcony. Striped ivy in green wine bottles hung from chains along the eaves; philodendron choked planters and window boxes; wisteria twisted on the gallery and spilled down the side wall. In each corner of the patio a washing machine tub bursting with elephant ears sat in a swampy dump of other broken appliances that were slowly being sucked down and covered with lush green. The broken concrete under Lilah's feet didn't feel quite solid, weakened as it was by creeping roots and seeping water.

Mrs. LeBlanc led Lilah up a curving outside staircase. They reached a landing separate from the main house, but connected by a gallery. "This is the slave quarters," said Mrs. LeBlanc.

The room for rent was small with one narrow, rectangular window. The bed was a home-built affair flush up against one wall. It gave very little. Pushed up against the wall next to the bed was an old washstand. A white pitcher in a green washbowl sat on it. The only other furniture was something Mrs. LeBlanc called a "Chifforobe." All the pieces were reddish brown. Painted often, one coat on top of the other, with mahogany deck paint. The chipped corners exposed white enamel paint over wood. The bathroom across the patio was enormous, featuring the biggest bathtub Lilah had ever seen. A bare lightbulb hung from the ceiling over it. She wondered how many tenants had been electrocuted pulling the chain. She said, "I'll take it," and gave Mrs. LeBlanc twenty dollars.

As she unpacked she thought about tradition, the only tradition ingrained here was grime, the same kind in the neck of a shirt worn too often. The room was impersonal in a personal way like a public toilet. No one had left a mark and everyone had. Joe, Eddie, and Mary lived here, left some dirt and moved on—gone. Gone—gone. She splashed water on her face to make herself believe she lived here. There were plenty of towels, but the frugal Mrs. LeBlanc had cut them in half, and neatly re-stitched the ends. The towel was wet before Lilah was dry. After changing clothes she walked down the interior corridor beside the house. The air along the dark brick-lined alleyway was cool and damp, but when she walked out into the humid, hot street she started to sweat again. That was when she'd found the cool doorway of Nan's bar.

As she wiped the mahogany bar with the luminous cloth, Nan said, "You're going to like it here. You can be yourself—whoever or whatever that self is. What you've got to remember is: You can get old in the French Quarter, but it's hard to grow up. See that woman at the end of the bar?"

"What woman? Where?"

"That's what I said the first time I saw her."

The woman in question, sitting at the other end of the bar

in an indolent, comfortable position, leaned over a drink as if she spent most of her time on that stool, was youthful and slender. Even in the perpetual gloom of the bar Lilah could see her glowing shirt was a man's shirt and she wore trousers.

"First time she came in here, somebody said, 'That's Krakatoa's aunt.' I said, 'Looks more like an uncle to me.'"

"Who's Krakatoa?" Lilah asked.

"You *are* new in town. Krakatoa's the most famous stripper on Bourbon Street. She's gorgeous and she can dance. I mean, she can really dance and Marnie there trained her, managed her and waited on her hand and foot. She was in love with Krakatoa. But Krakatoa, like everybody else, is getting older. She was thirty-two, so she goes out and gets herself a twenty-two-year-old Colombian transvestite who looks just like her. But she doesn't have a two-week fling. Nope. She marries him. Trains him to strip, designs his costumes, and teaches him her exact routines. The ones Marnie taught her. They play the same nightclubs. They played the 500 Club as Krakatoa I and II. So now Marnie's out of a job. She picked up a young girl who looked pretty good but couldn't dance. All she could do were basic bumps and grinds. Frankly, Marnie's used to something better. So that didn't last too long. There's always some woman in here looking for Marnie. They buy her gold cigarette lighters and keep her in pocket money. They don't come any nicer than Marnie. You want to meet her?"

"Not now. Some other time. I'll have to digest some of this," Lilah said laughing. "I'll come back when I'm hungry for some good stories and you can tell me more." She paid for the lemonade and went back out into the daylight.

All of that was nine lives ago. Lane Clayley was the only real link with herself, but how could she think this self was any less than that self. Only different. All of it was still there. With Lane she could talk about anything. No questions of right or wrong, just friendship—enduring friendship. When she'd go to Lane's all her nostalgic memories went out the window. Lane was piled up in the bed in several places, a jar of Vick's Salve, a bottle of Wild Turkey and another of Jack Daniels black label on the end table.

"You sick? asked Lilah.

"What a stupid question? Of course, I'm sick."

"Well, you could be drunk. You've got enough booze around to make it debatable."

"I'm sick. I've got some miserable New Orleans allergy, cold, asthma deal, and I don't feel like any of your disgusting optimism this morning. Why don't you just go on and be cheerful elsewhere."

"Oh, no. I'm here to dispense hot tea, and talk about going on a ski trip. If I don't go down a mountain soon I'll go off a bridge—-"

"That bad, huh?"

"I'm not exactly dead, but I'm some distance from alive."

"Maybe you ought to get your Galatea costume out of mothballs. Shake up that lawyer you married."

"God, wouldn't that be funny. Wouldn't it be wonderful to walk around like that at Holy Name of Jesus or even a supper dance." She sat down at the end of the bed, kicked off her shoes and began to laugh saying, "Oh, God, wouldn't it be funny—?"

Galatea

IN THE DARK CONFINES OF THE BOX LILAH COULD feel a rush fluttering like wings against glass as the inside of her body tried to escape, but the body itself stood stock-still in the proscribed statuesque position as the band attempted an abbreviated version of "The Pines of Rome," and the M.C. whose last joke had been to come out in beaver ear muffs and call himself, "The Old Muff Diver," began a breathless description of "Galatea, the statue who came to life."

He said, "Ladies and Gentleman. It is our pleasure at The Champagne Club to bring to you one of the premier erotic illusions of the twentieth century. An illusion based upon the myth of the classical sculptor Pygmalion, who without a living model created an unparalleled sculpture, the exquisite body of a young woman, a statue of such pristine and roseate beauty that he fell in love with it." The MC's voice broke, as if overcome and unable to go on. "You will now be privileged to witness that astounding beauty."

Lilah felt the lights thrown on the black box where the full-length statue stood in the niche like a classical Greek sculpture in the Louvre. After a concerted intake of breath from the audience, there was a slight "oh," as they saw that the statue was nude. Expectations rose. The voice of the MC went on:

"Pygmalion was obsessed with the beauty of his creation. His hands caressed her; his mouth kissed the cold lips, the tender nipples, the curve of the inner thigh. In an agony of desire Pygmalion begged Venus, the goddess of love, to bring his perfect woman to life, and he was rewarded by Venus for the excellence of his art. Ladies and Gentlemen, it is with great pleasure the Champagne Club presents: Galatea—" Lilah got ready for her entrance "—the statue come to life." She could feel the hot lights inside the box come on as the marble statue projected on the mirror appeared to change to the audience watching from both sides of the runway. Slowly, as the light intensified, the illusion worked its magic and, in the eyes of the audience, her own body slowly replaced the white statue. She held exactly the same position. Her own dark brown hair caught up in a classical Grecian style that mirrored the sculpture. Her arms posed the same. The lights rose, the statue faded, and she stepped from the box onto the runway in a long, graceful stride accented by the long panel of black silk jersey hanging from a small belt at her waist, the jersey moving silkily against her bare legs. A dark halter with a high color encircled her neck. Lilah walked slowly in black high heels against the swinging panel of cloth, against the heavy waves of sensuous music, amid the avid stares of the heavy-eyed couples sitting below the level of the walkway. She loved the feel of the music against her legs and arms; the breathless voice of the M.C.—fruity, melodic, who said:

"Ladies and gentlemen, for your aesthetic enjoyment, the living body of Galatea." She swayed up and down the walkway feeling the eyes on her body, the music; feeling her mysterious body—an exotic creature—untouchable, a goddess who walked to flutes. She danced in a slow whirling motion, as if propelled by gusts of slow wind. The silk panel swinging freely, hypnotically, as she whirled across the runway to the black box. She stopped suddenly as if transfixed, then walked slowly back inside, and once more the music swelled, the lights rose, as she was transformed into marble.

Backstage Marnie waited for her with a hot towel to rub down her arms and back. "You were great—beautiful. You kept it clean. Remember, don't ever give them any flesh. Don't give them the hots. Don't give them the satisfaction. Give them a dream."

"I felt like a statue, but human inside."

"That's it. That's what you've got to be. That's who you are—Galatea—a goddess. Above them. If they can have you, they don't want you. Let them sleep with their wives. What they want is fantasy come to life."

While Marnie rubbed her shoulders, Lilah looked into the small mirror. Her face was not there. An opaque mask appeared in the mirror; the eyes outlined in kohl, like a startled cygnet on point. Somewhere upstairs she could hear "Night Train," as Sherry, a young girl who'd come in on Greyhound last Saturday bumped her way across the stage. Sherry didn't have Marnie. She had to dress up with three other strippers and drink with customers. Marnie cut through all that. Lilah did three shows a night, had her own dressing room and five hundred a week, two hundred of which she gave to Marnie who spent a hundred to rent the illusion. The illusion was the act. She was the latest of dozens of Galateas; some man in Slidell had built the box and rented it out to dancers, but as Marnie said, "It's a classy act. Anybody can bump. I can bump. They want, as the song says, 'A dream walking.'"

When she thought about it, Lilah was gleeful. Her first job. Her very first job in her whole life was as a statue come to life. That was something for the grandchildren to find out about. It was true. She had come to life. She liked the glamour of her new profession, and thought of herself as a myth. At three o'clock every afternoon she and Marnie went to the Bourbon House for breakfast. At one o'clock she had her hair done at Passion Hairy's on Bourbon Street so it was usually past three when they got there. She would brush past the other tables with a superior look on her face to get to the booth Jerry the waiter held for them, and she liked hearing the voices, "That's Galatea—Galatea. You know the one who comes to life. Yeah, gorgeous—some kind of gorgeous. Yeah, that's her aunt with her."

And she and Marnie would sit there and eat breakfast, Marnie calling Jerry to tell him just how Galatea wanted her breakfast. "Jerry, last time you had too much butter on the whole wheat toast. Remember, just half a pat per slice. One poached egg. One six-ounce juice, and black coffee for both of us. I'll have the number four breakfast."

Lilah liked being taken care of. The tender concern, the sure knowledge of what was good for her; what was good for the act. The slow sensual massages Marnie specialized in; she'd been a masseuse at one time; the special mixture of rose water and glycerine with twenty drops of phenol that Marnie prescribed to keep the clear bloom to her skin, and which Marnie had to order from Dorignois' Pharmacy on Louisa Street in the Ninth Ward. It was only after three weeks of lessons in makeup, dance, expression—professionalism—that Marnie had allowed her to dance. All this personal attention, combined with a partnership which seemed to develop the sensual side of her being, made her happy and, as she relaxed into it, developed into something more tender and loving. Sometimes she dreamed of Marnie as a young man. A young man, who put his arms around her and kissed her. A young man who said, "I love you. I want to marry you."

But in the daylight—the smoky, greasy daylight of the Bourbon House, where bacon and hamburgers smoked on the grill, Marnie's face was tan and wrinkled like the weathered face of Malissa Daw, the old woman in Texas who sat on the fence post at her ranch and scared the cows through a gap by beating a tin dish pan with a soup spoon. Marnie had lived with a succession of dancers until she'd hooked up with Krakatoa; she'd lived with her for fourteen years. She was a professional manager who tenderly cared for all the needs of those women — sensual as well as technical.

Marnie called Jerry over to give him two dollars in quarters to feed the juke box — even that with a practiced air. "Okay, Jerry, give us 'Round Midnight,' some Ahmad Jamal, and the lady singing 'You're My Thrill.'" She looked at Lilah with a deep, penetrating stare of her grey eyes. "That's what you are, Galatea — my thrill, my sweet thrill."

When the song came on they were drinking coffee, and there was a thrum to Lilah's being as the reedy voice sang, "You're my thrill. You do something to me," and she stared deep into Marnie's grey eyes and Marnie's face began to change like the statue changed to the beautiful young man in her dream. The man who sang, "I love you, I want to marry you." But the dream didn't go further because a voice said, "Marnie, it's about time you stopped playing with dolls and came on home to a real woman."

Lilah looked up from the planked, scarred boards of the table into the oval, severe face of Krakatoa, who stood tapping her black, high-heeled boot in front of Marnie. Behind Krakatoa stood another Krakatoa dressed in the same black, skin-tight motorcycle suit, a slightly less imperious figure with masses of long, black hair and red lipstick shaped with a brush above the thin bow of a peaked upper lip.

Marnie's face changed. Bright red blood charged up to her hairline. "What about your fancy Dan over there?" she said, motioning with her head to the other Krakatoa.

"That's strictly a professional relationship. I just bought a new trailer. We're doing six weeks in Vegas, and then a tour. We need a good road manager. All of us can take turns driving — same deal as always."

"I've got an act," Marnie said, but Lilah could see the blood pulsing in her temple.

Lilah said, "It's okay if you want to go."

"Galatea's not an act, it's an institution," Krakatoa said

without acknowledging Lilah's presence. Posed against the Wurlitzer like a hood ornament, the other Krakatoa said nothing.

"You coming, Marnie?" It was the slightly unsteady pronunciation of her name that seemed to impel Marnie out of the booth.

She said to Lilah, "This is blood calling, baby. I'm going. But listen, I love you and you're got a great act. But don't ever sit with the customers," and she walked out of the Bourbon House following Krakatoa I with Krakatoa II trailing behind, leaving Galatea to toy with a poached egg while the whole Bourbon House watched to see how she took it.

That was the last night Galatea came to life. After the show, the owner, Joe Toledano, came into her dressing room without knocking and said, "Hey, Galatea, I got a john who wants to buy you a bottle of champagne. Put on your evening dress and come on out and show him a good time."

Driving back from Lane's apartment Lilah felt good. Lane was so down to earth. In her married life Lilah had never managed to develop the same kind of friendship with another woman or, for that matter, with her husband. He was closed, no opening to that safety deposit; he kept the key. And she'd never gotten interested in Louisiana politics which was one of the main topics of conversation after food, sex, and renovation. She did try to use her mind. Lilah belonged to an uptown literary club called simply "The Club." They each read the same book and once a month had a woman in to review the book they'd all read. This month's book had been something dismal by Céline. She'd hated it. The club had started years before when a few women, with small children at home, who like to read met with no other refreshment but cokes. Now those women had children in college and money in the bank so the luncheons had become elaborate. It was Lilah's turn on Thursday. She had to plan a luncheon and get someone in to serve it, and she didn't have help except for Helen who came in once a week to mop and dust.

She stopped at Langenstein's market where she picked up some nice crab salad in cartons. Langenstein's had great deli items. They would order anything for you and send it. Everyone had a favorite Langenstein's story, they told them at meetings of "The Club." Mrs. Eads Gaudet had lost her diamond earring in the produce at Langenstein's and it was promptly returned to her. The other women nodded, "Where else but Langenstein's."

Davis and Elise were ready to leave when she got to the school. Davis looked like a little old man carrying his brown leather schoolbag in a very precise manner. Lilah thought he looked more like her than Elise did. Thin, with dark hair and eyes, she didn't know where he'd gotten the nose. It was rather large for his face. An aquiline nose, which some kid had already told him he would like to have it full of dimes. The kid's father must have said it. Elise, who was hanging upside down from the jungle gym, had on a clean pair of underpants Lilah had sent with her. The teacher's aide handed the other pair to Lilah in a slightly damp paper bag that smelled of ammonia.

They scrambled into the jeep with some confusion; both wanted to sit in the front next to her. "No." said Lilah. "Get back there. I need to think straight." What she needed was to think back.

White light and a strong reminiscence of childhood. Lilah drifted on a featherbed. The sun blazed in the room, as if a door had been thrown open, and someone shouted, "Get up."

She felt drugged, only wanted to lie there, daydreaming, slowly pulling herself together for coffee and doughnuts at the French Market, but her eye caught the fancy script of yesterday's paper — the *Times-Picayune* banner — the other section of the paper was Classified. A job — she had to get a job. Her money was almost gone and going every day. She'd fallen into the habit of drinks and dinners bought by friends at Nan's, no obligation, just conversation. She'd become a regular — in the bar every night. It was a simple life. For the four months she'd been in New Orleans there had been no responsibilities. It was routinely pleasant; her short stint as Galatea had fed her for quite a while. There were new, fascinating people to meet.

Every day was sunshine. Winter would never come. She loved the streets, the shops, the artists with their pot boilers on the square — something always going on. She ate when the mood struck her. And every night she landed at Nan's to talk and drink lemonade — sometimes Champale. It wasn't an ambitious life, but it suited her and a lot of other people — remittance men, out-of-work entertainers, and dinner-pail pimps — night people who lived the same way.

But she had to get a job — the sun went under a cloud throwing the room into black and white like a James Cagney prison picture. Her bones felt still and cold. Old beer and cigarettes, a sweetish sickening smell permeated the room. She forced herself to jump out of bed, and race to the bathroom, where she filled the big tub to the brim with water. Once she'd forgotten to watch it and it overflowed, and ran down into the patio. There was no drain below the faucets.

After her bath she felt human again, and took her one clean dress and the inevitable spectator pumps out of the chifforobe, hunting around in the dresser drawer until she found a pair of short, white gloves, gloves she'd bought at the Volunteers of America. Whatever the current style, somewhere there would be a man whose mother had dressed just this way. He would recognize the uniform — the pumps, the simple dress, which announced just as simply: I had a grandmother, and a great-grandmother, and I know their maiden names. She would modify her Texas accent. He would hire her no matter how badly she typed. She knew this, but she didn't know how she knew it.

ACE EMPLOYMENT AGENCY, written on the glass door facing the elevator on the fifth floor of the Pere Marquette Building, opened onto a waiting room full of people in straight-backed chairs. As she walked in, she saw a row of men lined up from the door to the water cooler. On the other side sat a line of smartly dressed women with haggard faces, most of them very young. They all looked slightly sick, even the receptionist. The fluorescent light lingered in the lines and blotches on the faces of the men, hollowed and greyed the cheeks of the young women. Angry pink pimples stood out on vulnerable chins. The people looked consumptive or syphilitic—she couldn't decide which. Lilah's confidence drained under the lights. Her lipsticked mouth felt as if it levitated above her face like the mouth on the cover of the frayed and dog-eared copy of Vogue one applicant was reading. Lilah licked her lips to moisten the dry cracks caking up with indelible lipstick.

The receptionist said, "Your name, please?"

"Lilah Hahn Rule."

The pie-faced woman wrote with her left hand and pulled at her brassiere strap with her right. "Miss Clayley will see you in a minute. Please be seated. I'll call you."

The women looked Lilah over suspiciously; the men appreciatively. A statistic—she was now one of the unemployed, but she hadn't been paying attention. Was the percentage up or down? She didn't know. From the look of the people in the room, it must be up. She felt rejected before she started—knowing she had to trot out her talents—type, recite—do something to prove she was worthy of a nine to five. If only she could still be Galatea without drinking with the customers. The longer she sat the more miserable she became. Her head settled back into her shoulders. She slumped down in the chair. As her eyes circled the room, she noticed an uncommon number of balled up Kleenexes surreptitiously applied to dripping noses, almost as red as the pustulant chins. They all had colds. They coughed liked a pack of seals, handkerchiefs and tissues waving a constant surrender. Her eyes began to water; her throat felt scratchy—a cold coming on. Just as she decided she was too sick to stick it out, the receptionist called, "Miss Rule, Miss Clayley will see you now."

The office was a cubbyhole. Behind the desk sat a munchkin. Lilah turned her knees to the side so she could fit into the space allotted for the applicant. She didn't fit but neither did Miss Clayley. If the world was too small for Lilah, it was too big for Miss Clayley, whose feet didn't touch the floor.

"Can you type?"

"Not very well."

"You never tell that. Act like you can."

"Do you have a degree in anything?" Clayley coughed three times—staccato coughs.

"No. Two and a half years of college. Flunked out."

"Well, what can you do? You look good. Great teeth, blue eyes, dark hair—what a combination. I don't have to send you out to have your dress cleaned or tell you to polish your shoes." She coughed again. Three times.

"I guess I can't do very much. I've never worked." Lilah's voice had sunk to a whisper. She didn't think the job as Galatea would be a big help here.

"How old are you?" asked a brusque Miss Clayley.

"Twenty-two."

"If you're twenty-two and you've never worked, why the hell are you looking for a job now? Aren't you just going to get married?" The words were tough, but she leaned over her desk and looked at Lilah with a gentle expression in her hazel eyes.

"I left home. I need a job—I don't—I don't want to ask my family for money—money means strings."

Miss Clayley nodded. What's more, she looked as it she understood. She picked up the phone. "I'll see what I've got." She cradled the phone on her shoulder, looking like a hunch-backed dwarf, and dialed numbers without looking at the paper in front of her.

"Mr. Scherer—Lane Clayley, Ace Employment. I've got just what you want. Great looking girl. Very smart looking. Right kind of voice, right tone. Yes, and she can type, too. College woman. Right—right. I'll send her right over."

She hung up the phone and paused with her hand over it. "Alright. Now listen. I want you to go over to Atlantic Travel Agency, 504 Carondelet. It's right down the street. You're going to be a travel agent."

"But I don't know anything — ."

She interrupted, "You're right. You don't know anything, but you've got the job. Harry Scherer deals in little old ladies with lots of money. All they want is to go where they didn't go last year. You make trips by formula — they've all been done before. But you've got to look right and talk right. You do. Now go over there with your head up and drop a few cultured you-alls and you've got it. Good salary, good bonuses and some trips — you're not going to do any better. Believe me." Miss Clayley coughed, got up from the desk and moved toward the door.

As she walked out of the elevator, she heard a bell ringing above the door. Strident, it resounded down the vacant shaft. The travel agency was directly across the hall. A glass partition plastered with posters began waist high; SEE SPAIN and WORLD CRUISE ELYRIA LINE. Pictures of mountains and streams, flamenco dancers, castles — adventure, excitement. Lilah's blouse moved visibly, as if a nervous frog had taken up residence where her heart should have been. Cheered by the signs, she still wanted to walk out of the empty room. Reluctant to sit, she roamed around looking at posters. The elevator bell rang again. A tall, grey-haired man walked in. At first she thought he might be Mr. Scherer, but he said, "I'd like to arrange a flight to London on the twenty-fifth. Can you help me?"

"I don't work here," she said in a small voice.

"Oh, I beg your pardon. I thought you worked here — obviously you don't — you're carrying a purse. They continued to stand around staring at the travel posters. Lilah wanted to be anywhere in the world but in the travel agency. Where was that idiot Scherer? she wondered. How did he expect to sell trips if he didn't come into the office? What an ass.

The elevator bell rang three times; the tall man and Lilah turned expectantly: The man who came in was short, pudgy, with a high forehead and a baby face. "Sorry to keep you people waiting but I'm short-handed right now." He turned to Lilah with an ingratiating smile, "I'm sure this gentleman will excuse me while I talk to you about your trip. The smile was pure *bon voyage.*

Lilah pinked to the ears. Why does this cretin have to take me for a customer? Aloud she said, "I'm Lilah Rule. Miss Clayley sent me to see you about a job." She said this as quietly as possible.

"Oh — well — ah yes. Oh —" He was dumbfounded. "Well, Miss Rule, if you'll have a seat here. I'll speak to this gentleman, and then I'll talk to you about the job."

The other man had heard the conversation and seemed puzzled, as if someone had deliberately misled him. "I wanted to talk to you about a flight to London, but I'll come back. You go on and talk to this young lady." He backed toward the door. "I'll be back. I'll be back after a while."

Lilah knew she'd just lost the agency trip. The man wouldn't come back. He was embarrassed and he wouldn't want to repeat the experience. All he had to do was walk into another agency. Scherer was staring at the man's back as it entered the elevator.

When the elevator doors closed, Scherer threw up his hands, "Well, that's that," he said.

He turned back to Lilah with a nice smile. "You know you really look like a customer. First time I've ever taken someone for a customer who wasn't. You look perfect for the job. If Clayley sent you, you've got it if you want it. She never makes mistakes."

"You don't want me to type or something? Lilah asked.

"There's not much typing — I mean there is a good bit, but you can do it with two fingers if you want. The main thing you have to do is work with the customers — that is — the clients." He smiled again. The skin of his forehead was smooth and when he smiled, his eyes lit and the shiny, tight skin gave him a radiant look, as if he must be terribly kind. Suddenly, he looked worried. "Do you think you'll like the job?"

"Oh sure. I know I'll love it. When do I start?"

"Let's see. Today is Thursday. Why don't you start Monday? I'll give you some travel literature. Steep yourself in our mystique and come back Monday at 9 a.m."

"Okay — that'll be fine." She felt herself smiling back at him. She was so relieved. Mr. Scherer was a hero — a fine and noble man. Miss Clayley was her fairy godmother. "See you Monday," she said.

The little bell rang as she plummeted to the street below and walked out into sunshine. She had a job! Mr. Scherer had said, "If Clayley picked you, you have to be right for the job." She had to find a pay phone to thank her.

In the Maison Blanche arcade the telephone booths lined up like guard houses. Lilah rang several times before the receptionist answered, "Ace Employment."

"Miss Clayley, please." Lilah heard a pause and then someone's muffled cough. A strangled voice answered, "Lane Clayley speaking."

"Hi, this is Lilah Rule. I got the job."

"You did! That's great. Now I tell you what. Some people are coming to dinner at my house tonight. Why don't you come too. We'll celebrate."

"Hey, that's my first dinner invitation to someone's house. I thought everyone in New Orleans ate out. I should study all this stuff he gave me."

"Aw, come on now — you won't study anyway and the bars will keep. Come see what the lost and lonely do when they cure their bar-itus. About 8 o'clock at 909 St. Philip Street. Have you got it?"

"Sure... 909 St. Philip Street. I'll be there."

That was the first time she met Lane Clayley. It was Lane who introduced her to that other special world of crazies, the nine-to-fivers without children, church, or family, stumbling through a series of short, intensive affairs or long, emotional one-sided relationships that never got better. People, who after five lived as they saw themselves—unmodified for public consumption. The Quarter was tolerant, forgiving—there was no front to keep up for the children or anyone else. Most people in the Quarter didn't bother with driver's licenses, taxes, or bank accounts. Although, it did have its share of solid citizens. People who owned property, paid taxes; but even they had a certain attitude of: Let it pass. What's it matter. Who'll care a hundred years from today.

Lane's House

THE HOUSE WAS ONE OF THOSE CYPRESS DOUBLE cottages New Orleans has so many of in the old neighborhoods. The front was dark—no outside lights. There was a loud bar next door. Lilah was almost ready to leave after ringing the bell several times, when a side gate opened and a tall, thin woman wearing a caftan and carrying an ice bucket came out. The woman walked into the bar next door without seeing Lilah. After a few minutes she returned with the ice bucket full. Lilah stepped forward as the woman opened the iron gate with a key.

"Oh, hello," she didn't appear to be startled. "I didn't see you in the dark. Are you looking for Lane?"

"I'm looking for Miss Clayley. This the address she gave me but I'm not sure I have the right house."

"This is it," smiled the woman. "Lane Clayley lives here. I'm Eve Abbot. Come on in; the party is in the patio."

Lilah followed Eve down the long alleyway. It was completely dark—uneven bricks threatened to trip her. A cool, dank smell of earth exuded from the close walls and the slippery surface underfoot. After walking the full length of the house they came into a space with some light where Lilah could see dim figures sitting around a garbage can lid filled with chalky coals glowing red at the center. The voices were low, a murmuring sound interspersed with the clink of ice being dropped in glasses. There was a large patch of light from an open door. "God damn it. The soufflé fell." The small figure of Lane Clayley appeared in the doorway in a pair of slacks and a bra, sweat glistened on her chest as she brandished a dismal looking mess in a pan. "Every time I make it it falls. Looks like I'd give up. Oh, hi, Lilah. Do you know how to make a decent soufflé? Do you want an iced-coffee or a martini?" "No. I don't know how to make a soufflé, and yes, I'll take an iced coffee." Lane disappeared into the kitchen; when she came back she had put on a red pullover. She carried a glass of dark iced coffee shot through with seeping veins of cream. Lilah nearly choked when she took a swallow—the cream was ice cream. "I always drink my coffee black."

"Well, give it back."

"No—I like it. The coffee must be like pitch but with the ice cream it's delicious."

"Come on. I'll introduce you to some people. This is Ben, my old man. He sometimes plays the piano." Ben stood up and Lilah thought he'd never stop unwinding—at least six feet five. She couldn't help laughing.

He took Lilah's hand. "You know, Lane, I'm either a terribly funny person or people must get an immediate picture of us in bed together."

"Oh, shut up, old man. Nobody has any visions of you in bed with anybody. Now this is Tony Tit," she introduced a small man sitting on the edge of a flower bed. "Tony Tit is not really his name, but that's what everyone calls him. I don't think it's supposed to be obscene but short for Titmouse, which is his name. You met Eve Abbott." Tony Tit sat with his head leaning against Eve's legs. She was still smiling, but her smile crumpled to one side of her face, and it was easy to see she'd had one too many martinis. She said, "For God's sake, Lane, fix us something to eat. I'm absolutely crocked and you keep farting around introducing people. We need food; you promised steaks. Sit down, Lilah. We've heard enough about you." She reached up and pulled Lilah down bodily beside a man she hadn't met.

"Okay, Eve. Keep your pants on. Ben's doing the steaks now, and I made that eggplant deal, and salad's made. I was just doing the soufflé for fun." Lane backed off and headed for the kitchen.

"Hello." It was the man sitting in the shadow, and he spoke softly. Eve was already deep in conversation with Tony Tit. Lilah got the feeling that she was the extra woman for the extra man, and she hadn't even met him. She tried to peer at his face in the dark as she said, "Hello." He moved forward so that he was right beside her, and as he did, the firelight seemed to set his beard on fire. The figure was slender. His hair and beard were red. "I'm Kaleb Borland," he said.

"I'm Lilah Rule."

"Yes, I know," he said and stared at her intently. She wondered what Lane Clayley had said about her. It had to be Lane. She was the cook and the matchmaker, whether she was any good at either one remained to be seen. Eve and Tony had gotten into a violent quarrel, and were too busy fighting to join in any sort of conversation. This left Lilah to make conversation with Kaleb.

"You haven't been here long, have you?"

"You mean in New Orleans—no not long. It's a great city. I've never been any place where people are so kind to strangers," she said.

"Are you making a joke?"

She flushed, "I don't think so."

"That's what Blanche DuBois said in *Streetcar*—she depended on 'the kindness of strangers.' We're all strangers. You seldom meet a native. New Orleans is a dirty old city—

half whore, half saint. She smells sweet like the overripe melons thrown out behind the French Market." He leaned back against the patio wall and stretched out his legs. "You're Galatea. I saw you in the Bourbon House." He crossed his legs at the ankles like a dancer.

She decide to fake it. "Who's Galatea?" she said.

"Oh, just a statue that came to life."

"Well, that's not me. I'm just beginning to have a life."

"Pardon me. Mistaken as usual."

"I was ready to go through my—And how do *you* like New Orleans?—conversation. Apparently, you don't like her too well." She leaned back against the wall, also.

"Don't get me wrong. I love New Orleans. Where else could I live such an easy life—drinking and eating well, and sleeping late on the pay from my art work? I'll never really know New Orleans or the Quarter, but I do just as I please here."

"Yes, I suppose that's what I've done—just as I pleased. It's like being in a foreign country. You feel absolutely no responsibility for any of your actions. There's no one to disapprove. As if you were born over, but full grown," she said. He leaned forward, and she could see in the light that his eyes— even the pupils—were reddish brown—dark with thick lashes. Any woman would have found him interesting. He had a comfortable way with a woman; the manner of a man who'd been around them a lot—sisters—and, she was sure, a lot of women after that.

"Lane said you got a job in the travel agency today. She must like you. She saves her bookstore and travel agency jobs for people she likes." He smiled at her.

"Did she ever get you a job?"

"As a matter of fact, she did, at Doubleday Bookstore."

Lilah started to laugh. "What a silly conversation," she said.

"Oh, so you think my bookstore job was silly?"

"No. I was just thinking how none of us ask any of the questions we're really thinking."

"Don't be so sure. You're liable to hear anything tonight."

Suddenly, there was salad and steak, and of all things, Sangria. She was saved by the food. He was a secret person and her greatest weakness was curiosity. But they all got busy balancing plates on their laps and glasses on a short ledge of brick that edged a few plants. Everyone was laughing and talking too loudly, as if the food had come a little too late. They were all rather drunk except for Lilah. Lane gave her a martini instead of sangria. "Drink this. You're too damn sober. Catch up. You make us look bad." In Texas Lilah was notorious as a wild two-drink drunk, and now she embarked upon debacle with an insouciant "What the hell."

She plowed into the steak and sloshed down the drink.

"Martini in not good for washing down steak," she said.

Kaleb went to get her sangria. There was no doubting her own intention; whenever she didn't want to feel responsible for something she was going to do she would have a couple of drinks—lose what few inhibitions she had, and do it. "Put the policeman to sleep," she said.

He handed her the glass, "What does that mean?" he asked.

"It doesn't *mean*. It's a fact," she said. Something had been building since she saw his face. Every time he moved, she wanted to touch him. She was dizzy from trying to carry on a conversation with him. He talked about everything but nothing. She really wasn't very interested in what he was saying. It was some kind of animal magnetism that kept her focused on him.

The party had progressed to spastic-gaited dancing. Lane Clayley was clinging to Ben somewhere slightly above the knees. Billy Holiday was wailing "Fine and Mellow," and Lilah felt that way. Suddenly Eve Abbot, who was dancing with Tony Tit, started pummeling his chest with both fists. Kaleb and Ben jumped up, but then let it go. Probably embarrassed to go to his defense because he was such a small man. But when Eve picked up a brick from the flowerbed, Lilah called out,"Eve! Eve don't do that." Eve turned toward the voice with a glazed look.

She said, "You know me? You really know me?" She put out a tentative hand to Lilah, who took the brick away from her. "Do I know you? Do you know my husband?"

To pacify her Lilah said, "Perhaps I do."

Eve's hair was falling in her face and when she swept it back with her hand her eyes were blank. "He's crazy—bug-fuck," she yelled and thrust her face in Lilah's. "They put him in Jackson. They put him in, and he'll never get out—never. He tried to kill me. Did you know that?"

"No, I didn't know that." Lilah didn't know what else to say. Kaleb stood beside her saying nothing. Eve grabbed his hand and kissed his fingers. "You two are married—that's so good—but he's crazy. What can I do?" She looked from Kaleb to Lilah. "What can I do? I cry all the time—all the time. Then I end up here." Spent, she sagged down against the patio wall. "God, I'm so drunk. Lane? Lane, get me home—"

Lane, who had been standing to one side waiting for Eve's fit to exhaust itself, came forward with a wet washcloth and wiped her face. "Come on, baby, we've all got miseries and gin doesn't make them go away. Ben, help her up. You and Tony had better take her home."

Lilah looked at Tony Tit. He was nursing a bad scratch on his cheek, but he rallied, and they began trying to walk Eve out of the patio. The doorway was narrow, and three people couldn't walk through. Ben picked her up in his arms. Tony Tit followed behind carrying her purse. He looked as if he'd done a great deal of following after Eve Abbott. Lilah, sober now, turned to see Kaleb staring into the fire. His face was so sad she hesitated a moment then walked back to him. "Are you okay?"

He looked up slowly, "I wanted to tell her—Lady, get a cat or a dog—some dumb thing to comfort you. People talk, but not to each other—suffering embarrasses us—and mental suffering—we can't do a goddamn thing about it. That's what everybody needs—some dumb, soft, furry thing that'll come when you call it to be touched and held onto. We don't want to get too close because, well, hey—the lady's got misery, and misery rubs off. That's what I wanted to say, but all I could do was stand there while she kissed my hand." He gave Lilah a shove and she landed against the wall.

"What's the matter with you?" She was stiff and angry.

"Oh, God, I didn't mean to do that." He began rubbing her cheek gently with two fingers, and she softened now that he was finally touching her. "Come on, baby, let's go home. I need you so bad." And she walked out with him into the fog that had rolled in from the river. The iron street lights were soft white globes of angel hair floating above the mist. There was a chill to the air, a clinging dampness, which made them huddle together. She couldn't see the winos asleep in the doorways under the grey down. Fog horns sobbed as ships on the river blew warnings.

Lilah walked with Kaleb until they came to a carriage entrance. The huge door hanging by one hinge opened with a scraping sound as Kaleb pushed it and then pulled Lilah inside. They were in a dark carriageway; discarded furniture stacked to the ceiling thrust sharp legs into the narrow passage. To get past it they walked sideways in the dark holding hands. Kaleb felt his way cautiously pulling Lilah until his foot hit the bottom step of a stairway and he stopped to light a candle. The banister, which whirled gracefully upward, was gap-toothed, the stairs littered with broken plaster and dust. They walked further back to climb a second set of stairs, which exited the main house and led to a slave quarter where they crossed a rickety balcony without a catchrail. She shivered. He turned to her and the candle lit his soft eyes. "Cold feet," he asked.

"No," she said.

When they reached the end of the balcony, she followed him into a room of the main house. There was no furniture but a few boxes. He stopped and lit a kerosene lamp. They went on through another room of canvases and cardboard boxes. The last room had an ornate wooden door—hand-carved cherubs picked carved camellias. He opened the door, and she walked into the room holding his hand. The lamp threw their linked shadows around the room. They were moving awkwardly like Siamese twins. The massive bed looked like a ship in full sail. Carved posts of rosewood reached up to the high tester draped in gold silk. Above it a gold and yellow parachute bloomed from the ceiling. She looked at Kaleb in surprise. He put the lamp on the table, threw matches down beside it. "I got it from a junkie," he said. She stood there, mute—arms folded, staring at the bed.

"This is the music room," he said, "but there's no music. I'd like to buy an old phonograph that doesn't need electricity..." He left the words hanging between them as he reached out his hand. She walked to him uncertainly. "Let's try the bed," he said.

She lay in his arms passively. "Too much liquor, I think." He undressed her slowly and carefully. Folding her clothes as he took them off. When she was stretched naked beside him, he stood up looking at her as he unzipped his jeans.

"I knew you were different," he said, "even with that serious look, but I didn't know how different. I'm rich—no doubt about it—I'm rich." He laughed and pressed the length of himself against her. He was gentle, and she found herself rising up to meet him, feeling pleasure in a hard sweat.

He was asleep. She crept to the window and watched the light come in. The damp air was cool on her skin. She picked his shirt up off the floor and threw it over her shoulders. The long sleeves hung exactly to her wrists. She didn't put it on. The apartment overlooked Decatur Street. From the window she could see the tops of ships sliding by on the river. She couldn't see the dock or the water, but the ships were clean forms moving, their booms of intersecting angles like sculpture. Below on the street, the night people began going home. At first only vague forms moved from doorway to doorway, but now as the hard light of morning hit the street two people came into view.

"God damn it, I said I don't want to go with you, and I don't want to go with you. I got my own money." The woman's hair had been combed into a sticky mass on the top of her head. Yellow strands escaped from two bright blue combs pushed into the sides. Lilah couldn't see the woman's face, but she wore dusty black pedal pushers and an ill-fitting beige sweater. Drunk, she leaned heavily against the building across the street, rummaging into her purse for something. Lilah could see dark, crusted sores on her ankles. The man with her was about fifty, the top of his head bald, the round shiny skull vigorous as a cue ball. The hair surrounding the bald spot was grey, but his body looked fit under a limp brown suit. Squat with heavy, slightly bowed legs, he appeared younger than the woman who could have been forty or sixty.

Lilah wondered at the mystery of sex—a healthy man, probably a seaman, pleading for the favors of this sick-looking woman who had no charms beyond basic equipment.

"Come on, Lily. Let's go upstairs."

"I'm not going up any fucking stairs with you. I got my money for the night. I don't have to take no shit off no one."

"Aw, come on, Lily. Just a short time."

Lily finally found a cigarette and lit it, and they both wandered unsteadily down the street, stopping often, until they turned the corner and went away forever.

Lilah shivered, wondering what power Lily had. What was her own power and how could she use it? Was it only sexual? Kaleb lay stretched out dreamless, yet far removed from her. A small movement of his chest, a tensing of one finger and she knew he was coming back from wherever he'd traveled. As the new light caught his body, she realized she'd never seen the relaxed penis of a grown man by daylight. It was an intrinsic part of his body, not the insistent force which leaped out of him with a life of its own demanding from both of them. She loved him then. But as she watched it, the organ appeared to gather force and rise out of his body like the head of a plant photographed in slow motion, alien—her first impulse was to laugh—it had nothing to do with either of them, and yet she loved to look at its vigor. To know it was hers when she needed it.

He woke with a start, covered himself, then lifted his head and looked over to her side of the bed. His face forlorn and young.

"I'm here," she said, as she pulled herself up from the cramped position by the window.

"I'll be back," he said, and jumped out of bed wrapped in the sheet. She heard a toilet flush in the distance and felt glad there was some plumbing somewhere.

He came back in a striped, wine-silk bathrobe, the silk so old it had shredded at the sleeves. He had two oranges and tossed her one which she caught in surprise. "Hi, you look nice. Have you been awake for long?"

"Before daylight." There was something about Kaleb's face that moved her. Perhaps, it was because he smiled so seldom. He smiled now, and she knew she had been waiting for it. She would have sung songs, tap-danced — anything for that smile. She didn't know it then, but that aching smile would be the keynote of their time together. And she left herself no defense — she wanted the real experience. Kaleb was an open wound — he walked around bleeding — he only smiled when he hurt a little less. She wasn't equipped to bind a wound of this size, but she was excited at the thought of knowing him — the depths of his hurt self. It hadn't been a casual night.

"I have to dress and go home," she said.

"Not now. Stay with me. Let's go have breakfast at Battistella's." He reached for her hand and held it. There was something of her mother in that restraining hand holding her — *I need you — ease me.*

"No. I have to go. I have to get things ready for work." She pulled her hand away and began putting on her clothes.

"Why can't you give up one day. Just one day. You haven't started the job yet. Are you on some sort of schedule or something?"

As she moved away from him, he grabbed his shirt off her shoulders. The movement was so sudden it left her exposed, but he wasn't looking at her. He began gathering his clothes up from where he'd thrown them the night before. He buttoned his shirt, then held his jeans in front of him, pulling them over his naked body and pushing his genitals to the left with an impatient hand. He shoved in the shirt tail, stepped into thong sandals, and was dressed before Lilah could get over a certain reluctance to put on the same underwear she'd worn the day before. She thought of Lily—the man looked better than Lily. Her eyes began to swell—she knew there were tears there. "Oh, God," she said. "Why am I crying? I don't know why I'm crying."

Kaleb watched—waiting with an angry look on his face.

"Don't cry. Let me. I'm the man who cries. Do you know how disgusting and sissy a man is who cries? Well, I do. My father told me at least once a week. So, please, please, don't cry." He put on a mock serious face that made her laugh. He smiled too, and she picked up her limp clothes to put them on, but her face immediately turned down.

"I know what's wrong with you. You need some soulful clothes. You can't wear those again, can you?"

He swaggered around the room bopping his forehead like one of the three stooges. "You need something southern—southern Japan maybe?" He opened a door on the rosewood armoire, which took up half the wall, and began sliding hangers over a metal bar. She could see a bright purple tulle skirt sticking out from a row of costumes. He pushed it aside and pulled out an orange kimono with a writhing magenta dragon embroidered on the back. "Kee-mo-no? Missy."

"Can't stand orange."

He was flinging down costumes—cheap, carnival satins in day-glo colors, an elaborate blue velvet cloak with hundreds of rhinestones, pink harem pants—throwing them onto the floor, the bed, anywhere. The armoire was a costumer's shop—outlandish outfits piled up until he pulled out something that seemed to unfold forever—dark green silk with gold embroidery, he wrapped himself in it while trying to get it out of the armoire. She tried to help him, pulling at the silk, and then she found herself on the floor in folds of silk kissing pink lips edged in red beard, and she rolled with him playing, the way she'd rolled with Poppy her dog, and then she was helping him under the silk to get out of his jeans, and when she sat on him astride it was an ache, a fever, and a chill—she couldn't ride fast enough.

Afterwards, they bathed on the back gallery, pouring buckets of cold water over their warm bodies. After she dried with a beach towel, her body felt clean and bright. She held the end of the dark green sari, and he pleated its length around her waist, tucking it into the top of a petticoat, throwing the embroidered end over her shoulder.

"Me too," he said. "I'm going to be beautiful," and he dressed himself in a white shirt with dark velvet slacks, and a soft cream Panama hat.

It was still early and Battistella's restaurant was full of working men, some of whom worked in the French Market, and a few longshoremen. Big men, but quiet, leaning over the counter drinking their morning coffee. The rest of the café was empty—row after row of empty tables covered in green and white oilcloth held down by a circle of condiments: sugar, salt, pepper, oil, vinegar, and a bottle of Crystal hot sauce.

No one stared at them when they came in. Lilah was conscious of being out of place in such flamboyant clothes, but no one gave them a second glance. They sat at a table and the waitress brought biscuits and coffee with hot milk. Kaleb's pleasure in the place was contagious. He made expansive gestures with his hands, "You know I've never brought anyone here for breakfast before. I get coffee here every day before I go to the square—no tourists."

She was quiet—really didn't have anything to say. He kept watching her, as she began to turn inward.

"You're not talking," he said.

"I don't know what to say."

"Who are you? I mean I know who you are to me, but who are you to you?

"I don't know. I think I came here to find out."

"Oh, well, that's too bad. I can't think of a worse place to discover yourself than New Orleans."

"You say New Or-lee-ans. Some people say something like N'Awlins."

"Remember, I'm an implant. You may not want to listen to anything I have to say. This town is all light and shadow — you chase them around — even the real people here dress up and act crazy at least once a year. I think people are in the Quarter because they're not real enough for any place else."

"I don't like real people. Rule is full of them. I'd rather lights and shadows. Besides, you're real — the men at the counter — they're real."

"No, I'm not. I don't go to work every day and I don't have any kids to feed and I don't intend to have any kids to feed. Besides, real people don't hurt all the time unless they can't eat or the rats eat them. I hurt for everybody no matter who the rats eat."

"I think you have some very romantic image of yourself. Like a great doomed painter — Van Gogh or Gauguin — somebody like that."

He shrugged his shoulders and ordered more coffee.

A tall, soft looking man in a red and black dashiki came in the front door. She knew she was staring — he looked so much like a picture of Oscar Wilde in his latter days, but she didn't think he was gay. Not the way he looked at her.

He came over to their table. "Kaleb! How are you? Will you be coming out on the Square today? Letitia looked for you all day yesterday like a cat in heat."

"Yeah, Bud, well you know how it is. I didn't feel like working." Kaleb didn't look up, but kept his eyes lowered on the coffee he was stirring. Bud continued to stare at Lilah as if waiting for Kaleb to introduce them. "I don't believe I've met this subtle beauty. I'm Bud Thompson. Kaleb won't introduce us because he doesn't want anyone to move in on his territory, but then Kaleb has so much territory to cover — " He sat down in the chair next to Lilah. Kaleb scowled, but didn't say anything to Bud, absorbed with getting his coffee right, he put his spoon back in to stir it again.

"I'm Lilah Rule," she said.

"I *am* fascinated, Miss Rule. I'm fascinated by the fact that Kaleb Borland always squires the most beautiful women. Now from this fact I must assume that Kaleb Borland is a remarkable, significant man. I am not quite prepared to admit that. I would prefer to think that fate is fickle and Kaleb is getting my share of the world's beautiful women. This time he has outdone himself." He leaned very close to her. Lilah put out a hand to get him out of her territory, but he took her hand and kissed it. "Exquisite. Skin like magnolia petals. I *am* right. You *are* Southern. Not one of our Northern hollyhocks — they seem to grow like weeds in the Quarter. Texas — I would imagine from your distinctive speech?"

"Yes."

"You see, Kaleb, I'm a seer. I'm wasting myself as a sidewalk artist. I should invest in a cloak and a crystal ball — give hope to the aged and love to the lovelorn." He smiled and showed dazzling teeth between his fleshy lips.

"Oh, shut up, Bud. You're an ass. You should have been gay, then I wouldn't have to listen to your womanless lament." Kaleb pushed at the table, the hot sauce shook but didn't fall, as he stood up. "Come on, Lilah. You'll get stuck in molasses if you stay here. See you later, Bud. Try to cut the flowers. This is my girl. Okay.

"Goodbye," she said awkwardly as they left.

Kaleb was marching along a half-a-block ahead. She hurried to catch up. "Kaleb, why don't you like him. He's harmless."

"Harmless! About as harmless as an elephant — big, soft, and harmless, but watch out if he decides to step on you. He likes to be seen with good looking women, and he can afford them. He doesn't have to paint, but he's good at it. He's good at women."

Lilah raised an eyebrow. Bud Thompson was physically rather repulsive. "He's not very attractive."

"Yeah, that's what every woman thinks when she first

meets him. When Letitia met him she said, 'He reminds me of a jellyfish.' Now she lives with him."

"What did he mean — Letitia's looking for you?"

"Letitia lived with me before she moved in with Bud. It was all over anyway. Bud was just a way out and she took it. He likes to talk as if she still looks for me. Just his way of romanticizing — Bud has some strange streaks. He always wants what someone else has. Particularly, if he thinks you really care. The minute I saw him I knew he'd heard about you through the grapevine. I got jealous — I just didn't want him talking to you."

"How could he hear about me? We've only spent one night together."

"They see things. Somebody at Lane's party. They always seem to know if it's casual or not. They're probably giving odds on how long it'll last." He took her arm and tucked it through his. "It isn't casual is it?" He stopped walking and gave her a hard look.

"I don't know. I'm not a casual person. At least I don't think so. But I don't know too much about me. Someone else was always telling me who I was."

Moving In

It seemed like a year since she'd been in her room at Mrs. LeBlanc's. There was something condescending in Kaleb's attitude as he walked in with her. Lilah kept checking his expression. He sat down on the hard edge of the bunk and started to laugh; then he threw himself back and stared at the ceiling. "I love it. I would never have believed I'd see you, the elegant Miss Rule, in a flea bag like this. How in the world did you ever find this glorious dump?"

"Oh, a wino I know told me about it," she said as she gathered up clothes for the big move. Something told her she was making a mistake, but she couldn't think of a graceful way out. Not now—not after Kaleb had seen where she lived. No longer believable was the argument that her place was more comfortable than his. He could see it wasn't, even if it did have hot water. Lilah felt dull, lethargic. She didn't want to pack. There was something cozy and uncomplicated about her room and her life. She didn't think living with Kaleb would be uncomplicated.

"Miss Ruuu-eeel, Miss Ruuu—eel," a shrill voice called.

"Oh, no. It's Mrs. LeBlanc. You're not supposed to be up here."

"You're kidding? You mean you can't have men in your room?" He started laughing again.

"Oh, for God's sake, Kaleb, be serious. She's a nice little old lady who used to be in show business. She's still living in the twenties."

"The twenties? Show business? Where have you been? The twenties were wild. If she was in show business, at least she's been around." He stepped out on the gallery, "Bonjour, Madame LeBlanc."

Lilah didn't understand the rest of the conversation. It was in French. Suddenly, a fervent "La Vie En Rose" was being sung by a husky voice in the patio. When Kaleb walked back in, he was grinning and chewing on a cigarillo.

"Where'd you get that?" she asked.

"Mrs. LeBlanc. She says I'm the type of man who should smoke a small cigar—of course, she said *teep* of man." He swaggered like a bullfighter, puffing and blowing the smoke around the room.

"What about all the singing? Edith Piaf?"

"Wasn't she great? Just gave me a sexy look and started singing." He leaned back in the chair and put his feet on the edge of the bunk.

"Well, now that you've seduced Mrs. LeBlanc you don't need me. I can't sing, and I can't pack." She was trying to stuff accumulated junk into two cardboard boxes, a couple of Schwegmann bags, and the two original suitcases. "I don't think I want to move in with you. It's too damn complicated."

"Yes you do. You don't have to sing. You have enough talents to keep me entertained forever." Suddenly, he got up and put his arms around her. "Let's stop playing like this doesn't matter, Lilah. You feel like you're being trapped—you are—neither one of us will be as free. But we won't be alone either—I mean the kind of alone where you don't want to get up in the morning. I want to wake up and see you."

She had begun to respond—not to what he was saying, but to his hands and mouth, which talked to her more eloquently than anything he said.

He let go. "Come on. I'll help you pack. I went to military school; I can fold anything." The long fingers carefully smoothed the dresses on the cot and folded them until each one fit the suitcase. He tucked lipsticks and her hairbrush into the side pockets. It was quick and neat.

Lilah watched him with the amazed attention she would have afforded a virtuoso playing a Stradivarius violin. "I've never been able to wrap packages or pack. My mother would never let me do it because everything muddles up in my fingers and my clothes look like they're dirty when I get where I'm going," she said.

"Don't apologize. I went to military school. It was supposed to make a man of me—it did teach me how to pack and how to hate anything authoritarian." He was tying up the box of books. She sat with her chin in her hand as he took down her print of the Chinese horse, rolled it up, and secured it with a rubber band. Within the hour he had packed everything and put it into one pile, then charmed Mrs. LeBlanc into calling a cab—a courtesy she'd never extend to Lilah.

As the cab stopped in front of Kaleb's house, Lilah had another moment of panic. By daylight there was no charm to it at all—anywhere. The house was a condemned fire-trap; she could smell urine before she opened the cab door; every bum who needed to urinate used that doorway. She didn't want to live here anymore than she wanted to live in her mother's house. She hated her own passivity—her willingness to step off solid ground to follow Kaleb into unknown territory. He took her arm possessively and ushered her into the courtyard which was littered with broken shutters and shattered glass panes, which had separated from the dried putty in window frames. In the windowless gable a bevy of pigeons danced, sliding their necks back and forth in a hypnotic trance. Pigeon shit covered the old bricks of the patio with a heavy coat of white lime splats leading up to the back steps and continuing up the first two steps. Lilah and Kaleb stepped on it as they went up the rickety stairs carrying boxes of posters, books and a celluloid dresser set. In Rule she had walked out on a lifetime of possessions without a backward glance, but here she felt tied to a few dollars worth of prints and a few books.

It was the first time she'd really seen the studio. There were rolls of canvas in one corner; a square paint table with a clean-shaved glass on top stood near an easel at the window where the light was cold and intense; dusty worms of oil paint gobbed the sides and edges. The disorder of the room stood out in harsh relief, but the most unsettling objects were the huge, grotesque canvases leaning out of the filthy corners with a persistent obscenity, demanding attention. The colors and shapes were not eye pleasing, and the emotional content frightening. There were huge female body parts disjointed at the hips with large buttocks, and enormous breasts supporting abstract geometric shapes. Kaleb followed her around the room as she looked at his work. His own eye was affectionate. She couldn't help thinking how like a mother of deformed children he was. He loved his paintings. It would never occur to him that she would find them strange. She stalked into the bedroom. Moving in with Kaleb had already destroyed her independence and her disposition.

"Are you mad?"

"No," she answered.

"What's the matter?" He kept following her.

"Nothing."

"How the hell can you say 'nothing' when you look like that." He was getting angry.

"Because nothing's the matter." The more he tried to reason with her, the more sullen and shutdown her face became.

"You've been funny ever since we left your room. Now tell me. We're not strangers." He took her by the arms and made her look at him.

"I don't like it here," she said at last. "I hate the dirt and the ugliness. I'm not ready for it in the daytime. I can stand it at night, but I can't take it in the daytime." She sat down on the bed and began to cry.

"It's alright, baby, we'll clean it. We'll clean our part of it, and hang the world outside."

"You can't clean it, Kaleb. There's no way you could clean this house. I have bad feelings about this house."

"Look now, it's really a great house. I know it isn't suburbia, but neither are we—and that's the life we're trying to get rid of. You have to make adjustments to this house, but it gives you a lot in return. I can see it in my paintings. I didn't paint as well before I moved here. Now I get lost in painting. I come into this room and I want to paint—I really want to paint. For that I can do without hot water." He was so earnest clutching her hands until they began to hurt.

She pulled them away. "I'm not talking about hot water. I'll probably curse and scream because there's no hot water, but I mean something's wrong here—for me—a feeling that I shouldn't live here. I won't be happy here."

"Try it with me. You may hate me after a month, but let's try. We can always move if it's *really* bad. I mean really bad." He put his arms around her, and she leaned against him.

"I love you, Kaleb, and I'll live here, but I think I've made some enemies." She kissed him, but over his shoulder she could see the paintings like disorganized meat in a dirty butcher shop.

But he made it wonderful. On Saturday at the Morning Call, waiters in white hats and aprons passed with trays of coffee and hot beignets; while droves of people waited for tables, Kaleb stood quietly and expectantly beside a couple at an inside table as the man put a quarter by his empty cup. Lilah, who stood by the door to the inside café, was not alert to the ritual of getting a table at the Morning Call; she watched as the man picked up his paper, and Kaleb slid quickly into his empty chair. Flashing her his smile, he motioned for Lilah to join him. "That was quick," she said. They sat down—two empty coffee cups and a fine mist of powdery sugar covered the table. Lilah sat facing Jackson Square. Kaleb knew everyone on the square—the artists, the cops, the guy in the wheelchair, who was always there. Earlier they had stopped to talk to an artist named Hal, who had a bland face—a pale wash like the watercolors he hawked.

Now she asked, "Do you like Hal's work?"

"You don't like or dislike somebody like Hal's work—he's a paint factory. He does the same street scenes over and over to make a buck.The tourists want to take home something from New Orleans for Aunt Ida—something cheap, so they buy a watercolor from Hal. I don't think Hal's had any illusions about his art for some time now."

She could see Hal sitting by the fence on St. Ann Street. "I bet he does. I bet he really cares." From where she was sitting it looked like a picture of a Paris street scene. Hal wore a black beret, and the watercolors were colorful hanging on the square's iron fence.

The waiter had come by and wiped the sticky table with a damp rag. Now he brought the beignets piled in stacks of three covered with a dense layer of powdered sugar—white, lumpy sugar—at least half a box, dumped on the square donuts. He swirled the coffee cups with a flourish from the tin tray as he put them down before Lilah and Kaleb. Small plumes of steam rose from the white cups. The chicory coffee foamed with milk the color of warm sand, and Lilah thought of the beach as she sipped it. There was such a strong sense of leisure here. They didn't need to talk much, like cats leaned near each other in the sun, and when they were finished moved out onto the sidewalk still powdered with sugar. He kissed her, and she could taste the coffee.

They passed through the Square, crossed Chartres Street and walked down Pirates Alley. Lilah heard a raucous laugh and a voice called out. "Kaleb? Lilah? Are you tourists come to see the freaks? Letitia, here's Kaleb with his new conquest. Come here, Lilah. Let me introduce you to the other most beautiful woman in the Quarter." It was Bud Thompson.

Kaleb and Lilah stopped in front of the gallery. "Come in. Come in," Bud said. One wall was hung floor to ceiling with paintings signed THOMPSON. She looked at them with a critical eye. They were large canvasses with splashes of primary colors. She couldn't see any of the man's sarcasm or surface attitude in the paintings. "I like them" she said. Kaleb glared at Bud as he had the day before. A girl walked out of the back of the shop. At first glance Lilah thought she was oriental, her black hair long and straight, the bones of her wrists fragile. She wore faded blue jeans and a Chinese-red silk shirt. The features or her face were so perfect Lilah began to wonder if there was even a tiny flaw, but as Letitia smiled at Kaleb, Lilah saw that her canine teeth were long and one folded neatly over another. Rather than spoiling her, it gave her a vulnerable look. When Letitia looked at Kaleb, Lilah could understand Bud's antagonism. Whatever held Letitia to Bud, it wasn't love. She was still in love with Kaleb.

"Letitia, this is Lilah Rule. Pretty isn't she, and from what I can understand witty, though I must admit she hasn't said anything particularly clever to me. Kaleb is still his same raunchy self. I can't for the life of me see what you women see in him."

"Hello, Lilah," Letitia nodded but hardly looked at Lilah. She was looking at Kaleb. He looked down at Letitia, but with the same glowering eyes he'd turned on Bud. "He's sexy, Bud. Can't you see it?" she said.

"I must confess I can't. Let's say I prefer not to see it. Now I see how sexy I am." He laughed his raucous laugh again.

"No, Bud. Sexy is what you feel. Sexy — is what Kaleb is," Lilah said.

"Let's get out of here," Kaleb said.

"Don't rush me. I'm waiting for Bud to say something clever about life and love. Bud, your work doesn't look like the you I've met. When are you going to let your true self show?" Lilah couldn't help needling him. He acted such an ass to Kaleb.

Bud looked startled. "Never," he said. "I can't afford to."

"I said let's go." Kaleb was pulling at her by the sleeve of her blouse. She moved his hand with her hand, but held it and allowed him to pull her away. Letitia followed them with her eyes. She was still staring at Kaleb when Lilah looked back.

She and Kaleb had been together such a short time, and yet she felt explosive emotions. She had been unreasonably angry with Bud Thompson and felt something close to envy when she looked at Letitia. Beneath the surface ease of her life in Rule, there had been emotions, but her father and mother kept things under control. Tidied up, at least the surface of her life was serene there. Her feelings in Rule had eaten at her from the inside out. She hadn't realized her father was an alcoholic until he died of a cirrhotic liver; he was always drinking but never drunk. When he died, the cause of death was never mentioned in the house, but when she saw the death certificate she knew she'd always known.

Living with Kaleb was the edge of a volcano; there were rents in the surface and deadly vapors kept rising. Trembling on the edge, she had become, without knowing it, a vulcanist, willing to risk anything to find out what was under the surface. Her feelings frightened her, but she knew she was living.

"The careful life dries you up," she said to him, but he was lost in his own thoughts and didn't answer. She hated her parents' life. She couldn't believe anything interesting had ever happened to them. They were so careful, but she'd noticed as a child, even the most careful people got hurt. In Texas there was always something in the bushes; her father riding his mower cut his grass like a flat-top, there was always something in the bushes. Here she was—out to meet the bogeyman on his own territory—tweak his nose—ask him to dance. Bud Thompson was a bogeyman. She felt it in her bones. He could hurt them—at least she was in the arms of some she cared about.

"You're thinking," he said quietly.

"I'm scared of all this letting go, but I'm whistling. You know—in the dark."

"We both talk a lot of shit," he said. "Let's go somewhere for a drink."

"Let's go to Nan's Place."

"You mean that gay bar?" He looked surprised.

"That's the first place I went to in the Quarter, and I was so fascinated I sat there every night. It's another world—surrealistic. The conversations are poetry. Dramas are acted out every night. They begin in the bar and end in the bar. You can see it all. I learned about roles. I've always known everyone is caught up in some sort of pattern they're forced to play out. I thought if I could just see some of the patterns, maybe I could break them. In Nan's bar you can see the roles reversed—men are women and women are men, and men mother other men and women father other men. You can see some of the things we're born with, but mostly you can see all the garbage we acquire when we're kids. It's like dreaming one of those dreams where you think there's a great truth, but you can't quite remember what it is, and every time you try to tell it—it slips away."

"Do you think you could be bisexual?" he asked, a note of worry in his voice.

"Maybe, but I don't think so. I like some of the women, but I don't think I want to sleep with anyone but you." They walked to Nan's Place, but it was too early and the bar was closed. It didn't open until 4 p.m.

"Let's go see Lane Clayley. She's always nursing some emotional cripple and the conversation's good." He started to run. She hadn't run since she was a kid, and she couldn't run fast—swimming was her sport. Running, she felt heavy and hot. He raced down the street, grabbed a lamp pole and swung around it; at the corner he came to a mailbox, put two hands on top, and vaulted over it. She didn't try to keep up, but when she came to a school yard on Royal Street she went in and climbed a tree. He was still racing on. She couldn't see him, but she knew he was probably in the next block. She didn't care. The leaves were green and there was a breeze where she sat on a branch on the second tier and swung her feet in thin air. She heard him walking back. He stood in the middle of the sidewalk. Through the leaves she could see him, but he couldn't see her. Looking up and down the street, he didn't find her, and was so disconsolate she called him, "Kaleb, I'm up here."

He loped over still breathing hard, stood a moment and then looked up.

"Hi, green fairy. Is there room for a troll?"

"Nope, no room for trolls or Bavarian princes who leap mailboxes. However, I'm partial to intelligent frogs. Were you ever a frog?"

"Sorry, but I'm coming up anyway." He pulled himself onto the branch in one gesture. She had seem swimmers get out of the pool with the same grace.

They sat in the high, green world as a few tourists passed, but none looked up. They were invisible, the world an underground movie stuck on beautiful. Time with Kaleb was children's time—it stretched on forever, and neither of them spoke to spoil it. When Kaleb leaned out and caught a branch to swing down, he called her with his eyes, but she leaned her cheek against the rough bark of the tree, and thought about plants responding to love; if so then the tree should burst into hundreds of blossoms in the spring. She swung down and they walked down Royal to Lane Clayley's house.

Work

LILAH STOOD CLOSE TO THE ELECTRICAL HEATER trying not to burn her bare thigh as she struggled into her pants. The heater was connected to a long extension cord that connected to a longer outside utility cord, which ran from their house across the patio to another house that had electricity. Kaleb still slept under the feather bed. Only a supreme act of will had made her throw back the striped ticking and get up, and now she hated him with a burning passion that outdid the puny filament in the electric heater. Harnessed, her anger could run power stations and light cities. A tangle of dirty shorts, socks, and shirts piled in one corner contributed to the damp, goatish smell of the room.

Their hours never seemed to mesh. He painted until three in the morning; she had to be at work for nine. Late as usual: Bathing, washing—any hygienic activity was an infinite chore in the old house. It was January and a cold drizzle fell constantly. She had a bucket of ice water to wash herself in, and the room, even with a tall, glowing electric heater, was cold. Kaleb would go to the Square only if the weather was good. The weather had not been good for six weeks. Some of his paintings had been farmed out to local galleries, but his work had become more stylized and few people were brave enough to hang it on their walls. The tourists bought bayou scenes or street scenes—not garish women bald and plucked as strangled chickens. The big galleries hadn't picked him up. He hadn't made any real money for six months.

"Lilah?"

"No. The abominable snowman."

"Come back to bed. Let's make love. It's too cold to go to work."

He stretched in the bed and yawned, then sat up. Under the feather bed he was wrapped like a mummy in a pink double-down comforter her mother had sent. He leaned forward, and his red beard stuck out of a beach towel he'd wrapped around his head to conserve body heat. As he talked a stream of vapor stretched before his mouth like the conversational bubble in a comic strip. He didn't look real.

"Come on, Lilah. You're being goddamn silly to go to work on a day like this. You've probably got goose pimples on your goose pimples. Come on back to bed."

"I can't. Somebody has to make some money. Anybody can see it won't be you." She hated saying it, but she hated Kaleb more. She hated him for being out of work, complacent, and physically unattractive. She hated him for wanting sex when sex was the last thing on her mind. "I don't know whatever possessed me to move in with you. You lie in bed and wait for a patron to come along and buy your paintings."

He threw off the comforter and stood up stark naked; unwinding the towel from his head, he threw it at her. "What the hell gives you the right to stand around lecturing me. You don't have to work. How many times do I have to say it. There's no rent here. We'll eat. You're a tight-ass puritan, why the hell do you think you have to go work every fucking morning. I'll sell a painting, and we'll eat until I sell another painting." He skipped back and forth—leaning toward her to jab a finger in her face. The cold didn't faze him.

"Fuck off, Kaleb. I said I'll be there and I will. She picked up her bag, fluffed her hair out over her red coat, and sailed out onto the wet balcony. She could hear a shoe hit the door behind her, but she felt wonderful. Now that she'd gotten him up and mad, the mad had gone out of her, and she felt great as she ran down the stairs.

There was a restaurant next door. Garbage cans full of smelly oyster shells covered with damp burlap sacks blocked the front gate. She pushed them aside. Both hands came up with dark, oily looking catsup; pushing on out with her elbow, she wiped the catsup off onto the restaurant's cardboard BOILED CRAYFISH sign.

This grey morning the street was slick and full of fat, closed automobiles. At her feet the sidewalk was mottled with black rounds of old gum, but she could smell chicory coffee from the French Market. The shot of adrenalin from her argument with Kaleb had set her up for the day. She grabbed a go-cup of coffee from the Golden Star and stepped onto the crowded bus. "You can't get on here with any drinks," the bus driver said.

"Yes, Sir," she said, paying her fare. "I'll throw it away next stop." He didn't say anything but slammed the door and pulled out. She had almost finished it by the next stop, but he acted like he didn't see her so she didn't throw the cup away. By the time she got to Canal Street, she had finished the coffee and tossed the cup in a trash can as she stepped out.

She liked her job; it was a pretty good job, but when she saw Mrs. Mackinaw weaving toward her from the elevator all she could think was: "God, why me? Why today? What did I do to deserve Mrs. Mackinaw today?"

Mackinaw was seventy-five. Lilah knew that from her passport. She could have been a hundred or sixty. A black leather shoulder bag hung over the shoulder of her jaunty St. Laurent jumpsuit. By her gait Lilah knew she'd had several bloody Marys for breakfast.

"Lilah! I am lucky. I thought that fat old Scherer person would be here. What I want to know is exactly where am I going?"

"You mean you didn't get your itinerary, Mrs. Mackinaw?"

"That list?"

"Your itinerary?—with the date you'll be in each place—who will meet you—what you'll do."

"Oh, I didn't read that. I hate lists. That's why I hire you people. Where do I land?"

"Well, let's see. I have a copy of your itinerary here. I'll check it out for you."

Lilah kept hoping she'd just go away—go have another drink. She wouldn't. Lilah usually felt old and inadequate when she came up against Mackinaw's zest for life. Today she felt like keeping up with her.

The bright, dried-apple face watched Lilah struggle through the file. Lilah wondered why Mackinaw had never had her face lifted—her figure was as trim as a girl's. "Here it is," she said, and pulled out the folder. It was a three-month trip, and the folder was made like a thick, college syllabus with a blue cover.

"That's fine. Now let's just find some comfortable chairs and go over it. I haven't anything to do until lunch."

"You land in Lisbon"

"Where's that—Italy?

"No, Lisbon is in Portugal."

"Oh, yes. That delightful Mr. Salazar is in charge there. I met him once at a Hector party. Such a charming man, so accommodating. I probably should look him up."

"I think he's dead, Mrs. Mackinaw."

"So many people dying these days. Must be something going around. What do I do after I land?"

"You'll be met at the airport and our representative who will see you through customs and take you to your hotel. Where you'll rest awhile, and then he'll take you on a tour of

Lisbon."

"Is he Latin? I'm really very fond of Latins."

"He's from Portugal. I think that's pretty Latin."

"What's his name?"

"I'll have to look that up." Lilah began riffling through the pages of the itinerary. She began to feel disoriented, as if she'd had the bloody Marys for breakfast. "Here it is—his name is Luis Fuentes."

"Now that *is* a lovely name. It means fountains. He must be a Spaniard. I really do like Spaniards. They're all so noble.—very noble people." She tilted her head to one side. With her blue hat cocked on her neat hair, she looked like a blue jay perched on the chair. How old is he?"

"I'll have to look that up." Lilah started back through the itinerary, which looked like the telephone directory of a medium-sized town. "He's forty-two."

"Oh, no. I can't have anyone that old. I don't mean forty-two is old. It's just so—mature. People that age are quite cautious. Conscious of doing and being the right thing. They really can't have any fun, and I won't be able to have any fun with him. You'll have to have him replaced. I think I'd like someone about twenty-one or twenty-two. Male and Latin."

"I'll make a note of that," Lilah said.

"Where do I go after Lisbon?"

"You take a private car to a little town called Evora where there is a very interesting church hung with the hair of women who have promised 'their crowning glory for favors granted,'" said Lilah, reading from the itinerary.

"What bull. I hate churches. Positively loathe churches—so many of them. All that gold on the altars—poor women scrubbing the floor, back and forth—endless—they scrub to one side and scrub back to the other."

"Well, I guess you could pass up the church. Just have lunch in Evora and go on to the border."

"What border?"

"The Spanish border. Portugal borders on Spain."

"I can't remember geography. I used to cut that class all

the time. First time I went to Spain I was twenty-one. I had an affair with a poor boy. He kept following me on the street. I just picked him up and took him back to the hotel. I was a virgin and he was a virgin. I didn't want to be a virgin anymore, and he was very passionate so it was a successful affair. All we did was make love every time we met. He was poor, but noble and handsome. Everyone else liked the bullfighters, but bullfighters are always getting virgins. I'm sure Julio never forgot me. It's very important to be unique to someone."

Lilah couldn't help wondering maliciously if Mackinaw thought she was going to repeat the Spanish affair. Aloud she said, "That's interesting."

Mackinaw cocked her head and laughed. Lilah had the terrible feeling Mackinaw had heard that thought. "No, I don't intend to have anymore affairs—at least not with a twenty-one-year-old guide; I don't like to be regarded as a ruin, but I do like to hear the thoughts of the young. It keeps me au courant."

Lilah blushed. "You know Mrs. Mackinaw, I don't feel well today."

"Oh, yes. I know—I know. *Malade d'amour*. You really need another lover, my dear. The painful ones are for extreme youth. After that we never enjoy hurting as much. I know a perfectly delightful young attorney. Solid but imaginative. Very good for your late twenties. He might even be husband material."

"That's alright, Mrs. Mackinaw. I'm not in my late twenties yet. I'll do with what I have. Now about your itinerary. Maybe you'd like to look over it."

"Oh, no. I'll just be surprised when I get there. There aren't too many surprises left—except the ultimate surprise. She laughed and her black eyes glittered like the ebony beads in her antique stick pin. She hopped up and slung her bag over her shoulder. "Don't forget now, Miss Lilah Hahn Rule—attorneys." She turned smartly and walked out. Her little behind bouncing as jauntily as a basketball in the hands of Meadowlark Lemon.

The day was shot. Lilah felt shaky and a little stupid. She made a fresh pot of coffee, and sat in a chair behind the file cabinets drinking it and thinking about Kaleb. They were only good in bed. They were safe there—warm and close. The gaps appeared when they got up. She wondered how she could get close to him. At times he was her best friend. She could tell him anything, but when they fought he used it all. After every quarrel she swore she'd never tell him anything again. She'd never loved anyone as much as Kaleb, and she'd never hated anyone as much as Kaleb. Full of ambivalent feelings, she knew Mackinaw was right. Their affair was past feeling good when it hurt, but she hadn't reached the sensible stage yet. Kaleb was her first real lover. Those white lightning fumblings in the back seats of cars didn't count. Oh, the enormity of that—her first real lover.

Someone had come in and walked to the counter. She tried to pull herself together before she talked to another client. When she walked out front she saw it was Kaleb—completely wasted. It was still raining out and he was soaked—a light green slicker black with rain, curly hair plastered to his white forehead like old leaves. So wild-eyed anyone who saw him would think him unbalanced. He frightened her. She had never seen Kaleb as others might see him. It was a revelation, as if she'd fallen in love with an aborigine in his own culture and then tried to bring him back to hers. All her small-town prejudices were still intact.

"Lilah, Lilah—look. I couldn't let you go off like that. I mean—I love you—I've been miserable all morning, but then we got lucky—" She realized he was waving money around in his right hand. "Steel Trap sold a painting for me."

"Steel Trap! I thought you said you wouldn't sell through him anymore because he always cuts you short."

"Yeah, well. He can sell things. He gives the tourists a spiel. Tells them the artist is starving, which is usually true enough, or the artist is a warlock. Like I'm a warlock. Do you think I look like a warlock?"

"Hmm. Look, I'm glad you sold a painting. But I don't

know how Scherer would take it if he came in here. I'm not supposed to be entertaining friends here. I'm supposed to be selling trips."

"Oh, ho. Look out of place do I?" The wet, wild-eyed smile was satanic. "Maybe I should take my warlock notices seriously. If good old Lilah Hahn Rule from Rule, Texas, doesn't approve of me, I probably have definite possibilities as a warlock, because I can't think of a thing that would really shake up old Lilah except Beelzebub."

Bob Scherer walked out of his office. Lilah was surprised to see him. He must have come into his office while she was drinking coffee. She could see him sizing up Kaleb the way he sized up most clients, and he walked over with a purposeful air. He thought she needed help with some bum off the street.

"Miss Rule, do you need any help in planning this gentleman's trip?"

"No, Mr. Scherer. This is Kaleb Borland, a friend of mine." Kaleb wiggled his ears.

"Oh." He raised one eyebrow slightly, but shook Kaleb's hand.

"Are you planning a trip, Mr. Borland?"

Kaleb straightened up and smiled. He had tremendous charm when he wanted to use it. "Well, yes, I am planning a trip to Greece to paint, but I'm afraid I won't be able to afford the sort of trip your agency offers. I'm an artist. Not quite starving, but thin. I thought I might be able to persuade your travel consultant to have lunch with me. That is, if she'll be seen with me. I'm soaked through." He sounded Ivy League. He'd thrown off his hang-dog appearance like a raincoat.

"If you can talk her into it, she's free to go. I'm not Simon Legree. Just selling trips. Besides, you might sell her a painting for the office. Hey, you know we really could use some paintings—something besides travel posters. Could you do something modern that might make an old lady want to go to Tahiti? Paintings would add a little tone to the office. Sell a little culture with a trip. Give me your number and we'll talk about it. I'd like to look at some of your work."

"I'll give you the name of my gallery. You can get in touch with me through them." He wrote out Steel Trap's number. "His gallery" — Lilah made a face at him behind Scherer's back.

"Fine. Fine. Look now — I'm keeping your from lunch. Scherer clapped Kaleb on the back as if they were old fraternity brothers, and shook his hand.

Lilah said, "I'll get my coat." They rode down in silence, Kaleb smiling like a smug Mephistopheles.

Felix's Oyster Bar wasn't far from the office. When they walked in, several people turned to look at them. There was something about Kaleb that made people look at him, and they had looked at Lilah all her life. She was used to it, but today the stares made her think of the relative anonymity of Battistella's. Good looks were such an affliction — they never allowed for anonymity. She knew they didn't look like they belonged together. Lilah tossed her hair, "What the hell," she said.

They had martinis before lunch and oysters for lunch — "To celebrate the sale," he said.

It wasn't long before they were leaning toward each other.

"You know, I don't think you should go back to work," he said as he carefully straightened the silver, lining it up on the table.

"Why is that, Mr. Borland? Why shouldn't I go back to work?"

"Because you're going to be so fantastically sexy, so fine from these good, good oysters and deeeelicious martinis that you will tempt, yea, entice and corrupt that clean-cut boss of yours, and if you turn those bigggg eyes on him the way you turn them on me, you'll blow his mind — I mean you really will." He leaned confidentially across the table.

"I think you're crazy, really crazy and I'm crazy because I'm crazy about you — really crazy, isn't it?" She felt a wonderful glow.

"I think you're really marinated and I'm marinated, too. Would you marrini me? We could raise an olive for you, an onion for me." It was nonsense, but his eyes were holding hers, and when she looked down she saw his fingers stroking the stem of the martini glass and she could feel it. His long fingers were tapered with blunt thumbs, the knuckles sprinkled with reddish hairs. Each fingernail had a rim of dark paint. She held tight to her own glass because she had such an overwhelming desire to touch him. He watched her. And when he brushed the tips of her fingers with his, she shuddered. He stood out in painful clarity, but the rest of the room was drunk and distorted.

He leaned forward and slipped his hand behind her hair, and she leaned toward him and kissed him gently, sweetly. The waitress came up at the small sign he made. He paid and they left together.

Carnival

They'd been drinking all night, gone home to sleep a few hours and now, Kaleb and Lilah were out on Mardi Gras morning headed toward Canal Street. They'd dressed out of the *armoire*: She wore a tail coat over a tee shirt, with baggy checked pants, and tucked her hair up under a top hat. Kaleb sported a brown bowler and suspenders holding up similar baggy pants. He'd painted their chins with heavy, five o'clock shadows of eyebrow pencil.

A hard wave of people on Bourbon Street moved toward Canal; the force of forward movement pushed Lilah into the gutter where she waded through a sluice of discarded beer cans. A tower of those cans had been erected by a door, stacked around a blond young man who'd passed out in the doorway. Kaleb pulled her back toward the center of the street as the crowd veered out to pass the cans and the kid in the doorway. She saw it all through a haze. Kaleb had a wineskin they were passing back and forth, sharing it with a gorilla who had fallen in beside them. The gorilla had only a small opening for his mouth, too small to pour a drink in so he held onto the wineskin, draining burgundy they'd bought into his hairy face. It was cheap burgundy, but they didn't have much cash. Kaleb gently disengaged it, saying, "Hey, monkey, take it easy."

Lilah was drunk. It was wonderful to stagger down the street arm in arm with a gorilla and Kaleb. Two pink rabbits pushed a blue baby rabbit in a stroller through the crowded street. Music poured out from apartments and glass beads rained down onto the wet sidewalk. "Hey," yelled one of the maskers on a balcony. Lilah looked up, as the daddy rabbit managed to snag a handful still wrapped with a brown paper band. Lilah didn't bother. To her it was silly for people to go so crazy for a few glass necklaces. A faint drizzle had begun to come down. A constant clatter rattled empty cans on the wet sidewalk as people threw down their empties and others kicked them forward. In front the street was blocked solid at the corner of Bourbon and its cross street, St. Peter. There was a syncopated roar coming from the crowd—chanting. Lilah couldn't tell what they were saying.

"Are you game for this?" Kaleb asked.

"For the crowd? What's it about?"

"If you can stand it, it's worth a look."

"What are they saying?"

"Listen."

"Show your —."

Now they were caught up in the crowd and Lilah realized they were mostly young men with beers in hand. Gathered like men in a football huddle, they were repeating in unison, "Show your tits—show your tits."

As if the crowd had one face, all looked up toward a corner balcony. On the balcony a girl with brown hair wearing black shorts and a pink sweater leaned out from the balcony smiling. She had a drink in her hand. Toasting the crowd she straightened up, then put down her drink and crossed her arms under her breasts pretending to raise the pink sweater.

The crowd roared its approval but she shook her head, still smiling and picked up her drink again and walked back into the open window on the balcony. As one breath, the crowd wailed, "Oh, no." Then they started again. "Show us your tits—show us your tits." She came back out again with a few other people, and waggled her finger at the crowd. The refrain quickened in beat like a football cheer wanting a touchdown:

"Showusyourtits-showusyourtits-showusyourtits."

The girl turned her back and walked toward the inside. Then she suddenly lifted both arms and pulled the sweater off revealing a naked back. There was an intake of breath from the crowd as if someone pulled a plug. The girl turned around smiling uncertainly and showed her breasts—fleshy and well formed, there was an undefined tenderness to the pink nipples which had suckled nothing and seemed too young for sex. The men on the street were whooping and throwing beer on each other. Engrossed in the tableau on the balcony, Lilah hadn't spoken to Kaleb, and now with a panicky feeling she realized he was out of sight. The crowd shifted and jostled and started a new chant. Now they were saying, "Show *us* your ass—show *us* your ass." Lilah's panic quickened in time to the words, but the men were not interested in her. In the crowd she was just another face fixated on a balcony. Lilah caught sight of Kaleb who had moved to the sidewalk. He pointed to the other balcony. She relaxed and looked up. A young woman stood there with one foot up on a kitchen chair. She wore a short, strapless bodysuit of red satin with jet beading. The suit was cut so that both cheeks of her buttocks were revealed as she leaned toward her foot tying an imaginary shoelace on her high-heeled boot pulled tight and laced up the leg. She smiled over her shoulder at the crowd, now divided—one half singing, "Show us your ass—Show us your ass"; the other chanting, "Show us your tits." The confluence of the two suddenly split and Lilah was spit out like a log and washed up on the sidewalk. After a few minutes of gathering herself and pawing through the crowd she managed to find Kaleb. "How did you like that?" he asked. "Your kind of thing?"

She didn't answer, just started walking ahead of him toward Canal Street, but within two blocks she had come upon another crowd massed around a small wooden stage completely blocking Bourbon Street. The jam here was brilliant with costumed gay men. Kaleb caught up with her, and they watched for awhile as contestants in towering feathered drag were called to the stage in a beauty pageant. Most of the costumes were fantastic mythological creatures.

"Who makes these costumes?" Lilah asked a moustached man with fine skin.

"The Queens make them out of thousands of feathers. See her?" He pointed to a tall blond, whose dress was made of iridescent shades of midnight blue, teal, and turquoise.

"She's from Houston. Her outfit cost $10,000 dollars. She and her lover have been sewing it all year. If you really want to see the costumes, go down the side street. It's not so crowded. That's where the queens line up to go on stage." Lilah thanked him, and they pushed through the crowd to Orleans."

On Orleans the crowd thinned out, but a brilliant train of rainbow feathers and lamé stretched down the street as the contestants lined up. Two men dressed as sun god and goddess posed for a photographer. Their thirtyish faces and bodies were painted with gold stage makeup, and they looked like sweaty ballerinas as the sun and exertion melted their makeup. The photographer said, "Let's see it." And then art took precedence as the exquisite costumes of gold and cinnabar were suddenly activated by graceful arm sweeps as they posed and fanned their feathers into a huge corona like a massive setting sun behind their heads. The photographer said, "Hold it—that's it. I got it." And the two wheeled around again, gracefully swirling their trains around their feet as tourists, too, snapped photographs.

Lilah and Kaleb wandered on down the side street to Royal and back toward Canal, in and out of bars talking long, serious drunken conversations that seemed to exist on a higher plane. Kaleb had been popping pills. Lilah couldn't quite catch up with him by drinking wine. Near Canal Street Lilah smelled chili, and suddenly felt ravenous. "I want a Lucky Dog," she said. "I'm starving. Doesn't it smell good?" They stopped and wolfed down two Lucky Dogs slathered in mustard and covered in chili. Lilah had the vendor pile on soft onions which smelled faintly of perspiration but tasted delicious on the hotdog.

They moved inside. "Let's go see Rex. The crowd is getting thicker. The parade must be coming." She was trying to get Kaleb out of a hole-in-the-wall bar where he was talking to a huge man dressed as a black praying mantis.

"Nah, baby, nah. You see a parade is the truth. People on the inside aren't real. Masks are real. Today we're real. Music all over and everybody high. Anybody'll talk to you. It's important to talk to as many of your nightmares as you can. When you see one of your bad dreams go by, you've got to stop 'em and talk — good dreams, too. Otherwise they pass and they're gone, and you don't even get to work 'em out. I could walk and talk all day and all night. Just float up right out of these people holding onto my baby's hand." His eyes were red and his words spilled out.

Lilah tried to grab onto this vision by taking pills but they made her heart beat too fast and she felt a quick nausea. She wanted to unstick her brain, get out of whatever boundaries Rule had sealed around her. They staggered back out onto the street, still headed toward Canal. She gagged and spit up one of the bitter pills, and there was nothing to wipe her mouth with but the end of her tail coat. Kaleb found the next doorway, and they wandered in. People were pressed four deep at the bar. He had to buy two beers so she could use the restroom. Moving slowly the line of women stood well out into the room waiting to get behind the plywood partition into the narrow, smudged pink door. Spittle had dried on Lilah's face, and she kept rubbing the corners of her mouth, which smeared the eyebrow pencil on her chin.

It was finally her turn and she squeezed in the tiny room. An overflowing toilet crammed full of paper towels and musty brown soup stood within six inches of the lavatory. A bare bulb illuminated a pink-bordered mirror. As she leaned down to the lavatory to wash her face, rivulets of black water ran down her shirt, and she got a good view of the floor which was papered with transparent trails of wet toilet paper. When she saw the floor and the smell rose to meet her, she threw up into the lavatory. A woman beating on the door kept saying, "Get out of there. You had your turn." Lilah wiped her face again and rushed out. She came face to face with the woman, a furious drag queen in mountains of pink tulle. Lilah said, "All in pink — a good match for the toilet," and ran. She could hear him holler when he got in the bathroom. "My god, the bitch threw up in the sink."

Now Kaleb was deep in excited conversation with a tall blonde leaning against the bar. Lilah looked for a place to sit. The room had emptied out as most of the crowd went to the parade. There were colored lights going around and around. A whole room of colored lights going around, but when she looked up it was only a double spot of blue and yellow above the piano. She sank down the floor behind the upright. It was noisy there, but she was out of it all for awhile. The piano player had a large pustule on his cheek, something on the order of a carbuncle. It stood out like a dueling scar and gave him a dangerous air. His long, greased hair had been pulled back into a pigtail at the back of his neck. Hard, fast piano without pedal, poured out. He beat out the music, banging the floor with his right foot. There were three dancers whirling in the light which reflected blue and green on the wet tile. Two tall young men dressed as flappers danced; one had a gigantic lantern jaw and wore an orange cloche that shaded most of his face but for his purple lipstick and huge jaw; the other wore a pink slouch hat and a yellow long-waisted dress. They both had on very high heels and tottered around trying to do the Charleston, which was not what the piano player was playing.

The third man, a Siamese temple dancer, wore a magenta velvet body suit with heavy metallic trim, fitting his short, heavily muscled body like a second skin. Tight black curls peppered his short legs which were able to leap without effort onto tables. A grotesque dead-white paint masked his face, and he wore a peaked gold hat. His penciled eyebrows and thick lipstick grimaced and smiled as he jumped up and down in acrobatic leaps with the music, jumping to the top of the piano and turning flips to the floor. The leaps became wilder, more daring, as he jumped from chair to a table to the back of the piano, which rocked as if it would soon be off the floor, and then back-flipped off, coming down next to Lilah where he loomed up in her face like a wave in a funhouse mirror—a monkey dressed like a man. She couldn't see Kaleb at the bar anymore—the deafening music, the wine—the scary monkey-man. In her corner nothing was real, and she waited for some terrible climax to the dance, but suddenly the music stopped and the men wandered away, out the door. She sat in the sudden silence afraid to move.

After a while the piano player came back and began to play "La Vie En Rose" very softly—wrapping her in a great blanket of peace. Someone turned the spotlight onto the partition hiding the ladies room. A hand appeared on the side of the partition wearing a full-length glove. It waved in time to the music—Lilah the only person watching. The hand called her—a seductive hand, her mind focused and it held her. As the music came to a crescendo, the hand slid around and suddenly there was a small man standing in the spotlight wearing an orange wig made like a dust mop. He was very old, and his face cascaded into a thousand small seams as if rivers had eroded his face. He began to sing "Je t'attendrai" in French. His voice almost a boy soprano; now there was no other sound in the room as attention was drawn to the man standing by the partition to the ladies room. Lilah couldn't stop the tears pouring down her face—*Je t'attendrai, Je t'attendrai*—where was Kaleb? She wanted him.

And then his body leaned against hers and thrust a beer into her hand. Kaleb didn't say anything until the last notes of the piano tinkled off into the corners of the room. The little man blew kisses to the crowd, bowed and disappeared.

"That's Aggie," Kaleb said. "He was once a famous female impersonator—he and his twin brother performed for the crowned heads of Europe until the brother was killed in a diving accident and Aggie lost it and ended up in Le Rendez-vous with a mop on his head. Let's get out of here. Maybe we can still catch Rex."

Canal Street was packed solid. They pushed their way in toward the curb. Lilah tried not too push too hard, and then the people let them in. The bands marched, floats were strung out along Canal while others still turned onto Canal Street from St. Charles Avenue. Maskers tossed throws, as they walked into it, the sky seemed to be raining small toys. A wizard in a tall hat next to them kept leaping up like a basketball player, snatching beads out of the air. From the floats the blank-faces threw beads, on a float with a moving dragon one short fat man did a little dance as he hurled packets of beads to people he pointed to in the crowd. He would dance around threatening to toss until the crowd went crazy. The parade stopped so Rex could toast the Queen at the Boston Club.

The float with the fat man stood in front of them while Rex made his speech and toasted the Queen. The short masker picked Lilah out of the crowd and began pointing to his heart, and then to Lilah while doing his bandy-leggy dance. He was thick in the middle and the gold lamé costume clung to his belly, but he was light on his feet and his animated body shook to the music of the band. The mask was expressionless except for full painted lips. Lilah put both arms up as he signaled her again. His toss was true and the blue beads lobbed through the air directly for her. As they came toward her the basketball player jumped up, and she jumped too. But she had a good hold on them, and she gave him a slight push with her other hand. He laughed and said, "Happy Mardi Gras," and let go. She yelled, "I got them—I got them," to Kaleb.

"You sure did. What are you going to do with them?" He was not impressed. "I should have caught them for you," he said. The parade started up again. As the crowd prepared for the next float, Lilah ripped off the paper and gave some beads to the basketball player who took them eagerly although his neck was solid with glass and plastic necklaces of different colors. She hung the sparkling mass of blue around her own neck and felt a tremendous satisfaction that she'd caught so many.

"There goes Ivan Kotterman," Kaleb said. "He's got a temple on his head." She looked where he was pointing and saw a man limp by in a gold leotard, his head bent from the weight of a full Mayan temple made of *papier maché*. The temple bobbed by on an angle. His friend, wearing a reindeer suit with huge antlers, bobbed along after him. They watched the temple and antlers appear and disappear again and again in the crowd.

"Ivan has the Disgusting Group, the longest running discussion group in the Quarter, twenty years—or something like that," Kaleb said.

"What do they discuss?" she shouted as a band went by.

"Anything—is there sex after death?" he said over the music.

"What was the conclusion?"

"Oh, the conclusion is always the same—everybody got drunk and didn't care."

"That's me—I'm drunk and I don't care."

"That's not you—that's carnival. It's a blow-out. You've got to let go—tomorrow's Ash Wednesday. 'Ashes to ashes—dust to dust.'"

Lilah leaned against Kaleb in the cab. It was close and she felt small leaning against Kaleb's shoulder.

When she closed her eyes she could see him—he was so big he blocked the sun and his mouth was teeth, and laughter, and a big moustache. He smelled so good—suede, whiskey, and sometimes a wild smell like dove feathers or dogs. He'd come back from hunting and the house crackled with the excitement he generated. They fluttered back and forth getting things for him. He ate salad and drank the juice. He ate a large purple grape and spat the seeds into his hand, then leaned back in the kitchen chair laughing and talking while her mother moved silently around the kitchen getting dinner ready. He'd brought wonderful things with him: a coconut, two pineapples and sweet orange-bread in a can.

After dinner her heart jumped when he grabbed her up from the table and took her with him in the pickup. He drove out of town—she didn't know where they were going—they stopped at little grocery stores, old houses, barrooms, whatever caught his eye—he stopped to talk to anyone. And in the dark, cool barrooms with long, gleaming bars—the men were always nice to her. She wasn't supposed to be there. It was a secret from her mother—the drinking and the long, dark cool rooms where men laughed and talked.

And then they were hiking—his legs so long she couldn't keep up, but she tried—her braids flopping on her back with each step. Long steps—long steps, she thought as she stretched her legs to match his stride.

"You know that old man we talked to—well, that old man knows a lot. He told us about polk greens and where to find them. Just imagine something to eat, free for the taking. Not everyone knows that."

She nodded her head and concentrated on walking. The greens were sticky, and she was tired of carrying them, but she couldn't give up. He was so disappointed when she gave up.

But the sticky greens were not greens, the sticky greens were the clothes wadded up on her lap—her tail coat and hat, and he was not as big as she remembered, and now she was in a cab Kaleb had managed to find on carnival day because she was sick from too much burgundy, and then not in a cab—going up the stairs with Kaleb, and it was over—carnival was over.

Ben's Gone

ON ST. PHILIP STREET THE PATIO GATE STOOD OPEN.

"Hello — Clayley — Lane? Lilah called. No answer, but Dinah Washington sang, "Salty Papa Blues" at full volume on the stereo. Lilah liked to drop in on Sunday. A cup of coffee with Lane could answer a lot of questions. Today she'd brought Kaleb with her — that changed things. "She's home. Do you think we should go in?" she asked.

"Sure. Lane doesn't stand on ceremony. Just go on back to the kitchen. I don't think she can hear us for Dinah."

Along the walkway blue-green ivy ran up the wall, a satyr's head leered out of the ivy, spitting water with a scowl. They stepped onto the patio, a small jungle of orange bromeliads and staghorn fern.

Lane stood in the back doorway ironing. The sun streaming in the side shutters patterned her bare breasts with slats of light. She slapped the ironing board and iron in hard, nervous runs, wrinkling her brow and closing one eye, as she avoided the smoke of her cigarette without taking it out of her mouth. A glass of iced coffee balanced on the end of the ironing board shook with each slap of the iron. She glanced up and saw Kaleb and Lilah standing there slightly embarrassed; her quick smile was a child's smile of utter delight.

"Hello people. I was just wishing for company . Come on in. I'll fix you an iced coffee in minute." She disappeared into the bathroom and came back wearing a white cotton blouse. Lilah wished her own mother had this ease. Lane's smile was childlike, but her face was not much like a kid's, more old-young like the midgets of The Wizard of Oz. Sloshing coffee and ice into tall glasses she poured in cream, and presented them each with a glass. "What have you two been doing? You're the talk of the Quarter. I don't know what's so unusual about two people moving in together, but the grapevines talked of nothing else."

"I'm in love with this lady, Lane, and it's your fault."

"Is that so? Good. I consider you one of my more successful meddlings. I'm glad for you. You got lucky—I'm not so sure your lady friend is lucky. You're a handsome devil and probably good in the sack, but—you've got such a far-out head." She shook her own head and grinned again. "How do you like living with Don Juan?" she asked Lilah.

"I don't know Don Juan—I'm living with Roderick Usher. Have you seen our house? No hot water or closets—just hot and cold running ghouls."

"Yes, I know," she said quickly. "Ben lived there for awhile." She turned to Kaleb. "Bud Thompson told me you put some of your paintings in Steel Trap's gallery. Doing any good?"

"Great. People come to Steel Trap's looking for something different. They're not looking for pot boilers. Believe me, at Steel Trap's my paintings look conservative."

"Hell Kaleb. There's nothing conservative about a woman with a square tit," she coughed three times, "unless she's a John Bircher. What you mean is—they look a little less odd than they do hanging on the fence with a bunch of grapes and a swamp scene. Or how about that one with the tippy-toe mouse prints all over it and the dead cat in the corner. You're not exactly Norman Rockwell, you know."

"You can get off my case, Lane."

"Where's Ben?" Lilah asked. She'd reared back in a kitchen chair listening and sipping her coffee, but she felt it was time to change the subject.

"He didn't come home last night," Lane answered. "Probably found himself a younger piece. Saturday night is a night for a little extracurricular screwing around. God, I hate Sundays. What a stupid day." She got up and poured herself another glass of iced coffee, coughed three tight little coughs, and suddenly looked older.

Lilah hadn't realized how much Lane cared for Ben. Their relationship was long-standing, so stable she couldn't imagine Ben with anyone other than Lane. "He's probably just out on a drunk," Kaleb put in quickly. "You know everybody needs a good drunk now and then. You've been telling him where to get off so he thought he'd have a few quick ones. You know how that goes — it gets stretched out." His voice had a jocular tone, and there was something in it Lilah didn't like. "He's probably under the bar somewhere on Decatur Street."

"You know better than that, Kaleb. That's not a pretty picture, but neither is strung out — Ben's strung out. He kicked and was clean for a long time, but he's strung out. I know it. We ought to stop this — Lilah doesn't know what we're talking about, Kaleb. Let's skip it." The smoke coming into her mouth was inhaled in short gasps, and some of it returned through her nose. Finished with the smoke, she began to drink coffee in the same staccato movements, but suddenly put down her cup and removed a small piece of tobacco from her mouth. Her movements were so nervous she looked like she was getting ready to bolt.

"I can find him, Lane."

"I said, let's skip it."

"Let's not skip it." Ben's in trouble — he needs us. Lilah is not an innocent who has to be spared Ben's problem. If you don't want to tell her I will."

"Tell me what? Ben drinks. We all drink—tell me what?"

Lane didn't answer her, but yelled, "Kaleb, goddamn you. Goddamn your self-righteous hide." Kaleb shrugged his shoulders with an elaborate pretense of disinterest in the whole affair. Lilah got up and put her arms around Lane whose head came slightly above her waist. "You don't have to tell me anything, Lane."

"Ben's an addict. You know, dope. Heroin—smack—whatever you want to call it. It wouldn't be such a terrible habit. I mean, it's not as if he's mean or anything. He just needs it. I'm not quite enough for him," she said miserably. She moved away from Lilah, put her arms around her own little body and rocked back and forth.

"Do you want him back, Lane?" Lilah asked.

Lane looked surprised. "Oh, sure. I always want Ben. It's just part of him. Like taking insulin or something. He's sick without it, but it's illegal—he can't afford it—I can't afford it, but I love him. You leave him alone, Kaleb. He'll come home, when there's no place else to go." She went to the sink and began taking the coffeepot apart. Her hands were shaking and the grounds fell on the floor. "Oh, shit," she said, and when she tore off a paper towel to clean them up, she was crying.

"I think we ought to go, Kaleb. Lane doesn't need our advice." She took his hand, but he was staring out into the patio. Lilah could tell he was angry, but she couldn't put her finger on why. If he wanted to find Ben all he had to do was go look for him.

"I'm sorry, Lilah," Lane said. "I'm not very good company today. You kids come back when my nerves aren't so raw." She smiled and even with her red eyes she looked like she meant the smile.

"Come on Lilah, let's go," Kaleb said.

"We'll come back, Lane. If you need us you know where we are."

Out on the street Lilah asked Kaleb, "Why were you so

rude? You have no right to treat Lane that way. She's worried. Why give her such a hard time?"

"She's a silly bitch. Ben could be dead somewhere, and she's just going to wait until he shows up. He's done this before. She's had him in DePaul's before. He kicks it because he has to, but as soon as he has a few gigs and makes a little money he goes back on the needle. Then he takes off. Lane just makes money and pours it down the drain. Puts him in for a cure and gets him out to do it again. Fucking needle freak hanging out in shooting galleries. I can't see it. Sticking himself with a needle—a needle. He has to push a needle in his arm or his leg just to stop being miserable."

"Why are you so indignant? You take pills to get high. Lots of people get needles stuck in their arms to stop feeling miserable. What's making you so righteous?"

"It's not the same thing. I don't stick a needle in my arm." He stalked ahead.

Lilah felt tired. They seemed to swing back and forth. In the light now he was dazzling, his coloring made him reflect light like an iceberg, but the dark parts floating submerged in the depths—no one knew those parts. Kaleb was like deep ice.

"Let's go to Steel Trap's," he said.

They walked through the gallery. Steel Trap wasn't there and Kaleb nodded to the woman at the counter. "We're going in the back," he said. They went up a steep, crooked stairway in the back courtyard. Lilah followed Kaleb. There was a utility door. Kaleb opened it but stopped at a black velvet curtain hanging in the doorway. There was no opening in the curtain; Kaleb had to lift it from the bottom. It was heavy with lead weights in the hem, a musty mildewed smell came from the velvet. They struggled under it into a room, dark except for a soft pink light at the far end. Lilah noticed a strong smell of rotten fruit, her foot slipped on something on the floor. An insistent humming sound filled the silence—an electrical hum Lilah couldn't place. Sound became a presence in the room, combined with the eerie light and fetid smell, it made her feel uneasy. She wanted to stop following, but didn't.

"Ben," Kaleb called.

There was no answer. Omnipresent, the sound became more insistent as they progressed slowly through the room, which was full of obstacles, mostly couches, odd chairs, and cushions. It was a long room and the floor uneven terrain. Lilah stepped on a cushion and nearly fell as her foot sank into it; the other foot searched tentatively, not knowing where to step in the darkness. What they finally reached was a lace boudoir lamp with a pink bulb in it. They found Ben lying beatified by the soft light on the couch covered with an Indian silk coverlet. The sound came from a seventy-eight phonograph whirring around at the end of a record. Ben's eyes were open and he had a half-smile on his face."

"I didn't realize Ben was so good looking," she said. It was hard to believe shambling old Ben, the poor man's Jimmy Stewart, could look like a young god dreaming of virgins and nectar. There was a spoon, an eyedropper, and a book of burned matches lying on the table.

"He's on the nod. We'll have to leave him here," Kaleb said as he lifted the needle from the record, which left a void — a dark silence.

"What did he take?" she asked.

"Heroin. Lane told you, didn't you listen?" he answered sharply.

"Yes. I mean, I don't know much about it. He doesn't take anything else?" she asked. "I know more about drunks."

"He smokes a little pot when he's clean, which is never very long and he always takes downers. He's been on an involuntary cure anyway — they cut the stuff with milk sugar and barbiturates. When he goes into DePaul's they can cure him in a week for a small bundle. But he always feels better if he's got some kind of junk coursing through his veins. Damn it. Lane is broke — flat broke. She makes good money but she just bailed Ben out — cured. Here he is two weeks later. Damn."

He looked at Ben as if he were an expensive tropical fish that had just died without giving him his money's worth.

"Lane says he's sick. She loves him and she wants to take care of him. I don't think it's any of our business if she doesn't want our help." Ben lifted his head slightly, as if to look around, but his expression never changed. He was still smiling at something in another dimension. "I must say, he looks better than he did the first time I saw him." She smiled back at Ben. Of the two men—at the moment—Ben, in his sweet dreams, was more appealing than Kaleb in his righteous anger.

"Something has been left out of my moral code. It looks like what we're talking about is lack of money. You're mad at Ben over money, over wasting money, not over what he's doing to his life or Lane's."

"What's the matter with you, Lilah? Aren't you disgusted? Lane Clayley is the best friend you have here, and this goddamn asshole is giving her a royal screwing. Don't you care?"

"No. She told you to leave Ben alone. She said he would come home on his own. All you wanted to do was show him to me and get my shocked reaction to a 'dope fiend'—it's probably some kind of a sexy feeling for you. Well, sorry, if it wasn't what you wanted. Maybe she likes the kind of screwing she's getting. You're not exactly what my mother would pick out for me." Lilah started working her way back to the door.

"Here," he shouted, "you'll never find your way out of here without me."

"Oh, yes I will. You're just someone I met on the way." She staggered over the pillows and toward a thin line of daylight where she lifted the curtain and struggled out. She could hear Kaleb cursing behind her.

Lilah knew her first hunch had been right. Everything she thought of his paintings she could now see in him—she felt hair rise on her arms. The paintings that bothered her most were miniatures—tiny paintings in infinite detail, little worlds within worlds—studies of the microcosm—bacteria with terrible faces—electric viruses. She knew those paintings were Kaleb, and she loved Kaleb so the paintings were a part of her. It had been a constant state of electric excitement—stinging, loving, hating, empathy—his body. Was there empathy? He was callous with Ben, judging him with too little understanding. How could he begrudge Ben his escape, his running—they were runners too—more people killed in the panic than in the fire. Just someone yelling fire—and everybody running—piled one on top of the other—dead. The Quarter—a sink—not a kitchen sink, a sink of runaways—all fleeing the fire, smothered in the pile-up. Too many people piled on top, some stronger ones making out—all these poor nuts running around trying out their little peculiarities—

"and man must have his mate." Those songs catch you; you want to believe.

She tried to sort something out of the images. Lane pretending everything was alright—no different than her mother in Rule, then telling Kaleb to leave Ben alone. Kaleb with his righteous anger, mean humor, moods flickering back and forth. Petulant as often as anything.

She walked down Toulouse to Nan's bar. The sweet beer smell delivered on a breeze caught her nose and she followed it in. Nan was behind the bar. "Miss Lilah, I thought maybe you'd gone back to Rule, Tex-ass, but you just got yourself a boyfriend, didn't you? Man troubles. I can smell them a mile off." A lemonade appeared in front of Lilah.

"No lectures, please. I'm tired." Lilah pushed her stool back into the corner. She didn't want company or conversation. There was always something comforting in Nan working in the background. She soothed without doing anything. A competent presence, someone who could sweep up the pieces if she suddenly shattered. Part of a song Anita Ellis sang kept turning over in her mind—"I'll call up my used-to-be. He'll straighten out my affairs." The only trouble—no use-to-be. She went over her affairs—adolescent—none of them could even ride a horse much less a white charger. What needed straightening out was Kaleb—that affair. She couldn't figure him out.

The bar was beginning to fill up with the afternoon regulars. They pushed in, talking mixed with hyperkinetic laughter. Smiling at everyone—always a part—visions of young girls in summer dresses waving from boat docks—the gay boys swept in for their five o'clock-tails—gay beers. Nan set them up—beer on tap. They checked themselves in the long mirror behind the bar. A tall figure with a slight stoop said, "I've taken up needlepoint—given up tranquilizers." "Does it help?" "I don't know, but it's a hell of a conversation piece." He had a sudden braying laugh.

The other man was small and quick with dancing gestures. "Mrs. Duckworth and I did needlepoint at the bar on the last cruise to San Juan. I didn't get a tumble, just snide remarks until we got off the boat. First night in port I had the second mate and the Doctor."

"Was the old lady a pain?"

"No. I like old ladies. I'm going to be an old lady one of these days myself."

"Soon—soon. You're twenty-five."

"Twenty-four."

"Twenty-five. I count, darling. You know last year's trade, tomorrow's competition."

The tall young man took his beer and his slightly stooped frame to the other side of the bar where he said, "I've taken up needlepoint and given up tranquilizers."

The other man spun on his heel and began talking with great animation to a man in glasses who looked like an optician or accountant—someone precise. Nan hastened up and down the bar setting up drinks with a deft hand, saying, "Drink up. It's been a slow night."

Lilah drank her lemonade and thought about attorneys.

There was some sad joy in it. The constant ache had gone. She was left with something she knew and tolerated like a long-distance earache on the edge of sensibility. It could reach a throbbing pinnacle at 3 a.m., but resided back to a dull hurt during her busiest hours. When she moved out of the apartment she left everything they'd bought together. Lane said, "You've been took, Sweetheart. You had the job. Kaleb never had two nickels to rub together. You paid for the new stuff. Why leave it? I hate to see another woman act as dumb as me."

But Lilah didn't want the few sticks of secondhand furniture, didn't want the task of rearranging her past life. She loved the new apartment—loved the aloneness of it. Awakened in the morning by peach-colored light falling across her pillow through the green flaked shutters; the kitchen's shocking white appliances and white-washed plaster with black morning coffee; and the patio's green elephant ears weighted with crystal globules running down the seamed leaves to the red St. Joe bricks. Even the street, a short, one-block street called Madison, was unique and her own. At the Volunteers of America on Toulouse Street she found a tired oriental carpet, and spent hours dying its worn patches with red and blue markers until the color revived and endowed the living room with a rich look. She padded around the apartment barefooted wearing cotton pajamas, glorying in her own body, its sensual freedom from the demands of another, and she drank cup after cup of jasmine tea steeped from the same leaves until the tea became pale golden water. Then released from the pleasure of her own company, she left the house wearing a cloud of her favorite perfume, Magnolia by Hové on Royal Street—a perfume she had given up because Kaleb thought it too "loud." Dressed in a fresh ecru silk blouse and a wool skirt she'd bought from Kreeger's with her own money at a half-price sale, she went off to her job.

It was surprising how easy it was to avoid Kaleb. After two months she stopped expecting to see him and got careless. On Tuesday she went to the Chinese shop to buy jasmine tea and walked right into him, but after he'd pushed past her with a savage expression, she realized she didn't love him anymore—it had gone out. His red beard looked silly and theatrical to her.

One day she ran into Bud Thompson who was talking to the owner of the Voodoo Shop on St. Philip Street. "What are you doing here, my pretty? Looking for love potions?"

"I'm through with love. I'm looking for gris-gris packets for some tourists who came through and fell in love with New Orleans. They thought Voodoo was the most fun of anything after they went to one of those tourist Voodoo rituals on Bayou St. John where a woman danced with a snake she called Damballah, and they gave this guy some *gris-gris*. Now they're convinced Voodoo helped them win five thousand on an Exacta at the Dog Races."

"How about you?"

"I'm the one who should be burning candles. Letitia left me. She moved back in with Kaleb. It was inevitable," he said. "She's quite masochistic, you know. I was entirely too good for her."

Lilah began to go out again. Twice she slept casually with men she met at parties, finding the best way to allow herself that careless pleasure was to drink a little more vodka than she cared for. This made her bold, able to talk to a man who pleased her physically, able to say, "Why don't you come home with me." These nights at first seemed harmless, but then they began to take on an aspect of courtesy, something she did for men she thought were rather nice. In the morning she usually fixed them breakfast but had little time for them when she met them again. They were bewildered by her attitude, and found her more off-handed about sex than it appeared fit or proper to them. The would-be writers or painters were most put off by her new attitude, her self-assurance. They couldn't place her in the hierarchy of women as they understood women; she was a mystery. The men who inhabited the Quarter were still attached by nearly invisible umbilical mores to tract houses in Metairie and Angst Park.

Her reputation, however, was not of a woman who would sleep with anyone. In fact, if a man talked about her sleeping around he was considered a flagrant liar, and her reputation was more as heartbreaker, a woman someone fine would marry, and it was said of her that she was deadly honest—whatever came into her head came out of her mouth, and "Well, if that hurts, I'm sorry." For some reason they loved it, and lined up to be told if they'd made the grade as men, and this was a silly thought to Lilah because she didn't know what made a man anymore than she knew what made a woman. As she told Lane, "God, I'm sick of being the oracle. It's all bull."

The truth was, nobody knew her, with the exception of Lane who knew her a little. But they were peers now; she didn't think Lane had all the answers either. Lilah had taken off tradition like last year's bathing suit. She reveled in being herself. The self took Turkish lessons at the International House, folk-danced in Greek bars on most Saturday nights, slept with whomever she damn well pleased, and began to think in terms of a long commitment to her own eclectic education.

It was a year and a half before she looked up and realized she was twenty-six. Something like a shadow began in the corner of her mind, and like a dark bruise on the side of a nice, fresh peach, began to widen. What had been her fine, chosen life became repetitious and dull. Her night courses were less interesting, the men she met gay or divorced, and her own conversation sarcastic, impatient. She was tired of parties, but went anyway, and one night she went to a gallery opening and felt herself edging closer to a man she hadn't met with panicky feelings in her chest, which translated to desperation and sent him in search of a drink or, another occasion at a party, a man excused himself from her quickly to look up an old friend in another part of the room. The one area of life which broadened, and in which she felt most secure, was her job. She now managed the agency, and she was able to take trips. On Easter Sunday, 1967, she decided to go to Turkey.

With her discounts, trade-offs and trip allowance she was able to plan a full month if she could get a stand-in at work. This turned out to be easier than she supposed. Lane Clayley sent in a young woman named Suzanne Joiner, a trainee who had been laid off at Eastern Airlines. Lilah's assistant, Darcy, would slide temporarily into Lilah's job, and Suzanne would take the job Lilah had when she first came to New Orleans. After she said, "You've got the job," Suzanne immediately asked if she could use the phone. Lilah heard her say, "Hello, Miss Clayley, I got the job. I don't know how to thank you. To dinner? At your house? I'd love to come."

Lilah felt old, as if she'd worked in the agency for twenty years, as if nothing ever really changed in the long-term overview of things. Two weeks before her trip her depression received a bludgeoning *coup de grace* in the form of an official letter from the company, which read:

All employee allowances for trips to Western Europe, Turkey, and Greece will be discontinued until further notice. It's in the interest of the company and American tourism that our employees explore our Caribbean neighbors. Substitute trips are available to Jamaica, Haiti, or Puerto Rico.

A month later Lane received a card from Lilah in Haiti. The picture on the card was an ugly one of some official building. On closer inspection it appeared to be a hotel or pension with a red, inked spot at a window with an arrow pointing to a printed, "Me."

In a scrawly handwriting across the top, Give my regards to the count, or something to that effect—something Lane couldn't understand—who was the count? Next an address: Petit Grove, P.O. Box 316, Cocoyer Beach, Haiti. The message read:

A large wine red tile thing with rooms and rooms, sun porch, the harbor and all that's part of it in front. The sun always there, beach too. Very fun making. Say, hello, soon. Yes, Lane, tell me something of the city. Lilah.

Lane missed her. Lilah had become her mainstay—her

best friend, and left a vacancy almost as large as the one left by Ben's passing. Lane's insomnia had become a monstrous thing. It rushed into the bedroom to curl in the corner before she'd even turned back the covers. She tried not to take the downers until ten p.m. so she could sleep until two a.m. If she didn't take the downers she'd think—think about what life would be if someone hadn't thought Ben was an informer, if someone hadn't cut heroin with battery acid, or what if Ben had never taken junk at all, or if she'd never met Ben, just been some sort of housewife with kids. Someone had once asked her, "Is that what old age is—regrets?" Regrets—regrets. She was old. She was older than old. She was old.

Dozens of books were piled on the night table. Books and cats weighed down the blanket on the bed. Never enough books to lead her to sleep. She was afraid she'd run out of something to read, would be left with her own thoughts at two a.m. For hours she turned the pages, sometimes letting the book fall forward as she dozed—the fall instantly jerking her back into the room. At the first sign of sleep, beautiful sleep, she would hopefully put out the light. Immediately, the beast jumped on her chest to palpitate her heart, each beat a racing horse's hoof on a lonely highway in the hinterland, galloping into dangerous night.

Her eyes opened mechanically like the Shirley Temple doll she'd had as a child—it was a hinged, artificial wakening that could only be reversed when she changed positions—sat back up—opened her book, which reset the cycle—the heaviness of the eyelids, the falling of the book—a panicky start. Sometimes now she brought in a bottle of claret and drank herself to sleep. Lilah's card was a penny inside an empty well. She had been deserted by everyone, even by Lilah who mothered her since Lilah had stopped needing mothering herself.

Haiti

ELLIOT DIDN'T KNOW WHY HE WAS IN JACMEL, BUT he was glad he was. The air had a sensuous smell of flowers and something slightly foul like a dog who'd rolled in dead jay bird, like musk used to make perfume, it added something to the fragrance, a dizzy depth, a sense of sexual well being as if a beautiful woman were in the next room waiting for him. He'd been homesick for this place although he'd never been here. He'd felt a longing in his gut for the Caribbean, as if he'd been sent away from home by some awful happening and only now was able to return. The smell of the place made him feel comfortable and secure.

He stretched in the white sheets and thought about how he'd suddenly left New Orleans, packing in the middle of the night, and leaving on the first plane for Haiti. His last semester at Tulane had been more night life than midnight books — too easy. He didn't need to study; some supernatural sense of being on top of things had colored every moment of his this year, but the last month, the last month had been hell. He'd had an affair. A sloppy, messy, stupid affair with a woman old enough to be his mother, if his mother had been a drunk-pillhead who slept with sailors off visiting ships, gay men, lesbians, pimps, and him.

He had met her at Ivan's discussion group in the Quarter. She had hair like a black poodle, creamy skin, and a red mouth with a black mole at the corner like a chocolate fly sitting on ecru silk.

When he first saw her she was sitting on a battered green sofa stuffing cotton back into the holes with one hand while feeling up some big guy in Bermuda shorts with the other. She'd come up from kissing the big guy to flirt with Elliot who was trying to keep up with the discussion on the extraterrestrials who, according to the fuzzy-headed chair of this discussion, had first landed in Pontchatoula and had now moved into Goat's Castle on Dauphine Street, where they gave great parties and took methedrine.

He'd left the discussion group with the woman, so drunk she had to stop in the patio to throw up behind the elephant ears while he held her head. As he wiped her mouth with his handkerchief he felt tender toward her, even when she gargled and rinsed her mouth out with bourbon from the glass in her right hand, preserved in spite of her unsteadiness and the elephant ears. When they walked out into the glare of Bourbon Street, he noticed small white curds spotted his black shoeshine. He was fascinated by her. She had the air of someone who was born damned and pursued her destiny as an art form. She took him to her Conti Street apartment furnished with rosewood Mallard antiques and stacks of dirty dishes which meandered throughout the rooms. Soiled china and baccarat glasses with dregs of old wine leaned in unsteady piles on every flat surface. As they went into her bedroom, she stopped at the doorway, balancing against him on one high-heeled shoe, took off her peach satin panties and slipped them down over his head. His erection had received an immediate jolt like the jerk upward of a noose, and they'd stumbled halt and blind to the bed. He could still smell her, and that was what Haiti smelled like this morning.

Ultimately he'd run away from her, not because of her, but because of Camilla Jane. What he wanted from the other woman—passion beyond good sex, beyond sane sex, beyond anything he'd ever had, he found, but not, unfortunately, beyond what he'd imagined with Camilla Jane. He was a prisoner of his dreams. No woman's body could compete with his dreams.

And here he was in Haiti, not where his ancestors had come from, but Haiti where Moo's ancestors had come from, maybe Took's ancestors, too. A place his Irish ancestors had never even heard of, although there was a Frenchman back there somewhere, maybe he'd dreamed of Haiti like Gauguin had dreamed of Tahiti. Elliot knew he wore the skin of his ancestors, but he didn't wear their culture. They hadn't handed down stories. The stories he'd heard were from Moo, and the French he'd first learned at home, secondhand, was Creole third hand and his religion was not Irish Catholicism; it was Catholicism mixed up with "Eh, Legba." Caribbean loas had called him home.

The hotel Tres Jolie was a rundown, mildewed affair that could have been off St. Charles Avenue on Carondelet Street except for the sound of the ocean in the distance. It had been a *grande maison*. Now it housed student Americans and hippies. A friend of his from Tulane had given him the address. Dressed now he walked out onto the veranda, big as a tennis court, before setting out for downtown Jacmel. The yellow-skinned woman with red hair who'd given him the key to his room the night before called to him, "*Monsieur,* how do you take your coffee?"

He sat down on the veranda with a cup of *café au lait* and studied the patio. It was foreign but familiar like the woman he'd left in New Orleans. He loved it. The scents and people passing gave him a feeling of home without the responsibilities of home. It was like Took's kitchen where he was most comfortable, where anything untoward that happened could be manipulated by ritual, by *connaissance*, by the intercession of spirits who could handle things. He thought about that kitchen, the breeze blowing through the door, a cross current through the kitchen window, refreshing, comforting, rinsing the air until it was clean but still human.

From the veranda he could see a clump of little houses, *caillies*, one door, one window. The shutters and door were painted — blue, pink, green. The shotgun houses in the old neighborhoods of New Orleans were first cousins to the *cailles*.

Elliot felt primed by place. Tulane was far away. The other life he'd been educated to didn't fit. It was a hand-me-down. Someone else's life. He'd come to look for Erzuli in her home-land. The woman from Ivan's — Eugenie was her name. At climax he'd called her Mama Erzuli, and she'd come out of her own world long enough to say, "I'm not your Mama, boy."

He went out of the hotel to walk around the sun-drenched town looking at three-storied houses with balconies painted every color of the rainbow, and stopped to watch the women under the porticoes sorting coffee beans by hand — sizing and sorting huge piles of beans for export. Women on the street flashed hungry smiles at him, open glances of invitation. He was used to women looking at him, of responding with the lift of one eyebrow and an extra rhythm to his walk, but as he watched the women sort beans under the portico, he began to feel lonely and out of place. The sense of not fitting into his life had come back upon him and now rode his shoulders like a restless child.

He walked back to the hotel. The admiring glances of the women he passed fell on him unacknowledged. He felt re-sentful. They saw his blond hair, fair skin. They responded to a handsome foreigner. No kinship here. They were not of his skin, but he was a man who had come to understand his culture, to find out where his soul had come from. At home, when he and Camilla had tried to find their way between the kitchen world and the world of the double parlor, he'd felt hurt and alone except for Camilla. They'd played double-deal-ing games. It was the two of them against both worlds, and he smiled when he thought of the things they'd said — the things they'd done to the family — those foreigners.

As he walked back into the hotel, Ginette called out from the little cage that enclosed the front desk, "Do you like Jacmel? It's a beautiful town, oué?"

"Yes, it's a nice town, but I need to visit a more spiritual place. I'm here to forget a death," he improvised. As he watched her face change, he knew he'd said the right thing. "Yes, it was a death that brought me here."

She was all warm empathy now, ready to help him through a difficult passage. "Was it your Grandmere who died?"

He passed his hand over his eyes. "Closer, closer," he said choking on the words.

"Your Mama?" She whispered wide-eyed at the enormity of his loss.

Elliot appeared to be overcome at this question. His thoughts turning to Eugenie, who had said, "I'm not your Mama, boy," and he whispered, "Yes."

"Aiee —." She sucked in her breath in a profound expression of sorrow.

Elliot felt better. His mother had been dead five years. It always seemed to him she'd gone some place to paint, but this was true, there had been a death. His childhood had finally died, and he'd been forced out into a hostile world of law offices and papers — a world where everyone in the office on a daily basis moved forward toward goals as finite as those two goal posts at the end of Tulane stadium. The lazy child in him begged for immersions — spiritual, carnal — a plunge beneath the waters.

Ginette said, "You should go to the Bassin Bleu." He started right after dawn — climbing. The trail to the grotto led along a steep chasm, and he crossed and recrossed the same stream, at times fording as deep as his thighs in cold mountain water. He was a tennis player not a mountain climber and the climb was more than he'd bargained for, and when he got there and found what he'd bought with his energy he felt short-changed.

The sun was high, and the place was swarming with people. The climb had been difficult. He'd expected a reward — a quiet place where there were no tourists and few Haitians. He'd come for a spiritual experience and found the body — vulgar, triumphant — eating, drinking, and shitting — just like home.

There were vendors everywhere hawking medicines, oils, *gris gris* bags — a whole table of High John Root — almost a supermarket shelf of High John Root laid out on a table presided over by a black Haitian with a Chinese face. Elliot touched a root, but felt nothing sucking at his fingers, nothing drawing him — his fingers didn't stick. The vendor gave him a big grin. "Hello, Mr. America. You looking for something to freak out on. Some herb, some woman to freak your leaves. Some big mystery. I think this is the big mystery," and he tapped his wrist.

Elliot said, "Yes," stiffly and walked on to look at the falls and the pools of water where he could see swimmers and a few young men standing without clothes under the direct force of the waterfall. Elliot looked for the goddess sitting on a rock combing her hair with her golden comb, but the person he saw combing her wet hair was a young woman, probably American, in a blue-green swimming suit and sunglasses. She was sitting on a side boulder closest to the water — close enough to dip one foot in while splashing water on two Haitian boys, no more than thirteen years old, who were splashing back in a joyful, noisy water fight. Although the young woman was tan enough to be Haitian, he thought she was not.

He didn't wait around for dark to see the candles around the grotto. He didn't wait for a transformation, for magic to arrive. He was tired and disgruntled. The *magi* he'd searched for had turned out to be ordinary. The woman with the children was the most interesting thing he'd seen and she was bound to be American. He hadn't left the States to hang out with Americans.

He hiked back down to the hotel and, when he got back, without even lingering for a chat with the landlady, paid his bill, and made his way down to the square where he hired a tap-tap to a small harbor called Ti-Mouillage.

It was lunchtime when he arrived. There were no tourists at the small seafood house near the water. He sat at one of the two tables where he could smell the oily ropes while he ate a fresh lobster. The claws were huge and red. It was as delicious as any meal he'd ever eaten. It was the first time anything in Haiti had been completely different from New Orleans, and he savored the meal, although he savored it alone. As he stared at the water, and closed his stomach with a little cup of coffee, he thought of Camilla Jane — her electric curls flying out from her face. What would they have seen together if she'd been with him?

The hotel he stayed in at Ti-Mouillage had more *vevert* drawings on the posts than he'd seen elsewhere. They were crude drawings, but the manager was a scrubbed and manicured Creole man of the elite class with a body like a shot glass. The first thing he said to Elliot was as out of character as the drawings on the front columns. He said, "Do you want to see an authentic voodoo ceremony?"

"Why not?" said Elliot.

They went up the hill in a tap-tap diving into the dark over tire-swallowing potholes and rocks that hit the underside of the tap-tap like coconuts. Elliot wondered what he was doing in a taxi in Haiti with other American tourists on his way to a phony voodoo ceremony for which he would pay top dollar when he could see the same thing at home for free. They were all squeezed in together in the back of the taxi, his companions slightly hysterical with excitement. In the crush with them was a guide named Marcel who kept saying, "Authentic, very authentic ceremony. You will like it."

"I hope so," said the man who was the quietest member of the party. He and his wife were from Rome, Georgia. She giggled at anything the woman from New York said. "We have terrific voodoo in New York. In fact, we have everything in New York." The woman from Rome considered this hysterically funny and continued to laugh. It was not contagious. Elliot shared glances with the other tourist, who looked like the woman from Bassin Bleu, although she was wearing a cotton skirt and sweater instead of a bathing suit. He peered through the gloomy van, pretty sure it was the same woman.

"Did you stay for the candles?" he asked her.

"Oh—at the grotto? Yes, it reminded me of Lourdes."

"You've been to Lourdes?"

"No."

He didn't follow it up. She sounded shallow and the bouncing tap-tap didn't lend itself to easy conversation. They stopped at the top of a hill and piled out the open back of the taxi. There was no electric light on the outside. A fire of what looked and smelled like old tires burned in front of a corrugated tin building. There were many people in white milling around in the dark, and Elliot felt his pulse quicken as he heard two drums—one calling, the other answering. The music shifted him back to a restless, horny puberty by the church on River Road. The other tourists huddled together, and he got a glimpse of their startled faces by the firelight; apparently they'd expected something slicker—less basic. He began moving to the drum with a certain uptown abandon. In spite of his wild memories, his tight-assed dance was not too far beyond a hip, self-conscious secondline. He'd lost something somewhere. The guide motioned them inside the building.

Once inside, where he could see the ceremony, he could have been visiting any spiritualistic church in New Orleans, and now he moved to the drum as easily as the women dancing, and they were dancing as if their bones were aspic and their tongues red peppers. The tourists had walked into the middle of things. The houngan now strode in crackling like cellophane; the dancers bent in deep backbends to greet him, and the excitement in the room escalated exponentially as he began to sing. Elliot peered into the inner room for what he could see of the mysteries—*le mot d'enigme*. It was decorated in heavy white linen; near the throne was a table with fine napery. A heavy damask tablecloth reached to the floor, even the feet of the table were swathed in white linen. Everything set in white except the banners which were white and red. On the table a huge loaf of white bread, Erzuli's bread, waited for the knife. Elliot, deep in his own study of the place, had not been watching the tourists or their reaction to the ceremony. As the houngan sang, Elliot heard the singing voice behind him, and he turned to look at the tourists. The young woman of the blue-green bathing suit had lifted her voice, throaty and deep, in what sounded like the same song as the singer. Her words were in Creole — it was the same song. The dancers bending and twirling as the voice of the singer moved with them. There were calls for Legba and Ogoun Badagris as the dancers circled the *poteau mitan*. But no loa arrived and Elliot felt a deep disappointment. The drums beat on for hours like a warm-up act for a star who is drunk backstage. The houngan continued calling and singing with desperation now. The tourists, obviously bored, hadn't realized voodoo took so much time. It was as boring as church at home. They huddled together like wet chickens and looked completely out of place. Elliot knew he was out of place — another of those long-haired Americans who tried to go native with the aid of a little herb.

"What's your name?" Elliot asked Blue-green.

"Lilah," she whispered back.

"I'm Elliot Gilbert," he said.

As he spoke, one of the dancers behind her was struck a stunning invisible blow to the head. Her body convulsed, shivered and shook, as she sang with her eyes closed of how Ogoun Badagris now possessed her.

Opening her eyes after a few minutes, there was a swash-buckling gleam to them which had not been there before. She made a deep bow to the congregation, "*Messieurs, dames, bonjour,*" she said. She then went into the inner chamber. He could see her change into a red shirt and red cap, then pick up a stick and a wooden-handled machete left on the floor of the room. She disposed of the stick and kept the machete. This was immediately noted and whispered about among the other tourists who pressed together more tightly as they eyed the machete in Ogoun's hand. She took several practice swings in a mannish way with her legs braced and akimbo like a pirate. The singing and drumming continued and the loa posed and swung the machete in time to the music.

Elliot's body shook in time to the drum as he watched the girl, now Ogoun, as he, Ogoun, presented himself to the congregation. While Elliot watched intently, he felt something like a mild electric shock at his side as Lilah convulsed and sagged against him. He quickly caught her and with the aid of one of the women in white helped her to a chair. To his amazement, she opened her mouth and sang the song of Erzuli Freda Dahomey. There was a tremendous swelling of voices like cellos as the hounsis and members of the congregation sang out the three responses to the three Erzulies.

Lilah jumped up from the chair, left the big room, and went into the sanctuary where there was a sound of water running and splashing, and the friction of vigorous scrubbing: Elliot remembered with some excitement how clean Erzuli was and how feminine, always anxious to make the most of her attractions. He could hear her brushing her teeth and gargling. At last she came away from the basin and he could see her shadowy form robing herself in the costume of Erzuli Freda Dahomey; it was mysterious, exciting. With an ivory backed mirror in one hand she put perfume at her collarbone and behind her ears. The fragrant bottle of white lotion was familiar to Elliot, and he thought he recognized it from D.H. Holmes. He'd once picked up a bottle of Aphodisia body lotion for Eugenie. He believed, with a small thrill, that it was the same lotion.

Erzuli seemed very taken with herself—with the three rings she removed from a small jewelry box, she posed with her hand out, examining the hand with each ring as she put it on. The rings were all on the left hand: one for marriage to

Ogoun Badagris, the second a token of her marriage to Agoue, the third her future union with Damballah Wedo. Slowly, she turned around and opened her arms to the congregation in the exact manner of a Roman Catholic priest. Elliot felt a magnetic projection of self from Erzuli. He knew it was to show her beauty. There was a murmur of appreciation from the congregation when she bent to kiss the cheeks of Ogoun Badagris, standing at her side with a macho air. Amazing—the woman he'd known as Lilah had been strengthened by the spirit of Erzuli Freda Dahomey, and she seemed bigger—taller.

In his head Elliot tried to add it up, why had she, a woman who was not Creole fallen into a trance, been possessed so easily? At the same time he felt a tingling activate his groin—how easily the body became possessed. Erzuli Freda was now parading herself for all the men to see. When she looked at the women it was with an open mockery—disdain transformed her face into the face of a scornful *Haitienne*, and she crooked a little finger at them as a sign of her complete disapproval, how dare they compete with her for the men.

Some of the women came over to Erzuli and touched her finger in the salute of the loa—a submissive attitude which she accepted, and which seemed odd in light of the powerful presence of some of the women. A hounsi took a seat next to Erzuli. She carried a fan for her; at Erzuli's command the woman passed the food—the *mange-loa* to the men.

Erzuli then motioned toward Elliot, and he saw the congregation part like the waters of the red sea, waves of blurred faces pushed back, as he made his way up front. The hounsis showed him to a place of honor next to Erzuli. She bent over him in her white negligee and placed both arms around him in a gesture both protective, all-enveloping, and tender, and she pulled him, to his great embarrassment, upon her knees and began to whisper in his ear. Elliot, in an agony of embarrassment and desire, heard her whisper, "I am Erzuli and you are mine."

But that was when he'd seen her face collapse as if her

skull had dissolved and rebuilt itself in the fraction of a second. She had been Erzuli, but now they were being led to a small hut lit by a kerosene lamp and where they were given mats to sleep on. Now she was Lilah again. Marcel the guide and the other tourists had disappeared. At first Elliot thought they might have gone for help, but then he realized his exotic dancing and Lilah's extravagant fondling of strange Haitian men — taking him on her lap like a ventriloquist's dummy — probably just looked like crazy hippies gone native. And were they? He didn't know himself or her well enough to know. Normal — she looked whatever passed for normal, enhanced perhaps, a beautiful woman more beautiful because she had revealed some hidden side to herself. At the moment she looked too docile for his taste. Erzuli would have wrapped those long arms and legs around him. There was still heat in his spine. His nature had come tumbling down and the loss of control worried him. She was quiet. Her face impassive.

"Do you know what happened?" he asked.

"Sure. They danced me to death. I can't believe I danced so much, but they never did get the spirits in, did they?"

"Well, actually, they did."

"They did? You mean that butch girl who went jumping around in the pirate outfit?"

"Yes, she's Ogoun Badagris. That's one of Erzuli Freda Dahomey's husbands."

"You seem to know a lot about this. It seems to me with all those good looking men around Erzuli Freda Dahomey could have found herself another husband."

"Well, it depends on who the loa decides to ride. How do you feel?"

"Tired. Why did they bring us here? What happened to the tap-tap?"

"The tap-tap left with the other people. I think they thought we were having too good a time."

"I was having a good time. I love to dance."

"Do you remember saying you were Erzuli?"

"You're kidding. If I said that I must have had too much

Clairin—they're pretty generous with their rum." There was a loud banging on the tin door. Lilah looked startled and Elliot noticed dark circles under her eyes. He felt protective toward her and went to the door. "Who's there?" he called out in Creole.

"*A serviteur, a serviteur,*" answered the voice, and the door, which had no lock, burst open. A tall man with a spongy white patch of hair in the front of his head came in. His eyes were red and Elliot knew immediately he was a worshiper still in a trance.

"What do you want?" he asked the man.

"You should not have come. You do not belong here. The *blanc* is not Erzuli Freda Dahomey and should not put on her clothes. You are impostors pretending to be loas. Go back to your own country." He spoke this speech with great animation, waving his arms as if angry, but the words came out like poured molasses. When he finished his diatribe, he turned and left the hut.

"Who was that, and what did he mean I shouldn't have put on Erzuli's clothes? I didn't touch her clothes."

"You don't remember saying you were Erzuli?"

"Don't be ridiculous. Why would I say I was Erzuli? I don't know anything about voodoo. I've only been in a voodoo shop once in my entire life at home."

"Where's home?"

"Home is New Orleans, but I was born in Texas—I don't count Texas."

"I live in New Orleans, too. I've been going to Tulane."

"You mean two people from New Orleans end up meeting each other in a voodoo hut in Haiti?" She laughed at him.

"Sounds about right to me."

There was another banging at the door. This time it was the woman Ogoun Badagris who came in with eyes flashing, whipping her machete around in a theatrical manner and using it to point at Lilah. "Where is Erzuli Freda Dahomey? What have you done with my wife?"

"Listen, Mack, she went home—took the first train to

Guinee," Elliot said. "I'm here with my friend. Erzuli left. I promise." The woman had thick cheeks and long greased hair; she flashed her eyes and staggered a bit as she brandished the machete. After uttering a few empty maledictions she left.

Lilah, who had appeared scared at first, now seemed relaxed and even laughed when the woman asked for her "wife." But she still didn't seem to realize she'd recently been the wife.

"I think," said Elliot, "we ought to wait until daylight and then skedaddle out of here. No one seems to be hostile, but the ceremony is still in full swing, and the drums are going a mile a minute. They're resentful of us for taking positions of honor at the front of the room."

"We didn't take positions of honor. They offered us positions of honor."

"You remember that?"

"I think so."

"Yeah, well, whatever. They've forgotten all that now." "Let's just go as soon as it's daylight. In the meantime why don't you try to catch a little sleep and I'll keep watch for your husband, Ogoun. She is your only husband, right?"

"Right," she said laughing, and put her head down on the mat and, like a tired child, immediately went to sleep. He sat up smoking a cigarette and looking at her. He could still see Erzuli—how she had looked as Erzuli, her gestures painfully feminine, ethereal—not like an American woman. He stared at her face; she was good looking in a patrician sort of way, as Erzuli her character had deepened—an earthy quality overlaid with an extreme femininity—almost a caricature, like some sex goddess tripping around in extremely high heels, a deep décolletage, and talking in a little girl voice. Something appealed to him on an irrational physical level. He looked at her, trying to figure it out and he still wanted her. It was even crazier than the woman in New Orleans. He moved closer to her and felt ashamed when he moved. The room was tight with sexual tension—time had no meaning, it was endless and the night miserable, he would hike down to the village in the morning with a pair of aching balls.

They had jumped out of time—this was time out, but he knew they'd caused whatever happened to them. They'd both made crazy choices, which brought them to this place where he sat in a corrugated tin shack smelling dirt, woman, burning rubber, and music. He could smell the drum, the hide of the animal thumping away in the night. The top layer peeled off everything and laid out like a dead animal on top of the drum. He felt intensely alive and male and he wanted the woman lying beside him. He wanted her so much he reached beyond himself and touched her slightly curled fingers. She straightened her hand and stretched her body, opening her eyes to his swollen face pulsing with the drum.

She smiled at him, a huge broad-lipped smile, and reached her arm up behind his head to pull his face down to hers.

It was a night right out of dreams. They'd taken their clothes off in a frenzy, but he'd stopped suddenly to stare at her body, at the dark triangle between her legs, while her arms grabbed at him, supplicating, begging for him to cover her. Her face feral in the lamplight, lips drawn back; he felt drawn into something too deep, too elemental for his manhood, but desire hadn't left him. He was terrified, as if he were holding the raw ends of two electrical power cables together to light a city. He felt electric, powerful, and scared. He was beyond his depth and he knew it. The crazy thing was, he was finally going to have her—the woman he'd wanted all his life, but she wasn't here in body, she was in Louisiana with So Busteaux, but sex has no logic; his face blazed; the dark slit was an entrance into another world—a dip beneath the waters, the mouth of mystery, and he was drawn in with a powerful magnetism, as powerful as the High John root, and he threw back his head and laughed like a drunk until he cried. Kneeling above her he pressed forward and plunged into darkness.

He was hung over, unsure of where he was, when a loud

banging on the door brought him to. Lilah was sleeping on her stomach, her hair fanned over her back in a mass of tangles. He pulled his rumpled shirt over her bare buttocks and answered the door. Elliot could hear the drum as the door opened and the Houngan walked in stately as an archbishop. Two men in a trance were with him.

The Houngan bowed to Elliot and addressed Lilah's back. "*Maitresse*, we have not recognized you with proper respect. We have not shown you honor. Stupid, bad men came here last night and defiled your wedding bed, your place of honor with the man of your choice. *Maitresse*, I know that you ignore your servant out of disgust. We beg your pardon for treating you badly, but we come now to do you honor."

Elliot stared at Lilah's sleeping back, and the gleeful child in him could hardly keep a straight face as the archbishop addressed her back, but as he laughed to himself, Lilah turned over and sat up in one graceful motion. She held her hand out in an imperious gesture. One of the men handed her a white negligee which she put on while standing buck naked in front of them without shame. And holding her hand forward to be led, she followed the Houngan back to the ceremony with Elliot trailing behind.

Morning

THEY HAD COME DOWN FROM THE HILLS. GOING back on the trail in the morning was stranger than going up in the dark. They rode in a spotless red Ford belonging to the Houngan. The car was old, the paint job faultless, the velour upholstery like new. Layers of drawings, paintings, small statues of saints, and decorations covered the dashboard. Lilah in the back was driven in state like a queen. There was a driver and the Hougan in the death seat. Elliot couldn't bear to look out the window as their insane descent scattered chickens and goats down the hill. He sat beside Lilah, honored with a seat beside her since he'd been chosen by Erzulu. Nothing was said about the second ceremony, or how easily she had fallen into the part of Erzuli after she said she didn't remember anything. He didn't ask her to explain because it was too exciting unexplained. They were delivered like royalty to the Tres Jolie.

There was a month left to Lilah's vacation. They spent

most of it in bed. He, in a constant state of silly excitement, and she, although in complete control of her emotions, just as content to spend her life in indolence and sexuality. They did not go to other ceremonies, but everyone in the hotel knew she'd been ridden by the loa and everyone knew he'd been chosen by Maitresse. Physically, they completed the circle, but neither of them knew anything about the other.

"Coffee" her muffled voice called. She was lying on her stomach in the darkened room with one hand hanging over the edge of the bed. "Coffee," she called again without opening her eyes. Elliot got up and threw open the shutters. The sun splashed into the room and drenched her back with waves of light. The fan over the bed hissed with an off-center wobble. Elliot stood at the window with the breeze caught on the fan blade caressing his naked skin; the washboard of tight muscles on his sides ached with the pleasant catch of exercise, and he looked out at the garden jungle green — grass, myrtle, lime. He knew suddenly he was happy.

"I'm happy," he said grinning at the empty garden.

"Hm — hm, coffee," came the wail from the bed.

He laughed, ran over to the bed, and jumped astride her back. She didn't move, just giggled and raised herself up, pushing against him. Elliot held himself up so that his full weight was not supported by her back. "Coffee?" he asked. "You expect me to get coffee for a lazy, gorgeous woman who stays abed all day, every day? What's in it for me? What's in it for the coffee *serviteur*?"

"Don't be disgusting. All you have to do is push a button."

"As I said, 'What's in it for me?' Will the goddess Erzuli awaken and fuck me cross-eyed or will she smite me dead? I'm scared," he said softly. "Oh, oh," he said kissing her back. "I'm scared." The body beneath him wiggled and pushed until he fell over on one side still hollering, "Oh, oh."

Lilah sat up and pushed the hair out of her eyes. "Where's my coffee? Can't you do the simplest thing without making it a voodoo ritual? This place has gone to your head."

He made a serious face like the *Houngan* and said in a deep voice in accent, "No coffee for the goddess. She sips the nectar of the gods. Would you like some?"

"Hm, what did you have in mind?"

"You're suspecting me of unclean thoughts." He snuggled his face between her breasts, as she folded her arms around him, he kissed the skin between her breasts and then moved to the nipples. The aureole stained the paler breast and raised into an erect nipple that fit his mouth like a chocolate kiss.

He looked up into her face. The eyes were hooded, her mouth open as short bursts of breath came from her lips. A faint flush passed over her neck and chest. He slipped his hand down her legs and found her as he'd found her since that first night in the hills, wet and ready.

He slipped in and began squeezing his tight buttocks toward the center of the earth, as his eyes sewed themselves shut, and he fell into his head where Erzuli walked toward the room of the mysteries in a white dress. As she turned to call him and he saw her face and it was changing to Lilah's and he screamed, I love you," as he plunged toward climax, and she answered him in a whispered moan, "Love," she said, "love," and he closed her mouth with his and he felt closer to her than he'd ever felt to a woman. When they moved apart, she kept her legs stretched toward the center of the bed looped over his. They didn't move to wash but stayed together holding hands.

"Let's get married," he said.

"Married? I don't think I'm ready to get married."

"Why not? You like me. You like to sleep with me. What else is there?"

"Marriage always looked like prison to me." She shook her head. "What about my job?"

"What about it?"

"You'd want me to stay home and have babies."

"Not me. Who said anything about babies? I said, Come live with me and be my love. Let's get married."

"You didn't say that. You said, you want me to come sleep with you."

"Well, isn't that part of marriage?"

"Yes, but people don't sleep together after they get married. They change. They become their parents."

"How could I become my parents? I hardly knew them. Moo and Took were my parents."

"Who were they?"

"Two women who worked for my family. Moo ran our house and Took tried to run my Aunt's house. If it hadn't been for them, my cousin and I would have been weeds."

"Negroes?"

"Yeah, I guess so. I never thought too much about that. They were Moo and Took. Really it was Moo, and she was about your color. Took reared my cousin and she was black-black. The rest of the family was absentee. My father lived in New Orleans, and the only thing he ever wanted me to be was a good tennis player and join the Krewe of Comus when I came to New Orleans. I did do a lot of dancing with debutantes last year."

"He's in Comus?"

"He was. He's dead. Had a heart attack playing tennis. Most of them are dead except for Moo. I came to Haiti because of Moo. *Connaissance*—power, knowledge. It's here. New Orleans is just another Caribbean country. It all comes from here, from Africa to Haiti to New Orleans. I'm not quite ready to be an attorney—that's the other thing he wanted me to be. I wanted to go back to Africa. I was there once on a ship. That's where we all began you know."

"What I like about New Orleans—is—it's not Texas, and as far as negroes—this is the first place where I ever spent any time around any, and I've had a good time, but I don't know any and never did. Are you really going to be an attorney? One of my clients told me I should marry an attorney."

"Safe—right? Well, she's wrong. Nothing's safe."

He got up from the bed and rang for coffee. "I'm going to take a shower. I can tell a bad idea when I get one."

"It's not *such* a bad idea."

"Don't do me any favors," he said as he stepped into the shower which was in the corner of the room over a bubbling drain in the floor. He soaped himself down and drowned out any further conversation with the force of the water. The dented shower head deflected water sideways; a thin stream shot out to the center of the room where Elliot could see it hit the side of her suitcase. He didn't care — better yet, he did care. He rejoiced in the water hitting her suitcase while she pretended not to see it. Her calm exterior belying annoyance escalating to anger — he waited for her to let it show. When she let go, when she screamed and hollered at him for being inconsiderate, for ruining her suitcase and wetting her clothes. When she let him see just how mad he could make her she would give up and marry him. She'd fill up any empty spots in his life; pack in all the things he couldn't pretend; Camilla Jane would cease to occupy his thoughts, and he would be able to make believe, just as well as anyone else, that he was in control of his life. As he walked out of the shower a pillow hit him in the belly, quickly followed by Kenneth Patchen's poems, and a hairbrush. He smiled at her and headed back to bed.

Even thinking about going back to New Orleans made him sick. Everything he believed about himself would fall apart in New Orleans. Only when Lilah agreed to marry him in the Catholic church in Jacmel, was he able to bring himself to buy a return ticket. The marriage was more complicated than he'd supposed. Father Martin insisted that the banns be posted and all formalities observed. After the banns had been posted for two weeks, he and Lilah went to a dusty government office which was usually closed; on one trip there they waited in line with a petite Creole women with three children. She shook her finger at the clerk, "Where is my paper? You promise before the first child you would give me the paper. I am to marry and still no paper."

"Madame, who do you know? I think you do not know

anyone except the father of these children." And he closed the small mahogany door in their faces. It took three trips and the special intercession of Ginette, who whispered *"Maitresse,"* and gave the clerk fifty dollars, which she'd gotten from Elliot; only then did they finally get the forms recorded. Allowed to marry at last.

Lilah wore a white eyelet dress with a white gauzy veil on the back of her head. Hardly the type of dress Camilla would have worn. Their witness was Alcide Desiones who had arranged the voodoo trip. The maid of honor was Ginette, the red-haired woman from the hotel Tres Jolie. "Do you see the bride is like a postcard of *Maitresse*? Do you see it?" She asked everyone, and everyone but the goats nodded *Oui*. Even Father Martin.

The wedding was quick, and they all went off to drink Clairin at the hotel. As they drank, Elliot watched Lilah's face change to the expression of disdain she'd worn as Erzuli and before she left, Ginette went up to Lilah and touched her fingers in the expression of submission he'd seen the night of the ceremony. There was something odd about the gesture. He drank more Clairin to quiet his nerves, and soon found the room jumping around like a fever dream. When he fell against a table and shattered two glasses on the red tile floor, Lilah asked Alcide and Marcel the guide to help him upstairs. They half-carried him with his legs hanging down, feet dragging behind. His legs were boneless, and he couldn't get his feet to stand flat. They dumped him on the bed where he passed out and slept through his wedding night.

The next day he awakened to a hammering headache and a cheerful Lilah who didn't chastise him or even seem concerned that on the first night of their marriage she'd slept alone. She was walking from the bureau to her suitcase, packing cotton sweaters, jeans, and incense for the return trip home. And when he came up behind her to put his arms around her, she said, "Not now."

Everything was different in New Orleans. They moved

into a double on Prytania Street and Lilah went back to work. Elliot went to work every morning for the law firm of Lawson, Haynes, and Broussette. Beginning a life of doing what he'd always known would kill his soul if he had one. He quickly developed a taste for afternoon Ramos gin fizz at the Roosevelt bar, for introspection, for amazement at the change in his wife, who no longer wanted to lie abed all day in sexual dalliance, who dressed now in blue suits with white blouses and joined the Junior League. It was not what he had in mind when he'd danced to the drums in Haiti and stared into the room of the mysteries. What had happened to *connaissance*? What had happened to love? His soul shriveled and split like a soaked red bean waiting to be thrown in the pot and cooked to mush. And as he became his father, Lilah got pregnant and became her mother, a woman he'd never met but she'd always hated.

Sometimes he sat up talking with Moo in the mother-in-law's house in the rear of the double, two rooms and a bath, which she insisted on calling "the slave quarters." Lilah didn't want Moo in the house.

"Too crowded," she said. "We need our privacy."

"I don't know what for," he said. "We never do anything the neighbors couldn't come and watch."

Lilah did the housework with an air of martyrdom, which Elliot hated, and Moo made fun of. He knew in his new life he looked like a dog someone had thrown a shoe at. All Moo would say was, "Now you've gone and done it. You got stuck. I bought you back but you had to go to Guinee to see what it was...."

"I didn't go to Guinee; I went to Haiti."

"...and now you know. You went from hot-hot to cold-cold. When you lie down with Erzuli Freda Dahomey, you never know who you're going to get up with. This one's bad enough, but she's the puppet. The real *Maitresse* is still in Baton Rouge, and every once in awhile she is going to pull your string."

"God, I hope so," he said.

River

THE TENNIS COURT RADIATED A TERRIBLE HEAT. Graham reached up and served a ball that scored the rubicon. Elliot scrambled to reach it but couldn't. "That's set. I'm thirsty," he said, and wiped his face with an already smelly towel. They went into the clubhouse, where the air conditioning was so low it turned the sweat running down Elliot's temples into ice water. Elliot ordered two gin and tonics at the bar. He and Graham threw themselves down into chairs by the windows overlooking the lawn bordered by a high hedge of ligustrum. Red hibiscus bushes lit the green lawn like stations on a pinball machine. The drinks arrived with ice cubes piled to the rims. Cut spheres of lime floated somewhere in the middle like green bobbers.

"Tennis," said Elliot lightly, "has been my profession. I'm going for a new one." He held up the glass and eyed the lime now sunk to the bottom like a bright tennis ball.

"What're you saying? You'd starve if tennis were your profession. You're a lawyer and a damned good one," Graham growled back.

"No, law's my hobby. It doesn't mean anything to me. I could cut it tomorrow. I'm a lawyer because somebody else wanted me to be one. It doesn't mean anything," he repeated, as if repetition would make Graham understand.

"It means sixty thousand a year to you. That's about as meaningful as you're going to get. It means your wife has decent clothes and your kids can go to good schools—I don't know how anything could mean any more."

"You're wrong. Tennis means something to me, but it's ephemeral, and I wouldn't even make a good clubhouse pro. My hobby pays me sixty thousand, and I'm sick of my hobby. But I may continue to let you beat me at tennis."

"What crap. Let me beat you! You can't help it. No matter how bad you want it, you can't win except when I'm tired or your wife gives it to you. In court I win one sometimes. You've got the serve and the backhand there. I wouldn't even hire me for my lawyer." His laugh was apologetic, and he bent forward sucking at the ice cubs rolled forward in his glass."

Graham sank into his drink, turning away from Elliot, and looking out toward the tennis court where he'd won. A line of heavy flesh from from Graham's ear downward was the first physical expression of age on a body that had been leaping hand outstretched over a meshed net for twenty years. Elliot knew he was right to quit now before the sixty thousand a year meant more than what he thought of himself, before all he aimed for was seventy thousand a year or eighty thousand. Life expressing itself in increments of ten thousand increases, which bought more things he didn't care about. "I've got a chance to go on the river," he said to Graham.

Graham got up suddenly and went back to the bar for another drink. Elliot waited to talk to him in the kind of late-night deep conversation they'd had as fraternity brothers, smoking pot, drawn together by their inability to deal with the expectations of their fathers—distant autocratic men who expected large, perfect chips off the old block. They had both tried to be their fathers' sons, admiring them from a distance like gods with miraculous gifts and sudden, unpredictable rages that rained down on their people like scourges and plagues. He and Graham had been able to talk of their fathers; of their impossible hopes to emulate them; of their deep desires to knock them into the other side of kingdom come; but Elliot had gotten out, gone to sea for three years, escaped Moo, escaped his father. Graham never got out of New Orleans for more than a few weeks skiing.

Elliot knew, as Graham walked around the room with his drink, relaxing muscles by shaking out first one leg and then the other with the unselfconscious movements of the born athlete, the conversation was over. Graham had retreated into his own regrets. Elliot would never be able to talk to him about this subject — ever.

It was the summer after his freshman year at Tulane, he'd told Graham he was going to do it and he did. Graham was his roommate, and they often talked into the night about the adventures they were going to have in the real world. But they didn't call it adventure. The conversation would start off with a few beers and a joint.

"I'm going to Alaska," Graham said. "My dad's wasting his money. I'm not going to stick around this place until I flunk out. I'm going to Alaska. Boz Denechaud's got a cousin who has a boat up there. He takes people out on fishing trips and prospecting trips. The guy's a geologist and he sets off charges of dynamite for semi-precious stones. I'm gong to go up for the summer and work as a deckhand and set off dynamite in my spare time."

"Sounds good, Grab. Did you ever read a story called "Youth?"

"No."

"It's by a man named Conrad. It's about this young guy who goes out on a ship, and everything happens that can happen. The ship's a floating junkyard. It's got a fire in the hole and they're limping all over the ocean. They've got storms and floods and pestilence. Now the guy's telling the story when he's old, and he keeps saying, "Pass the bottle," as he tells this story, and then when he takes a swig off the bottle he says something like, "Ah, youth" because all through these terrible things happening to the ship he's happy and this is a great time in his life. That's what I want to do. Go out and have something happen to me before I'm too old, before I'm a lawyer and dead. I've got a cousin and she always said you have to make things happen to you. Not just wait around until you're almost dead and then be sorry that nothing ever happened to you."

"Man, when you're a lawyer you'll have the money to go where you want."

"It'll be different when I'm a lawyer. I won't go anywhere. Right now I want to sleep with all kinds of women and eat curry in India and cous-cous in Morocco—all those things you read about." He got up and got another beer from the six pack on the desk.

"All those things *you* read about. I didn't have Moo on my back."

"I want to see where those ships come from. The ones that come in on the river from Greece and Peru. I want to go there and see it."

On his nineteenth birthday Elliot went down to the Thalia Street wharf. There was a huge rusty looking ship called the Khios at the dock. He was scared, knew he looked young—too young for a job. They were unloading rubber and loading cotton. He'd never seen a cotton gang work before and he watched them while he got his courage up. Their rhythm was smooth and quick. Longshoremen drove squeeze machines clamped onto five-hundred-and-fifty-pound bales of cotton down the open wharf, and threw down the bales, strapped. Wire hooks drew up four bales at a time to a sling, which they pulled up and stuffed unto the upper tweens. Twenty stick booms stuck out all over the ship. The speed of the men with hooks stuck out all over the ship. The speed of the men with hooks kept the weight from stopping and the rhythm of it kept men moving the weight down so quickly it seemed effortless. They were big men: black, tan, and some men the color of bad milk all moving five-hundred-and-fifty pounds like it was easy, like it was nothing, and the cotton got loaded and stacked.

Elliot watched mesmerized until he saw a man coming down the gangway. He worked up the nerve to go up to him to ask about a job. "Pardon me," he said, "I'd like to talk to the Master about a job." He was embarrassed because he didn't know if the man spoke English. Half afraid he might answer him in some foreign tongue he didn't understand.

The man answered with a smile out of his black beard. "So you want to work the sea. The Old Man's crazy now. We're late. All is broken, even one of our deckhands, who has broken his arm. The Master — even crazier than usual." He spread his arms and shrugged his shoulders. "Maybe he will hire you. Who knows. Nothing could be worse. Anything would be better. Go up. There — he is the one cursing. Pay no attention to his curses. No one does. This is a Greek ship. Every man is Master. We are the true democrats. Perhaps, even you." He laughed again. "I am Yanni Stavros and I am the third mate."

"I'm Elliot Gilbert," he shook the mate's hand.

"Good — good, Elliot Gilbert. Go up. We'll sail together. Who knows?" He smiled again and waved as he left the ship. Elliot went up the shaky gangway. A man holding a raw onion and Greek olives in one hand, and a knife to carve the onion in the other, met him at the top of the gangway. His forehead rolled in creases like a dome over a messy desktop of papers and late bills. It took a second glance for Elliot to realize the worried man was the master of the ship.

"*Gamisi,* you're late. All agents are the same. Where are you to make calls — to tend business. Where are you, you *Skata*?"

"No, sir. Not me. I'm Elliot Gilbert. You've got a deckhand

with a broken arm. I can do his job. You need a man and I want to go to sea."

"This *Poytsa*, the agent where's he?"

"Listen, you give me the job and I'll make the call to find him."

"The captain started to laugh as he cut himself a big slice of onion and ate it with the black olives, which dripped olive oil down to his elbow. His laughter was as raw and strong as the onion. Dark eyes shining, he clapped Elliot on the back and said, "*Skata*, you've got balls. I like you. I hire you now on the spot. We sail at midnight tomorrow night. You got a passport?"

Elliot, nose full of the rusty ship, the olive oil and onion, said "Yes, Sir."

"All right—all right. You're hired. Tonight we go to the Acropolis and get you some *Moyni*. You like *Moyni*?"

"Money—sure, everybody likes money."

"No money—not much money on Greek ships, but lots of *Moyni*—pussy—you say. *Moyni* loves Greek men because we're so good to them. You learn too. You meet us there to-night and we'll drink on it. Now I've got to find that *poytsa* agent. You make a call, O.K.?"

Around midnight Elliot found the Acropolis—a narrow doorway on Decatur Street with a neon sign over it—not too far down from a mysterious message carved into the side-walk: "Alligators, furs and pecans." He didn't know the name of the company specializing in those three commodities. He still pondered it when he walked into a doorway that opened onto a flight of narrow, red-carpeted stairs. As he ran up, the stairwell was suddenly crowded with a group of smoking men and laughing, perfumed women. Hand-clapping and music followed them down. Upstairs, the landing was dense with smoke and people as they struggled to get into the room. A band of smiling men on stage played stringed instruments Elliot didn't recognize, and in front of the stage dancing was the Master of the Khios. He was leading a dance holding up a handkerchief, which he used to balance the next man, who jumped down in a squatting dance step as a line of men snaked down the center of the room. A heavy man, powerful in the neck and shoulders, the Master stepped lightly and jumped up slapping his ankles behind him; the others followed step, and Elliot, overwhelmed with a feeling of joyous abandon, followed the dancers with his eyes, knowing with happy certainty he would learn this dance on the Khios, and he wanted to throw himself into the action now as he watched them dance around the edge of the clapping crowd. The tempo increased as the Master picked up a table, steadied it on his head, balancing a young seaman on top. The seaman swayed back and forth in a dance step of his own, and again the Master lowered himself into a squat. When he raised himself, and the table with the dancing seaman in another turn of the dance, the musicians played feverishly as he squatted and stood in quick succession, while the seaman balanced on top. Elliot thought the old man would fall from exertion as cords stood out on his neck, but all he did was laugh through his beard until the seaman jumped down lightly. The Master brandished the table triumphantly by one leg as the music changed tempo again. Two women in shiny blue costumes came from the back singing in Greek. Each woman had a handheld microphone; they sang in close harmony, a lamenting song—Thessaloniki. The women were not beautiful or young, but their figures were voluptuous, with tight, muscular waistlines accented by slight mounds of exposed belly. Harem pants began well below their navels and, as they sang in unison about Thessaloniki, the men of the Khios, sitting at a long table ringside dotted with five bottles of red label Scotch, threw dollar bills onto the floor. The women smiled broadly and sang their throbbing song, "Oh Thessaloniki." The Master spotted Elliot standing by the door and motioned him over. At the table he pointed to an empty seat next to a woman with long brown hair, "Here we hold your berth," he said.

Elliot saw at the table several big women with huge breasts

and dark lipstick, and he felt supremely happy to be going to sea. He would write to Camilla Jane to tell her all about it. When the line of men got up to dance again, he danced too. He stayed on the Khios for two years before he went back to Tulane to become a lawyer.

Elliot got up, drained his glass, picked up his cigarettes, said "See you" to Graham and left the clubhouse. After putting his racket in the trunk of the car, he drove out of the tennis club down St. Charles Avenue to Carrollton and up Oak Street with its shoe repair shop, antique upholsterer; past a lunch restaurant called Entre Nous, a bride shop, a frame shop, beauty salon, the Maple Leaf Bar, and a Woolworth's dime store — down to the end of Oak Street where he wheeled up the shell road onto the levee.

It was the gut of the city he came to — the river. The houses there, on tall, spindly pilings wet in the water, distant as cypress docks, were not what he came for — not cities or towns, or squatters encroached upon the very body of the river. For his life he wanted an opening wide as water.

Slicks, boils, and tarred ropes had been slung upon the bank like thread: a sound like a heartbeat began in his belly — a huge, dark shape came gliding by. A beat at the base of him like the thrum of his belly when he kissed Camilla Jane.

As a boy he'd gone with Moo to fish on the bank under the willows, saw the catfish she'd pulled up with their slit eyes, blue-steel skins, their old hooks and window shade poles hanging off their invincible lips, the reins of river horse gods transmuted and hanged, like devil fish with finny pitchforks. This was the river he came for. The river he'd found with Camilla.

The city's houses, huddled under the arm of the levee, hugged the soft-bellied land with the tyranny of the weak. Here he'd seen flood stage rise up and threaten, sink down and tranquilize, and the old desire was in him, at the root of the root, and power was the river, which could not be held or bound—could whip around, change course, and leave New Orleans dry, breasting a crescent of mud, a swamp of malarial malaise, dry boxes of yellow fever and no trade.

This was promise and threat, as she was, and it was in him and of him to love the body of the river with ships. The muddy power of the Mississippi was the dust circulating in his bloodstream blown into his nostrils by the brown-rose lips of Moo circulating good earth through him like the larvae of some flies in Africa are hosted by other organisms until, transferred by the bite of a fly, they awaken in the bloodstream and take over a man's life with dreaming until he dies. This was true of his own past where black and white was like coffee milk, good and sweet, and they had all grown together suckled on the same milk. And he had gone to sea to find the different cultures flowing in on the river intermingled in his brain. And soul had flowed in from France, Scotland, Haiti, and all waters of the Caribbean. The dances: the calinda, the jerk, the monkey, a Cajun two-step at Fred's in Mamou on Saturday morning. The Greek dances on the Khios. It was in Elliot when he danced—it was in him when she danced a slow drag. They all came together and became the hex on the milk cow, the mojo, and High John the Conqueror. People came up the river—frightened, superstitious. They stood up against forces that couldn't be contained or denied—base forces—storm and flood—hurricanes blowing them away or drowning them like cats in a bucket.

What was sweet was also bitter. All the graces bestowed upon him by the city could not bind him. He was still held by the root, by water, by the woman, by the house that wasn't there, and by two old women who served power from little black bags—who saved fingernail parings, and menstrual blood as holy and terrible things. Those old women owned him. And they would hold him until he could find his own way, fill his fetish bag, pass his puberty rite and pass to manhood. But these were his nightmares and his sweetest dreams. He knew his place was on the river and in her arms, and his terrible dream was that the river would change and she would die before he came to them.

The river was different now, as her face has transmuted and changed. He walked barefoot in his own footprints, dwelling behind his own eyes like St. Francis, the mambo, the monks of Buddha—those who won, disdained, and walked on. Elliot had come to the pinnacle of his desire. It came out of his mouth like fog in the bend: He wanted the river, and still, when his life was wood ashes in his mouth, he wanted her.

Dinner at Galatoire's

"TASTES LIKE A SKINNY HURRICANE," LILAH SAID.

"Skinny — skinny? This is a full-bodied woman of a drink," said Graham, who was already feeling his.

The two couples had been waiting in a long line on Bourbon Street for dinner at Galatoire's. There were no reservations at Galatoire's. For the past two drinks they'd been drinking some awful drink Graham had tried before he talked the bartender into making this for them. It was a syrupy concoction of several different liqueurs and rum.

"What do you think Jane? Do you like it?" Elliot asked Graham's wife. Lilah watched him as he tried to include Jane in the conversation. Jane so seldom had an opinion Elliot felt obliged to elicit one. If he didn't, the evening became a three-way love feast and she was always the one left out.

"This is sweet. I like sweet things," she said.

"I don't," Lilah said. "I think I'd like a raki. You know that

Turkish drink that tastes like licorice. I just had a sip once and I liked it."

"Licorice is sweet," Jane said.

"I like them all," said Graham holding out his left hand for the other drink. "I'm a two-fisted drinker."

"I knew that," Elliot said. "I doubt if Galatoire's has raki, but I'll try." He started in to get fresh drinks. "Anybody else need anything?"

"I've got two, thanks," said Graham grinning.

"Me," said Jane.

Elliot "pardoned me'd" through the line to the front where he waved the glasses as he pushed with his shoulder and waltzed in backwards for the drinks. Lilah watching him thought he was still the best looking man she'd ever seen, and tonight he was full of energy and a light touch, which made him especially attractive to her. She felt a constant grin on her face. She smiled at Jane, who was overwhelmed by the attention and gave back a misty, smiley look somewhere between tears and laughter. Lilah looked at her again. Jane had glanced down as she hung onto Graham's arm. Lilah wasn't sure what she'd seen there; she knew they'd been having some problems. Graham chased women and made no attempt to hide it. He'd tip any skirt, and Jane knew about most of them. Lilah was one of the few women of their acquaintance who hadn't had some sort of an affair with Graham. He specialized in one-night stands, and Lilah had come upon him at parties coming out of vacant bedrooms and once an upstairs powder room with a woman she knew.

"Lilah, what's this about Elliot changing his profession? He was raving on about becoming a tennis pro the other day at the club," Graham said.

"Don't be silly, Graham. I know Elliot loves tennis but he'd be the first one to tell you he's not up to a professional career. He's a good amateur. That's it."

"Yeah, that's what I told him, but he's talking about changing his life. I thought maybe you might have a clue."

"Graham, you could be a pro," Jane said.

"A little late, Sugar."

The Maitre'd called out "Gilbert party" and they went in to dinner.

"One of these days I'm going to give that old fart a big enough tip to get in without waiting," Graham said in a stage whisper, as they followed the Maitre'd to their table where Elliot was waiting with drinks.

"Become a tennis pro," Jane said.

"I don't think it matters how big a tip—you wait in line."

"They didn't have raki so I got you a Sazerac. It has that sort of flavor but it's red."

"The drink's fine. What's this about changing professions?"

Elliot's face changed from his lighthearted grin to an icy frown at Graham. "Thanks, friend," he said.

"I told her you were kidding," Graham said quickly.

The waiter laid napkins across their laps and offered each a menu. He said, "Let me tell you about our specials."

"Let's talk about this later," Elliot said.

"I want the Crab Yvonne," Jane said staring at the menu.

"I want to hear about this new job," Lilah continued without opening her menu.

The waiter standing behind her raised one eyebrow at the tone of her voice.

"Do you need more time to think about this?" he asked.

"I think so," Graham said politely and the waiter walked off with his little book.

"Look, kids, this is no place to discuss your life's work."

"You're right, of course. But this wouldn't have come up if you could keep things to yourself, Graham."

"You're right, Elliot. I apologize but I think you ought to fill your wife in on your plans."

"Lilah, we'll talk about this tomorrow. Right now let's try to make this a pleasant meal." Everyone became very busy reading the menu and deciding what to eat.

Graham ordered a bottle of some trendy California wine and the conversation took off on his choice, but except for

Jane's ability to ignore whatever was going on on a secondary level there was tension. Elliot motioned to the waiter to come back.

"I've changed my mind," Jane said to the waiter. "I'd like a Shrimp Remoulade, and Trout Marguery."

"You always have Trout Marguery," Graham said.

"Yes, but I always like it."

"Would you like a salad?"

"Yes, I'd like a Caesar Salad, and do you mix it here?"

"Of course."

"And what would you like?" he asked Lilah.

"I plan to drink," Lilah said.

Lilah didn't bring the matter up again until the next day at breakfast. They were sitting in the sun room. Lilah with her usual pear and toast, while Elliot cut away at a piece of black-ish-red blood sausage surrounded by a valley of grits filled with a tablespoon of melted butter. He relished each bite. She hated him when he ate things like blood sausage. She hated him for relishing every bite.

"Is that good?" she asked.

"Delicious. Moo fixed it the way I like it."

"I'm glad she likes to cook things the way you like them. What's this about becoming a tennis pro?"

"Who—who's becoming a tennis pro? Graham should. He's a lousy attorney."

"Graham says you are. That's what we were talking about last night."

"So much for communication. He misunderstood me. I said I was changing professions but I wasn't talking about tennis. I'm going to be a river pilot."

"That's even crazier. You're starting a new profession? Now?"

"Thanks for the vote of confidence."

"You haven't even bothered to discuss this with me. Don't you think I should have some say-so in such a drastic change in our lives?"

"Sometimes it's not easy to talk about things. Especially when you're working from some inner logic. I've always known the river was something special and mysterious but I've never had the nerve to go after it." He stumbled in his effort to make her see, and from his eyes Lilah knew he was shutting down on the subject. She always had trouble getting a fight out of Elliot. He'd shut down.

He went on slowly. My cousin and I used to play on the river at High Castle. Pilots were the most respected men in town. There were only two who ever lived there, and they moved to New Orleans because of piloting. But everybody talked about them. What they did. Where they went. Who they married. They were like master craftsmen. Running the Mississippi river is an art form. I want to be that good at something."

"How are you going to do this? I thought the association was closed to outsiders — don't you need to be someone's son? Do you have to go to school? Do I need to go back to work? Private schools are expensive. What do pilots make?"

"Their wages are comparable. You won't have to do without in the long run, but it's like going back to school. First, I have to get turns, a job, on a line boat, get a sponsor, get elected by a majority, and then a year at one hundred and fifty dollars a month for the length of the apprenticeship. That's if I pass the test. I think I can get it. I've got a sponsor."

"One hundred and fifty dollars a month. That won't pay our house note. Are you crazy? Why would you throw away a good career for something you don't even have a chance at. Do you think Moo's going to do some hocus-pocus and get you in or I'm going to change into Marie Laveau and make you a river pilot? What are we going to do while you're off on some boat — get welfare?

"I don't think you have anything to worry about." He was sitting in the shadow now, a colder part of the room. "We can live for six months on savings. I get the test results Friday, and I don't mind telling you it was the hardest test I've ever taken. I had to draw the river to scale from memory: Every pipeline, light, and electrical crossing on it. I don't think we have anything to discuss until we see if I've passed."

Lilah stood up suddenly, blood rising in her neck. She could feel it in the roots of her hair. As adrenaline shot into her bloodstream she wanted a fight.

But he didn't give her time to argue. He crossed the silver on his plate, got up, lifted his jacket off the back of the chair and went out, leaving Lilah with no one to fight with, and the feeling that she'd lost control of her life.

It was still dark. Lilah rolled over in the bed and noticed a pale light coming through the voile curtains. Elliot was a dark shape against the light. He was dressed.

"What time is it?"

"Early."

"Do you have to go?"

"Yes."

He sat down beside her and cupped his hand under her hair to lift her for a kiss. She leaned against him. They had been fighting ever since he'd told her about going on the river. Last night they'd had a farewell dinner—just the two of them, and the tension that had begun at Galatoire's threatened to make the evening miserable for them again. But somewhere during the meal, after many glasses of Chateauneuf de Pape, they had moved into the bedroom for the most intense physical expression of love since Haiti. There was no sexual play-acting involved, just a deep need to express feeling. Lilah ached at the thought of his leaving. He'd passed the test, and today was the day. The first day on a Mississippi river line boat. He'd be gone for a month.

"A lineboat doesn't stop for anything," he told her. "It comes in and gets emptied and heads back up North. All focus is on the river—whether the river is high or low—if there's traffic. The man with the least experience gets the worst sleeping hours. I'll be working my ass off, but I should be in good shape when I get back. It's a working job. I'll have to carry a thirty-five foot cable as much as a thousand feet. Every fleet has a landing signal." He was flushed with excitement. Lilah had never seen him this excited about any kind of job. "Ours is two shorts, a long, and three shorts. It tells them to get ready at the landing." A distance had set itself up within her. He would be gone a long time and far away.

He kept talking about the lineboat, a note of nervous excitement in his voice. "Lineboats carry anything: General cargo, containers, grain. Flanking is an art form. I can't wait to learn about flanking. Most marine engines, when you go astern only have forty percent power. A lineboat has eighty percent. Long tows couldn't turn—their turning radius won't allow it if you don't flank. So what happens? They stop the tow above the point on the point side—at night that's hard to tell. They have work lights—and a painted white can floating on a line which shows them headway, sternway, or dead in the water. The object is to stop above the point, then nudge the bow out into the current, and since the stern is in slack water—what they call duck water—it pivots you. Takes about twenty to thirty minutes to do that. You just keep backing on the point engine and pushing on the bend engine, and she comes around."

"Will you do that?"

"No, I'm going to be the working stiff, but I get lots of hours on the bridge with the pilot. I need twenty trips on the bridge before they'll even consider me a candidate. I have to go," he said.

"How long will you be gone?" she asked, although she knew when he would come back. It would be November. Too late for Thanksgiving.

"Thirty days and then I'll be in for ten."

"I don't know why...."

"No," he said and stopped her with his fingers across her lips. He left then. She couldn't see his face well enough to know his expression, and she felt a quick rush of tears to her nose and eyes. The bedroom door closed with a soft click, and she felt afraid—afraid she might never see him again. The river was full of danger and darkness. She'd never felt any of that when he went to a law office.

Apprentice

AT BURNSIDE THE RIVER WAS DARK AND MOVING.
Elliot could feel it there behind him as he picked up his pilot's
bag from the back seat of the Belle Chasse car. From the top of
the levee he could see the flooded batture, and boils working
against the slick surface like small rutting animals under a silk
sheet. He heard a car door slam and a man got out of a car on
the shore side of the levee. The office had said to meet the pilot
at Burnside. Elliot was dead tired when he got the call—three
hours of sleep isn't enough for anybody. It was two o'clock
in the morning and Elliot didn't want to go, but he had dis-
covered that pilots and apprentices were always hungry for
sleep. Sleep had become his priority. The other man hitched
his radio, hooked it to his belt to ride his hip at the proper
angle, slung his pilot bag over one shoulder and strode out to
the launch rocking the dock. Elliot raced after him and at the
last minute jumped the two-foot space of black water to ride

out to the ship. Now the pilot looked at him and Elliot knew what he was thinking from his limited experience with other pilots. He was thinking Elliot looked like a company man—an executive. Elliot had been at pains not to look that way, but something in his manner remained Tulane lawyer. Elliot shouted his name and the other man, who shook his head as if he didn't understand or want to understand over the sound of the launch's engine.

Elliot leaned over and stuck out his right hand while holding onto the rail on the gunnel of the boat with his left. The pilot shook his hand cautiously. After a five-minute ride the launch came upon a dark mountain which leaned out over the boat. The driver flipped the launch directly under the pilot ladder and the pilot motioned for Elliot to go up first. He stepped on like he'd been up before—grabbed both sides of the ladder—not a rung at a time, which might have thrown him into the mouth between the ship and the launch if the ladder had broken. Ladders often broke. If a pilot was lost over the side the family and the insurance company waited months for the body to surface—a naked floater, miles away. There was something terrible about the way the river ate the clothes off a man.

They stepped on deck. The pilot headed up to the next ladder, and, taking a deep breath, began to run up the six decks pretty good, but when they finally got to the bridge they were both winded. The pilot because he was forty-five years old and getting a little tired, and Elliot because he didn't do this every morning for breakfast. The young mate came up to the pilot and asked him for his name for the bell book. Still out of breath, he said, "Jack Hawley" between huffs and gasps for air, but the mate didn't know how to spell Hawley, so the pilot went through it a letter at a time between breaths.

Jack shook hands with the captain, a short, hard-nosed Norwegian who stuck around for awhile to see how competent the new pilot was. Elliot shook hands with him, and introduced himself. The pilot he'd gotten on board with looked glad to hear the name because he didn't catch it at the launch boat. The pilot Jack relieved shook hands all around and gave Jack the skinny on the ship. "She's making eleven. There's a lineboat, The Charles E. Peters flanking Sugar House Point. Your E.T.A. in Red Stick is 9 a.m. in the Harbor. She handles pretty good, but you need to stay in the current streak. The Peters asked us to hold below the point. I don't know how many barges she's got, but the captain's nervous. Have a good one."

Jack Hawley switched on his radio and announced his position," N.O.B.R.A. 81, Northbound, Burnside Anchorage coming up on Sunshine Bridge." The orders he gave to the mate were in English so there'd be no confusion on his part. The mate repeated them to the helmsman who said them again. He said to Elliot, "Something's developing. There's a lineboat Northbound under the point. This is a seventy-thousand-ton ship and it's high river. Hold on, Elliot, we're going to button and unbutton our assholes just like trying on a new suit of clothes, and the Peters is going to get on the radio asking us to hold up. *Roger, Cap, take what you need. I'll work off you. Slow up under Houmas Point. I'll stick to one whistle and let you travel where you want.* Let's give him the river." Elliot watched the Peters' searchlight slowly scanning the bank. "Coonass radar," Jack called it, and the lineboat glided past. The Peters comes on the radio again, and says, "Thanks, Captain Hawley. Why didn't you tell me you had a big one?"

Jack can't hear him. Says, "Sorry Captain. You're coming in broken up."

Elliot finally said something. "He didn't have twenty-five barges—sixteen I counted. Did he need all that room?

"Maybe not, but some people get nervous. They always think that what they've got is worse than what you've got. So you let them have the river. On the river you always let a man have what he says he needs." After they made the point and traffic slowed down, the master of the ship, who had been standing around watching Jack's every move, said, "Mr. Pilot, I leave her to you," and went below.

Jack said, "Mr. Mate, how about some coffee for us? "He said to Elliot, "I guess we've got time to shoot the shit. Things aren't so hairy now. You asked a pretty intelligent question there — better than most. Sometimes apprentices are underfoot worse than terriers. Ask dumb questions like 'Isn't it better to run in fog without the radio?' I usually tell them to go to Vietnam if they want brave and stupid. The idea on the river being to get there with the cargo intact and everyone still alive. Who're you related to, Elliot?"

"Not anybody on the river."

Jack stepped back and took a good look at the apprentice. "Is that so? I don't know how you got in. I don't remember voting for you. Relatives have been the rule on the river since before I got in. I believe in it and I don't believe in it. I'd like my kid to get a good job out here if he wants it, but my kid's pretty smart and not interested. He'll probably do a good job anywhere. Some of these kids can't parallel park a VW, but Daddy gets them out here and makes sure they learn how to be pilots."

"They can't be too stupid. I had trouble with the test — a week long — eight hours a day. Draw the river to scale — free-hand." Elliot's voice had an indignant note.

"Trouble with most apprentices these days — they're not hungry. Daddy gets them right out of that warm, soft bed — gets them out here on the river to park a sixty-thousand-ton ship. You ever see a twenty-five-year-old man with white hair? We've got one in the pilots. You've got balls to get in if you're not related. It's not easy even if you are. You still have to have the trips and pass the test. But if you're not related you must have something going for you? What is it?"

"It's something I've always wanted."

"Hell, that's something, but that's not enough. I've known guys who did everything right — passed the test, got the turns, kissed ass and mowed lawns for pilots, and still didn't get in because somebody with a block of proxies didn't like the way he combed his hair."

"I was brought up on the river. Watched the ships — swam in it with my cousin. She's the one wanted it first."

"No women. We'll have blacks before we have women."

"There are two things I've always wanted—being a pilot is one of them."

"Who's your sponsor?"

"Captain Turner."

"Good man, Captain Turner. He came up from the push boats, didn't he?"

"Yes, Sir."

"You take your turns there."

"No, I didn't come up from the push boats. I did some legal work for Captain Turner, and we started talking about the river. I rode with his son-in-law on a lineboat to get my turns. I came up from the Tulane law school." He laughed when he said it.

"You got a wife?"

"Yes."

"Kids?"

"Two—boy and a girl."

"Hell, Elliot, you got it all. How'd she take this piloting business?"

"Not too well. She can't see us living on a hundred and fifty a month for a year, and she thinks attorneys are more socially acceptable."

"She's right about that, but wait until the real paycheck starts rolling in. She'll warm up quick."

"I doubt that, but I hope so. Right now I don't like to go home."

"Who does? After you've been out here—gotten a taste of real life—who wants to go home?"

"It all depends on who's there."

"Well, I tell you one thing, Elliot, you keep your eyes open or you might get a chance to use all your legal skills to get yourself off the levee one of these days."

"Aren't we coming up on High Castle?"

"We are. Look sharp. There's hospital point—Carville. Where the lepers live." Jack spoke again sharply to wake him. "The lepers live there."

"Yes, I know." The apprentice kept staring at the bank

where the long, low Panama-style buildings of the leper colony shone through the cedar trees.

"You're looking up on Point Clair. It's important not to meet traffic on the point — now you're going to see her. Three hundred and sixty-five openings — doors and windows — one for each day of the year."

"Nottaway?"

"There she is. White as a government building and twice as big. Biggest plantation house anywhere — been there a hundred years. A lot of them houses done gone pecan."

"High Castle's my home town. My grandmother's house used to be there — where those lights are. Right there — this side of Nottaway. But that's all gone now. By river you realize how far New Orleans is from High Castle. How everything comes in on the river. How it's all still in your bloodstream like the river."

The ship passed on — past the tow head, past Nottaway — in a blur of commands: "Port five, port ten, midship." The helmsman silent except when he repeated: "Port five, port ten, midship." There were long stretches of river where silence reigned. And Elliot's dreams of Camilla's attic room, and the attic were more real than the river. He didn't know how much he'd learned about piloting, but he'd learned High Castle was never behind him. They docked in Baton Rouge eight hours from the time they'd left Burnside — by river — seventeen hours from New Orleans.

Driving back East with the sun in his eyes — Elliot wanted to talk. He was still high from adrenalin. He wanted to talk about the trip and the docking where men on bicycles — fifteen arrogant, slow guys on old balloon-tire bicycles rode up and down a tremendous dock tying up the ship.

"They were pretty slow tying up."

"That's a bicycle graveyard, slowest dock on the river."

"I don't know how you managed to keep your cool with that guy on the radio who was getting you to move the ship twenty feet forward, a foot at a time."

"I don't have the energy left to get mad — mad takes energy. Talk takes energy, and I'm tired, Elliot. Bone weary. I'm going to snooze now, Elliot, and I'd advise you to sleep while you can, because we're going to be back out here quick. There's a lot of traffic out there, and one of them's for us." He settled back against the pillow in the corner of the car. Elliot couldn't think of sleep.

The light flooding Elliot's senses was golden, pink — part of the sky blue, as they rode toward New Orleans he felt alive — tuned into color, sensitized as if he'd been smoking — higher than he'd ever been. Later, as they came in, he could see across the city in the distance, a thick vertical rainbow of green, yellow, pink — thick but softly melting like a stick candy that had been in the mouth too long.

The clouds above were languorous grey — downy. To the left of the rainbow, the sky was a paler grey, almost white, extending in oblique waves to the cloud, and suddenly he realized — over there — where the colors were — it was raining. But here, embracing his vision was a bowl of splendid light which lit each tree and blade of grass to its most vivid hue. And before him — billows and sweeps of clouds always — some of the sky — blue.

Parade

ELLIOT WALKED OUT OF THE PILOTS' OFFICE ON Canal Street. The conversation he'd had with Captain Sam Darrow filled his mind, and he couldn't help thinking they were talking about two separate professions. When he spoke of the river, Elliot felt as if a powerful force had redirected his life; Sam spoke of good turns and bad turns, and whether or not the pilots would get their raises from the steamship association. The elevator descended, Elliot walked out into the chilly October afternoon; he wondered if his idealism was a protracted adolescence which made him think in more romantic terms than other men or if his idealism was born of some innate gift for piloting the river, as much an art as music or poetry. He had to laugh at himself at that thought. He realized he'd been on the river long enough to develop a pilot's inflated ego. The variables of the job excited him.

He'd described it once to Lilah: "Pretend you're driving

a car that weighs eighty thousand tons on I-10 at rush hour, but you don't really know how to drive, all you know how to do is steer, and you don't have any brakes, and you have to coast the red lights, but you've got me sitting next to you, who knows how to do all those things and I'm telling you how to do it—so you're the helmsman and I'm the pilot."

"That sounds more like the kind of thing twenty-year-old males play on the highway. You're now in a macho profession that bears a distinct relationship to chicken. Teenagers play chicken."

"Hardly. Piloting depends on a cool head and good judgment."

"If you had good judgment, you wouldn't get into anything without brakes to coast to red lights." He gave up trying to explain it to her, and she never rode on ships with him. It didn't matter. His life on the river had nothing to do with her. Ships from other countries were like time capsules carrying mysterious and different time. Each meal that he ate on a ship was another cuisine, another sustenance, even the meal he'd once been brought: Two slices of white bread with lettuce slapped on and bloodied with catsup. He'd been a pilot for a year now. Each turn brought him stage fright, death fright, and a tremendous sense of being up, on top of something which took every brain and nerve cell he possessed to get it right. Alive in the most real sense of the word.

Canal Street was filled with people. They congregated on the curbs and looked up the street with a curious air of carnival expectancy. They were waiting for a parade. A list of holidays and occasions ran through his mind—not Mardi Gras—it was the end of October—not the Shriners. He had parked his car in Holmes garage on the opposite side of Canal. He wouldn't be able to get out anyway. From the size of the crowd he figured the parade was close enough to wait for, and he was prepared to spend a pleasant half hour listening to marching bands. A parade was as much a part of the climate as rain.

He didn't ask the woman waving a small green pennant what or who was parading, that would soon be revealed. His mind still revolved around the conversation and his own image of the river—what pleasure he knew standing on the wharf at Governor Nichols and watching the big ships pass, each ship describing its own path, coming in shape or sliding broadside according to tonnage, steerage, the height of the river and the skill of the pilot, and knowing that he could do it.

In the distance he could hear the weak bleat of sirens, as the crowd moved restlessly around him, but he still kept to his own mind, and paid little attention to the surge forward as two police cars with flashing lights passed, a sure sign the parade was coming. It was some time after the police cars, a gap in the distancing of vehicles, before a utility truck passed measuring for clearance, which meant there was something in the parade as high as a float. A high school band from Crowley, La., passed. There were sixteen drum majorettes in white satin jumpsuits with polar bear shakos. Tassels on their white boots stamped and tossed with every step. The band was playing the "Washington Post March," and Elliot was surprised to find himself grinning with pleasure.

A long stretch of police on motorcycles passed. So Busteaux placards were being held up in the crowd; it was then it dawned on him: So Busteaux was up for re-election.

In his own preoccupation as a new pilot—his intensity toward his goal as best pilot on the river, he had forgotten that, because of the scandals of the past four years there was some speculation So Busteaux would fail—the other man win. To Elliot there was no real contest—So Busteaux would be governor for another four years and then, in the tradition of Louisiana governors, select his own successor.

Elliot's cool evaluation of Busteaux's chances had little to do with Camilla Jane. After his fall—the fall from the bicycle so many years ago, the summer of *Les Fleurs du Mal*—he had never been jealous of So Busteaux or drunk Jack Daniels daily. In his own mind it was as if she'd never married. Soltice Busteaux was not the power who kept her from him, just as he never thought of Camilla and So's marriage to her as an impediment or his own feelings as duplicity. His relationship to Camilla Jane was so fixed and inviolable, any other contracts that either of them had entered into were null and void in the light of the original contract. The only obstacle which ever arose was Camilla Jane, her desire to have some power over the disposition of her own life. There was a common thread which ran through them as vital, basic, and unromantic as the dark vein in the transparent flesh of a raw shrimp. She was his cousin, almost all that was left of their family. Whatever other relationships either of them entered into were extraneous and unimportant, and what they knew of both worlds kept them riding on a current like a cushion or air between what passed in the real world as powerful and what they knew from their own past as powerful. And when they were drawn together to press their mouths upon each other it was an affirmation of the past and present, as whole and sealed, and had nothing to do with their other lives. It was physical and it was spiritual like the river.

The convertible carrying Soltice Busteaux approached so slowly as to appear barely moving. The band walked a slow drag as they would at a funeral, but instead of playing a sad song, they played "Gotta Go For So Busteaux" in double time, while walking slowly—a time distortion. Rows of helmeted police rode motorcycles on either side of the car. They managed to keep upright in a military formation in spite of the slow procession. Their yellow Cadillac convertible held three men in the front seat, the driver in shirtsleeves wearing a red tie, the other two men in suits. In the back seat stood Soltice Busteaux, two men crouched below him holding his feet steady. Gargantuan now, his face reminded Elliot of *Le Boeuf Gras*, the papier maché figure that rode, turning its huge head from side to side, illuminated by the distorting flames of the flambeaux, before the Krewe of Proteus at Carnival. Time had altered the handsome lady-pleaser of Camilla's party beyond recognition.

There was something over-ripe about him now; a grey

suit, seamless as a balloon parted around his belly; his white shirt wrinkled under the figured tie. He held a straw hat in his right hand, which he waved up and down at the crowd in a monotonous motion. He didn't smile and his lips were large, petulant, and red. The crowd surged against the motorcycles, and one cyclist appeared to lose his balance as he put one foot to the ground to hold the heavy bike upright. As the crowd shouted and waved, the governor's mouth opened, and his expression of open-mouthed pleasure might have seemed foolish in a less powerful man. His eyes arrested any speculation on the rest of his physique; they were light eyes, but Elliot thought the white surface of the eyeball to be larger than ordinary, sculptural. As he swung his great, cow eyes back and forth like the head of *Le Boeuf Gras* Elliot looked away from the Dionysian figure with a certain disgust, and he realized with a start that the small figure behind Soltice on the top of the back seat was Camilla Jane. Her white, gloved left hand waved as mechanically as any carnival Queen. Her arms were covered to the elbow, each wrist fragile as a crystal stem. The motorcycles rode between her and the crowd — arms reaching out to her, threatening in their multiplicity and their obvious urge to touch. She passed within a few feet of Elliot, but didn't see him. Her eyes had a distant look, an obvious glaze, as if she didn't see anyone or want to see anyone. Her smile was fixed. Elliot recognized the expression.

As children in High Castle, they'd been required to attend mass at the Catholic church each Sunday. Whenever Camilla Jane was ordered by her mother to do something she didn't believe in or didn't value, she'd put her eyes out of focus — wouldn't see. Originally, it was the product of a slight myopia, but as she became more displeased with certain aspects of her world, she would do what she called "going blind." She would deliberately not see what she couldn't change. In order to protect her from Aunt Mag's righteous wrath, Took had arranged for Elliot to lead her. He would keep her as far from her mother as possible when she was "going blind." He would lead her up the steps of the church and guide her into the pew, keeping her at all times just far enough away so Aunt Mag wouldn't recognize her willfulness, but would know she was there in body.

Took and Moo sat in the side pews of the church reserved for the black parishioners but away from the family. Camilla Jane would not accept their position since it separated her from Took. As a small child she had cried through the whole service, years of subterfuge had pressed Elliot into service at an early age. Aunt Mag's absolute dedication to the church was born not of conviction, but of a passionate desire to lead, and she led the ladies of the altar society to glories of decoration. The altar was a mogul's garden of lilies and gladioli banked upon cutwork of the finest linen. The parish priest was a soft-handed, moderately intelligent man deified by the iron whim of Aunt Magdalen into a holy prince of the church.

Camilla sat as she was supposed to with the family near the front of the church while her mother performed miracles of discipline and leadership in the interest of the altar society where she ordered around women who tended the vestments in the sacristy. In the general congregation, it was whispered that Camilla Jane Maynard had a slight affliction of the eyes, but no one would ever have brought up the subject of such an affliction to the girl's mother; instead they often prayed for her rather than themselves.

Camilla Jane attended the convent, but she didn't like nuns, except for one, Sister Matilda, and she didn't like Father Godine, the pet and confidante of her mother. She would not deny Catholicism, but accepted it as only one part of her religion, as she accepted Aunt Mag as only one of her mothers, and if pressed would have said the one she liked the least; Took had reared her, and Took had time for her.

When Camilla Jane married So Busteaux, Elliot had not attended the wedding, which was huge and formal. Today, as Elliot watched her pass in the car, he imagined her walking down the aisle in Baton Rouge with this same zombied expression, her face hidden under a veil of Alençon lace. In spite of his own seeming indifference to her marriage, he felt a wave of happiness overwhelm him, as he imagined her walking through the ceremony — blind. As the dreamlike parade passed he found himself peering into her face. It had been a long time since he'd taken coffee to her room and made her tell him about High John.

In broad daylight now, he saw her passing before him riding beside So Busteaux in her role as governor's wife. Blind — that he'd seen already, but as he studied her he noticed her hair, the mass of silky wire which leapt from her head in it's own magnetic field of crackling energy, combed now in soft waves, and the palpable thickness or her skin was less dense, as if she'd been slightly worn away, still beautiful, but less contained than the woman painted by Corot who always reminded him of Camilla. The painting was now more the girl he remembered than this distant woman. Foreign as she was — as far as she had removed herself — she appeared more vulnerable than he'd ever seen her, slightly bruised like the skin of a Cape Jasmine on the second day. If anything, more beautiful — beautiful had not been the word before. He'd always thought of Camilla Jane when he thought of life — a leaping and whirling of dancers, a chase after lightning bugs in the evening grass, of swinging as high as the swing would go then dropping into deep green water, or his own body coming alive in his hand as he thought of her. She had been to his body as it was connected to spirit — the child's spirit which is connected to body in a simple and pure way. Without that connection the body was nothing and the spirit gone. He looked at her and felt a pull of his inner being to the surface of his skin, as if all nerves were moving to the outer layer of flesh. He'd waited too long — it was a terrible hurt — as if he hadn't gone to see Moo and she'd died. He had allowed his adolescence to drag on into his thirties, rejected his place by passive resistance. This had left him too weak to act when the time came. Camilla Jane, who had been to him the epitome of the body inhabited and loved by the spirit, had somehow lost light. She was wearing out young. It was important for him to find his true place so that he could save her. He could do this on the river. He would become the ship and the river would be his life; he could offer this to her as that power over the unknown she had always longed for, and he could do it without High John. As the parade passed he felt it had all gone on too long; he wished she could pilot a ship, steady up on something solid and sure. As the last band filed by, the drum majorettes dragged their feet, and only one boy kept the beat with a large padded stick on a muffled drum.

As Elliot turned to go back to his car, he spotted Captain Sam Darrow, standing at the light. Darrow's sloped shoulders straightened as he saw Elliot and he gave a crooked smile. "Good," he said. "Hey, Elliot, there was one more thing I wanted to tell you about piloting." Elliot walked over to him. "What you've got to watch for are sharpshooters on your watch. Guys who are in front of you, but give their time of arrival behind you. It means you get the shit end of the stick. It means he goes down on the books after you, and when you get a Baton Rouge turn you're out all night while he's in bed with his wife or somebody else's. Just a word of warning, bud-dy—just a word of warning." He waved and walked on. Elliot crossed Canal Street on an angle, wading through stragglers from the parade to get to his car.

It was the same week as the parade that Elliot got a letter from Camilla Jane. The letterhead read: DePaul Hospital, New Orleans, La. But it was dated January 27, 1965. It had arrived ten months late. It read:

Dear Elliot,

It's very cold here. January is a terrible month; my bones are cold and aching. I thought today how we swam naked in the bayou, how warm it was. The water a dark greenish-brown—no way to see the bottom. We had to trust ourselves. The bayou wasn't as wide as the river, but you were afraid to swim across because you thought a snapping

turtle might get your bird. I told you your
bird wasn't big enough for a turtle to notice
yet. I didn't have a bird so I wasn't afraid.
I was so much stronger than you then—I
swam and you followed. I even swam out to
the tow-head in the river alone, sat there
in the sand by the willows all afternoon
and watched ships. I thought I could do
anything. How things change.

Somebody—I can't think who, said you're
married and have kids. Good for you. I had
a baby, but lost him. I feel more alone now
than ever before, while the psychiatrist tries
to patch up my nervous system. There's
no remembering how you were—only bits
and pieces like us in the bayou—me on the
river. Nothing useful for my present life.
The psychiatrist doesn't remember anything
so he tries to make a new me. The old one
got smashed. He says, "This is the way you
were—no, on the other hand, you must
have been like this."

So is very sweet. He plays bourré with
me and a couple of friends here—lets me
win—I'm getting very rich. It shows how
much he loves me—So never let's anyone
win. I had to get sick to beat him. Elliot,
I loved seeing you that time by Moo. Moo
still hates me. I even felt good about that—
made me feel sassy and full of myself the
way I used to be. I told you I'd get sick if I
ever left home—I didn't know how far I was
going or how sick I'd get. I've still got my
High John, but he's lost a lot of strength. I
hope to get out of here soon, maybe we can
get together for a little soul search.

All my love, your cousin, Camilla Jane.

p.s. I'm sick of T.V. First it was sit-ins—I
wish Took had sat in at mass—wouldn't
that have fractured Mag—now it's war
every day, and me right there. So doesn't
watch it, says he can't keep up with the
miserable people in Louisiana much less take
on a bunch of miserable people in another
country. He says he's got to stay focused.
Nobody else here mentions it—the doctors
all seem to think what's on T.V; is normal,
I'm the one who's sick—except one nurse
who's husband is over there. Sometimes I
think I'm the only person who thinks about
certain things, but I remember you always
did think about those things too, like the
time we bought the starving Chinese babies
who were going to be baptized and named
after us. They've probably blown them up—
blown up little Camilla Jane and little Elliot.
These babies on T.V. are Vietnamese, but
they look Chinese. I don't think our country
should blow up babies. I'd love to have a
little baby. So says he'll take care of that
after he gets Louisiana straight—that's bull.
So's a little off the track, and I'm not up to
getting him back on it. Maybe next week.

p.p.s. Mag got married. A Mr. Dawson
who is a contract bridge whiz. They travel
all over playing bridge. She's been here
once. She said, "All you do is feel sorry for
yourself. No matter how good you've got
it you still want more." I said, "I sure do."
And she left.

Little Rum Boogie

LILAH PARKED ON NORTH RAMPART STREET AND walked over to St. Philip. Monday's paper lay on the step. Lilah picked it up for Lane who was off Mondays and slept in. She stopped for a moment to look down the street. It all looked the same—Johnny Matassa's bar still on the corner, a convenience they'd all needed in the years past—cars parked bumper to bumper down St. Philip Street, a fact of life in the Quarter, which left all but automobile fanatics without cars.

Lilah opened the iron gate with her own key and walked down the gangway, a moist, green passage, like being under-water, a feeling most French Quarter alleys retained on even the hottest day in July. English Ivy grew over the wall to the next patio and Lilah noticed tumescent salmon-pink brome-liad stuck into the masonry like a brilliant anemone on coral. She remembered the first night she'd come through this alley as she walked into the patio and came in through the open kitchen door.

Coffee beans she'd bought at Langenstein's were quickly poured into Lane's old coffee grinder, and ground while the water boiled for slow-drip coffee in the white enamel coffee pot. She poured the first tablespoons of boiling water through the coffee in the top of the pot.

"Coffee?" called a voice from the other room as the aroma drifted through the apartment. Lilah didn't answer, but poured a demitasse of black chicory coffee into a small, thick cup—put nothing in it, and carried it to Lane in the next room. Holding the cup out near the head of the bed, she peered at the bed clothes. Lane pulled her head and neck out of the rumpled covers; she looked like a small, sick chicken. Her short hair stuck out. The bags under her eyes packed for a weekend trip.

"You look like hell," said Lilah.

"Thanks. Sorry I can't say the same. You look pretty good. Hand me my cigarettes." She coughed hoarsely three times, and lit a Benson and Hedges from the pack Lilah threw at her. Lilah went back into the kitchen to lace her own coffee with hot milk. She came back to settle down cross-legged in a full lotus on the blond leather sofa, pushing crumpled newspapers and magazines to one side in order to make room for herself on one end of the couch.

"Jesus, how can you do that so Goddamn early in the morning?" Lane's voice had a petulant edge. "My legs feel like ancient toothpicks left over at the bottom of last summer's picnic basket. I don't know if I like you visiting so damn early in the morning. You're too damn healthy."

"Healthy is as healthy does."

"Tell me about it," Lane said as she shook three pills into her left hand, threw them back, and chased them down with chicory coffee. "That sure is profound."

Lilah watched without comment. "Elliot's got another woman," she said.

"How do you know?"

"You know."

"Oh, yeah. They're all the same. Ben was so junked up he couldn't get a hard-on at home, but he'd go out and find some barmaid and screw her all night. Come rolling home at 6 a.m. and sit up writing pornographic sonnets in honor of her tits — with illustrations, yet. Then he'd expect me to edit for him when I got home from work."

"Are you going to go on the ski trip for Mardi Gras this year?"

"Hell, yes. Where else can I get warm in February. This apartment's colder than a witch's tit that time of year. The walls drip water and the street is full of beer cans and tourists. I can curl up in the lodge in front of a log fire and get toasted on brandy."

"Elliot doesn't want to go. Captain Turner wants somebody to work for him so he can go to Arkansas, and Elliot says he has to do it since Turner sponsored him as a pilot. I think he's going somewhere with her."

"Who is she?"

"I don't know. Probably one of the women at the Pilot Station in Baton Rouge. There are a bunch of women who hang out around the lounge and shack up with pilots."

"Come on, Lilah. Captain Ice-Blood, the young hawk? I don't believe it. The one thing I can tell you about Elliot, and believe me it's all I know — he's particular."

"That's right — he is. But piloting's a crazy profession — power, adrenalin shots of danger in the bloodstream — exhausting, insane hours — most of them seek some outlet — some sort of blow off. They's professionals and dead serious about the work, but after work — that's another story."

"In other words, he's no Kaleb — there are no explosive works of art?"

"No — definitely no Kaleb, but he's plugged into a socket with some kind of power we can't even dream of."

"So — no master works of any kind — hobbies?"

"No, but you don't see pilots doing much in the master works category. There's something different with him. He's got a power leak somewhere. But it's not an obvious one —

something very secretive."

"What are you going to do?"

"Nothing — unless he wants to divorce me and marry her."

"Do you love him?"

"Of course I love him. He's the father of my children, and when he gets around to me, he's a fantastic lover, but I don't know him. I never met his mother or his grandmother; they were dead before I came along. He thinks Moo is his mother. Elliot is the most mysterious man I've known in my life, and that's probably why I married him."

"I always wondered why."

"Listen, Lane, you're in no position to wonder why anybody marries anybody. Ben was hardly Mr. Right Guy. He's been dead for two years and you haven't looked at anybody since. Women start off looking for a father, a mother or an alter ego, and end up with an adversary. I got lucky. Elliot isn't an adversary. He's mysterious, but he's my friend, and I'm damn lucky to be married to a friend."

"Must be boring as hell."

"A boring man would have stayed a tax attorney all his life. God, I think it's sick the way women trivialize men no matter what they're doing. He's been moving all the time — all that volunteer work for five years keeping guys like Ben out of jail, and now the river..."

"I never trivialize Ben. He was lots of mixed up things, but he wasn't trivial. Elliot wants control. He's a pilot because it's about as close to being God as he or anybody else is going to get. All that power under his feet, between his legs — 80,000 – 100,000 tons — the ultimate motorcycle on the ultimate highway. He could wipe out New Orleans with a light tanker."

"Let's get this straight, Lane. I can talk about Elliot. I can curse him — call him every kind of son-of-a-bitch in the book, but I don't appreciate when anyone else does, particularly not my best friend. Come on — get up. Let's go. Elliot doesn't want to wipe out New Orleans. Another minute of this, and we'll both be basket cases. Let's go check out the honky-tonks in Pierre Part. I've got the jeep. Mrs. Heywood is going to pick up the kids and take them to her house. I told her I'd be back about six. All I want to do is dance with somebody I don't know — be single for an hour or two. And I want to go with you because you're not going to talk about me tomorrow — you're not going to run down my husband — and you're not going to try to steal him, while I'm uncertain about what I'm going to do, and I know what I'm talking about because you're my friend."

"Hallelujah, Sassy Ass, let's go."

Lilah and Lane were sitting at a table spread with newspapers eating crayfish out of a Dixie beer case in a place called Little Rum Boogie. Lilah could look out the door and see the bayou. "Jolie Blonde" was playing on the juke box and Cajun French was being tossed back and forth at the bar by a middle-aged woman with dark, soulful eyes and no makeup; two young men leaned their narrow blue-jeaned hips against the bar while hanging over it on one elbow, getting as near the barmaid as possible without climbing into her lap.

"They look like a couple of book-ends," Lilah said to Lane who had her eyes downcast on the pile of red crayfish in front of her. Lane looked up over her glasses which had slid down her nose. "You must be horny as hell to be checking that out."

Lilah ignored the remark and continued to watch the goings on at the bar. One of the men was only about nineteen, the other somewhere around thirty-five. The jeans on both were worn to a light blue, but a general dark greasiness spread around the pocket seams. Lilah imagined they were oil-field workers, although she didn't know if there was an oil field nearby. "Do you think they work in an oil field?"

"Who knows — lots of oil in Louisiana. Wish I had some." Lane took a swig off her Dixie.

Lilah liked looking at them. They both wore straw cowboy hats pushed to the back of their heads. The younger one had very curly, black hair that dipped down his forehead. Every few minutes he would turn around quick, lean back on the bar, push his hat back and stare at Lilah and Lane. Lane looked right through him. She leaned her straight-backed chair away from the crayfish, braced against a green sheetrock wall under a Dixie beer light. Her thong sandals rested on the top rung.

Lilah had a large pile of rusty crayfish shells in front of her and kept reaching in the beer case for more. Two half-empty bottles of Bud stood guard over her stack of shells. Grabbing a handful of crayfish out of the beer case, she selected the largest one, a big old man with a reddish, black shell; breaking his claws off first, she laid them in a neat pile she was saving on her left. Pulling the head off next, she put it into her mouth and shoved her tongue into the cave of the shell, sucking out the hot, yellow fat. Tossing the head with the other shells, she turned her attention to the body. With her left hand she peeled as she went down the side of the shell toward the tail. A quick squeeze on the tail gave her the tail meat in one neat piece. She didn't eat the claws, but left them piled up to eat later. Occasionally, she would peel a crayfish in a lazy gesture, pass it to Lane, who would eat it without comment.

A man came into the bar, tipping his hat to the barmaid, "*ça va?*" he said to the two men, without emotion. Lilah couldn't tell if he knew them or not. His hair was dark, and he had a reddish, leathery tan that left a strip of white at the back of his neck near his collar. Lilah found herself looking at the way his jeans wrinkled at the top of his leg and noticing that he wore a black shirt. He looked heavy in his jeans but not fat. He was tall enough. Carrying his beer bottle in his left hand, he walked over to the jukebox with the deliberate movements of a high school quarterback. He put in a bunch of change and punched buttons with one neat bang of his fist, a gesture she'd never seen before. She knew he was used to women watching him.

Hank Williams' voice came out of the jukebox singing "Hey, Good Looking." The man sat down at the table directly across from Lilah with his back to the bayou. He stared squarely at her face, then took a heavy slug of his beer.

Lane looked at Lilah and said, "I think you've made a

friend."

Lilah said, "I think I need a friend."

"Well, you'd better decide what you're going to do with him before he comes over."

Lilah continued to eat crayfish, but found herself changing her technique. She would break off the head and throw it onto the pile of shells, quickly peel the body, but not eat until their were five pieces, then she'd eat them slowly, chewing deliberately. She straightened her back and closed her knees and the man continued to stare.

She got up from the table and walked slowly over to the lavatory which was available in the corner of the room for customers to wash their hands. She squirted soap into her palm from the dispenser, ran water over her hands, and dried them on a paper towel. She could feel his eyes on her back through the whole operation. As she walked back to her place, she looked directly into his face and narrowed her eyes. He had a slight cast to one eye. He lifted his eyebrow over that eye. She felt a little weakness in her knees. Lane grunted a funny little laugh and took another swig off her beer as Lilah sat down.

After a few minutes, he came over and asked her to dance. She didn't know the song. It was French, and the only expression she recognized was *ma coeur*, which was repeated many times in the song. The man was a smooth dancer. Holding her left arm behind her, he moved her through the quick patterns of the cajun two step, as if they danced together every Saturday night. He smelled faintly of diesel oil and some kind of shaving lotion. She knew she smelled too — a combination of sweat, crayfish fat, and Aphrodisia, the incongruity of the smells made her feel sexy and desirable. She imagined that the rough material of his jeans, as he brushed against her leg, was an extension of his body and his desire for her, but there was no indication in his good eye or in his manner. She had no surge of sexual feeling toward him, only a general sense of sensual well-being like the feeling after swimming hard in a cool pool on a hot day. A sense of the good stuff of her body.

After the song ended, he took her back to her seat, pulled

out her chair for her and bowed slightly. "*Merci beaucoup*," he said and went back to his own table.

Lane said, "Do you want to pursue this avenue of self-expression or do you want to get out of here?"

"Let's go home," Lilah said.

Lane pushed the glass door toward the bayou and walked out onto the white shell parking lot. Lilah trailed behind. Before she stepped out, she gave a smile and a little wave of her hand toward the man drinking beer alone at his table in the corner. *Ça va*," he said.

Lilah picked the kids up from Mrs. Heywood who was angry with her because she left them so long. She charged Lilah double time for every hour after six p.m. It was nearly ten thirty by the time Lilah let herself into the kitchen door. Both kids were asleep in the car. Elise was draped over her shoulder and carried in first, as Lilah shielded her eyes from the kitchen light with the blanket. Afraid to leave Davis sleeping in the car while she took the baby upstairs, Lilah left the back door wide open, which made her feel even more vulnerable as she laid Elise down on the floor next to the couch in the living room while she went back to get Davis. No longer a little boy, he was heavy. She slammed the door with her foot as she came in. Elise sat up with the blanket held under her nose and began to cry. Lilah was trying to hush her when Elliot walked in from the sun porch. His eyes looked like a pair of matched cat's eye marbles. She stood still waiting for him to say something. Elise continued to cry. He walked over and picked her up, wrapping the blanket gently around the back of her head. Elise put her head down on his shoulder and began sucking her thumb.

"I saw a parade today," he said.

"Oh, where was that?" Lilah said over her shoulder as she moved quickly through the kitchen with Davis making him walk up the stairs.

"Canal Street," he said to her back as he cuddled the baby.

Lilah took her time before she came back down for Elise. She didn't know what she would say to him if he acted jealous or asked where she had been.

When she came back she said, "Was it a nice parade?"

"I saw my cousin."

"Oh, the famous cousin who's married to our fine governor?"

"Yes—Camilla Jane."

"How does she look? She's much older than you, isn't she?"

"Not anymore," he said.

She laughed, "That must be nice. Is she getting younger?"

"I guess not," he said.

Lilah took the baby from his arms and went to the foot of the stairs, walking briskly. "I had a fantastic day," she turned and said deliberately. "I went dancing in a bar called Little Rum Boogie."

Elliot was standing by the mantel lost in thought. His hair was a pale lemon color in the dim light. He laid one hand on the mantel and leaned in a similar pose to the one held by his father who stood by a mantel in the painting overhead. Shaking his head in wonder at some picture in his mind, Elliot said, "Camilla Jane is still the most beautiful woman I've ever seen."

"Thanks," she said, "That's just what I needed to hear." She turned on her heel and ran up the stairs.

Now she drove like a madwoman. The night seemed to part for her and the car grooved on the highway like a train on a monorail. It drove itself. The hurt and fury made her mind cold and clear. There was a chill to the night air that roared through the open window as she crossed the twelve-mile span—the desolate stretch of road over the Atchafalaya Spillway where cypress trees and snaggy stumps stood up out of the creeping waters of Lake Pontchartrain. It was a long time before the headlights caught the sign for Pierre Part where she turned off down the narrow road to Little Rum Boogie and the man who danced to "Jolie Blonde."

She knew she would find him. There was no doubt in anything she did now, and she didn't think of New Orleans. She thought in the moment. No seduction needed. He wanted her as she was. No Galatea. No Erzuli. She stopped at Little Run Boogie but it was dark. The Rainbow Inn had fifty cars huddled like sleeping dogs on the shell lot. A Cajun accordion set up a crackle in her veins, and she turned into the drive electric with the rhythm of the dance. She hit the front door whirling and picked a man with a little moustache who danced her into the back room where a swirling mass of people were dancing a Cajun jitterbug as she slipped her arm along his in the quick patterns. She looked around the room searching among the dancers for his face and when she didn't see him, she paid attention to the man with the moustache who was in his smooth fifties. He danced the jitterbug faster than she'd ever danced before, and she was caught up in the exhilaration of the moment. But when the piece was over she headed back to the bar for a beer and the man went back to his table and friends. Someone stepped out of the dark and said, "*Ça va?*"

"Just fine," said Lilah and paid for her beer before she put the bottle to her lips. She stared straight into his eyes.

They danced like old lovers and the evening thrilled her, satisfying every vision she had of herself as separate from her husband and children. She went with him, ferried to a little house across the bayou in a pirogue in which he stood stolidly, his back to the soft kerosene light, the dark "V" of his legs above her as he paddled.

She learned there that his name was Amedee. He said, as they made love, "Call me Amedee, cher." At dawn he ferried her back across the bayou, and she drove to New Orleans still married to Elliot but as lighthearted as a girl. She was prepared to fight now for what was hers. She and Elliot had each drawn blood.

When she walked in the back door of the house, she expected Elliot to still be sleeping, but he had been called for a turn and stood drinking coffee in the kitchen.

"Have a good time?" he asked.

"Yes," she said, and went to bed.

Moo Dying

MOO WAS DYING—WAS DYING AND HAD BEEN FOR six weeks. Elliot and Lilah were exhausted from hospital sitting. The tension in their relationship dissolved into mutual support as Elliot tried to deal with the thought of a world without Moo. He and Lilah had been there in shifts, around the clock, helped out by Alita LeCroy. The old woman preferred Alita to Lilah, who she hardly knew, and since the children were young, Lilah was needed at home—Alita stayed and Lilah went home more often.

Alita came in for an evening shift at nine and would stay the night. After work she'd go home, have a quick bite to eat and a shower, and come back to the hospital where she'd worked all day. She didn't know why it was important for her to be with the old woman, but it was. She washed Moo's eyes out with a boric acid solution she prepared at home and brought to the hospital. For the past two weeks Moo had been blind. Her eyes bulged behind stained lids. The doctor said it would not be long. Elliot couldn't believe it. She hadn't spoken to them for some time. She didn't eat. I.V. tubes connected her to life. The catheter between her legs continued to fill a plastic blob, attached to the hospital bed by a metal clip, with straw-colored urine, which daily became more cloudy.

Late at night when there was only a little light in the room, and the floor nurse seldom came in, the old lady would rouse herself and talk to Alita. She said, "I got some things to pass on."

At midnight she would rise on one elbow, and say, "Are you there, girl?"

And Alita would say, "I'm listening."

"You can't give yourself away or sell yourself. They tried to say my Mama gave me to Miss Elise, but she didn't. She cried. We were moving all the time in the country. Any house that was vacant or where somebody had some room. I wanted to live in a nice house, and I didn't want to marry an ignorant man, so I gave myself to Miss Elise when she got married. I knew who she was; I saw her when we went to church, and I liked her face and her husband's face. I was just twelve years old—you got that? Don't give yourself away for something too comfortable."

"I've got it."

"And you don't let them patronize you—don't let nobody patronize you. If you do then you got to find somebody to patronize. Closest I came was Elliot, but I wouldn't even do it for Elliot. I was never a Mammy, and he was no Mammy's child. Almost—'cause of Took and her hoodoo bitch, but I caught on when she was giving him the powders, and binding him to her. I sent Took to Miss Mag—that family was coming apart. You got to watch all that stuff. You hear me? I don't believe in no gods. They couldn't be any—not the way things are—not even Catholic."

Alita was shocked. She had never doubted her religion or known anybody who did, but she didn't want to fuss with a dying woman. The old lady settled down again and seemed to sleep. Alita turned on the little T.V., pulled the long, mechanical arm down so she could watch it from her chair. Johnny Carson was talking to a young woman. Everyone on the program seemed congenial, kissed each other on the cheek. Another young woman was announced and got the kiss. She was wearing a tight, beaded evening gown. As she sat down and turned to Carson, her body seemed to leap out of itself to get closer to him, but he was smiling and nodding at the band while they played an up tempo show tune and he drummed two pencils on the desk like drumsticks. The woman wiggled her beaded fanny in the chair, anxious to begin her conversation; it made Alita think of Thelma, the smart kid in school no one liked, who waggled her hand up in the air, and screamed "Me—Me—I know—Ask me, me.' The music stopped and Johnny made a deadpan shrug at the camera before he looked at the woman who was now practically wiggling out of her chair. "Looks like a pissing female puppy," Alita said aloud. "She'd do anything for him to throw her a bone."

The old woman seemed to rouse again. Alita got up and leaned over her to see if she was awake. "Miss LeCroy?" asked Moo.

"How'd I get to be Miss," asked Alita as she turned off the T.V. "You been calling me girl for two years."

"You got something to be proud of. I had to learn to read off medicine bottles when I was nursing the old doctor. They were afraid I'd kill him with the wrong medicine so they showed me how to look for patterns on the labels. In two months I could read the newspaper. That was in 1923. One time I was reading to him about the statue—they were going to erect a Mammy statue in Washington, D.C., dedicated to the black Mammies of the south. All he would talk about then was how proud he was for his Mammy that she was going to have a statue, but then he got disappointed because two thousand black women protested to Coolidge, asking him not to do it, not to remind us that we come from a race of slaves. And that old man, he looked at me with tears in his runny old eyes, and he said, "It's good to have you with me. I miss my Mammy.' I decided then I wouldn't be one."

"But what about Elliot?" Alita whispered.

"He's not my child. I saw to it. He can love me all he wants, but he's not my child. He's the last one—Miss Ann Elise's child, so everybody made him special."

"He says he's your grandbaby."

"Sometimes I say so, but I know it ain't so. A grandbaby you can take up or leave down like you want, but not Elliot. He was my responsibility—he was a monkey on my back." She slept again.

Alita went to the bathroom. She was almost afraid to go. Afraid she might miss something the old lady said. She used the high toilet, flushed it carefully with a piece of tissue on the handle, and put her rings in her mouth while she washed her hands with green soap. When she came back Moo was awake again.

"Once I thought I wanted to sleep with Miss Elise's husband because I thought he was so fine. She was all worn out from having all those babies, and I was like the wife in that house. I did the cooking, and I nursed for him sometimes when patients came, and I nursed all the kids—Miss Elise just kept having them babies that died. She was working all the time too, and she didn't want to sleep with him because they was so Catholic and believed in as many children as God gave them, and God gave them thirteen. I went to his room one time when he had a cold, and I was rubbing his back for him. I started rubbing to make a little fire, but he said, 'Moo, you're too good for all that.' And he was right. I never went with anybody."

"You mean you're a virgin?"

"Somebody always thinks they've got to put a name on something. Naming things only tells you one thing—what somebody calls it. It don't really tell you anything. Like I could say you're an old maid."

"I'm too particular, that's all."

"So was I. *Light's all right, brown stick around, black get back.*

You stop worrying if they're light as you, and worry more about smart and good. You'll get a better one. House niggers all the same. They worry more about color than white people."

"Not me," said Alita, but she knew she lied.

"They used to say the lighter you marry the richer you get. I was going to marry so white he wouldn't have to work, and my kids could *passe blanc*, but I didn't marry nobody, and I didn't go to school except with Elliot. Every time he had a book to read I read too because there wasn't any new baby, and I had a little time. Miss Elise got tired. Her womb fell and her titties fell, and right after the hoodoo bitch got married she just went to bed, and pretty soon she was the new baby. From here it hardly looks like it happened. You hear?"

"I hear you."

"You've got to make more plans. Don't listen to your Mama. She don't know. Just wants you to fit in. She wants you to do it the way she did it. She's got a full belly and she knows her place. You're still carrying bed pans. Why're you carrying bed pans when you could be a doctor? I knew when I used to help the doctor—my hands were as quick and sure as his—quicker. I said to myself, 'I could be the doctor—better than him,' and I could—maybe next time."

At seven a.m. the nurses changed shifts. The nurse came in and checked the I.V. and cleaned the catheter. After she left Elliot came in with a white paper bag with coffee from the French Market and a bag of donuts. The beignets had shriveled down to hard, greasy lumps covered in white powdered sugar. Alita took one to be polite, but it stuck in her throat.

"Has she said anything?"

"She mumbles in her sleep sometime," she said.

" I wish she'd tell me something," he said. "She's the only family I've got."

"Maybe she'll come out of it before she goes. Sometimes they do," she said as she put on her cashmere coat.

"You really think she's going to go? I haven't given up hope."

Alita stared at him, wondering how he could look at Moo

and think she was going to live, but she said, "There's always hope."

After Alita left Elliot stood over Moo looking at her face. It was a clear face; there was something elegant about the line running from her cheekbone to her chin. He remembered how he and Camilla Jane had drawn straws to sleep with her. No one had wanted to sleep with his third cousin Kathleen because she wet the bed, but everyone wanted to sleep with Moo, and they drew straws for the privilege.

There were things he wanted to know, but there was no one to ask. He felt a division in his life—a cutting off from everything he'd known before. It filled him with longing and regret for things that had passed and gone away. Now his childhood was dying, but he still loved it and hated to give it up—old feelings he continued to nurse and cherish. He couldn't help crying. He put his head down on the bed near her hand—hoping. But she never raised it. He cried until his throat ached. He heard the nurse come to the door, but he didn't raise his head, and she went away again.

Blue ribbons, pink ribbons—lavender—streamed out of the windows of the streetcar as it rocked toward them. It began small—now it was rocking down on them in all its beribboned olive majesty like a jubilant army tank. There was no sound or he couldn't hear it. The streamers stood out from the windows in a brisk breeze. Whose birthday was it? He didn't know or care; he loved anybody's streetcar party.

She held his hand tightly. As the white hold-bar dividing the doors separated them, she dropped his hand and paid seven cents for each of them. He said, "Bread and Butter," as the bar divided them and he followed her as she walked toward the front of the streetcar. There weren't many people on the car, and he lagged behind looking at them. She pulled at his hand until their arms outstretched, and they became a two-link human chain as she dragged him to the front.

Then he saw Moo, she was sitting in the back of the car,

very serious—her eyelids closed. He pulled his hand away from the other woman to run back by Moo, but when he tried to sit beside her she pointed to the wooden screen on the back of the next seat and hissed, "You can't sit back here anymore." She never opened her eyes, and the only way he could tell she was in there was by the reddish-pink of her mouth when she opened it. He was hurt when Moo wouldn't let him sit by her. Staggering up the aisle against the motion of the swaying car, he went looking for the party and the woman he got on with. There was no music, no cake, no children—there didn't seem to be a party. About halfway up on the lefthand side of the car he saw Took. When he stood beside her he noticed she had one eye closed, which gave her a comical look, although she wasn't laughing. Holding out a closed fist, she opened it and gave him a rabbit's foot. "Good luck," she said, and closed the other eye. Nudging her knees with his he tried to push past her to sit down beside her. She pointed to the wooden screen and shook her head. Again he moved forward to find the woman he'd gotten on with, but he didn't see her and he didn't know where to sit. Way up front—near the driver— wearing a grey straw picture hat with ostrich plumes and a little pink roses, his grandmother sat on the beauty seat, which ran down the side of the front of the streetcar. She waved gaily and called out, "I have to sit here."

He stood in the aisle holding onto the brass hand-hold on the back of the varnished seat until the car came to a full stop at the end of the line. Moo and Took immediately got up and got off, when he looked up front his grandmother had gone too. The motorman passed up and down the streetcar pushing them over. After changing the seats he got off and changed the position of the shaft with the stiff cord of electric line to link with the overhead cable, so that what had been the back of the car became the front.

The motorman's curly black hair curled around a military hat. Quick, deft gestures completed the transformation, and when Elliot looked again, he realized the motorman was a woman, now set to go, standing with her back to Elliot. He listened for the bell to clang as they started. With a familiar wave of one hand she started without the bell, and now that she was busy driving the streetcar she didn't turn around again.

He looked to see where the moveable screen was now that seats were reversed, and he saw that the woman he'd gotten on with had the screen in her hand. She didn't seem to know what to do with it. While trying to fit the little brass pegs into the seat in front of her, she had turned the message so that it was facing the front of the car.

He came and sat down beside her to tell her what to do. He said,"You can't do that—it says 'colored only.' "

"Oh," she said, and put it on the seat behind them. He said, "I can't sit here if you do that."

"Well, for goodness sakes, have it any way you want," Lilah said, and threw it out the window.

He heard a small sound from Moo, and he lifted his head from the sheet to listen, but she turned her head away from him. He thought she said, "Next time," but he couldn't be sure, and by the time he got up—disoriented—and went to the other side of the bed, she was gone.

Scottlandville

ON THE DOCK AT BATON ROUGE THE BLACK TELE-
phone in the booth had been scarrified like a youth for a cir-
cumcision ceremony—names and numbers—Boo & Linda,
Runey and Arlene scratched in by hand or cut in by small
knives. A stale, sweetish smell of urine, which reminded him
of the hospital, forced him to leave the phone booth open. He
put in a dime and called her. A switchboard operator asked
him if he had an appointment. He did not. "I'm Elliot Gilbert,
Mrs. Busteaux's cousin from High Castle. If you tell her my
name I think she'll want to speak to me." He said this too
quickly. There was always the possibility with Camilla Jane
that she didn't want to be bothered, and he had the same feeling of not being wanted he'd had when he tagged after her as
kid.

"Hello, Elliot?" Her voice on the line was hesitant, a vulnerable, little girl quality which denied her split-second daredevil

self, who'd climbed to the top of an oak tree, and dropped into the bayou without regard to height or depth, who came up laughing, her hair and face decorated with green waterweed and she hardly bothered to pick it off. This same little voice had said nonchalantly, "Look, Elliot, a cottonmouth," as the snake undulated swiftly within a hand's length of her body, until it pulled its muddy length up the bank and disappeared in the grass. She was braver than he was. If he had known her courage for his own, it would never have taken him so long to find his right place. He knew that.

"Camilla Jane?" he said, "Moo died."

"Are you here?" she asked.

"In Baton Rouge, yes. I'm here for a week, shifting ships. I'm a pilot now," he said.

"Oh, are you *here*—at my house?"

"No," he said, thinking when she said "my house" of the house on Leonia Street in High Castle, but she spoke of the capitol as "my house."

"I'm at a phone booth on the dock. I just got off a ship. I want to see you." He almost choked on the urgency of it—how much he wanted to see her.

"And I want to see you, Elliot—I want you. You're the only person I have now." And to Elliot, who had always wanted to hear this, her voice seemed to hold as much emotion, as much desire as his own.

"Where—how can you get away? It's seven p.m.," he said. "Can you come now?" He didn't care how many turns at double pay he had to trade another pilot; he wanted to be with her.

"No, not tonight. I go some place once a week. Bubba drives me, and he never tells anyone." She gave a convoluted set of directions, which would take him there by the longest, most circuitous route. "I always go the back way, in Bubba's old black Ford, so no one will see me. The highway is called the Scenic Route," she said. When he hung up he tried to remember the directions; he had agreed to meet her Wednesday night in a place called Scottlandville.

• • •

He was parked, under the oak tree she had described, in a rented car. It was dark and he was about ten feet behind the highway sign that named the town. Two tire widths of shell led under the oak tree. There was an overflowing garbage can lynched between two posts. It smelled of rotten chicken necks. Someone had been crabbing and had gotten rid of their bait here. His impatience to see her made him early, and he'd been sitting for forty-five minutes, sweating and cursing the mosquitoes and the rotten chicken necks, which forced him to keep the car windows up. In a sudden burst of heat and frustration he rolled down his window, the smell made him retch, and a swarm of mosquitoes buzzed in his ear before he rolled the window up again to boil in his own juices as he tracked down the individual mosquitoes biting his hands and neck. The car lights coming toward him were infrequent, and he had begun to think that she would never come when a car drove up and a man got out. He came over to Elliot who rolled his window down again.

"I'm Bubba. She wants you to follow us."

The Ford led him down a long, curved La. Highway bordered by open fields with a few huge, scattered oaks on both sides of the highway. He wondered when they would come to a town. There were some industrial tin buildings, and a train track with the empty black bodies of coal cars or cane cars left on a switch off. The Ford went over the stretch of track, and they went on into the quarters of what Elliot was sure was a bigger town ahead. He'd never taken this road or been to Scottlandvile. The road was potholed—not lighted; a bright gibbous moon shone on the quarters of what he imagined had been a sugar plantation—along a series of small cypress shacks with a patina of aged moonlighted silver where the yellow light of coal oil lamps smoked in the windows. Bubba's car slowed as they passed livid neon tubes strung around a peeling tar-brick bar, where black men hung around outside talking. Elliot braked, too. Cars were parked in front of the bar and on the other side of the highway. Both cars slowed as figures continued to cross the highway from the bar to the parked cars on the shoulder of the road.

Once more they speeded up. The shacks stretched for several miles on either side, only one building reared itself above the rest. It was the white steeple of a church with a full front yard of raised whitewashed tombs. Elliot's lights caught the sign as he turned following the arrow of a highway sign shaped like a yellow "S." The sign read SCOTTLANDVILLE BAPTIST CHURCH, and he realized the quarters did not belong to a plantation. This long road with no shoulder and deep ditches of sewage on each side was the town of Scottlandville. He followed the Ford another half mile until it stopped at a whitewashed house slightly larger than the rest. Pulling up directly behind Bubba on a false shoulder just wide enough for two cars, he braked suddenly to the crackling sound of oyster shells spread on the shoulder and crushed by the sudden stop. Bubba opened the door of the Ford and she got out.

"Elliot," she said running to him and throwing both arms around him. She was so thin, he could hardly believe her legs would support her, like the drooping baby mockingbird they'd once saved which later died of poison from the pecan worm they fed it. In spite of its bones, her body was a braggart with its own musky smell, and her kiss was as deep as it had always been. His electric thought was the same: I'm in.

She pulled away after a moment and turned toward the house. He followed her onto the porch's slated cypress boards. A door opened and a light rode out onto the body of the night. The arm holding it disappeared into the darkness; behind it he could see the immense body of a tall woman whose folds of flesh and hanging dark garment filled up the doorway like a soft boulder. Her enormous breasts hung down to her belly like unbaked loaves.

Camilla Jane said, "This is Took's sister, Mama Linda." Camilla embraced the woman as she had embraced him. Mama Linda bent her massive head to be kissed on her wide, gleaming cheek. Without saying anything the woman shifted her weight to move back into the house. Elliot felt the boards give as if they'd borne her weight too long and would soon break. He moved quickly to follow her, a fault in the earth had shifted, trembled under his feet, and nothing was solid or secure.

Inside the room was large, with a squat ceiling. Elliot, who was as tall as the woman, bent his head to avoid the aromatic herbs tied by leather strings hanging from the ceiling. The far corners of the room were dark and mounds of bundled clothes were piled on the floor or dropped carelessly without pattern around the perimeter of the room. Some of the bundles had figures sitting or kneeling on them, and he felt the eyes of silent faces on him as he tried to find his way through the dark, labyrinthine order of the room. The back wall was banked with glowing candles in colored glass, and a small, plastic radio gave off a yellow light and static while playing distant off-station music. A heavy smell of burning wax mixed with human smells in the room and settled his mind on the high altar built in seven levels of step-stringers to the ceiling of the back wall. Plaster saints gathered around plastic medicine bottles and cast-off plaster casts.

The woman stood near the altar still holding the lamp. Camilla Jane said, "This is my cousin, Mama Linda. He's the only family I have left." The woman nodded and came close to him. He had an unreasonable fear of her. She came so close he could smell her, and he was surprised, her body was as fragrant as Camilla's with a light perfume of something like Florida water, and the starchy clean smell of immaculate linen. Her face when she came close to look at him bore a strong resemblance to Took; the four o'clock seed eyes were the same, but the look was different. Took could not take Camilla past childhood. The look in these eyes was as old as the river. If she wanted, he knew she could lift him, take him on her lap and rock him, his legs would be no longer than they had been in Took's kitchen before he touched the root.

"Mama Linda," Camilla Jane whispered, "I want to be alone with my cousin." Mama Linda shifted from one heavy foot to the other, then led them to a curtained doorway where she held aside the flowered curtain for them to enter. He bent his head following Camilla. Mama Linda held her head upright; the small tufts of thread-bound hair compressed as she passed through. Lighted by the swinging lamp, this room was much smaller. An iron bedstead covered with a black quilt with a white star on it stood in the middle of the room. She motioned the lamp across the room where leaping shadows of their bodies appeared on the bare tongue and groove. A dresser with a statue of a saint stood in one corner; votive candles illuminated the saint's feet, leaving the face in conjectural shadow. The floor shook again and the light went out of the room.

Camilla Jane and Elliot sat on the edge of the bed. His pulse filled the darkness. It appeared to him that the candles beat against the darkness and flickered in time to his pulse like a deep drum—the way lights do to music. He could not bear to touch her for the hot violence of his desire. He tried to quiet his body, but it would not obey him. His body was like a drunken, vulgar stranger he could not control, but when she laid her cool hand on his arm, it was like his mother's hand on his forehead when he was feverish. The urge to throw her down and climb into her abated.

She said, "Elliot, High John was not a true giver. For everything he gave he wanted something back. First it was only red beans and rice. After So was governor High John was never satisfied. I even gave up my little boy—begged and begged, prayed and prayed to St. Jude for him, but he came sick and got sicker, and I bled clots of blood like red oranges. The doctors said I was going to die of childbed fever because I was shaking with a chill like the flu, and I wouldn't cry. I just kept begging High John: 'Take me, take me instead.' And he would have, and the baby would be here still, but So got a *traiteur*, who sent for Mama Linda and she gave me ergot to take and a kitten to nurse so my milk would steady my womb-Jesus, until she fanned out all the fever. Then I cried, and my soul came back to my body.

"With So in the capitol I can't do anything for the people

but pray. Mama Linda says my power comes from an African god, and I should do something for the people who are cast down like before Moses. So is a good man, but willful. He doesn't know how to help all the people. He just helps the people he sees, like his cousins and his friends, and their friends. I try to be a friend to the poor people, but Mama Linda says I'm too ignorant—that my High John's gotten weak, and the power is passing from me. That it will pass from So until someone with grace comes. She says she gets disgusted with me—I should be reading all the books I can get my hands on instead of buying white linen dresses. I've registered for college. Political Science. She says I like white linen dresses because I'm dead now—became I'm not a grown woman, just some dead little girl. And she makes me mad, she makes me sick, but she makes me think. And she says if I think maybe I can grow up and do some good. I've been studying need."

Elliot tried to follow what she was saying, but his body had only one thought and he pressed himself against her. His left arm was around her body, and he felt his hand under her arm where the first swelling of her breast began, and his right thumb hooked the inside of her waistband—the beginning of an urge that could rip her skirt. But she continued to talk in the childish whisper of the things Mama Linda told her; how she had not been able to lead So Busteaux out of the system of patronage, petty graft and kick-backs, which was his heritage—which went back to the beginnings of Louisiana to the first governor. How So loved her and she loved him, but that he had thickened and coarsened so that now Mama Linda said, "He's a double-headed boil ready to pop. His blood will pour out of his mouth and ears, and he'll die. You won't have anything of him after he passes because too many children are hungry, and you can't have a baby unless you feed them. High John will see to that."

Her voice droned on liked a child reciting a litany of bad dreams until he felt older than she and protective. "I have to grow up, Elliot. I have to grow up and use High John when I know I'm right and not let High John use me."

His hard urge drooped and a terrible *triste* overcame him as if they'd lain in bed for a long time after good sex fueled by a close death. Old bandages wrapped an inextricable truth, and he recognized the body of that truth as one he could not save. She was still a child, but not the child he'd known. His own desire for her, which had led him down so many strange roads, was only an adolescent's fantasy prolonged through years of his own uncertainty and yearning for his childhood. He'd found everything on his journey — Lilah, their children, the river — some dreams were the true dreams of childhood, and he had been drawn to them while following her. And he hugged her to him like a sister. She said again, "You're the only family I have." The light came back into the room again. Mama Linda said, "Bubba says it's time to go."

Camilla Jane turned to Elliot and kissed him as she always had, but High John was old and weak. Elliot's body had resigned itself to its true pleasures, and he kissed her on both cheeks and said, "Any time you need to talk to me — call." He followed the light and the hem of her white skirt out of the room. The wheels of the Ford turned loosely in the shell until — at last — they caught. He followed Bubba in the black car back down the highway, where he saw again how weak High John really was, how weak all gods were, as shack after shack melted into darkness with only the lights of the coal oil lamps breaking the night. And suddenly with a twinge like an earache he remembered: Moo's dead.

Green Trout

ELLIOT SAT IN THE GALLERY OF THE STATE HOUSE of Representatives. None of it made too much sense to him yet. His mind wandered. Politics had never interested him. Not even when Camilla married So Busteaux. He knew that his life was often affected by decisions made by small-minded men, but he'd never had a passion for fighting them. As a lawyer he knew how, but it all seemed so petty; he turned instead to the elemental—the river—which changed slowly. Camilla had the fire, but she banked it.

There were Representatives on the floor debating a bill on fish farming. The gallery was packed with Cajun fishermen. One man wore a bill cap and white tee shirt with *Captain Richard, Hog Hunter* printed on the back.

Captain Richard whispered to a woman with a large beehive hairdo, "He's lying through his teeth. You can't shop in more than one grocery store at a time."

The page shushed him and Elliot tried to tune in on the debate on the floor.

"Mr. Jackson."

"Mr. Speaker, I rise in support of this bill. There are mothers and fathers without jobs. Fish farms put a lot of those men and women to work."

Elliot found himself looking at the mosaic ceiling, precise flowers in subtle shades of blue and pink. At the right of the room, huge windows with see-through scrim shades were intersected by wrought iron beanstalks of flowers and leaves which climbed the outside of the glass. Four light fixtures heavy with bronze filigree hung from the ceiling. Huey Long had built a temple to himself. Elliot admired the temple, but had a hard time keeping up with the clergy, the combative legislators talking below.

Someone was saying, "Yesterday, they were against it. Today they're for it. The only promises the governor made was for fiscal reform and educational reform. I don't know where fish farming fits in."

Another representative was recognized. "Well, I'll tell you, Ron. I don't change my mind unless somebody gives me something, and you don't change your mind unless somebody gives you something."

At these words the fish farmers in the gallery clapped loudly and there were loud exclamations of "Ohhh and Ah." The speaker called for order.

A reluctant lobbyist to start with, Elliot quickly grew tired of sitting. He was there because of pilots' fees. The governor held the pilots' commission, but the pilots were self-governing. By holding the commission the governor could control the pilots—a fact Elliot hadn't been aware of when he became one—that he would be controlled by So Busteaux just as Camilla Jane was. There was always some weakness; he had followed his fate but it still lead here. The rumor at the Pilot Station was that certain legislators were in cahoots with the Steamship Association and that there was a move in the legislature to grab the pilots by the balls and hang on. Denut them. The governor could be gotten to. With power in the hands of the Steamship Association, they could dictate rates to their advantage—put the pilots in the position of taking whatever the Steamship Association wanted to dish out. Elliot, as well as pilots from his own and other associations, were there to lobby. He looked down but couldn't see the bullpen from the gallery.

Below the president's bench was the representative's rostrum. On the back walls were ventilators cut in stone, designed in a sugarcane motif. Again he was amazed at Huey Long's power which still persisted in this monument. He thought of it as an edifice, building was not pompous enough. All the door frames and the wainscoting of the walls were made of marble—beige and black marble. Long had scoured the country for the materials and practically thrown the Capitol's walls up overnight. Hundreds of railroad cars had arrived daily with tons of materials for the new Capitol. Elliot looked at what Huey Long had built and a slow anger built in him—not at Huey Long—Huey Long was dead, but So Busteaux ruled this now, and his arm was long.

In the center of the room behind the president, a small clock smiled against the backboard of mahogany where the House's roll call ticked off and was tallied. There was a Quorum call now. It was thirty-nine to sixty-nine and the amendment on the fish farming bill failed. The fish lobbyists trailed out of the gallery in disappointed solidarity.

Elliot left the gallery and found himself in a crush of disgruntled fish farmers. "What's happening?" one man asked.

"We've got to find seven votes," Richard the Hog Hunter said.

"Hell, go out in the hall and promise them some free shrimps and you'll get them votes tout de suite. Some of them legislators is hungry. That's what makes them mean."

Above the crowd Elliot could see Richard Dejean, one of the pilots from the Crescent Association. He loomed over everybody. Richard was six-foot-five and weighed around three hundred pounds. Nobody could figure out how he climbed the pilot ladder, but he did and he could dance like a Baby Doll. Everybody called him Lightfoot.

"Captain Lightfoot, how're you making out?"

"Captain Gilbert, if you know anything you'd better tell me. All the president told me was he wanted a show of strength in Baton Rouge. I been flexing my muscles all over this show, but nobody but a cute little blond lobbyist paid any attention. I've been over in the Senate. It's slower than a high school double-header."

"The bill is due to come up this afternoon."

"That's what Captain Ricks told me."

They walked into the bullpen where the other pilots were strung out like linemen. Most of them were big, but the president of the association was a short, square man with a red nose named Slater. During his last work week Slater had called Elliot at home and asked him to come into the office on a business matter. Elliot knew little of the inner workings of the Pilots Association but read the notices and petitions to change things from the other pilots, and voted as he thought fit. It took a majority to change anything.

The Pilots Association was a real democracy, and like most democracies it took forever to change anything, and everyone had an opinion. Their quarterly meetings were shouting matches as big egos bounced off each other. Every man was Captain and every man knew he was right. The one thing they agreed on was to do the best possible job. It was a matter of honor for a pilot to consider human life above any other factor. They were often at odds with the Steamship Association. The president of the Pilots Association had the unenviable job of trying to keep them all on track, and working amicably with the ship owners. About every three years they negotiated tariff with the Steamship Association by a Fee Commission.

Elliot liked Slater, the president, although he didn't always agree with him. Last week Elliot had gotten a message that Slater wanted to see him, and when he walked into the Association's office on Canal Street, the secretary told him Slater would see him right away.

"Captain Slater," he said, shaking the other man's hand. "How can I be of service?"

"Well, Cap. I hear you've got a useful cousin."

"I've got lots of cousins."

"Well, what I hear is one of them is married to the right guy."

"You mean Camilla Jane."

"It's nice to be on a first name basis with the governor's wife."

"That doesn't mean I'm friends with the governor."

"You don't need to be his friend. All you need to do is get us an early appointment before our bill comes up. He's been playing hard to get, and our bill comes up next week to increase our fees. The Steamship Association has a coalition of representatives and senators. They've put out big bucks to lobby against us. We need an appointment with the governor. All you need to do is get us his ear."

"For what? What does the governor have to do with this?"

"You sound dumb, Cap. How'd you pass your pilot's exam?"

"Don't worry about it. I did."

"Let's put it this way. The only commission the governor hasn't sold is the Cosmetology Commission. He's commissioned us from the beginning. Way back then it was considered alright. He owns us now so he can't sell us a commission, but we've got to get his ear or we're out of business. The Steamship Industry makes a bundle off our backs and treats us like poor white trash. You with this association or against it?"

"With it."

"Well then, why don't you give your cousin a call. We're overworked and they won't raise our fees so we can make new pilots. We're just trying to play politics too."

"What about the other pilot's associations?"

"They're with us as long as it's to their advantage, but the governor has always been closer to the bar pilots. They're the oldest association, but they've got the easiest route. They're the ones rode the rowboats out to the first ships that came into New Orleans. They had the reputation then of fighting off other men with knives if anybody else was cheeky enough to try to guide a ship. They wear their tailored suits now, but they're hand in glove with old man Perez who runs his kingdom down there in Plaquemines Parish. They're still hard men no matter what they wear. Right now we're all agreed to do whatever it takes to beat out the Steamship Association. But if the Steamship Association offers them some goodies to throw us over, I'd bet my license they'd take it. You get us his ear and all you've got to do is pilot ships from then on out—hopefully, for more money."

"I'm not too badly paid now," Elliot smiled.

The other man did not smile. "If you're willing to risk your life moving iron for peanuts when the big shots in the Steamship Association are sitting at the Blue Room eating steak and caviar, then you haven't got the balls I think you have."

"I didn't say I wouldn't like to make more money. I'm just thinking how much we make compared to the average guy."

"The average guy doesn't move iron, can't wipe out the city if he makes a mistake. You just call your cousin. I'll do the rest."

He called her.

After he told her why he was calling, there was a long silence and then she said, "So now they've got you pimping, Elliot."

He couldn't say anything, then he said, "It's my association—they just want an appointment to get an even break. They need to talk to the governor before a bill comes up."

"So—they just want to talk to him? They're going to pay him."

"No—there was nothing said about money."

"Of course not. Who'd say it aloud? The governor's office sells all commissions but Cosmetology Commissions, and I don't know why he doesn't sell those."

"That's the second time I've heard that today."

"Believe it." She laughed down in her throat. "Well, if you want it you've got it, baby cousin. But it makes me sick. Good-bye." And the phone clicked off before he could say anything else.

He went to the governor's office in the Capitol with Slater, but only because he was the governor's cousin once removed. So Busteaux smiled a big smile at them and shook hands all around. He winked at Elliot, and said, "Good to see you, Cousin." Elliot was surprised because they'd never been friendly.

Busteaux said, "I'm glad to see you. I've been shaking hands with pilots all morning, and I don't think you have anything to worry about. As I said to the Crescent boys, I'd just like to have some of them green trout you boys catch on the river. The bill's going to pass, and when it's passed we'll just enjoy ourselves some green trout."

"Green trout?"

Elliot was amused to see Slater just as confused by So Busteaux's political double-talk as he'd been by Slater. Slater was out of his depth.

"That's what I said." Busteaux was enjoying himself. He leaned back in his blue leather chair with his hands folded across his stomach.

Slater couldn't believe his ears, "The bill's going to pass."

"No doubt about it. You boys just enjoy yourselves. Go over to the beer distributors and eat some free oysters. Go to the Capitol House and spend them oysters on some nice girls. Pass a good time. You got nothing to worry about."

The rest of the pilots went on over to the Capitol House to celebrate. Elliot didn't go. He was still thinking about Green Trout. He went on back to the Senate. It was a funny request "Green Trout." He thought about what Camilla Jane had said. He knew he hadn't seen any money passed, and from the look of Slater's face he hadn't passed any, but somebody had, and they would benefit from it. It didn't make him glad. In fact, it made him sad.

He went on back into the Senate. He wanted to see the

pencil. Someone had blown up the Senate about a month before. No one was hurt. The place was empty at the time, but one of the lobbyists for the AFOL-CIO, a guy named Red, told Elliot about cracks in the marble pillars and a pencil stuck in the ceiling from the force of the explosion. Elliot had heard everyone from Red terrorists to Civil Rights activists had done the deed, but no one had managed to find out.

In the anteroom to the Senate there were a number of women standing at the rail. One woman with hair tinted an indelible black smiled at him as two tight lines descended the edges of her mouth. She had a shrewd look as she passed over him and quickly went back to listening. A slender, long-waisted woman with brown hair, in a white linen dress in a style that looked too sexy for the Senate, wore neat black pumps to make the whole subtle effect. There was a third woman about thirty-five taking notes. She wore a pink linen suit, and a white blouse with a lace cravat. Her hair was parted in the middle and two devilish horns of white hair swirled upward. Elliot realized he was looking at women and not listening to what was going on; these women were lobbyists, smart career women who spent their evenings with legislators or the supplicants who'd come to beg for something — handmaidens to power. It reminded him of Haiti. He ran on up the stairs to the gallery and looked down at the scene from above.

The floor of the Senate was grey and mauve marble. The square supports for the room were embraced on either side by round fluted columns with long grooves running from floor to ceiling. In the ceiling were six-sided depressions for lights — each one contained a star.

The South and North door lintels were of deep brownish-grey marble; the doors were brass. The main door was of sculptured bronze, but Elliot couldn't make out the scene depicted there. The pages moving around downstairs wore light striped seersucker trousers with blue blazers. There was something different about the Senate. Not as noisy. Elliot could see Red the labor lobbyist below. Red was pretty distinctive in his wine slacks and blue-green jacket. His red hair a dark mahogany from the hair oil he'd slicked it down with. Elliot chuckled to himself as he looked up to the side of the big lantern with its delicate swirls of iron work where a yellow No. 2 pencil stuck in the ceiling like a dart. He could see it right away and marveled at the force of the explosion. He noticed a few cracks in the huge marble pillars. There were a couple of other guys in dark jackets talking to Red now. The brass bell sounded for votes.

The Sergeant-at-Arms handled the blue velvet rope with ponderous dignity. The sign was up: SENATE IN SESSION. PLEASE, NO TALKING. NO STANDING AT RAIL.

One of the senators was saying, "Isn't life difficult. My father said to me, 'Al, all I want you to do is the right thing'. Little did I know that wasn't one of the choices. How can we cut $100,000 more out of government? We did the less bad thing. I suggest to you the alternative is completely, irrevocably unacceptable, untenable. Gentlemen, we are in the Senate, as Thomas Jefferson talked about this august body as the natural aristocracy of the elected body. It will not be so if we turn away from our natural society."

Elliot hadn't been listening when they explained the bill, and he couldn't tell what it was from the senator's speech, but he'd suddenly felt happy. He'd spotted Senator Dudley LeBlanc—*Coozan* Dudley LeBlanc.

Moo had always been for Coozan Dudley ever since he'd come out for the old-age pension. He also said he'd administer his duties without regard to race, creed, or condition, and to protect the rights of veterans. Moo was for him and Elliot had met him when he was a boy.

Moo had a sore toe and Elliot was sitting with her in her quarters to keep her company. They were listening to the radio which was playing "The Hadacol Boogie." Elliot was singing along with the radio:

> Down in Louisiana in the bright sunshine
> They do a little boogie woogie all the time.
> They do the Hadacol Boogie, Hadacol Boogie

Hadacol Boogie, boogie woogie all the time.
A-standing on the corner with my bottle in my hand,
And up stepped a woman, said, "My Hadacol Man."
She done the Hadacol Boogie,
boogie woogie all the time.
If your radiator leaks and your motor stands still,
A-give her Hadacol and watch her boogie up the hill.
She'll do the Hadacol Boogie, Hadacol Boogie,
The Hadacol Boogie makes you
boogie woogie all the time.

The announcer came on and said, "Do you recognize that tune?"

"Sure do," said Elliot. "I sang the whole thing."

"You did," said Moo.

"If you do you get a free prize. A bottle of something that most people say will cure anything. If you recognize this tune write in, and get your free bottle of something you won't regret. Now for a few of those testimonials." And he read letters from listeners claiming cures from "irritability, nervousness, chronic fatigue, dyspepsia, loss of appetite, loss of strength, inability to sleep, below-par condition, loss of weight, malnutrition, certain skin disorders, certain eye disorders, gassiness, and constipation, and other more serious diseases like blindness, cancer, neuritis, delirium tremens, beri-beri, arthritis, asthma, gall bladder trouble, swelling around the waist, swelling of the hands, epileptic fits, tuberculosis, brittle fingernails, cataracts on the eyes, and sores on the legs." And the letter which clinched it for Elliot..."and I haven't had a sore toe since I've been taking my medicine," said a woman from Clinton, Louisiana.

"Did you hear that, Moo?"

"Did I hear that? Of course I heard that. I'm not deaf. I've got a sore toe."

Moo chewed at the inside of her cheek when the toe pained her, and her cheeks had a hollow look. Elliot wrote the letter and waited. He haunted the mailbox waiting for the free bottle of Hadacol to cure Moo. But it didn't come. What finally came was a certificate for a free bottle from the drugstore. Moo sent Elliot to Dugas' Drugstore to get it.

Old man Dugas looked at the certificate, which was large and yellow, for a long time. "We don't carry it," he said.

Elliot, whose leg had begun to vibrate with the long wait, now shook in earnest. "Mr. Dugas, Moo has the gout in her big toe and it pains her terribly; she needs that bottle of Hadacol."

"Hadacol is nothing but alcohol. Get Moo a bottle of whiskey to cure her toe. Besides, gout is a rich man's disease, either Moo's been eating too high off the hog or she doesn't have gout."

"Moo's not going to like that."

"We don't carry it and we're not going to carry it no matter what. Put that in your pipe and smoke it."

Elliot trailed back home. The last thing he wanted to do was tell Moo they didn't have it.

"Where's the package?"

"They didn't have it."

"When they going to get it?"

"They're not. Mr. Dugas says it's just alcohol for people who want to drink but don't want anybody to know."

"Is that so? Well, they're going to be sorry, because they're going to have to have to get it."

That afternoon she got Elliot to write to Coozan Dudley Le Blanc personally, and he told Coozan Dudley how Dugas' Drugstore in High Castle refused to get Hadacol even though he, Elliot Braden Gilbert, had immediately recognized "The Hadacol Boogie" on the radio and had a yellow certificate for a free bottle.

Three days later a free bottle was delivered to Moo personally by Senator Dudley J. LeBlanc, who had his picture taken with his hat in one hand as he passed a bottle of Hadacol to Moo with the other. Elliot stood in the background of the picture which was printed in the weekly "Progress" newspaper.

But the best part was that was the beginning of the Hadacol Campaign in High Castle, and when the Hadacol caravan passed through with Mickey Rooney, Caesar Romero, and Maw Perkins, Elliot and Moo got free tickets and they went. Moo made a testimonial on stage about how her sore toe was cured and Elliot shook the senator's hand, and Minnie Pearl said, "I'm just proud to be here." At the end of the show Dudley LeBlanc made his disclaimer about the medicinal effects of Hadacol when he said,

"Hadacol will not cure everything. A friend of mine in Abbeville said he used it for antifreeze and he was mad as a son-of-a-gun because you know what? Hadacol can't be used as antifreeze in your radiator. It won't save your car." Elliot thought that was the funniest thing he'd ever heard even though he didn't know much about cars.

Right now Coozan Dudley was getting himself in trouble. Leander Perez was an old enemy. The bill up that had the whole Senate buzzing was state aid to private schools. Slater told Elliot about it. "A group of senators made up this bill to get around the new federal integration laws; the bill would offer grants-in-aid to those parents who didn't want to send their children to integrated schools. They could enroll their kids in private schools operating on a segregated basis." Elliot had heard talk about it from everyone. It was a key issue. Slater said the governor had contacted many senators asking for their vote on the Perez bill. The senators were afraid to be labeled "nigger lovers" if they voted against it. Everyone knew LeBlanc hated Perez. Elliot figured the governor had asked LeBlanc for a vote too, but he didn't know why the governor wanted the bill to win. Caught up in his good old boy network, he guessed.

The old man looked sick. Elliot had heard LeBlanc had kidney trouble. But Elliot was sitting right there when Dudley LeBlanc got the floor.

"Mr. Speaker, I demand an amendment to the bill. Let the amendment read that no grants be paid until the old-age assistance grants have been increased to $100."

There was a immediate uproar on the floor and calls for order. Leander Perez was running up and down the rail like a bulldog foaming at the mouth.

There was a long explanation of how much the amendment might cost the state—around six million a year. Elliot couldn't help laughing. No senator was going to go on public record opposing a humanitarian measure like the old-age pension that would lose him half his votes, and this was the governor's bill so he couldn't veto it.

One of the senators who was sitting behind Dudley got the hell away because the Perez crowd was moving toward Dudley's seat. The men were shouting at him and climbing over the chairs. Another senator who had supported LeBlanc's amendment scurried away as some of the crowd looked like they might hit the old man, but LeBlanc stood out in the crowd. Elliot jumped up in his seat with the feeling he ought to do something to help but the Sergeant-at-Arms managed to get the senators under control and the LeBlanc amendment was adopted 32 to 6 in a weird way. Angry senators voted for an amendment they knew would kill their own bill. Senator Adcock blasted them for their vote. He was so mad his voice trembled. "You've voted for the old folks amendment, and you've never been in that corner before. I want to tell you what happened here a moment ago was slick. It doesn't even help the poor people. All it does is to fix it so that people can't get a dime for a grant." Adcock then asked the President-pro tempore to return the bill to the calendar, and a recess was called to consider the situation with the governor. When Elliot got downstairs he could see Perez and his crowd racing for the governor's office.

Dudley LeBlanc was in the middle of a crowd of people talking at him. He looked a little ashen, but when Elliot made his way through to the senator he shook his hand. Elliot said, "I just want to tell you I like your style. You beat it by yourself, and you didn't back up."

"Thank you, Elliot. Why don't you go over to the Biltmore Hotel and have a drink with a few of our starlets. We're going to pass a good time. I've got to go in and get my shots from the governor, but I'll be there soon."

Elliot ran into Captain Lightfoot coming out of the House as he came out of the Senate. With all the excitement in the Senate he'd forgotten about the bill he'd come up to lobby for.

Lightfoot said, "The pilots' bill passed without amendment, and it looks like it will breeze through the Senate." The pilots would get their raise, but Elliot was more interested in Coozan Dudley, and it was a crazy scene at the Biltmore. Coozan Dudley LeBlanc had a big corner suite at the hotel. It was full of people — all kinds. Elliot had come on over hoping to learn about what went on in the governor's office after the floor fight. When Elliot was growing up, Hadacol and Coozan Dudley were household words. Moo said Coozan Dudley was a great man, and because of Moo he thought so too. Now Senator LeBlanc was an old man, and Hadacol had been sold off, but he proved today he still had dreams and schemes.

There was a bar at one end of the suite operated by two men in white coats. Everyone seemed to be half-loaded, but no one from the recent events at the Capitol had arrived yet. Most of these people had once had something to do with Hadacol when Dudley LeBlanc made millions selling patent medicine. Two real estate men stopped Elliot to try to find out when LeBlanc would arrive. They wanted to sell the senator some land for a big plant he planned to build. Elliot wondered about him building anything. The old man looked too sick.

In the middle of the floor were six dogs and a blonde middle-aged woman in a short blue spangled skirt. She was putting the dogs through their paces. A small black poodle in a blue skirt, matching the trainer's outfit, was walking on its hind legs across the floor. The dog wore a pointed cap and a strained expression. There was a young man in a pink leotard who backflipped over to the bar for a drink. Everyone talked at top voice. The other dogs, sitting on white barrels painted in zigzags of red and blue, encouraged the poodle with a chorus of frantic yips and barks. "The Tennessee Waltz" played incessantly in the background. It was the only record they had, Coozan Dudley's favorite tune, and when he finally walked in someone turned it up full volume. Flashbulbs popped and people ran up to the senator to shake his hand. Elliot heard him say to a reporter, "I wasn't trying to kill that bill I was only lovin' it to death. I didn't back down. The governor asked for a compromise."

The Senate reconvened. Back in the gallery lit by lightning daggers streaking by the windows, Elliot listened to Senator W.L. Rambo push through a resolution saying that the legislature would pay the old folks $100 "when the first money becomes available." There were constant loud blasts of thunder as LeBlanc objected to Rambo's resolution. But Rambo was successful and there followed an amendment from Senator Rayburn which eliminated LeBlanc's amendment. When the President pro tempore called for a final passage the Grant-in-Aid Bill was passed 22 to 15. Pandemonium broke out again and there were hot tempers all around but once again the master-at-arms made peace. Elliot was filled with a profound sadness. LeBlanc had lost.

The Governor's Wife

CAMILLA HADN'T SEEN SO IN THREE DAYS. HE'D gone with his friends to a camp near Lafayette to shoot doves. She stared from her bed at the pale, green drapes, the deep shadows like trees. Was he hunting doves — laughing, drinking whiskey, and playing *bourré,* or was this another working trip? Something she wasn't supposed to know about — plans for a new bridge ending in his friend's rice field or a dispensation of public service contracts. His ethics were involved and convoluted. He had an earnest desire to give his own *bonne cher amies* what their backgrounds had denied them. He wanted to give to the people, and the people were his own *cher amies,* but now they were rich, their hands still outstretched.

The ceiling fan's lop, lop, lop searched for a smooth rotation. She couldn't sleep without the ceiling fan; the air conditioning still set on 80. Reaching under her pillows for High John, she dangled a locket. It was small and insignificant.

At one time he had been satisfied with red beans and rice, but then he wanted meat—just a "length of sausage with his beans," Took said. Each year it was more. Camilla had given him masses and the fruit of her womb. What else could he want? High John and So blurred in her mind, the wants of one becoming the needs of the other. It was never money—So never really wanted money. He made it, finagled for it, but gave satchels of it away to his brother, his cousins, the thirty-year-old retarded son of his first-grade teacher.

"So, what is it you really want?" She'd asked when they were close, spent from real passion. She had gone with him, never to go home again except for a marriage after the fact—"What do you want, So? What can I give you?" She felt rich and giving. But he'd laughed and said, "What can a little boy from Crowley, Louisiana, want? Anything you going to give him going to be more than he ever expected." When they were alone he lapsed into the cadence of Cajun French, but when he stumped he suited his style to the audience, speaking French, bible redneck or Tulane English as he chose it.

His *cher amies* now were lobbyists from Washington. What could he gain from their company? Camilla didn't know, but when he had breakfast with her he scanned the *Washington Post* first, flipping paper with a quick rhythm as he skimmed page after page. So protected her from state business, saying he didn't want to spoil her looks, but Camilla had a head for it—knew the deals and leverage. She knew more than he ever dreamed, and now she had a diploma to back it up. Mama Linda said learn and she'd learned, but what she learned made her sick.

She leaned over and pressed the buzzer wishing for Took to answer or even Little Robert, but Took was still in the Leprosarium at Carville. She wouldn't talk to Camilla. When Camilla had ridden up to the gate and told the guard she had official business with Took Dodier, he wouldn't let her in. The Leprosarium was the only part of Louisiana she couldn't get into. It was another country. No closer than the gate to Took, whose case had not responded to treatment.

Little Robert, after fixing Camilla up with a new butler, one of his many cousins who wanted to be a politician, had opened a catering business called The Good Brown Crust. Now she waited for someone she hardly knew, a stranger from New Orleans with a degree in business, Alma Bryan, who would work as a maid at the mansion until such time as she could go to graduate school to get an MBA. This woman had a sharp, pointed chin, bright eyes, and treated Camilla like an ignorant, indolent worm. When Miss Bryan came into the room, there was no real conversation. Let her believe what she wanted. Camilla Jane would never fire her for being smart. It was hard enough for any woman to get to use her head directly without maneuvering or manipulating from behind the scenes without credit, but it made her lonely. Who were her friends? She always confided in Took and Took was gone.

An MBA's job was hands-on stuff; if Miss Bryan could get a better job more power to her. And something stirred in her when she thought it: a better job. Just want she wanted. They had come from different places but no one could realize more than Camilla what that meant.

Food was vended with machine-like efficiency: "What would you like for breakfast? The cook has some very nice figs, and is serving them with melon and prosciutto."

"Only *café au lait,* and a few figs. Is the governor here?"

"I don't know."

"I'll have breakfast in the sitting room."

The woman left and Camilla put on her ecru peignoir of Belgian lace, lifted her hair with both hands over the high lace collar and stepped forward to look at herself in the pier glass. She looked perfect — something she had never looked as a girl. Now she was thin and *soignée,* her long hair relaxed every four weeks by a hairdresser who kept it under control. The satin nightgown stretched flat across her belly. The baby fat which had curved her figure was gone, with it the girl's soft belly. Corot would never have painted her now or Renoir, but in 1967 *Vogue* had done a five-page spread on "the *svelte* first lady of Louisiana."

She walked into the sitting room with its soft shades of peach and green. At the big window she paused and looked out at the lawn. Rain was falling on perfectly green grass which sloped down to a curved drive. The rain made her long for the mushy garden, and sunken portions of her mother's yard, where her foot sank in the ooze just under the bright green grass, and for the vines climbing up and over—the morning glories, rose of Montana, and the bush of magnolia fuscata, whose bruised buds she'd picked and put in her little patent leather purse because they smelled like bananas and magnolias mixed together. Four-o'clocks, pink and yellow—peach and yellow stripes created by the yardman, who cut the seeds and buried the cut portions joined—a trick no one else in High Castle had been able to duplicate, a trick for when Took demanded full credit saying, "High John make it grow anyway I want." But that was when Took had power, before her nose began thickening, and her face too in the shape of a lion's muzzle. "Someone put a spell on me, *bébé*," she said.

And Camilla knew there were poisons in that garden, how often she'd been told never to string flowers, not even four-o'clocks which other children strung on long stems of grass. For her it was forbidden, as were the pink flowers of the oleander bushes dug up from the garden after her sister's death. In the front yard there was a sap sago palm, her mother and Took trimmed it with knives—a knife dropped in black dirt by her bare feet—the palm frond taken to church for Palm Sunday. After the palm was shorn of sharp points, there was a center of soft fronds shaped like curved fingers. Took said these were the hands of our lady folded to bless them for carrying palm to church. And when there was a hurricane, a frond was stuck in the frame of the mantel mirror directly over the holy candle burning to protect the house, and she slept well even when the windows rattled and rain beat the roof. There was no sap sago palm on the lawn of the Capitol. It was too old-fashioned a bush. She thought about her cousin Elliot. How he'd changed from the pale little boy who was so afraid of everything, so willing to follow anything she thought up. Elliot at thirteen, gangly, sensitive, suffering the torments of the damned because he was an altar boy and sexy, and she smiled to herself remembering how little she had to do to change that.

The figs put before her by Miss Bryan were served with the prosciutto and melon she hadn't wanted. She didn't complain, but thought of the long-legged red-bodied spiders striding toward her in the green tent of the fig tree she climbed for ripe figs, looking up under figs for that little button of pink ripeness which cried to be eaten, and she thought how So had called her Sweet Fig when they were first married, of how he'd always put his mouth on her before he entered — the fig in her own mind, opening with pleasure.

She left home in fear and power, fear she would go so far she could never get back, and in power over everything but her limited self. High John could get her anything she wanted, but she didn't think big. She didn't say *I want this*. She'd wasted wishes — she thought how all she'd ever wanted was the power to dispose of or build her own life, and she'd given that over to another. Now she had to wish sausages off her nose. Like the woman in the fairy tale, who kept making silly wishes.

Prescience, dark and intruding, loomed. She could hear the sound of it over her own thoughts. She pulled the green drapes and put on a record which didn't count on love. It was twelve-tone music, a composition contracting and expanding, sucking her in like a black hole.

She drew people — like So. She'd convinced him she was the most exciting woman in the world. It was just a question of drawing everything near. As a child she thought of herself as living on a reef, attached to it — around her were coral flowers, coral fish, swimming into her ken, the big fish after the little fish — anyone she wanted. So Busteaux came. She knew it the minute she saw him, and she hung on like a lamprey hanging to a shark. She swam with him eating the little bits. She saw and learned everything he did, but his world was still bigger than hers. She could never grow, even a shark as big as So couldn't let her get any bigger.

Took gave her High John, and High John gave her power, and So the power through her, but there was no book of instructions with High John; everyone said something different and nobody seemed to know. She always got what she wanted, but she didn't know what she wanted. There was a Chinese curse: *May all your wishes be fulfilled.* How many shoes could she wear? Diamonds, diamonds—how many icicles could she hang from her earlobes? How many dead animals could she wear on her back?

He came into the room with Tit Jean Hébert close behind him. Tit Jean's long nose and small eyes gave him the look of a hungry ferret. It was true—he could find out anything. Tit Jean was attached to So by something more elastic, an invisible cord which stretched or rebounded according to So's need like a corkscrew telephone connection. She glanced up but didn't turn around when he came in. "Go on, Tit Jean," So said, and the cord stretched outside. So walking into any room made it smaller. Kissing Camilla on the cheek he said, "Sweet Fig, we passed a good time at Disko's camp on the Delta ."

"Who was down there?"

"Everybody I wanted to see—Metsch, B.J. LeBlanc, Bobby Soustain, and Simmons Zervignon—the boys. We took Campbell from Washington with us. After we got our ducks, I played *bourré,* and made money, but they got Campbell out there creeping geese. The water came up and them big old geese were sitting out on those little marsh islands, all gathered together because of the water. Bobby Soustain came in and said, 'I'm going to creep me some geese. Anybody want to go?' Campbell pipes up and says, 'I want to go. I'd really like to do some hunting.' That's how he talks."

"Bobby says, 'Well, man you want to do some hunting—there's some hunting to do.' "

"Did Campbell ever hunt before?"

"Sure he did—them ducks we shot—maybe some pheasant under glass or some kind of sparrow, but I can tell you he never hunt no geese by creeping. Campbell got his waders on and some fancy hunting clothes and Bobby give him a shotgun they pulled the plug on. And they went out there about midnight by a full moon and they got Campbell crawling on his belly after them big old honkers sitting out on top a little island. Metsch said, 'Let's go see some fun.' But I say, 'Not me. I'm chasing my *bourré*...' Pretty soon I can't hardly get me a *bourre* because they so many people out there watching Mr. Secretary crawl on his belly in the mud. They crawl right up on those boogers, and then Bobby says 'Go' and they start popping them shotguns. Boom! Boom! Boom! Like an automatic. I could hear it and Bobby came back and told it. They got fifty-four geese not counting what was wounded and destroyed to bad to eat. Campbell came back covered in mud, blood and goose shit, looking like he'd been in Vietnam. I said, 'Maybe you better wash a little of that marsh skunk off of you before you get back into the game.' He was some kind of white in the face. He said, 'Is that legal?' I said, 'Man, where this camp is — anything's legal.' He never did get back in the game.

"Bobby and Metsch thought it was a good joke, since Campbell was so busy sending Louisiana boys to Vietnam. But when Campbell got ready to leave he was trying to take his geese with him in a pontoon plane. They had geese stacked to the ceiling and in the baggage compartment, but those babies are big. When they try to take off they can't get the plane up. They rev up again. The plane's got three props, but it's just sliding all over the marsh like a mosquito full of blood — belly so big it can't get up. So pretty soon they start throwing geese out — Boom! One goose. Boom! Two geese — they still can't get it up. Pretty soon there's geese raining out and Bobby's got a gofer or two out there picking up as fast as they throw them off the plane and pretty soon they throw out enough for Igor Metsch and Disko to have a fundraiser in Ycloskey. The government flies back up to Washington in their plane, and I feel real encouraged that that kind of managerial ability is going to take care of our boys in Vietnam."

"That's a good story. But it doesn't sound like much fun.

I'd rather spend time with real people."

"How about spending a little time with me?" He came up behind her, put his hand on her shoulders and kissed her on the neck. The belly he'd grown rubbed against her back. "Twenty years and your neck still makes me horny."

"Everything makes you horny, So."

"Come on now, Sweet Fig, you been reading my fan mail."

"No, I've been reading the papers. 'La. Governor craps out in Vegas with Cornato Mistress." You think you can cheat on me? I'm not one of those ladylike governor's wives who tells jokes on herself about her man sleeping around. I'm Camilla Jane Maynard and you have a commitment to me. Try to keep it."

His ear lobes turned red, "Who wrote that crap? That's libel."

"No, that's Benjie Turner. He can write anything he wants to and the paper will print it."

"Tit Jean — Tit Jean," he yelled. "Get what you got on Turner. He's back at it again."

Tit Jean stuck his head in the door, his big ears standing at attention."How many times I got to tell you I don't get any dirt on Turner. He used to be a seminarian — some kind of monk. He don't do anything — take anything. Sleep with anybody."

"He's an unnatural son-of-a-bitch. Make up something. I'm not going to let any unnatural son-of-a-bitch hurt my wife."

"He didn't hurt me. And you can't hurt me either." She turned back to the window, watching the rain fall on the green grass. He raised his hand in a helpless shrug, wheeled on his right foot, and left the room as quickly as he'd come in. Camilla knew she'd won, but what? She made him feel less. She didn't become more. She'd always known exactly who she was, and she knew now she wasn't who she wanted to be.

Whither thou goest Shark of my Heart — he was sleeping with other women. She knew it. And she knew she couldn't go to bed with him. Not just because of the women, but because he wasn't the man she'd married. Now the shark ate anything. What he ate she ate. She fed off people as easily as she swallowed the host. If the shark ate people, he fulfilled his nature, if she ate she'd become like the cannibals of New Guinea who dined on brains and got some terrible disease. Every day she read the papers—sightings, feedings, shark frenzy. Everything So did or said was in the paper. He said, "If you can't eat it, drink it or fuck it, what use is it?"

"Dead man," she said, but her heart didn't mean it, as she turned up the music and flicked the pages of *Harper's Bazaar* with one long, red fingernail.

It was after midnight, when she heard someone walking. She sat up quickly in the bed and switched on the light. It was So inside her room with his hand on the door knob, his eyes narrowed, squinting into the light. He wore a light robe, but his feet were bare. "I think I had a bad dream—someone's been calling me," he said. "I thought maybe it was you."

"I didn't call you."

He started back out of the room. But something about his back looked old. Without thinking she said, "Here," and turned back the soft green comforter on the opposite side of the bed. Sliding in quickly he didn't bother to take off his robe—his feet feeling for hers were icy. "Your feet are cold as marble!" she said, switching off the light and cradling him in her arms. "Tell me the dream," she whispered. "Who was calling you? What did the voice say?"

"I told you. I thought it was you, but there were several voices singing. It sounded like a choir in church and you were calling me over it. 'So, please, Soltice, please.'"

"Did you answer?"

"I don't know. I listened to it for a long time like it was on a radio; when I heard you—I think I answered."

"You answered! Are you sure you answered?

"No, I'm not sure but I think I said, 'Don't worry, Sweet Fig, I'm coming.' "

"You should never have done that—you should never have answered—now you're a riderless horse. Somebody's called you out—it wasn't me." Her voice was low and intense.

I'd never call you out even with High John. We're married, So. For me to call you out I'd have to damn my soul and I'd have to damn your soul. But somebody called you out—somebody thinks you wronged them, and they called you out. That's envy, So. A leader can't have too much of everything—maybe you've got too much—or maybe it's because you don't portion it out equally, and now they've called you out. It's Took. It's Took and she has a handle on you through me. I tried to see her and she wouldn't come out. That's why. She's in Carville. God knows what rotten spell she can put on you in Carville. You even bought my cousin, Elliot. She's telling you you're off track. You're not using your grace for the people.

"God damn it, Sweet Fig, don't you know this is Louisi-ana? The governors sold commissions since the time of the French when that was how he got paid—that's still how I get paid. I give it back to those who need it. I'm about as fair a governor as you going to get. Somebody calling me out is in your head."

"Then who called you?"

"It was a dream—I got a chill—that's all's wrong with me. You can interpret my dream all you want, but I think I got a chill at the camp—maybe it's the flu."

"That's probably part of it. Did you get a haircut at the camp?"

"Come on now, baby. That's enough of those kind of questions. I didn't get a haircut or my toenails or any of that stuff. All I did was sleep on the ground in a duck blind waiting on ducks."

"That's it—you left your imprint in the ground—you left an imprint and somebody took your measure and called you out."

"That's the craziest one yet, Sweet Fig. All I did was get a chill, and get stung by a wasp. The combination make me kind of sick. I just put my whiskey head under my jacket, and that old wasp he must have been trying to warm himself with my jacket—I put my head right on top of him. He got the *go go rouge* and stung me on the right temple. It throbs like a son-of-a-bitch. That old wasp was so sluggish and cold he was drunker than me. I pinched his head off. He's not going to sting anymore Frenchmen."

"Oh, my poor baby," she said, covering his face with kisses.

"I'd go back and do it again—you're going to kiss me all over."

"I'm going to have you undone—I've got too much power of my own to let them ride you. They must think we're divided. Don't you worry, So. I'm going to get it fixed as soon as the sun comes up. But you've got to be careful or you'll have a sacred experience—stagger speechless and naked with your arms and legs in the flames of wandering. Everything's going to be fine, but you've got to change your ways. Divide your pie."

"What kind—apple or pecan?"

Since Moo

SINCE MOO DIED LILAH SENSED A DIFFERENCE IN Elliot; she was sure he was not seeing another woman. Whatever had been was changed. He turned to her more often if he waked in the night. Not moving out of the bed to switch on the reading lamp by the chaise, instead now he moved to her, their sex primed by his sense of loss and need. They whispered in the night like new lovers and sometimes rose at five before any real light to go down into the kitchen, switch on the kitchen light and make coffee. Slathering big slices of wheat bread with sweet cream butter, she put it in the oven for toast, while he filled the top of the white enamel coffee pot—the old coffee pot—with coffee grounds for two, and then stood in a dark green robe, legs slightly spread, spooning boiling water into the pot with an ice-cream scoop. When the coffee was made, he poured it back and forth into another pot combining the hot coffee with hot milk until it became one, and they would move languorously from the kitchen carrying breakfast out into the sun room where there was little conversation. One morning he read a Spanish poem to her which he said was the most important poem he'd ever read in his life, although it was very simple.

Qué es la vida?

Es un illusion.

But she could not see how it applied to his life or hers. She said, "It's like a dream?"

And he said, "Yes."

"Sometimes it's real?"

"Sometimes."

They drank their coffee and ate the toast, while a public radio station played a Chopin étude and the sun came up, although they could not see the actual sunrise. And then suddenly it was day, and she heard the newspaper hit the front door. She picked it up to read the headlines, and he wandered off to take a shower. The extended moment had passed. They were strangers again, and went about their separate lives.

Soon Elise, who had been distantly quarreling with Davis, came in for breakfast, and Davis came downstairs to present himself starving at the kitchen table for the box of cereal he loved to pour in a shower of flakes and raisins that settled on the green-flecked pine table, an heirloom inherited from her grandmother Dean. Sometimes now she went to Texas. Her long resentment of her mother softened by time—still she could only stay a week before the place closed in on her. When she was there her mother wanted to give her things, and she had taken several pieces of furniture from home. Her kitchen now was more familiar to her, more her own, and more her own childhood.

She saw less of Lane, who worked hard as ever, but went directly to the Napoleon House after work, where she sat at the bar listening to Madame Shuman Heinke sing operatic arias, drinking Scotch and milk until nine p.m., when she would call Gin Lee's and order shrimp-fried rice to take home. Sometimes she forgot to order and didn't eat at all. A number of bar cronies looked out for her. If they thought she was too drunk to get home by herself, they would officiously order a United cab, walk her out to the cab and put her in, pay the cabbie, then stand on the corner telling stories about Lane. By the time they got back into the bar she was sitting there. She'd paid the cabbie to drive around the block, then come in the other door, and was now bent over the bar smoking a Benson and Hedges, drinking Scotch and milk. She did—always—finally go home because of her cat Sweetie-Face-Hearts-and-Flowers who had to be fed.

After putting down a bowl of chicken hearts, which had been defrosting in the empty refrigerator, she would eat fried rice from Gin Lee's, take two Seconals, and go to bed. But still she could not sleep, and one night when Lilah left the kids with Mrs. Heywood and stayed at Lane's, she heard her cry out. Before Lilah could get into her robe and into the other room, she heard Lane in the bathroom, the medicine cabinet shut with a click, a glass of water drawn, and the bare feet padding back to bed.

In the morning Lilah went into Lane's bedroom where the light was still on, pillows thrown from the bed onto the floor—covers tossed back even though the room was cold—Lane face down, as if she'd finally passed out from weariness. A black, clothbound copy of *Time and the River* face down on the night table.

Lilah had a hard time getting her up for work. "Do you ever make it on time?"

"Don't worry," said Lane. "This too is living."

And when Lilah went back to her own life, and the small sculptures she made on the kitchen counter, it seemed rich and full. The children were more distant now. When they were not in school, she was conscious of exactly where they were. She did a lot of work with the school and had to drive them to everything, but had help with cleaning—enough time left for clay.

The clay took form in her hands, a folding hibiscus flower—a bud-shaped the size of a small vase. She didn't open it from the top, however, hollowing it instead from the bottom so that she could still fire it in a small kiln—it would not be utilitarian. She pleased herself with reading books on glazes when the children were in school, and she searched until she found a glaze for the piece—a dull, old rose with a hint of fire. Only she would know where it started, as a dream of a folded hibiscus. As a small statue it had its own form and life. These were the things that pleased her now, and when she thought of Kaleb, she began to understand his work, and she felt she must have done harm to his art, but once when she was going into the ladies' room at Stephen and Martin's Restaurant uptown-- the food was not pricey but good--Bud Thompson was coming out of the men's room as she walked in.

He said, "My God, it's the Irish rose. How are you, little darling?" And he gave her a big, sloppy kiss on the cheek.

"I'm fine."

"Married? I heard you married an uptown lawyer and were given over to kids, Mardi Gras balls, and lunches in cute little restaurants."

"Like this one? Not quite. My husband was an attorney, now he's a pilot. And I do have kids. No balls of any kind."

His chest heaved in a dry, silent laugh. "Does he fly off great distances so we can dally in the afternoon." He chortled aloud and his eyes were the eyes of a wicked little monkey she'd seen at Audubon Zoo.

"He just flies off to Baton Rouge on the river—he's a river pilot."

"My God, what a rotten magnolia you've become. I don't imagine you're doing anything productive. Don't you think you're taking it a little too far—from the king of the avant garde to an old-world dinosaur—a river pilot? Wait until I see Kaleb. I can hardly wait to tell him." A man pushed past him into the men's room. They moved out of the alcove.

"Why would you want to tell Kaleb? I feel guilty as it is—I didn't understand anything about his art. How he felt—why he wouldn't take another job. Like the story Nan tells—I was too green."

"Oh, my dear, you flatter yourself. Art feeds on women like you. You're the beautiful woman who threw him over—the ultimate torture bitch, who was not ready to sacrifice anything to his art. And that's the kind of thing it feeds on. Letitia's not food for art. She's devoted. He'll never paint anything for love of Letitia." Bud's face was red and angry now. Lilah could see Bud still longed for Letitia. Kaleb had been wrong about Bud.

He continued, "Letitia follows him around blowing his nose and cleaning his brushes, and she's a better artist than he'll ever be. But when I made her lunch or bought her canvas she dismissed me as a lightweight. She's all for Kaleb—his dark moods and selfishness. You go on with your pilot and your babies. Forget about Kaleb Borland, and don't waste any regrets on how you messed up his life. This is a long train—the engine's at Carrollton Station and God knows where the caboose is—LaPlace maybe. Most people just watch a couple of cars go by."

"Okay, Bud. That's pretty heavy—relative trains and stuff. It's good to see you. I have to move on to more important things," and she laughed as she walked into the pink high-gloss of the ladies' room, which smelled of rose deodorant soap, wire to the side of the pink porcelain bowl, dissolving and perfuming the room each time a woman flushed it.

Near Christmas Lilah had a feeling she should go home to Rule, that she should spend Christmas as she had spent it as a child, her own children wide-eyed before the tree while her mother decorated it with old glass ornaments, and Burl Ives sang Christmas carols on the stereo. And when the cat climbed the tree, which it always did, and an ornament shattered, Elise and Davis could be the ones to take up for the cat, and see whose favorite ornament had broken. At last she could be with family, eat at the mahogany table, which carried its own memory of other Christmases in the tell-tale scratches made by the tines of forks in the hands of impatient children or the dent from the infamous carving accident of her father when the dead but still reluctant turkey slid off the platter. Her father's knife hand forced to make a wild sweep at the falling bird, struck the table instead, forever terrifying his children, who always after insisted that the turkey be carved in the kitchen.

She waited up for Elliot to tell him she wanted to go. It was past midnight, and he came in quietly without turning on a light. At one time she had been afraid and always waited for his footsteps, suspicious that they might be the footsteps of some other man—someone who knew her husband was not at home—afraid she might turn in her sleep to the stranger—the stranger in her dreams who was sometimes Kaleb. But that was before she'd breastfed children, and had to get up at all hours. For those years she was greedy for sleep, exhausted, and seldom awakened when he crawled in beside her, but Elise was no longer a baby, no mouth tugged at her nipples, and now Lilah felt the old yearning toward him—a yearning mixed up with love of babies and love of her husband who made the babies. Tonight she turned on the bedside lamp. There were dark shadows of gut weariness on his pallid face, surprised as she sat up wide awake, wearing his favorite white silk nightgown and negligee rather than a checkered flannel nightshirt. Perfume floated next to her skin.

"Aren't you cold," he said, as he turned on his lamp, and his voice was colder than the question.

"No, I thought it might be nice to go to to bed pretty for a change."

"You're always pretty," he said in a polite tone as he loosened his tie and pulled it off.

The shadows around his eyes looked like ground pencil lead or soot rubbed into the skin, the yearning in her chest shifted—moved. Perhaps the dim light of the room deepened the shadows, she leaned forward and laid her head at the other end of the bed as he sat down to take off his shoes, but as he bent to untie one shoe, she looked at him from that angle, and she saw with a small shock that the shadowed skin around his eyes was permanent.

She was lying on her back under the white silk, her thick, loose hair spread out around her head. She wanted to touch him. He glanced at her again, and she thought she saw his eyes kindle, but he bent down to take off the other shoe. Moving closer to him she inclined her bent leg against his back, and began to move the silken leg against him. When he came up again, she could see him grin, but when he turned around his eyes gathered her image as he moved closer and kissed her. It was an open kiss—a kiss of deep exchange, as if they had been brought together by something terrible which made them love each other more.

He turned out his lamp, but she kept the other one on because the look on his face excited her. Always an exquisite lover—what she demanded of him he could always give—his tenderness and his ability to wait for her to join him in pleasure had made their sex life rich and even, but except for Haiti he'd always been controlled, polite—almost impassionate. She called him "Everready" because he was. It was a laughing but hurt criticism because his ability had nothing to do with her. It was something he could do well like tennis. An athletic performance of style and grace that lacked emotion. Passion was what she saw on his face now, and his passion excited her beyond any regular caresses. He'd undressed quickly and she could see he was ready. His cheeks remolded themselves into gaunt hollows, a faint red flush spread across his chest, and his eyes were liquid—brimming.

He took no time caressing her. It was understood she was ready too, and when he began to stroke, her mind flashed on a time they had canoed to a small island in a river in Canada. She could see the bright lacquered paddle—strong, sure strokes of the paddle moved the boat along—the blade of the paddle lifting bright globules of water—hanging there as the poised paddle waited for the right moment to stroke again— as the paddle reached in again—a swift movement forward. But his strokes became more insistent, and her mind moved further down into the dark tunnel where sensation, speed, and pleasure became an intense feeling of union as waves and shudders finally shook them together.

They were lying quietly. "I'm going to Rule for Christmas," she said. "I want you and the kids to come."

"Fine," he said. Elliot in his dreamy way had no real argument against this trip, his own Christmases having evaporated with the breath of trees that were no more by the house which had given way to a drugstore and an insurance office.

The only way he could go home was by ship, when fog with its possibilities of collision in a smoky bend had cleared to a starry night, when the crackling voices from other ships were silent on his radio and he drove down the river like a man alone on a wide interstate at 3 a.m. with his own companions from the past crowding into his mind at a Christmas table burdened with turkey stuffed with oyster dressing, jellied cranberry in a special cut-glass dish, where the ambrosia salad was thick with lacy coconut, and the final—the ultimate—pie was pecan.

The women—Moo, his grandmother, Took, his mother—before Christmas in his grandmother's kitchen, cooked for days on this feast which would feed their whole family and send Took toting food home for ten others, and he remembered those meals not so much for the Christmas dinner, but for the leftovers that went on forever—leftover meals at the kitchen table with Moo. "You like bread, Elliot?"

"No, Moo. I like turkey leg."

"Now how'd I know that—I saved you one."

He ate turkey leg and she, from some ascetic preference, ate bread torn up and soaked in a glass of milk, putting it into her mouth with a spoon and pressing the bread against the roof of her mouth until the milk ran down her throat. This meal eaten in solemn communion gave him great happiness and a sense of place. Now that she was gone, every gesture Moo had made was memorable by the fact that she would make no more, and his thoughts now turned more often to the old woman eating bread and milk at the kitchen table than to any memories of Camilla Jane, whose every movement in the past had haunted him. And he wondered at his mind, its ability to move from the poetry of Camilla Jane, in a starched white pinafore dancing on the front walk, to music from the ice cream truck before they ran to buy a polar bar she sucked into a peak that melted down her arms in streaks, and back again to Moo.

When he came home from the river he'd taken that other trip and was ready to go with Lilah to Rule, Texas, to absorb through his pores a past not his own, in order to make a more perfect one for his children.

They came back to New Orleans on January 4, 1970, on Airline Highway. It was raining and sometimes sleeting. A long, dull ride through mile after mile of too-flat marshland where the swamp encroached upon the highway, taking it over by undermining the concrete—falling away from it, cracking it, leaving potholes as big as a man's head or by growing over it, creeping and crawling in long tentacles of crab grass. There was nothing scenic about a ride in such rain, not a turtle's head or an alligator hide showed above the brown water of the wide borrow pits on each side of the highway. Lilah, tired from her turn at the wheel and the bickering kids, turned all driving over to Elliot.

But after the children finally fell sleep, they came to the Airline Motor Inn, a restaurant and gas station in LaPlace—a milestone—only a few miles left 'til home. Not wanting to wake the children, they pulled the car in front of the forties glass-block section of the restaurant, as if they would be able to see the car and sleeping children in it from the green stools inside, and they went in for chicory coffee so black it turned green when the milk was added. They were cold and the big restaurant seemed comforting with its old counters and chrome-based stools. "I like the milk machine," she said.

"An ancient artifact—it has a counter weight to pinch the tube," he said.

She went to the bathroom, where a room with bluebird wallpaper and twenty mirrored dressing stations was ready for women in silk hose and felt hats if they should ever return.

Her face was bare, so she moved on into the tiled room with ten cubicles — all clean and empty.

"Airline is not a main highway anymore — the world has been diverted elsewhere," she said to Elliot when she got back.

When they came out the children had not been stolen by kidnappers willing to brave a storm — they were still sleeping, and Elliot turned back into the rain which obscured vision, giving the highway an existential importance beyond any other force in their lives. In this dry bubble they were drawn together by fear of the cold, rainy night, and their love of the children who slept through it all. At last, they came into New Orleans — still raining — the city down at the heels like a beautiful woman with a cold — no makeup and a runny nose — streets of grey tangled sheets and wadded kleenex.

They drove into the driveway, and carried in suitcases, paper bags of dirty laundry, and finally, the sleeping children past the pine wreath which had turned brown in their absence.

Lilah came back to a stack of limp and smudged mail rescued from the mailbox. Still shivering in the hall, she scanned through, and then threw it on the dining room table. The house was cold and smelled like old leather suitcases mildewed in a closet. A few pieces of wood were left in the woodbox. She brought it to Elliot who laid it in the fireplace and built a fire from balled up newspapers which burned fiercely, and finally caught on a piece of kindling for a real fire. They settled down before it in their own house relieved that Christmas was over — all the old pleasures and slights contained by the past year gone. Lilah stared at the wild geese burning on the tarry soot of the back bricks. Suddenly, they went flying up the chimney, and she felt something fly with them as tears rose in her throat for something — somebody — an unrelated sorrow.

It was not until the following Tuesday that Aubrey the bartender at the Napoleon House called to tell her that Lane Clayley had been found dead. "They found her four days before Christmas in her own bed. She was wearing a grey sweat-shirt and pajamas bottoms—her glasses still on. They said she was propped up as if she'd been reading."

"What was the book?" Lilah asked.

"They didn't say—just a book with a dark cover turned down on her stomach. The coroner says it could've been suicide because she'd been drinking wine and taking Seconals. We didn't tell him she does that all the time. It wasn't long before she was found because the people she worked with got worried when she didn't come in. There was no service for her in New Orleans, except for the people she drank with had a party at the bar. It was a good party. Lane would've liked it. The city released her body to her sister who came in from Cincinnati, and took her back there. I thought you'd want to know. She told me—one time—you were her best friend," Aubrey said.

Lilah thanked him, but it was so distant—Lane so real. Lilah couldn't believe it. She didn't cry. Instead she thought to call Lane, hear the dry voice make some crack about the reports of her death being wildly exaggerated or something funnier that she'd made up herself.

With numb fingers Lilah began to open some of the Christmas mail she'd stacked on the dining room table—bills, circulars, and a small, book-sized envelope which she opened last. A stack of polaroid pictures fell out. Pictures of Lane in an open casket surrounded by gladioli. Her hand shook when she read the note from the sister: "I knew you'd want to remember her as she was. It was a beautiful funeral. Happy New Year."

River Run

"THE OTHER GUY WON—OR TO BE MORE PRECISE,"
Elliot said, "So lost." Elliot read it to Lilah from the *Times-Pic-ayune* with a certain relief. It seemed for once a move toward
reform. The picture of the new governor was solemn, clean-cut. But Elliot knew he was humorless and lacked style, peo-ple believed him to be honest, and some—enough—had voted
for him. In the months that followed, Baker, the new guy, pro-ceeded with some lackluster plans for the state. He was not a
leader and he was not beloved. No one began a conversation
with "Did you hear what Baker said yesterday at the Gridiron
Club?"

The new governor settled in with a minimum of fanfare—
he didn't give a crayfish boil for two thousand supporters. El-liot wasn't invited to anything he did give—not even a party
to help pay campaign bills. He imagined it was because he
was Camilla's cousin and, supposedly, in the other camp. El-

liot hadn't heard from Camilla Jane since Scottlandville, and So had vanished like the Titanic. The past was getting taller—bodies stacking up—people he'd considered important had moved away or died. Elliot had always lived in the past or the now. It was the future he'd never believed in.

It was spring again and the river was rising every day. Ships converged on the port like mosquitoes. Elliot spent his week in the blur and cacophony of strange tongues, monstrous tonnage, and idiosyncratic foreign captains. The current at high river ran swift and dangerous. He came home from work sick with fatigue and the constant threat of wasting lives—of setting whole city blocks aflame with a light tanker that missed the point and slammed into the bend—or a collision—those cities waltzing past with their lovely lights ablaze had the power to send each other down—at Algiers Point two hundred feet into the deep belly of the river. Elliot hadn't had an accident, yet, and it was possible—it was possible—he never would, but he had little time for his children or his wife. They walked and talked quietly in the house so that he could sleep, and it was never enough sleep before he was out again at 4 a.m. praying there would be no fog, but knowing from the lilting tones of the weatherman on T.V. that there would be, and the points and bends of the river would be blacked out and impenetrable. Every nerve in his body strained to see—sense a way through, at best, to find a place to anchor out of the way of other traffic. Always there was at least one ship that lumbered full ahead, as if the river were free open water, as if fog were not the most implacable enemy. Elliot would call on all radio channels for the voice of the other ship to know what captain ran ahead like the Titanic trying to make a world's record in dangerous waters. The radio crackled silence and no one was there.

Tonight, his own ship was Artemis—a dirty, rusty tanker of Liberian flag and unflushable toilets, with a crew of Greek farmers who had the previous month still been moving stones from one rocky pasture to another. Farmers, who had, in desperation, gone to sea to earn a nest egg to marry the girl from the next village or to feed the hungry children gathered around an empty table. The captain, a short nervous man about forty, with a black, coarse moustache and full beard, his eyes shot with spots of cayenne still burning from three sleepless nights of doing everything for a run down ship and an ignorant crew, was reluctant to surrender the bridge to a stranger. He paced — veins still full of danger — his brain in a state of numbed disbelief that anyone other than himself could take the Artemis safely down the river.

Elliot had been listening for traffic ahead. He gave the order to change fuel from black oil to diesel and sent a crewman forward. "We're going to anchor, Captain. The river's blacked out," Elliot said quietly.

"No-no — it's very difficult — my charter requires me in Burnside tonight," the captain said.

"Then you've got it, Captain. If you want to sail to Burnside in blacked-out fog then you're the pilot. I'll go to the chartroom."

"But I don't know this river — I need your help."

"I am helping you — it's not safe. Don't sail."

The captain threw up his hands helplessly and left the bridge. Elliot anchored the Artemis wrapped in cotton batting in a bend of the Mississippi near willow trees. Below, the captain slept for the first time in three days. Elliot, too, went to bed, listening as he sank into the bunk, to the sound of a distant church bell.

The next morning, as the sun rose and the fog lifted, he saw the bell around the neck of a black and white cow grazing on the toe of the levee, which stretched out behind the ship like a backyard, the bell tolling mournfully as she ate the dewy grass with an occasional slight toss of her head. Elliot, after checking the radio for traffic, told the crewman forward, "Stand by the anchor; let me know when there's only one shot of chain left.

And soon — "One shot standing," came the call.

Then she was free, the anchor heaved.

He began maneuvering, calling, "Dead slow," and then "Hard to starboard," and she began a swing. He had to go half-astern to break the headway, but the torque of the wheel helped the swing and broke the headway. They were back down on her broad back where the sun shot the water with light that spun to light blue sky like a Kodachrome postcard, and Elliot was his dream, and when the captain got up, clear-eyed and happy, he sent the steward down for little cups of thick Greek coffee *metrio* in white china cups with gold rims. The captain now became the voluble host telling Elliot tales of Greek temples and how many bottles of wine it took for five men to roast a goat on the island of Chios where he was born and nights were two thousand years old. By the time Elliot docked in Burnside with the help of the tug Betty Shirley, he felt he'd done a good job. It was okay to be a pilot on the Mississippi River. Nothing else could make him feel time so worthwhile when it was running past.

But when the Port Ship car met him at the dock there was a message to call home. With a slight sense of unease, he went into the dock master's corrugated hut to use the straight line to New Orleans. Lilah answered in a distant, hurried voice. "Your cousin called and said she needs you right away. You're to call this number in High Castle."

It was Bubba who answered and said, "She wants you to come right now."

The directions he gave Elliot were to Tuolumne near High Castle on the river road, but he said, "The place is hard to find."

Elliot was not so tired that he couldn't wonder how things were in her life now — he was afraid something had happened. Unbuckling his radio from his waist, he threw the life vest into the back before he climbed into the Port Ship car that had come to pick him up. The driver was silent other than a "Good evening, Cap." Elliot settled down in the back seat leaning into the corner against a pillow put there for the comfort of exhausted pilots coming off a long turn on the river, but Elliot's mind was too restless to sleep, and he kept his eyes on the twists and turns of the road that followed the points and bends in the Mississippi.

It was near dusk again and the levee was a darker shade of green than in the morning. The big oaks that had been planted by dead men, the black-green shutters of old houses, and the twin tracks of dirt roads with grass growing down the middle fled off into clumps of trees where a tall brick chimney stood alone or where old houses cowered, passed over by the renovations of Texas millionaires and tourist hotels, as beyond repair, past regard. Brown historical markers flashed by, as always, he wished for the time to read every marker on the river road, to know who had come before, what they had done—what was set down in white letters flashing by slightly before dark from another man's mind.

All along the road, tall, grey weeds had fallen over like broken straws—everything a shade of brownish-grey except for sudden patches of brilliant green clover in a mat of yellowish grass. Soon rows of cane angled from the road stretched back, and the refinery Cora Texas reached up. He could see the tree line before the distant levee—they had moved away from the river here. Sticks and rubble left by cane trucks, old piles of *bagasse* turned to earth. They drove for an hour before they came to the town of High Castle, going far past the sign he had been told to look for—in town before he knew it. He recognized the Landry's Victorian house—a screened and windowed turret sat cat-a-cornered over the front porch steps. He'd played on those steps under the big pin oak trees, looking out through crepe myrtle trees. Riding past now, he saw there was mistletoe in the bare-skinned tops, spring not yet come to the branches. Down the street black men stood on porches, tinkered with cars, as always waiting for work to steady in the cane fields. The driver overlooked Tuolumne coming in, and now Elliot realized how long it had been since he'd passed some time in High Castle.

"Drive down two more blocks," he said to the driver as they came down Main Street. "Now turn right." This was the street. The only marker he had from memory was Kalisch's, a small jewelry store on the corner from his grandmother's house. The store was still there but the two houses had ceased to exist. The street now paved solid. In the past, gravel and a light pink dust had covered the street, filtering through fuchsia-pink crepe myrtles, the sweet olive and two large cedar trees, to layer the front porch, settling on the porch railings, the arms of the rockers, even the lip of the black mailbox which they swung up to touch numbers with their bare toes — tilted enamel digits under the mailbox, when the swing was at its apex in the wild game of higher, higher. He called while she pumped them up as high as anyone could go in the cypress swing — until — they touched 504 in wild exultation. He stared at the black brick face and empty plate glass windows of the two buildings set back in a double parking lot — nothing was there that he had known before.

He directed the driver up to the levee road. The White Alder sign was there at the foot of Leonia Street. It said WHITE ALDER MEMORIAL, but there was no other marker of the Coast Guard cutter that had gone down never to be raised, some said because of women and booze on board. Cane trucks had been along here — odd stalks of broken cane littered both sides of the river road. They drove up on the levee and got out, the driver walked with him. Here they were looking down on Point Clair at Hospital Point where he and Camilla had swum in the borrow pit. "There'll be terrific fishing after the river falls — river cat," he said to the nineteen-year-old driver who appeared uninterested like someone humoring an old man. Answering only, "You bet, Cap."

"See that tug and tow — when he sees daylight on the point he'll begin to drive on it — then you'll hear the turbo chargers kick in." The driver didn't know what he was talking about, but Elliot continued anyway, "It's important not to meet traffic on the points. See — he's got to drive her across the current streak or she'll set in the bend." He watched her make the point, and then they walked back to the car along the levee and down the small shell road across a cattle guard where there was a message scratched in the concrete culvert. It said,

"White boys ass."

They got in the car and went back to the river road where they began scanning for the sign that said "Tuolomne." It was a small sign—easily missed. They turned into a two-track country road like the ones they had been seeing for miles. The shoulder was soft and someone had placed occasional bricks and hunks of irregular concrete on the edge of the road to keep a car from getting stuck in the mushy earth. They drove for some time. The trees planted by the roadside were overgrown with underbrush, and the road instead of going straight turned off and followed a curve. It was getting darker now, and once they found themselves ending up on something that looked like a logging road ending in a stand of trees—nothing there for anyone. They then followed a maze of boxwood to a false turn that took them again into the dark wood, the driver leaning over the steering wheel, peering into the trees for some notion of how to go or where until they came to a dead end.

Wheeling and looking back over his shoulder, the driver backed out missing trees and bushes as branches slapped at the windows. They came back on the first road, and followed it until, by watching every tree they passed, they came to two low brick stanchions which they'd missed the first time.

The car stopped suddenly—brakes locked, "What's that thing?" the driver yelled. "There—on top of that stanchion."

Elliot leaned forward to look where the driver pointed: It was a figure—sinister in the distorting light of the headlights which left the eyes in shadow. The face stared at them with a wide open mouth.

"It's a warning—an African fetish. My cousin's idea, no doubt."

It was a wooden statue constricted by vine wrappings with medicine packets, and hundreds of knife blades embedded in the body blade side out. As they moved on, turquoise beads for eyes caught carlight and gave the thing a live-animal look.

"God, that's ugly. You sure you want to go in there? People got something like that might do you anything."

"That's true. But what're you going to do? It's family."

"You said a mouthful there. I'll drive you in, Cap, but I don't think I want to stick around."

"That's okay."

Now they were on a wider paved avenue bordered by giant oaks, and Elliot could see ahead—two lights on the veranda. It was not a grand plantation like Nottoway, but one of the smaller West Indian houses built by planters for their son or daughter who had married. The hipped roof and wide galleries gave the house a tropical air, as if the car had been transported to Haiti when it traveled the maze of little roads to get here. But when they drove up to the front door it looked familiar, and he found himself eager to see her again.

There was someone on the porch sitting back in the darkness away from the light, and without really seeing, he felt the darkness lift and move as it, a portion of it, had detached itself from night and come toward him like night moves over the countryside in a wave, and when it stopped, the shape of a head and thick shoulders rose above it and he recognized Took. She looked like an old lion; when he reached out to hug her she pushed him back.

"She's been waiting on you—be coming down soon," she said and moved inside the house. Some part of him waited for the wave of her leaving, but Took was not heavy, and she left without shaking this house. He was more steady here.

The driver of the car said, "It's not so bad; you want me to wait around?"

"No," said Elliot. "I'll call for a car on the radio, or I'll get Bubba to drive me back to town."

"I'm glad to hear that," the driver said, and gave a wave as he went around the circular drive and back down the road, his red tail lights bobbing as he passed over the cattle guard, and out of the grounds.

Elliot heard her running down the stairs barefooted. She came out of the house wearing a white cotton nightgown, and jumped into his arms like a girl saying, "You old Skinny Marinky Dink; I'm so glad to see you." And she kissed him right on the mouth, but there was no desire bubbling up in him like lava looking for any way to get out, only a sweet nostalgia for the past and someone who carried the same past. They sat down on the swing on the gallery.

"How do you like my house," she asked.

"Isn't this the old Glapion place?"

"Suppose it was; it's mine now."

"What's that thing out on the post."

"That's my watchdog."

"Now how did I know that? That's what I told the driver. He was scared to come in."

"He's right to be scared. Mama Linda got that for me. It's a fetish from Africa; it's to protect the village. The shaman collects iridescent beetles, bits and pieces of everyone's hair and nails, bones of our ancestors—whatever it takes to make big magic—a territorial claim, and he puts it in that box on the figure's belly, then he rubs fat into it whenever he eats and sometimes he pees on it. Maybe I should get rid of it, but it keeps the wrong people away from here."

"Bubba said on the phone that you needed me. What's wrong?"

"I did—I do—I really do, but I waited until things got better before I called, and now you're here and I can tell you something good, something so good it can't wait." He could see her white teeth shining in the dark, and she sounded like the girl whose words fell over each other because she couldn't wait to get them out. "But wait a minute. Come say hello to So before he goes upstairs. And she pulled him into the central hall which was white and well lit, the walls full of light-brushed paintings—a suggestion of flowers and Christian palm fronds, and then into a darker sitting room where one silk-shaded lamp shone on an open book in the hands of So Busteaux who sat reading. His hair under the light looked like the pewter of an old stein, and his face was thinner and more handsome than it had been since the coming out party for Camilla Jane. He looked up when they came in. Smiling he said, "Elliot, *comment ça va*?" And there was a faint slur to his words as if he'd had too many bourbons. "Pardon me, if I don't get up to shake your hand. I got a little Charley Horse decide to ride my leg." Elliot leaned down and stuck out his hand. So put down his book and shook it—lefthanded—the other hand limp in his lap. Elliott tried to adjust his face around surprise.

"How you like my woman? What you think—she looking fine? She's been bubbling all day about her cousin Germain from New Orleans, and her big news she's going to tell. Now here comes Bubba with his bad news. I got to go upstairs. She's going to tell you about our next campaign. It's a doozy."

Elliot was caught off guard. He didn't know what to say, but Bubba greeted him and shook his hand until he felt it in his armpit, the socket nearly disengaged like the brake on So's chair that Bubba unlocked now before he started pushing him toward the hall stairs. As they went out of the room, So said over his shoulder, *"Eh bien, mais on va ce revoir."* Elliot could hear the whirr of a motor that moved slowly up the stairs.

As she came back in to the room, he saw her dark hair in high tension—wild around her face; she was that old source of energy, and she said, in the same joyful voice, "You hungry, Elliot? You want something to eat? There's cold chicken in the kitchen and pecan pie. Come on." She led him to the back of the house down a long gallery to the kitchen where a nightlight burned. As he went into the kitchen he sucked air into his lungs as if he hadn't breathed for years. It smelled like coal oil and bacon grease. He sat down at the table while she lit a lamp. She walked back and forth from the ice-box to the table in her bare feet bringing out a platter of chicken, a quart of cold milk, hard French bread, and half a pecan pie. He was ravenous and stuffed himself, picking the meat off the chicken bones with greasy fingers and eating bread torn up in cold milk with a long teaspoon. It was the best meal he'd had, and all the time she was smiling at him from her eyes which were saturated blue like deep water.

Finally he asked, "Are you going to tell me or not?"

"I am," she said. "But don't tell anybody, Elliot. They think we're going to hell. They think So was beaten senseless by Baker and Benjie Turner—and then that little stroke he had—

Benjie Turner writing So Busteaux did this and So Busteaux did that until So almost burst his eyes, but I'm telling you, Elliot, it was time—we were so low before and we were so low after I thought he'd die, but old High John came to conquer, and he did. So, we're going home to High Castle to get you well. You can tell you're home, Elliot—smell the bushes—sweet olive, and smell the house—it's ours. And So is getting better all the time—he's not paralyzed or anything—just got slapped down—it's not permanent. He's teaching me and I'm teaching him—and this—this is the best thing, Elliot—the best thing is: I'm pregnant. So can make love, but just to me. He's not going to be less—just different. Like me. And this one took, this one really took." She pressed the white gown to the small mound of her belly for him to see, and she rocked herself with glee the way she had when she'd won all his marbles and even his tar. "And if you think I'm going to let Benjie Turner and Baker win forever, you're crazy. I'm going to come out of here running at a dead heat with a war chest you won't believe. Nobody pulls my string. I don't owe anybody any favors. A woman can get in office if her husband dies in office or is sick and can't run. I'll have So's vote in my pocket. People don't like this governor. He has no style. He's not a leader. I am. I don't have to worry about whether or not I have balls enough to do something because I never had balls to begin with. It's like that kid in High Castle who was born without arms. He said he'd never had any so he never missed them. I don't have to do things the way So did or any of the other Louisiana governors for the last couple of hundred years. I'm going to run and I'm going to win. I wanted to be governor when we paddled the towhead. I meant it then and I mean it now."

"I think you said you wanted to be a pilot."

"Not me. I've studied this state. When I'm governor everybody will be able to read. There won't be any little babies in Louisiana going to bed with their big bellies cramping and growling all night because they didn't have supper. Style and substance—So had style and substance. He just got diverted that's all. He was thinking it had to be the way it always was;

it doesn't have to be. I can change it and if old Wallace can be governor anybody can."

"You mean that bigot in Alabama? Why would you want to be like him?"

"Not him, Silly. Lurleen Wallace. She's a woman governor. If Lurleen Wallace can be governor anybody can. Now what do you think of that?"

And before he could answer she got up and twirled herself around the kitchen dancing to her own music the way she always had and Elliot felt young and old—real old—at the same time.

"Good luck," he said.

Acknowledgments

THERE ARE LOTS OF PEOPLE I'D LIKE TO THANK: Captain Ronald Grue, who gave me gifts of typing paper, manila envelopes, and a typewriter when we were living in a rundown, leaky rent-house in Anahuac, Texas, while he was going to sea and I was home having kids. Also thanks to my poet friends in the Poetry Forum workshop who helped me hone my skills, and to my dear friend, Valentine Pierce, who, out of the kindness of her heart, typed my manuscript for me. And thanks to Ken Fontenot for his hard work on this book, and Dr. Hazel Ward for her keen critical eye. And finally to Pamela Booton and Diane Wilson and Lowell Mick White for getting it out there.

About Lee Meitzen Grue

New Orleans poet and fiction writer **Lee Meitzen Grue** writes about the culture and music of her city. Her books include *Trains and Other Intrusions: Poems*; *French Quarter Poems*; *In the Sweet Balance of the Flesh*; *Goodbye, Silver, Silver Cloud*; and *Downtown. Live! On Frenchman Street*, features Lee's poetry accompanied by jazz musician Eluard Burt. Lee has taught poetry at Xavier University and Tulane University, and has performed her work and conducted workshops around the world. For over thirty years, Lee has edited and published the acclaimed *New Laurel Review*. She teaches poetry for the annual Alamo Bay Writers' Workshop. Owner of the celebrated B.J.'s Bywater Lounge, Lee Grue writes fiction and poetry from her Victorian home in the Bywater.

About Moonyeen McNeilage

Artist **Moonyeen McNeilage** created the artwork for *Blood at the Root*. Born in 1935 in Melbourne, Australia, McNeilage has been a practicing artist all of her life, winning many prizes, including the Diamond Valley Art Award and the Malvern Artists Society Award. Her work is on exhibit in The National Gallery of Australia.

Lee Grue at BJ's in the Bywater

Praise
for the Writing of
Lee Meitzen Grue

Lee Grue has established herself as one of the outstanding poets of this region. [Her writing] reflects a fine feeling for place—Texas, Louisiana, the music and quirks of the deep Southland we live in--along with the profound sense of displacement. This displacement, I believe, is a natural result of Lee's wandering, questioning spirit, her unrelenting intelligence, a spirit which recognizes the fact of home, but never too comfortably. In Lee's work there is always a reaching out to other selves, worlds, inner realities, which she absorbs, an expansion of identity which makes possible an extended understanding of her own self.

    —Tom Dent
        former Executive Director,
        New Orleans Jazz and Heritage Foundation

Lee Grue's poetry, like the roux that makes a good gumbo, is a perfect blend of spices—the right amount of New Orleans filé, a flawless mix of worldly wit and charm, the exact rendering of cayenne pepper that makes her art and craft unforgettable... Grue's poetic voice is one to be richly savored.

    —Sue Brannan Walker
        Negative Capability Press

www.ingramcontent.com/pod-product-compliance
Lightning Source LLC
Chambersburg PA
CBHW020941120726
47905CB00008B/2631